"Cameron, Cameron," Jackson whispered as he lowered his head to hers. She struggled against him, but he managed to press his lips to the sensitive skin of her neck.

"No," she protested. "No." She moaned aloud. How could her body betray her this way? How could she ache for his kiss even as she attempted to fight him off? She squeezed her eyes shut, ashamed of herself and her unleashed need, her wicked desire for this man.

"Open your eyes, damn it! I'm sorry," he whispered huskily. "Do you hear me? I'm sorry. I'm sorry for what I did that day. The way I hurt you."

He's sorry, he's sorry, her illogical heart cried out. She didn't believe him, of course. She would never believe him. She opened her mouth to spit a retort, but found herself leaning forward, reaching to meet him halfway. She threaded her fingers through his thick hair, the sounds, the smells, the very walls of the barn fading from her mind.

Jackson tore his mouth from hers, panting heavily. "Say it! Tell me you forgive r

His words suddenly hit hom
she realized what he was sayi
forget everything that had ha
and begin anew—at least un
again. Cameron gave Jackson
hands, so startling him that he stumbled backward. "Get off me," she shouted, wiping the back of her mouth with her hand as if she could wipe away her unbidden passion. "You try that again and I swear I will put that pitchfork through you!"

Tears filling her eyes, Cameron grabbed fistfuls of her skirts and ran from the barn, ran from Jackson...ran from herself.

ROSEMARY ROGERS

AN HONORABLE MAN

MIRA®

ISBN 1-55166-953-6

AN HONORABLE MAN

Visit us at www.mirabooks.com

Printed in U.S.A.

Thank you, always
My loyal readers over the years
And my new readers
I cherish you all

PART ONE

1

Elmwood Plantation
Jackson, Mississippi
April, 1861

Cameron Campbell shortened the reins of the spirited Arabian mare and concentrated on the spot between the gray's ears. This was where she was at her best, a fine horse beneath her, the scorching Mississippi breeze in her face and a split-rail fence looming ahead.

Mentally calculating the number of strides left until the fence, Cameron rose up off the man's hunt saddle, hunkering down over the steed's neck and threading her fingers through her mane. She could hear the skirts of her riding habit flapping in the wind, hear the steel-tipped hooves pounding the earth.

Cameron held her breath, thrusting out her arms to give the gray enough rein to make the daring jump, and suddenly she was airborne. For one long moment, time became elastic. As she sailed over the fence, all of Elmwood—its cotton fields and muddy rivers, lush vegetation and flat dusty deltas—stretched beyond the burning April sky. For that one moment, Cameron was a part of the magnificent steed beneath her. She felt Roxy's great lungs fill with air. She was free, free of the skirts and petticoats that tangled around her legs, free of the frustrations of being born female in a man's world.

All too soon, Roxy's hooves hit the soft grass and the two of them landed in Elmwood again.

"Sweet Mary, Mother of God," Taye cried, sinking to her knees in the grass.

"It's all right, Taye," Cameron called gaily, releasing the reins as Roxy trotted back toward the fence, proud neck arched, mane streaming. "I'm fine. Look, no hands." She dropped the knotted leather reins to her lap and waved with both kidskin-gloved hands.

"Please, Cameron, take the reins and stop scaring me like this." Taye covered her lovely face. "You know how much it frightens me when you don't hold on."

Cameron laughed as she slowed to a walk. "And what of this?" she teased, pulling her muddy riding boots from the stirrups. "Look, Taye. Does this scare you, too?"

With the practiced hand of a young woman who had tumbled to the ground many times, Cameron lifted one foot and then the other until she stood balanced on the seat of the English-made saddle, worth the price of a male field hand, her arms outstretched for balance.

Taye glanced up, her honey-colored skin flushing beneath her sunbonnet, her lovely features flashing from fear to annoyance. "Stop that, Cameron. Stop it at once. You know you only do that to frighten me."

"That's where you're wrong, Taye. I don't do it to frighten you." She swayed precariously as the mare lowered her head to nibble fresh grass. "I do it because I like to."

Cameron dropped to the ground, coming to rest before the young woman kneeling in the grass.

Taye—an innocent seventeen years old to Cameron's twenty-three—leaped to her feet and threw her arms around her companion. "Do you see why such nonsense is dangerous? You could have been hurt!"

"But I wasn't hurt." Cameron looked into Taye's pale blue eyes. "Look at me, you silly goose. I'm right as rain." She pinched Taye's cheek affectionately.

"Look at you indeed," Taye exclaimed, breaking into a grin. She worshiped the ground Cameron Campbell walked on and had since she was a baby on their mammy's lead strings. She handed Cameron her straw bonnet. "Best put this on before you're freckled beyond hope. The sun's hot today. What I was trying to tell you before you took off over that fence was that the senator has sent for you. A guest has arrived and just look at you." She indicated with a sweep of her gracious hand. "You look like a field hand. Your riding habit is covered in mud and your hair is tangled in a rat's nest. It will take me an hour to comb out those snarls."

Cameron caught Roxy's reins and headed along the elm-lined drive that led to Elmwood, the grand, white-columned house of the cotton and sugar cane plantation nestled beside the muddy Pearl River. Just south of Jackson, Mississippi, Elmwood was the only home she had ever known. The only world she had ever known.

"My appearance again? Taye, you know I could care less what anyone thinks of my appearance! I'm sick of always being the proper Southern lady. Sick of always being expected to be dressed suitably, to say and do what is appropriate, to smile when I don't feel like smiling. You should have been born Senator David Campbell's daughter instead of me. You are truly a lady in every sense of the word."

"Cameron, don't talk like that!" Taye's pale-blue eyes grew wide.

"And who is this visitor?" Cameron asked, running her fingers through her long copper hair. "Well, whoever it is, I'm so happy that Papa is home again!"

Senator David Campbell had been in Washington D.C. on and off since Mississippi had seceded from the Union in January. Though he could no longer attend the senate in an official capacity, he had been desperately trying to bridge the widening gap between politicians from both northern and southern states. Despite the secession of South Carolina, Mississippi, Florida, Alabama, Georgia, Louisiana and Texas, he still held out hope that a war over slavery could be prevented.

The senator had told Cameron only last night at the supper hour that matters were not going well. Just last month at a convention in Montgomery, Alabama, the seven seceding states had created a Confederate Constitution. And with the previous president's refusal to surrender southern federal forts to the seceding states, southern troops had recently seized them. The senator had been about to explain the ramifications of such seizures when her brother Grant had joined them and her father had changed the subject to discussing the new crop of cotton. Grant did not approve of the senator discussing politics with a woman, and on his first night home her father had wanted to keep the peace between them, at least for a few short hours.

Cameron lowered her hand to her hip impatiently. "Well, do tell? Who is my father's visitor?" She wrinkled her sunfreckled nose. "What's the big secret? Surely our newly inaugurated President Lincoln has not come to call! He's been president but a month. I would think he would be occupied elsewhere."

"It's not our president, silly goose." Taye glanced nervously away, smoothing the bodice of her new peach bombazine gown that seemed, on her, to be impervious to wrinkles. "Now remember, don't kill the messenger," she warned.

Cameron smiled lovingly at her companion. Though Taye was the daughter of their freed slave housekeeper, Sukey, and six years her junior, she had loved her as a sister since the day Taye had entered her nursery as a toddler. Because Taye had been fathered by some unknown white man, she had exquisite honey-colored skin. Her creamy complexion, pale-blue eyes and rich dark-brown hair gave her the exotic look of a woman who, like Helen of Troy, could launch a thousand ships.

"Tell me," Cameron said, halting. "You know I could never be angry with you, puss."

"Perhaps you should go to your father's study and see for yourself."

"Who?" Cameron demanded, her amber cat eyes narrowing dangerously.

Taye hung her beautiful head. "Captain Logan."

"Logan!" Cameron exploded. "Jackson Logan, that no good, son of a poxed—"

"Cameron!" Taye blinked in shock. "That is no way for a lady of your station to speak. Hush before someone hears you."

"My station, my rosy arse," Cameron shouted, starting for the house again. This time she took long, determined strides, her riding boots tapping on the dry, mud-packed driveway.

A yard boy came running to take Roxy's reins from her hands, leading the horse off in the direction of the stables.

"Jackson Logan," Cameron fumed aloud. "I should think he would have been sunk by pirates by now, that or killed in a duel over a loose woman." *Jackson,* she fumed silently. She hated the arrogant, egotistical, honey-tongued scoundrel. She hated his flirtatious manner and his beguiling smile. She hated him now as much as she had once loved him.

The summer Cameron had been seventeen, Jackson Logan, twelve years her senior, had arrived in a cloud of dust on a great dappled Thoroughbred. On business from his father, a shipping merchant, he had galloped up Elmwood's long drive with his darkly handsome good looks and his smooth tongue. Cameron had lost her heart to him before he removed his wide-brimmed hat and bid her good day.

Theirs had been a secretive romance of heated kisses and laughter on steamy July nights. They had ridden side by side, hunted side by side, even jumped fences side by side. Jackson had told her he didn't mind a woman who could shoot as accurately as a man, or a woman who rode astride and seated a horse as well as he did. He said he actually preferred it.

He had said many things, and she had naively believed him. He had said he loved her, told her he would love her forever. One night, after her father had gone to bed, Cameron had almost surrendered her virginity to Jackson Logan's sweet words and even sweeter kisses. In the end, she had refused him. The following day, Jackson was called back to Baltimore by his father. Cameron, starry-eyed by first love and inexperienced with men, had suggested they marry so she could accompany him.

But Jackson had laughed at her... She could still remember

the rich tone of his voice, the bored look on his strikingly handsome face.

He had laughed at her!

"Marry you," he had said, bending the brim of his hat in his hand just so, for he was always fastidious in a careless way about his dress. "I'm not going to marry you. What would I do with a spoiled little papa's girl for a wife? What would I do with a wife at all?" Again, the lazy laughter. "No, my little vixen, you had better stay here on Elmwood where you belong with your papa and your scores of servants."

"But you said you loved me," she had wept as she watched him don the hat, her heart tearing asunder in her chest. "You said you would love me always."

He had met her gaze with those startling gray eyes of his, eyes that could shamelessly undress her in a ballroom crowded with guests. "I said a lot of things, sweet, as did you, but we know we didn't really mean them, don't we?" He had held her gaze as her heart hardened. "Now give us a kiss, and I'll be on my way north."

She had called him names, vile names she had heard her brother Grant use, names she hadn't even fully known the meanings of. She had ripped off her new chenille headdress and thrown it after him. She had cursed him and every generation of his family to come.

And still he had gone.

Recalling that morning on the veranda brought the threat of tears to Cameron's eyes even now, six years later. But she took a deep breath and refused to cry, for tears were punishment, assuagement, relief from tension, and she did not for one moment want that release. She wanted to remain angry, to recall the pain. It was her only weapon against Jackson Logan.

"What does he think he's doing here?" Cameron demanded, wiping her eyes with the back of her hand, hoping Taye thought it was the dust from the ride that made them water.

"I don't know. The senator only said that I should fetch you," Taye said softly. "If you don't want to see him, I can make excuses. I can say you've a headache and you've gone upstairs to lie down.'' Taye knew what had happened between Cameron and Jackson Logan. She knew from nights they had lain beside each other in Cameron's great bed and Taye had dreamed of a man who would one day ride into her life and sweep her off her feet. But Cameron had given up on that girlish dream years ago.

''No,'' Cameron said firmly, entering the house through the towering front door. She strode across the formal entryway and down the elegant, portrait-lined hall toward her father's study, tossing her hat to a passing housemaid. ''Who does he think he is coming here after all these years?'' she muttered beneath her breath.

''I believe Captain Logan and your father are still well acquainted,'' Taye said.

''Captain? Since when is he a captain?''

''Since his father died and he inherited all those ships, I suppose,'' Taye murmured. ''Apparently, the senator and Captain Logan see much of each other when your father is in Washington.''

Cameron halted at her father's mahogany paneled study door. ''Whose side are you on anyway?'' she snapped, amber eyes flashing.

Taye immediately lowered her gaze. ''Yours, of course.'' She looked up, her chin quivering. ''Always yours, Cameron. You must know that.''

Pushing back a heavy lock of her tangled hair, Cameron reached out and gave Taye a quick hug. ''Don't cry,'' she said, feeling instantly guilty. ''I didn't mean to snap at you. It's only that after all this time…'' She didn't finish her sentence, too unsure of the emotions tumbling inside her.

For so many years she had dreamed of the moment she would meet Jackson again. This was the moment she had fantasized! She would tell him the things she had wanted to tell him all these years. She would tell him how cruel he had been to that young, innocent girl on the veranda, how he had taken advantage of her and known he was doing it! Now suddenly she couldn't remember any of the words she had rehearsed.

Her mouth was dry and her palms damp as an overwhelming fear washed over her.

"It's all right," Taye whispered reassuringly. "I would put you up against an entire army of ship's captains any day." She pushed the hair back from Cameron's face as she studied her gaze. "But why don't you clean up before you go in? Before he sees you for this very first time."

"Clean up? Why should I clean up for him?" Cameron demanded hotly. "He's not fit to wipe my boots!"

Taye squeezed her best friend's hand, keeping her voice low and, as always, ladylike. "You must look your best, so that he will see what he gave up." She hesitated, and seeing that Cameron was considering it, she smiled deviously. "Come, now. Just a quick wash of your face and hands, and a fresh gown. The new one your father brought you would be so beautiful with the color of your hair and eyes. And I'll do up your hair the way you like it."

Cameron glanced at her father's closed study door. She could hear male voices rumbling inside. Her father was there with his assistant Mr. Burl, whom Taye was smitten with, and there was another voice. She could still recognize that deep tenor and it cut through her like a dagger. "Jackson," Cameron hissed, her lower lip quivering with anger.

"Come on," Taye plied, leading Cameron away. "It will only take a few moments. Once he sees you in that green silk gown, he'll be blinded by your beauty. Awestruck by your grace and manners. He'll fall on his knees and beg your father for your hand right there and then."

"Ask for my hand," Cameron snapped, allowing herself to be led away. "I'd sooner give him my head on a platter than my hand."

"I know, I know," Taye soothed, wrapping her arm around Cameron's waist and guiding her up the grand staircase.

For a moment, Cameron relented and allowed herself to be comforted. She rested her head on Taye's shoulder, breathing in the soft, comforting scent of her skin as she slowly took the steps.

*   *   *

As Jackson listened to his old friend Senator Campbell, he kept his eye on the door that led into the hallway. Where was she? The senator had called for his daughter nearly an hour ago. A part of him couldn't wait to see her; a part of him dreaded it. What if she had changed? What if she had become an eyelash-fluttering, sweetly mannered Southern belle…a pale reflection of the vibrant flame-haired girl who haunted his dreams.

Cameron. He had almost cancelled his detour to Elmwood because of her. When he closed his eyes, he could see her golden amber cat eyes, could still smell her soft, pale skin, scented with magnolia. He could taste her mouth on his, full of fire and a sweetness he had never known before or since. All these years he had still not forgotten her, no matter how hard he tried or how many women's hearts he conquered. When he saw her eyes in his dreams, those tawny orbs were burning with anger and accusation.

Sweet, innocent Cameron Campbell. At the age of seventeen she had been able to match him astride, with a rifle, even at cards. For one lazy, hot Mississippi summer, she had been his constant companion, his equal, his first real love. Later, when he had closed his eyes, when he had tasted another woman's lips, it was Cameron's name that had echoed in his head—and he hated her for it. Hated himself. He had let things get out of hand that summer, for he, too, despite his age, had been innocent—innocent of love and its ravages. Even now, he was convinced he had done the right thing in leaving her then, when he could still get away. To give her his heart, his whole heart, would have been a terrible mistake. It wasn't that he didn't like women. He did. He loved them, but he loved them in their place. At the supper table, in a drawing room greeting guests, best of all in his bed. That was the one mistake he had not made, thank God above. He had not taken Cameron's virtue. Not that he hadn't wanted to, hadn't tried, but in the end her clear head had prevailed over his.

Now, after all this, he would see her again. What if she wasn't the girl he remembered? What if he'd spun his memory of her out of sugar cane and Mississippi moonlight?

Jackson fought back his reverie to direct his attention to his friend. Senator David Campbell, a man born on Southern soil who now sympathized with the north, was in a difficult spot, caught between the muddy shore and the paddle wheel. Jackson knew the senator had tried to help his constituents see their way through this dissent; he had attempted to persuade northerners to see the southerners' side of the position. David Campbell had spent many a sleepless night arguing with fellow Southern and Northern politicians in smoky hotel rooms, but to no avail. Even now, lines were being drawn in the dusty soil that was the South's livelihood, and men were being forced to choose sides, brother against brother, father against son.

Jackson glanced at his friend who was pacing the floor, waving a hand passionately as he had once done on the senate floor.

"Damn it, the imprisonment of another human being is wrong," the senator declared hotly, pausing at an open floor-to-ceiling window. "Damn, Logan, I'm glad to be home." He waved his hand toward the view. "This is where I get my strength, from this soil that my Scottish father staked out himself. The soil that as a young boy I hocd myself. And later, when the land had begun to prosper, and we were able to buy slaves, I rode these fields overseeing the planting, the picking and the baling of cotton. This soil of Elmwood is in my blood. In my soul."

Jackson listened carefully, nodding. Through the open window, he could smell the rich, upturned soil of the cotton fields of Elmwood. He could hear the slaves singing as they returned from the fields. He inhaled the heady, thick scent of rotting vegetation on the Pearl River less than half a mile away.

It was hot and stuffy in the study. He had forgotten how stifling the South could be, and it was only April. He was spoiled, of course. Spoiled by the more northern climate of Maryland and the winds of the Atlantic Ocean. He tugged at his starched white cravat, hoping the senator might shed his so that Jackson could do the same.

Damn it, where is she? Jackson turned to pour himself a brandy, fighting to keep his attention on what the senator was saying.

2

"Papa, it's me." As Cameron tapped on her father's study door, she felt a trickle of perspiration between her breasts, caused no doubt by nervousness.

She had begged Taye to come in with her, but Taye—always conscious of her place in the household—insisted that it wouldn't be appropriate for her to enter the study when the senator had a guest.

Cameron paused, feeling more like a second-century Christian thrown to Roman lions than a devoted Southern daughter attending her father. She opened the door and stepped inside.

"There you are," the senator exclaimed, walking toward her with open arms. "My precious."

Cameron lifted up on her toes, and he leaned down so that she could give him a hearty kiss on his cheek as he embraced her. She settled in his arms for a moment. How she loved Papa's smell—his tobacco, shaving soap—and solid confidence. It gave her the self-assurance she needed to lift her lashes and meet Jackson Logan's penetrating gray-eyed gaze head on.

"Captain Logan." The senator turned. "You remember my daughter, Cameron."

Jackson's gaze met hers, and for a brief moment, time stood still. She saw a flash of emotion in his eyes that she could not interpret. Was he actually as apprehensive about seeing her again as she was of seeing him? But the look on his handsome face was gone in an instant, replaced by a cocky grin. "It's been many years since I've had the pleasure to visit Elmwood," Jackson replied lazily as he strode toward them, his gaze never straying from hers. "But I would have known your lovely daughter anywhere." He took her hand, which she prayed did not tremble as he kissed it, dwelling just an instant too long for propriety, his warm lips pressed to her skin.

Cameron tugged her hand from his grasp, as if a cottonmouth snake had bitten her.

"Last I saw her, she was but a girl," Jackson continued as his eyes narrowed wickedly and his glance swept deliberately up and down the length of her body.

Damn him, Cameron seethed. He'd not lost an ounce of his arrogance. God Almighty, how she despised a man with such an insufferable superior attitude.

"But I see now she has grown to be quite the lovely *woman*," Jackson finished, his intonations apparently oblivious to everyone in the room but her.

"Good to see you again, Captain Logan," Cameron said coolly. She turned away, not so quickly as to be rude in front of her father, but to be certain Jackson caught her intent. "And, Thomas, how lovely to have you with us again," she declared warmly, meeting her father's assistant halfway as he came from behind the great carved desk.

"Why, Miss Campbell, thank you so much for having me." He nodded, moving stiltlike on his long, gangly legs. "It is so good to be here. I always know that I am at home again in Mississippi when I see the elm-lined drive."

Her father's assistant had a shock of sandy blond hair that was always immaculately kept. Thomas Burl's face was common in appearance, with hooded eyes and a long patrician nose. Though not unattractive, he was hardly the kind of man who would invite the attention of Southern ladies. But his warm brown eyes appealed to Cameron. They were honest, unlike the gray orbs she could sense now burning into her back.

"May I offer you another brandy, Papa?" Cameron asked,

headed already toward a snifter on a small table beneath the window.

"Of course, my precious," the senator chuckled.

She forced a mannered smile. "Mr. Burl?" she offered as she refilled her father's glass with a healthy dose of the rich, fragrant spirit he so favored.

"For me? No, no thank you," Thomas stammered.

Cameron forced herself to glance in Jackson's direction, trying hard not to look into his eyes. "And you, Captain?"

Jackson was a tall, lithe man, a full hand's span over six foot. He had broad shoulders and a narrow waist that were well fitted to the latest style. His tailor-made soft yellow coat and tan breeches fit him as if they were a glove, accentuating his masculinity. He did not wear his thick, dark hair short as Southerners did, but rather pulled back in a neat queue. On any other man it would have looked ridiculous in this day and time, but it suited him well, giving him an air of seductive mystery. Cameron recalled that his hands had been large and calloused, rough from the work he did on board ship and in his father's warehouse in the Baltimore harbor. They were sailor's hands, not those of a gentleman. She tried not to think about how shockingly magnificent those coarse hands had felt on her skin. She wondered if those hands were still rough or, if now, as his own captain, he ordered others to do the heavy labor.

"Me, brandy? Need you ask?" His lazy, drawled question brought a flash of heat to her cheeks.

The devil take him! Even after all this time, just a careless word from his mouth made her quiver inside. For six long years Cameron had done everything she could to deny the sexuality that this man had unearthed. She realized now, in an instant, that she had surrounded herself with all the things she loved—the plantation, politics, her beloved herd of Arabians— to escape this deep burning need for Jackson that had not vanished after all, but only lain dormant all this time. And seeing him here today, being this close to him, had fanned those sparks to a flame.

The insolent cad never moved from where he leaned against

a carved mahogany bookcase of law tomes. He waited for her, making her cross the study, which could have only been fifteen or sixteen feet, but seemed a mile to her as she walked it, her head held high, her layers of starched petticoats rustling.

His fingers purposely caressed hers as she refilled his glass. She jerked at the contact and the dark liquid leaped in the glass, threatening to spill over.

"Excuse me," she stammered. "I'm so sorry." Heat flashed again to her skin as she fought to regain her composure.

"Don't be," Jackson murmured, lifting the glass to his mouth.

Cameron meant to turn away, yet before she could, his lips skimmed the rim of the glass. In fascination, she watched as his mouth, which had once caressed hers, took in the liquid. Her breath caught in her throat. She turned, ashamed of herself, angry with her body, with her very soul's betrayal. Realizing that she had to make herself busy, she spoke. "If you gentlemen are hungry, I'm sure something light can be ordered from the kitchen."

"Cam is right. She has always been a better host than I could ever be. I forget myself." The senator smoothed his graying hair with his palm. "Something to eat, Jackson? I know it was a long ride to Elmwood."

"No, thank you, Senator. But another brandy would be appreciated." He lifted his glass to Cameron, in mocking, feigned politeness.

Cameron met his steely gray eyes, eyes that seemed to be laughing at her.

Her proper Southern hostess's smile still etched on her face, she retrieved his glass to refill it, taking care this time not to touch him.

"And then," Jackson continued, dragging his lazy gaze from her to the senator, "I thought we could speak, sir. *Alone.*"

Thomas's head snapped up as if he were a long-legged marsh bird suddenly startled by a roving hawk. He had returned to his seat behind her father's desk, where he was, no doubt, dealing with her father's correspondence. But one look at Jackson, who obviously intimidated him even more than Cameron did, and he was out of his chair, ready to make a retreat.

The senator's brow knitted. His gaze met and held Jackson's. "Please speak freely," he said. "I trust my daughter and Mr. Burl's discretion entirely."

"Senator Campbell, I understand your trust in Mr. Burl and in your *dear* daughter, but what I have to say must only be between the two of us. For *their* safety," he emphasized surreptitiously.

Cameron's back stiffened and the faux smile fell from her face as she met Jackson's gaze with fury. Not wanting to leave without speaking a word of opposition, she looked to her father. "Really now, Papa," she said in a teasing voice. She smiled in the way that she knew could get her just about anything from her father. "I do believe the captain exaggerates. He has spent so much time swashbuckling on the sea that I fear he imagines intrigue and plots where there are none."

Jackson said nothing and his silence made her even angrier than if he had hotly protested. Cameron ground her teeth, still gazing up at her father, purposely ignoring Jackson. How dare the cad come here to her home and insist her father order her from the room as if she were a child?

The senator lowered his hand to her shoulder. "Could you excuse us, dear? I'm sure the captain has some sort of dull political issue to discuss concerning shipping rights now that Mississippi does not consider itself one of the States. You'd be bored to tears in five minutes' time."

"But, Papa, you forget that I was milk-fed on political discussions. I relish them!"

The senator's gaze met Cameron's, and she knew she had lost. She might wheedle a new horse or another saddle from her father with that coy smile, but when it came to matters of her welfare or protection, no amount of cajoling would do. Her father had taught her well when to fight and when to gracefully withdraw.

"Mr. Burl," she purred huskily, turning deliberately on her

kid leather slippers. "Would you care to see the new Arabian mare Papa just had shipped from Ireland? She is truly breathtaking."

"Why, certainly," he managed to reply. His face turned as red as spring beets and his Adam's apple bobbed above his tight cravat.

She slipped her arm through his and boldly ran a hand down his russet sleeve. "What a simply lovely coat, Mr. Burl. Don't tell me it's another you've bought in France." She escorted him out of her father's study, giving the impression she was utterly enthralled with the young lawyer. "I must say, you *do* have the most superb taste in fashion."

Senator David Campbell watched the door close behind his daughter and he couldn't resist a bittersweet smile. "God, how I love that girl, Logan. I would give her anything, do anything in my power to make her happy." He turned. "If only it was in my power to keep this damned war from coming. But after this last trip to Washington, I know better. It's only a matter of time until the first gunshots are fired, Logan. That will signal the end of the privileged life my young, exuberant daughter has led here at Elmwood. An end to the life of all Southerners."

"She is beautiful," Jackson mused aloud. "But she is also intelligent. She will adjust."

The senator nodded. "Well, she is headstrong. You would not believe the things that girl has done, tried to do. She is so feminine in so many ways, yet she sees herself as an equal to every man in this county." He chuckled. "Truth be known, she probably is. I wouldn't want to race with her on the back of one of those high-spirited Arabians of hers." He cleared his throat. "But I apologize. You didn't come all this way to speak of Cameron, did you? What do you have to say that is so sensitive?"

"I think it would be better if we went for a walk, sir, away from prying ears." Jackson indicated the closed door with an arch of his eyebrow. "I know how walls can have ears in a home. I know mine do and what I have to say to you cannot go beyond you and me.''

The senator finished his brandy in one swig and set down the heavy crystal glass. ''A walk would be nice. Let me show you the new peach orchard we've just planted this spring.''

Grant Campbell watched from the polished stair rail of the second floor landing as his father and Jackson walked out the front door, their heads bowed, deep in conversation.

Grant pressed his back to the ornate papered wall so the men would not detect him. ''*Captain* Jackson Logan,'' he muttered beneath his breath. ''Captain, my hairy ass. He's nothing but a pirate in fancy breeches.'' He watched the door close behind them before coming out of hiding. ''Wonder what he wants.''

The sound of footsteps down the hall caught Grant's attention and he looked up just in time to see a swish of peach-colored skirting disappear around the corner.

''Not so fast there, my little chick.'' Grant hurried down the long hall as fast as his crippled leg would carry him and turned the corner.

Taye halted in the center of the hall, a straw bonnet dangling from her hand, but she did not turn to face him.

''And where do you think you're going?'' he drawled like the perfect Southern gentleman. The girl was so shy, so modest. He was enjoying the hunt immensely.

''Cameron's bonnet,'' she said coolly, still not turning to face him. ''She forgot it when she went to the barn with Mr. Burl, and she asked me to fetch it for her.''

Grant reached out and grabbed her wrist, twisting it, forcing her to turn and face him. He gazed into her pale-blue eyes—unusual for a darky. Her mother was that bitch, Sukey, who had always hated him. And her father? It had always been assumed he was one of his father's guests.

''She abuses your good nature, that sister of mine.'' He lifted her wrist to his mouth, pressing a kiss to the soft underside.

She tried to wrench away. ''Please...''

He bit her.

"Ouch," she cried as she jerked in pain.

When he looked up to meet her gaze, he was rewarded with sparkling tears brimming in those lovely blue eyes.

"Let me go. Cameron is waiting for me."

"She can wait," he snarled as he lowered his mouth to the red teeth marks he had just made. This time he was ever so gentle. He pressed his lips to the marred skin and then parted them to taste her with his tongue. "Oh, Taye, succulent Taye," he breathed, letting his eyes drift shut. "What an exquisite creature you are. If only you would let me take you into my room, I could show you the moon, the stars…"

She struggled, trying to pull free, but he held her securely. Just the thought of lifting her petticoats, sampling the honey of her nest, made him rock hard beneath his breeches.

Footsteps suddenly sounded on the staircase behind him. Taye yanked her hand and he let her go. It wouldn't do to let any of the servants see him. Next thing he knew, they'd be wagging their tongues to his bitchy sister, or worse, to his father. Now that Papa was home again, Grant knew he would have to curtail his amusements.

He sighed with already anticipated boredom at the thought as he watched Taye flee toward the stairs. Well, if he did get bored, he could always go to Baton Rouge. His father owned a house there, too, and Baton Rouge was such a fine town. Fine whores there, ones with all sorts of interesting appetites.

Naomi, one of the house slaves, came around the corner, a pile of clean linens in her arms.

Ah, Naomi. Grant knew her well. Knew every inch of her inky flesh and tight curls. He liked Naomi. He liked her relaxed attitude toward sex and the way she was so willing to fulfill his fantasies. He was also a little afraid of her. She was supposedly some kind of voodoo priestess. The senator did not allow voodoo to be practiced on Elmwood, but it was anyway. Any man with half a brain and one good eye knew that. If his father wasn't so busy in Washington, busy with those damned Yankees, maybe he would know what was going on on his own plantation.

Grant scowled at the thought. His father was a senator from Mississippi. Before Mississippi's secession he was supposed to have been representing his constituents in the senate in Washington. But what had his father done? What was he doing now? He was stirring up all kinds of trouble, talking with the other senators from the North, trying to sway the beliefs of honorable Southerners.

Free the darkies? That was the most ridiculous thing he had ever heard. What would become of the South if they lost their labor? The sugar cane would rot in the fields. The cotton would go to seed. The only way the plantations could continue to produce such labor-intensive products, continue to prosper, was to keep those black devils at work. What would they do with freedom anyway? Chop off more chicken heads? Stick more pins in little dirty dolls? He shuddered at the thought.

"I don' know why yer makin' such faces, Masta Grant. Ya keep that up and yer face'll stick thata way," Naomi said matter-of-factly.

Grant snaked out a hand and caught her arm. The linens fell to the floor, but she just stared at him with those black eyes of hers. She wasn't afraid of him, not like Taye was. "Shut your ugly mouth," he snapped. "You've no cause to speak to me in that manner."

"Shut up or what ya gonna do, *Masta?*" She mocked him, even as she used the proper address.

"Punish you," Grant said, licking his lips at the thought.

She didn't struggle or try to pull away. She just stared at him with those evil eyes of hers. "An' both us know ya'd like that, wouldn't ya, Masta?"

He let go of her and she leaned over to pick up the clean laundry.

"Come to my room tonight," he said. "After I turn in." He walked away, straightening his cravat. "We'll see how sassy you are then, Miss High-and-Mighty."

3

"Let me understand what you're saying," the senator continued as they walked in the direction of the river. "The president wants *me*, a man born and raised in Mississippi—the second state to secede from the Union, mind you—to be a war advisor?"

"Senator, everyone in Washington would like to think there will be no war, that we can settle this like civilized men, but…"

"But no one believes we will be that fortunate?"

Jackson frowned. "The president knows who his friends are. You would have to resign officially as the senator from Mississippi, of course," he explained. "You'll have to cut your ties with your home state. But in light of the latest developments, many in Washington assume that is your intention, anyway."

David Campbell leaned on an old weathered fence, its rails split by his own father when the idea of becoming a senator was beyond a boy's imagination. In the lush green meadow beyond them, he could see his precious daughter walking out to offer her new mare a tidbit while Mr. Burl waited at the fence on the far side of the pasture. Her skirts bunched in one hand, petticoats flashing, Cameron looked more like a girl out with a playmate than the capable young woman she had become.

The senator lowered his gaze to the rough-hewn rail of the

fence and grasped it for support. "You are right. The lines have been drawn and I must at last take my place in history. It tears my heart in two to think of betraying my friends, my constituents, my Mississippi this way, but I must." He took a deep breath, feeling suddenly older than he had when he awoke that morning. There was something about finally voicing his objective aloud that made it seem all the more real.

"It is my intention, Jackson, to sever my ties with the Confederate States of America, though I've told no one yet." He glanced at his friend. "Not even my son and daughter."

The captain nodded, lifting his booted foot to rest it on the lower rail of the fence. "I understand, sir. What passes between us will not go beyond here. I apologize for forcing you to even reveal this much to me. But when Mr. Secretary of State William Seward and certain gentlemen in Washington heard I was headed south to see my new ship in the yards in Baton Rouge, I was asked to carry this message to you."

David sighed, stroking the wood of the split-rail fence made gray and craggy by time. "I intend to set my slaves free and shutter Elmwood. Cameron doesn't know it yet, but she'll be traveling north to live with old friends in New York. I will not have her here when war comes."

"And it will come," Jackson said philosophically. "Soon, I'm afraid, sir."

"So I would be a war advisor?" the senator questioned, most definitely surprised, but pleased by the request. How proud his father would have been of him now.

"You would be working directly under Mr. Seward for President Lincoln. You are greatly respected by everyone in Washington, Senator. Apparently the president has had his eye on you for some time."

The senator laughed, but without mirth. "Every *Northerner* desires association with me, you mean. I had thought I was taking care with my words and actions, but apparently not enough care. I've seen the changes in my Southern friends. In Washington, even before the official secession, I wasn't invited to quite so many soirees as I once was." He held up a finger. "Oh, my peers are very careful to remain gentlemen.

Nothing has been said directly to me about my attitudes, but I can feel them watching me. Hating me.'' He closed his hand into a fist and brought it down hard on the rail. ''And I will not tolerate Cameron being subjected to that obscene hatred. What I do in the coming months must fall upon my shoulders and mine alone.''

Jackson removed his coat, hung it over the rail and pushed up his white sleeves. ''So you will accept the appointment?''

A smile caught the corner of the senator's mouth. ''I'm saying I will take the offer into consideration. First I must take care of things here on the home front. Once I'm back in Washington, I will seriously discuss the matter with Mr. Seward.''

''You know, sir, that Robert E. Lee resigned his commission with the United States Army.''

''A good man.'' The senator spoke quietly. ''Yes, I heard just as I left Washington.''

''He's been offered command of the military and naval forces of Virginia. They say he'll accept. Next thing you know, he'll be taking full command of the Confederate army.''

The senator nodded, drew a deep breath and glanced toward Cameron again. She had somehow managed to capture the mare and was now leading her across the grassy meadow with nothing but soft, encouraging words he could not quite catch on the warm breeze, and a thin rope thrown carelessly over the Arabian's neck.

''I don't know where my son Grant will fall into place here,'' David said, thinking aloud. ''It's the one matter I am most reluctant to address.''

Jackson gazed out into the meadow. ''I take it he does not see eye to eye with you on the slavery issue.''

''I fear my son and I do not see eye to eye on any matter these days, but this one least of all. He— Damn it, Logan, I would do anything to improve my relationship with my son, but Grant just seems to be drifting farther and farther away from me, from Elmwood and all that has ever been important to the Campbell name. Grant fell off a horse many years ago, and in the months of recuperation that followed, he changed.

He...he was demoralized by the accident, by his injury. He became so bitter, so angry. Nothing seems to matter to him anymore but the carnal pleasures he comforts himself with." David lifted a shoulder. "To Grant, as to most Southern gentlemen, slavery is simply an issue of economics. It has nothing to do with human beings. My son is correct when he says that, without our slave population, Elmwood's cotton and cane production will drop drastically. We could hire field hands, of course, but the cost would take too large a portion of our profit. So even if we could find men to hire to work the fields, we would fail financially."

"This is all about Grant's purse." Jackson made no attempt to hide his contempt for the senator's son. Grant and Jackson had always despised one another.

David nodded in reply. He wanted so badly to see his son happy the way Cameron was, but no matter what he gave him, Grant never seemed content. "I honestly do not know if Grant will consent to move north with us. I can't imagine he'd stay here, though. Elmwood means nothing to him but the cash she provides. Not like that one." He nodded in Cameron's direction. She was leading the mare through a gate, headed for the stable. "Elmwood is in Cam's blood. She's a Campbell through and through. I swear, the girl was born with Mississippi soil beneath her fingernails. She loves this plantation as much as she loves those horses of hers. Sometimes I think she's right, that she should have been born a man."

The two men chuckled.

"Do you think your son would join the Confederate army?" Jackson questioned.

The senator shook his head. "Oh, no, Grant could never join in the war effort," he said quickly. "His injury was too severe. No, my guess is that when the war comes, my son and heir will attempt to make me feel as guilty about my choice as he possibly can. He will then take the money I offer and go to our home in Baton Rouge. He'll sit out the war there, drinking and whoring, using the excuse of his injury not to fight."

"Well, sir, think over President Lincoln's offer," Jackson said, slapping the fence. He picked up his coat.

The senator turned to him. "Will you stay a week or so? Accept my hospitality?"

"My ship is being refitted in Baton Rouge, sir. I'm adding a couple of small guns. I should continue on and supervise the work."

"Come, now." The senator rested a hand on Jackson's shoulder. "You said yourself that she won't be ready for at least another month, perhaps even two. Stay. I'll throw a ball in honor of your arrival."

Jackson glanced out over the meadow.

"For me," the senator asked quietly. There was a sudden yearning in him to play the Southern host just one more time before his entire civilization crumbled around him. "Please. This is probably the last occasion I'll ever have to throw a ball. To drink and dance and laugh with my neighbors. Once I release my slaves, I won't be received in any home south of the Mason-Dixon line, and you know it."

"And you're willing to bully me into staying?" Jackson questioned with an arched brow.

"Absolutely." David offered his hand with the secure smile of a man who knew he had won the argument and Jackson took it. "Thank you."

"Thank *you,*" Jackson said. "And now if you don't mind, I believe I'll have a look at that new mare of your daughter's. She looks to be a fine beast."

"I see Mr. Burl headed for the house, so I had better go anyway. We have a lot to discuss." The senator turned to go. "We'll see you for supper in the dining room? Join me for a brandy in my study before, if you like."

"I'd be honored." Jackson offered a slight, respectable bow and watched as the senator strode across the grass and up the slight hill toward the main house.

Jackson headed for the stable, knowing he was playing with fire. He knew he ought to just excuse himself to the guest room, take his boots off and have a nice long Southern gentleman's nap to cool his heels.

But Jackson had never been afraid of fire.

"What a good girl," Cameron soothed, stroking the mare's long, graceful neck. Though referred to as a gray, clean and brushed, the new mare was as creamy white as Cameron's Sabbath day petticoats.

Cameron rested her cheek on the horse's neck and took a deep breath, letting her still shaky nerves calm. Here was the only place she was truly at ease; the only place she felt she could really be herself. With the great doors shut, it was cool and dark. Maybe she would just hide out here until the captain rode off.

She suddenly lifted her head from the mare. She did hope he intended to ride off. Surely he wasn't going to stay. The idea of having Jackson here, even for one night, was intolerable. How would she be able to stand his insufferable presence? His stares. No. To have Jackson at Elmwood again would just not do. He didn't belong here. Cameron didn't know how long her father intended to stay before returning to Washington, but she certainly didn't want to have to share him with a houseguest. She and her father had so many things to talk about. He had been gone so long and she was always so lonely without him.

Cameron walked to the tack room to get a hoof pick. There were plenty of grooms to see that her horses were well cared for, but she liked to do some of the work herself. She liked to have a purpose in life beyond drinking lemonade on the veranda and looking pretty for her father.

Still talking gently to the new mare, Cameron turned her back to the stall door to clean the hooves. "That a girl," she murmured as she ran her experienced hand over the horse's pastern and gently nudged, signaling the mare to lift her foot. "Nice job. Good girl, just let me get this stone," she murmured carefully cleaning out the area around the frog of the hoof.

"Beautiful horse."

Startled, Cameron lowered the hoof and turned to the door. "Don't look so distressed, my dear." Jackson stood behind her in the stall doorway, his coat thrown carelessly over one shoulder, the sleeves of his white linen shirt rolled up.

"I am not *distressed,*" she spit.

"Your father says you've a mind to breed Arabians and start your own herd."

"As if that's of any consequence to you." She met his gaze, her amber eyes sparking with barely curbed umbrage.

He lifted his dark brows. "Such a foul manner for such a truly lovely lady."

"Get out of my way," she said between clenched teeth, tightening her grip on the hoof pick. "Get out of my barn. Off my place."

"Off *your* place? Why, Cameron, dear, your father has just invited me to stay at Elmwood. A month if I like, until my ship is ready for me."

"I hope you politely declined." Her stomach knotted.

"Now why would I do that?" he drawled, still leaning against the door frame.

"Perhaps because I despise the ground you walk upon? Because I would like to gouge those mocking eyes from their sockets?" She gestured with the hoof pick. "Or mayhap because I would like to rip your intestines—"

"Enough. Enough." He lifted a hand, laughing. "I get the idea." He frowned. "What I don't get is why you detest me so."

She could feel moisture gathering at the nape of her neck and beneath the laces of her boned stays. Her skin seemed to tingle as she felt his gaze linger upon her mouth, her throat…upon her breasts. "Why I detest you?" She forced a laugh. "Don't tell me you have entirely forgotten that summer you spent here." She took a step toward him and pushed hard on his chest with the heel of her hand. She wasn't a rat and she'd damned well not be cornered by such an arrogant predator. "I mean it. Now get out of my way."

Jackson took a step back, allowing her to pass into the walkway, but she still felt trapped. Waves of heat shimmered over the surface of her skin, and she felt as though she were trying to breathe underwater. Her fingers trembled as she dropped the pick onto a hook on the wall, and it was suddenly difficult to think. She realized that the easiest solution here, of course, would be for her to go, but she didn't intend to. This was her barn, her horses, and *he* was the one trespassing on her territory.

"Ah, that fateful summer," Jackson chuckled. "The sun was hot, the swaying grasses green and you were so lovely. I had a good time, didn't you, Cameron?"

Insufferable! What gentleman would dare to remind a lady of her indiscretion? Numbly, she grabbed up a pitchfork and began to toss hay over the wall into the mare's stall. She truly felt trapped now. To tell him why she was still so angry would mean admitting how deeply she had cared for him. She'd rot in hell before she admitted the truth.

"But I sense we didn't part on as friendly terms as I had presumed."

She could still feel him watching her. The heat of his stare burned through her garments, scorching her skin, bombarding her with bright pinwheels of giddy sensations.

"So I must apologize for anything I did to offend you."

"What you did to offend me?" she flared, spinning around, the pitchfork poised in her hands.

Jackson dropped his coat to the stable floor and lifted his muscular arms to protect himself. She had drawn the pitchfork so close that it was a wonder she didn't take the buttons of his ivory waistcoat off with the sharp tines.

"Easy there!"

"Easy! Easy," she hissed, jabbing in the air at him.

Jackson lunged to one side, grabbed the handle of the three-pronged pitchfork and easily wrenched it from her hands.

Now *she* was defenseless. She grasped wildly at the weapon, her heart pounding, her blood pulsing at her temples. She couldn't stand to be so close to Jackson this way, to smell his clean hair, his shaving soap, his rugged maleness. "Give that back to me," she ground out from clenched teeth.

"What, so you can skewer me?" Holding her back with one hand, he set the pitchfork behind him. "Now just calm down!"

But Cameron was fighting mad. She swung her fists at him, the dampened rage of all these years bubbling up inside her. She caught him in the chin with her right fist and he gasped in pain.

"Ouch, that hurt," he growled, his anger rising.

"Good. I hope it did." She continued to flail, swinging her arms wildly, kicking, as he attempted to subdue her. "Give me back that pitchfork and I'll show you hurt," she challenged with a sense of false bravado.

Jackson captured both her wrists and pushed her against the barn wall. The back of her head hit hard, jarring her.

"That's enough," he grunted. "You're going to hurt yourself."

His face was so close to her, his stare so intense, that she had to close her eyes to avoid his gray-eyed gaze. Her head smarted from when it had bumped the wall and suddenly the heat of the afternoon was overwhelming.

"Cameron, Cameron," he whispered as he lowered his head to hers. She struggled against him, but he managed to press his lips to the sensitive skin of her neck. She was suffocating beneath the pressure of his body and her own torn emotions.

"No," she protested. "No." She moaned aloud. How could her body betray her this way? How could she ache for his kiss even as she attempted to fight him off?

Using his whole body to pin her against the pitted wall, he released one of her hands. He crushed his mouth to hers, forcing her lips apart as he ran his fingers roughly through her hair.

The assault of his tongue in her mouth was almost more than she could bear. Thrusting, driving, demanding. So utterly irresistible. She was breathless, dizzy. She had given up the fight for a moment, but began to push against him again in earnest. If she didn't breathe, if he didn't take his assaulting mouth from hers, she was going to faint in his arms.

Cameron clawed at his pristine white shirt, determined to gouge the flesh from his torso. The stifled sounds of protest she made, gagged by his mouth, were the growls of a she-cat as she devoured her prey.

He shoved her hands away, tearing his mouth from hers. "Cameron, don't," he said in a fierce whisper. "Stop fighting me and listen."

She could hear herself panting, feel her heart thudding beneath her breast. Perspiration trickled down her back, her gown suddenly scratchy and foreign against her skin. She squeezed her eyes shut, ashamed of herself and her unleashed need, her wicked desire for this man. She wanted to cry out, call for help, but no sound came from her lips.

"Open your eyes, damn it! I'm sorry," he whispered huskily, his intense eyes fixed on hers. "Do you hear me? I'm sorry. I'm sorry for what I did that day. The way I hurt you. I know what I did, damn it!"

Her lower lip trembled, and for a moment she feared she would tear up. The one thing she did not want to share with this man was her pain.

He's sorry, he's sorry, her illogical heart cried out. She didn't believe him, of course. She would never believe him. She opened her mouth to spit a retort but found herself leaning forward, reaching to meet him halfway. Instead of lifting her knee to strike him in the groin as she should have, she pressed her body to his. She molded her soft, betraying flesh to the hard, muscular frame of this man she hated so much and gave herself over to him.

Suddenly it was so hot in the barn that she felt as if she were suffocating. Her tongue darted out to explore the cool cavern of his mouth. She threaded her fingers through his thick hair, the sounds, the smells, the very walls of the barn fading from her mind.

He lowered his head to the swell of her breasts above the neckline of her gown. Cameron gasped and arched her back, feeling her nipples harden beneath the layers of her undergarments. He pressed his mouth deeper into the cleft between her breasts, his fingertips caressing the soft, eager flesh. He grabbed the neckline of the bodice to pull it lower and she heard the fabric tear.

Somewhere deep in her mind it registered that she should care that he'd tore her gown, she should care that he was handling her so roughly that the organza had torn. But nothing seemed to matter, nothing but his mouth upon hers and the burning heat of his hand on her breast.

Somehow he slid his knee between her thighs and she welcomed the pressure. She leaned against him, pressing herself to the strength and rigidity of his leg.

Jackson tore his mouth from hers, panting heavily. "Say it! Tell me you forgive me."

His words suddenly hit home. In one clear moment she realized what he was saying. He wanted her to forget everything that had happened that summer and begin anew—at least until he abandoned her again. Cameron gave Jackson a hard shove with both hands, so startling him that he stumbled backward. "Get off me," she shouted, wiping the back of her mouth with her hand as if she could wipe away her unbidden passion. "You try that again and I swear I will put that pitchfork through you!"

Tears filling her eyes, Cameron grabbed fistfuls of her skirts and ran from the barn, ran from Jackson Logan…ran from herself.

4

"I can't go to supper," Cameron declared miserably from the high, mahogany rice bed her father had commissioned for her when she was three and had outgrown the Campbell family cradle. Intricate carvings of leaves and stalks of ripe rice twined around each of the four posters, and fine white netting hung in billowing clouds from above.

She lay facedown. She was hot and sweaty, and the antique Irish crewelwork coverlet pressed into her cheek, but right now she didn't care. She felt awful and wanted to punish herself. She had let Jackson Logan kiss her and she had liked it. Even now she could taste his mouth on hers, feel his hard, lean body pressed against hers. She could smell the lingering odor of his clean, male essence on her skin.

"Don't be ridiculous," Taye said, walking around the room picking up Cameron's discarded clothing. "Your father is expecting you." She picked up shoes and stockings and retrieved a hopelessly stained hat. "You cannot possibly disappoint him."

Cameron rolled onto her back, irritably pushing her hair from her eyes as she stared at the netting that draped the bed, creating a filmy barrier between the tops of the posters and the high ceiling. "You don't understand," she cried passionately. "Didn't you hear what I just told you? I let Jackson kiss me." She shuddered. "I kissed him back, for heaven's sake!" She closed her eyes and groaned. "I don't know what came over me, Taye. One minute I was as mad as fire with him and the next minute—'' She closed her eyes and groaned again as shudders of delicious aching seeped through her bones.

"An error in judgment, that's all it was," Taye insisted calmly as she picked up the discarded green silk gown from the floor and began to smooth away the wrinkles. "You realized you had made a mistake and you put him properly in his place. You have nothing to be ashamed of. No reason to hide."

"I do not hide from anyone," Cameron argued as she sat up, sliding to the edge of the bed and tugging at the bodice of her shift, trying to ease the stifling heat that seemed to envelop her. "I just… Oh, Taye!" she cried in frustration as she flopped back on the bed again. "You're such an innocent. How can I make you understand the magnitude of what I've done?" This hadn't been a coy kiss on the cheek. This had been a *real* kiss, a mouth-to-mouth kiss.

"You just don't understand," Cameron muttered quietly, draping one arm across her forehead.

"So make me understand." Taye folded the gown carefully over a chair and knelt before Cameron on the bed, taking hold of both her hands and pulling her upright to a seated position. "Help me to understand."

"Oh, Taye, what would I do without you?" Cameron smoothed her friend's satin cheek, gazing into pale-blue eyes that were filled with a devotion she prayed she would always appreciate. "You're so good and dear. You've not really been kissed by a man yet. I don't know how to explain it to you. It's just that it can be such a—" she searched for the right word *"—violation."*

"Not if it's the right man, I should think." Taye averted her eyes.

Cameron couldn't resist a smile as she reached out to squeeze the younger girl's hand. "Don't tell me. Is it possible? Has Mr. Burl finally gotten up the gumption to kiss you? Is that why you're playing coy, dear sweet Taye?"

Color tinted Taye's cheeks as she laughed and rose to retrieve Cameron's gown. "Now you're talking nonsense. I would never kiss Mr. Burl. He's your intended."

"He is no such thing!" Cameron shot up off the bed. "I know it would certainly please Papa to see us marry, but I believe he thinks more of my security than my happiness. Mr. Burl is a fine man, but not the man for me." She slipped her arm around Taye's slender shoulders. She was so delicate, so beautiful. "Now you, you and Mr. Burl would get along well I think. You are both so genuinely good. Unlike me." *Unlike Jackson,* she mused but then pushed aside the unwanted thought.

"Don't tease me so." Taye's cheeks colored with greater intensity as she retreated to the chaise longue near the window and pretended interest in her sewing tin. "You know very well that Mr. Burl and I, why, we could never—" Her thick, dark lashes fluttered as she lowered her gaze, making an event of searching for a sewing needle. "A man such as Mr. Burl would never be an appropriate husband for a woman like me," she ventured shyly.

"And why not?" Cameron rested her hands on her hips. "You're well educated. You speak four languages." She looked to Taye. "I wager you speak better French than he does. You certainly speak the language better than I do," she laughed.

"Cameron, please, let us talk of something else." She threaded a needle.

"No. I will not talk of something else. I want to know why you think you could not marry Mr. Burl or any man like him."

Taye slowly lifted her gaze, her pale eyes suddenly dark with anguish. "Because my skin is black, Cameron!" she burst out. "Because I am a briar patch child, born without a father…born the daughter of a slave. You know that, Cameron."

They were both silent for a moment, and as Cameron saw the tears glistening in her friend's eyes, she became more aware of the pain she knew Taye experienced every day. For no matter how light her mocha skin was, no one could deny her African mother's heritage. Cameron's one wish was that they could live in a world where that wouldn't matter. She knew her father was fighting for that, would fight to the death for it.

"I'm sorry," Cameron said. "Truly sorry." She walked behind Taye and rested her hands on her companion's shoulders. "I didn't mean to upset you." She was silent for a moment, but then continued, "You're right, Taye, and I know all too well what you mean. But it isn't fair. No one should judge you by the color of your skin or even who your father was or was not. You should be judged by who you are, Taye, and nothing more."

"Please," Taye begged. She brushed at her eyes with the back of a delicate hand. "You know we're sheltered from so much of the outside world here at Elmwood. And you and I both know no such world will ever exist. No world will ever exist in which Mr. Burl and I could be man and wife. Now let it go, Cameron. Things are as they are...as they'll always be, and neither of us can change them."

"It won't always be, I promise you that. God won't allow such injustice to go on. Things will be better. I just know they will."

"You are indomitable." Taye forced a half smile. "A pity it wasn't you elected president instead of Mr. Lincoln."

They laughed together at the absurdity of the thought, and Cameron, eager to change the subject for Taye's sake, said, "So you really think I should join Papa for supper? Even with that beast still here?"

"I do. If you do not go downstairs tonight, if you don't face the captain, it will only be harder tomorrow." Taye sat down and spread Cameron's gown on her lap to mend the tear.

"You're right." Cameron walked to the window and pulled back the silk drapery to look out on the early evening that stretched before her. The slaves were coming in from the fields now, singing their spirituals. Through the open window she could hear their steady, comforting songs that marked the beginning and end of each day at Elmwood. "I should not allow Captain Jackson and his abhorrent behavior to keep me from spending time with my father," she said, trying to convince herself.

Taye's lightning-quick fingers whipped stitches in the fabric of Cameron's new gown. "Now that's my Cameron. That's the Mississippi-bred woman I know," she said proudly.

Cameron grabbed up an ivory-handled brush from the bed and began to pull it through her tangled auburn tresses. "Do you really think you can mend the dress? Papa was right. It is very pretty."

Taye bit the thread. "There you are. As good as new." She lifted the gown for Cameron's inspection. "I just stitched the tiny rent and then retacked the lace. The senator will never even see where I took the stitches in it." She rose to her feet and shook out the leaf-green gown with its three-tiered fringed flounces. "I must say, though, you really shouldn't wear such pretty things to the barn. It could have been ruined."

Cameron tossed the brush on the bed, armed with a new-found determination. She was so glad she had come to Taye and confessed her error in judgment. Taye always offered good advice. Taye understood her better than anyone, even her father. "Do help me get it on again and do something with this hair." She hurried to Taye. "If I'm going to supper, I don't want to be late."

A half an hour later Cameron glided down the grand staircase, her chin held high. Her gown was repaired and her soft kid slippers polished. Her long golden hair had been brushed until it shone and then pulled back beneath a white lace morning cap trimmed with white-and-green silk rosebuds. Taye walked a step behind her, in escort.

"Now, when we go into the dining room," Cameron whispered in a conspiratorial tone, "let us both give our utter attention to Mr. Burl and ignore Captain Logan. He'll soon realize what a terrible mistake he made in thinking he could get the better of Cameron Campbell."

At the bottom of the stairs, they encountered Taye's mother. Sukey smiled, her whole face brightening with a light Cameron always thought had to come from within the forty-year-old black woman. Sukey had been born and raised in Mississippi and had been granted her freedom by the senator years before in honor of how well she and her parents before her had served the Campbells.

Sukey was a beautiful woman, both inside and out. In fact, Elmwood's housekeeper seemed to be even more beautiful than Cameron remembered her as a younger woman. Petite in stature, she had an oval face, jet-black eyes with a dark fringe of lashes and her skin was the rich color of milky cocoa.

"There you two are," Sukey said, her smile making her all the more striking. "The senator and his guests have adjourned to the dining room. You'll have to hurry, Miss Cameron."

She offered her hand and Cameron accepted it, the comforting touch strengthening her resolve. Cameron's mother had been dead so long that she remembered nothing of her but a few glimpses of her face, perhaps more imagined than real. Here was the woman who had truly raised her. After Cameron's mother had died in childbirth, and the same fever had taken her mammy a few years later, Papa had not brought in a nursemaid, but allowed Sukey to care for both Cameron and Taye. It had brought all three women closer together, bound by threads that could not be severed by anything so trivial as the color of one's skin.

"You are so lovely tonight," Sukey said, her compliments always genuine. "Your father will be proud, but then he is always proud of you."

"You think so?" Cameron narrowed her amber eyes. "Lovely enough to make Captain Jackson insanely envious, because that is what Taye and I propose." Cameron threw a quick, sassy smile over her shoulder at her fellow conspirator. "He was a brute to me earlier, but he will not get away with it."

Sukey frowned. "Are you all right? Is this something your father should know?"

"No, no. I am fine. It was only that he made me angry and I should like to make him very uncomfortable for it now." She took Taye's hand. "We both mean to make him pay, don't we, puss?"

Cameron immediately saw Sukey's dark gaze meet her daughter's. Cameron turned back to Taye. "You *are* going to supper with me, aren't you?" She lowered her voice. "You wouldn't leave me to face the lion myself, would you?"

"Miss Cameron, dear," Sukey said gently. "It wouldn't be appropriate."

"Not appropriate? But Taye dined with us last night when Papa came home. As did you, Sukey."

Sukey lowered her lashes. She never demeaned herself, but she was well aware of society's laws concerning darkies and she behaved according to those laws. The rules were as important to her as any white mistress of any plantation in Mississippi. "It is the senator's prerogative to dine with anyone he likes in private," Sukey explained. "You know that, Miss Cameron. But it would not be appropriate for Taye to dine with you while he has guests."

Taye passed Cameron on the bottom step and stood beside her mother.

A part of Cameron felt betrayed. "I think Taye should come anyway. You know how Papa feels about all of these ridiculous rules. Taye is like a sister to me."

"It's all right, Cameron," Taye said sweetly. "Really. I don't want to go to supper with you, anyway." She slipped her arm through her mother's. "I want to go with Mama to the slave quarters. Naomi said her mother was ailing. Mama wants to take her soup and see if there is anything she can do to help her."

"Go then," Cameron said resolutely, realizing she could only fight one battle at a time. "But be sure to take a lantern. It will be dark soon."

Taye and Sukey walked past Cameron, headed for the back hall. As Taye went by, she brushed her lips against Cameron's cheek.

"Good luck with the captain."

Cameron waited until she was alone in the front hall. She took a deep breath, smoothed the pale-green silk of her gown and then, tossing her head defiantly, walked into the dining room.

The four men, her father, Grant, Mr. Burl and Jackson, all stood on the far side of the room near the floor-to-ceiling windows. They turned when she entered.

"I'm sorry I'm late, gentlemen," she apologized grandly. "It seems I suffered a tiny tear in my gown." She shifted her gaze to Jackson, then back again. "Silly me. But Taye has repaired it and all is well again."

"A beautiful gown it is," the senator said, coming to kiss her on the top of her head. "And an even more beautiful daughter."

Cameron smiled up at her father. He was a tall man and well fit for his age. He had an angular face, a long nose and a broad forehead. On more than one occasion it had been pointed out that he resembled President Lincoln. But the president was said to be a homely man, and Senator Campbell was most definitely not.

Her father turned to the other men. "Shall we dine, gentlemen, now that this exquisite lady has joined us?"

From across the room Jackson's gaze met hers. She could not believe he had the audacity to look at her that way, in front of her father, no less.

Mr. Burl pulled out a chair for Cameron and she smiled up at him with her prettiest, most ladylike smile. "Why, thank you, Mr. Burl. You are such a gentleman," she drawled.

As the men took their places at one end of the twenty-four-seat dining table, they picked up the conversation she had interrupted when she entered the room.

"You don't truly believe that sniveling nonsense, do you, Mr. Burl?" Grant asked, taking the chair to his father's right and directly across from Cameron.

"I...I do. Truly I do," Thomas stammered, seating himself beside Cameron. "With my heart I believe that when our forefathers wrote that constitution and the bill of rights, those freedoms were meant for all men."

"And what of you, Captain Logan?" Grant asked, almost sneering.

Cameron heard Thomas heave a sigh of relief as the senator's son set after another guest.

"Ah, Grant, you know better than to think you can draw fire from me," Jackson said lazily. As he spoke, he directed his response to Grant, but his gaze was on Cameron. "No one is interested in hearing my opinion on the matter."

She shifted in her Queen Anne dining chair, leaning back to allow Naomi to place a bowl of chilled squash soup on her plate. "I'm interested," Cameron said, locking gazes with Jackson. "Do tell us what you think, Captain Jackson. My father's table is always open to varying philosophies, even opposing ones. Is that not right, brother?"

Jackson grinned as if to say touché. "As Grant and I discussed on his last trip to Washington, Miss Cameron, I am from Maryland, a neutral state. We have chosen neither side of this conflict."

"But surely, Captain, should the war come, you will have to chose a side," she pushed. Cameron knew from a previous conversation with her father a few months back that Jackson refused to take either side of the slavery issue. To her, that was worse than taking the wrong side. To take no side at all was lazy and irresponsible.

He leaned back to allow Naomi to serve him his soup. He met the servant's eye playfully, as if they were already acquainted, before he returned his attention to Cameron. She immediately wondered how he knew Naomi and how well he knew her.

Though no one spoke aloud of the matter in public, everyone at Elmwood knew that one of Naomi's purposes here in the house was to see to male guests' "needs." Cameron thought the idea barbaric, but as Sukey had pointed out to her, it was a Southern tradition as old as sipping lemonade on the veranda on a hot afternoon. Sukey insisted that Cameron could no more change such traditions than she could uproot the elm trees that lined the plantation's long drive.

A thought fluttered through Cameron's mind and made her mouth suddenly dry. Had Naomi "serviced" Jackson that very afternoon? She had heard from one of the other housemaids that Captain Logan had taken a nap in the guest room. Had he had a partner? Cameron didn't care what the blackguard did, of course, but somehow the possibility rubbed her the wrong way.

"As I have stated previously, Miss Cameron," Jackson continued. "I am not a man of government politics, never have been. I am a man of economics. Mostly my own." He offered a boyish grin and lifted his spoon to sample the soup.

"So if war breaks out," Cameron flared, "you would carry goods to the South? You would run blockades that the North will put into place to cripple the Confederacy's economy?"

"If I am hired to carry goods and the price is right, frankly, my dear, I would ship to Hades."

Cameron swung around to face her father. The captain's words were almost sacrilegious to what she knew her father believed. She did not know how he could allow Jackson to speak so at his own table, and at least not argue the point. Yet her father appeared unruffled as he sampled his soup with obvious pleasure.

She glanced back at Jackson. "I cannot believe you would sit there and say such a thing, Captain! Surely no honorable gentleman would want someone to believe he was so unscrupulous."

"Miss Cameron!" He clutched his chest. "I am not unscrupulous. Even we blackguards have scruples." He sipped his soup, antagonizing her even more by taking his time. "Our scruples are simply different than yours."

Cameron's amber eyes narrowed. Was Jackson trying to tell her something? Was he warning her? She thought of the kiss they had shared in the barn and the emotions it stirred inside her. She knew he desired her, and knew that he understood she still desired him. Was he warning her to stay away? Was he telling her that once a cad, always a cad? She set down her spoon, her soup barely touched. She prayed she could heed his warning.

Later, in the senator's study, Cameron sat on one of her father's leather chairs across from him at his great desk. He was smoking a cigar, the smoke curling around his head before drifting toward the open window. From outside Cameron could hear crickets chirping and the brush of tree branches against the house. Most women took their leave when men smoked, but Cameron liked the rich, heady scent and she liked to watch her father enjoy his cigar. There was something eternally reassuring about a day at Elmwood that ended as her father enjoyed a smoke and they chatted in hushed tones. It was the time of day that she felt the closest to him, and perhaps the closest to Elmwood and the Campbell name.

The only thing that marred Cameron and the senator's time together tonight was Grant's agitated presence. He paced the study, walking back and forth behind Cameron's chair, the boot of his bad leg striking irregularly on the polished floor.

She glanced at her brother. No matter how Papa tried to make excuses for his son and heir, Grant was not the man the senator had hoped he would become. Never would be. Grant had fallen from one of Cameron's horses several years ago and broken his leg so severely that a physician had been called from Baton Rouge to operate. In time, the wound had healed and Grant had walked again, but always with a very distinct limp as the injured leg was shorter than the other. After that fall, all of the personality traits that Cameron had disliked in her brother had seemed to deepen. She and Grant had never seen eye to eye, but suddenly he had become pettier and more self-centered, even cruel.

With age, Grant had gained a roving eye, and though the household staff tried to protect Elmwood's only daughter from the sordid truth, she heard the gossip among the slaves. Not only did Grant have his way with many of the young slave women, but if they did not come willingly, he forced himself upon them. Worse yet, Cameron was beginning to suspect that Taye had caught his attention. The beautiful mulatto girl had been late to mature physically, but when she had, she'd blossomed as a spring magnolia opens to the bright sun. The thought that Grant might be attracted to her dear friend, that he might try to act upon it, disgusted Cameron. She had thought of speaking to her father on the matter but since she had only suspicions, she did not. She simply tried to keep Taye and Grant apart.

"I cannot believe you invited that cad to stay here," Grant fumed, still pacing the study. "You heard him. He cares nothing for anyone but himself. Why, Captain Jackson is nothing more than…than a pirate," he exclaimed. "And I want him gone from here. Gone tomorrow."

"Now, son, you know very well that the Logans and the Campbells have been friends for many years."

"I know, I know. Friends in the Highlands," he repeated as if he had heard the tale a hundred times. "The families traveled here from Scotland together, suffered hardships together, and so on and so on." He halted behind Cameron's chair, speaking to their father as if she weren't even there. "Well, this is not Scotland, and I don't care how well respected the man's grandfather was. This is Mississippi and the man does not deserve to be received!"

Though Cameron too wanted to be rid of Jackson, there was something about the way her brother ranted that made her want to take up for the captain. There was something about her brother's tone of voice, the hatred that seemed to drip from his mouth, that angered her. Cameron wasn't certain because she and her brother had never discussed Jackson Logan, but her guess was that he didn't like him because of how well he carried himself. How confident he was. How lazily superior he behaved. It no doubt made Grant feel inferior.

"I do not mean to discount your opinion," the senator replied, "but I have already made my decision. The captain will remain at Elmwood as long as he wishes, as my guest, and next Saturday night we will hold a ball in his honor."

Cameron couldn't resist a smile of pleasure. She always loved dances at Elmwood. Everyone said Senator Campbell threw the best ball in the county, maybe in the whole state of Mississippi. She loved the excitement of the preparation. She loved the hustle and bustle of the household with Sukey overseeing every detail. Cameron loved to see the guests arrive on horseback and by carriage, even by boat. And then there were the handsome suits, the lovely ball gowns and the exquisite music that wafted from the ballroom.

She couldn't help thinking nostalgically back on all the balls she had attended in Elmwood's ballroom. Did her father intend this one last celebration as a final goodbye, not just to his neighbors, but to a way of life they had always known? While she understood why her father would have to make a stand if war came, she could not help but be sad, not just for herself, but for him as well. How hard it had to be for Papa to take a stand against neighbors and friends, the very people who had put him in office.

"Grant," the senator continued, "you do not have to like Captain Logan. I have told you that before. You need only be polite to him, as I would expect you to be to any guest welcomed here in our home."

Grant let out a snort of disgust. "Fine," he declared, striding to the door. "I don't know why I even bother to voice my opinion in this room. It is not as if it is ever heard. Unlike *hers.*"

The senator rose from his chair behind the desk. "Grant. Son—"

Grant walked out and slammed the door behind him.

The senator eased into his chair again and his gaze met Cameron's. His face was lined with an emotion she could not quite put her finger to.

Cameron studied his face as he ground out his cigar in a tray on the desk. He looked older to Cameron than she remembered when last she had seen him. The lines around his mouth were more pronounced, the creases beneath his eyes deeper. It made her heart ache to see him like this, and it made her angry that Grant neither realized nor cared what he did to their father.

"I don't know what has gotten into your brother," the senator said, making light of his son's latest outburst.

"What's gotten into him?" Cameron rose from the chair to walk to the window. She needed some air. It was cooler outside now, but she could still smell the heat of the day and the fragrance of honeysuckle and night-blooming jasmine outside the window. "He is no different today than he is any other day," she said contritely.

"He has a great deal on his mind," her father said haltingly.

"I know he is concerned about the possibility of war and how it will hurt Elmwood."

"Papa!" Cameron turned from the window. "Oh, he's worried about the war all right," she cried, "but he's not worried about us, or Elmwood, and you know that. You know it as well as I do. He's just worried about whether or not the Yankees will cut off his supply of whiskey and new frock coats."

"Cameron, that is unfair." Her father spoke to her as if she were a small child. "Your brother has had a difficult life. His leg, his…"

"You're making excuses for him," she accused, her arms wrapped around her waist. "Don't you hear yourself? You're always making excuses for him. Always taking responsibility for his failings, or letting him blame us for them." She swept her hand through the air. "He is what he is, Papa, and nothing you say or do is going to change that."

The senator rested his gaze on the elm desk, his eyes sad.

Cameron gave a sigh, sorry for her outburst. "Oh, Papa," she murmured. "I didn't mean to hurt you." She walked up behind him and put her arms around his broad shoulders, hugging him tightly. She took a deep breath, breathing in the scent of starch and cigar smoke that lingered on his collar. "I had no right to say that. It was unkind."

"No," her father said quietly. He sounded so old, so tired. "You are right. He is my son and I love him, as I love you." He patted her hand, shaking his head. "But he is what he is. Your mother always used to say you can't make a silk purse from a sow's ear."

It was so rare that he mentioned her mother, Caroline, that it made her smile bittersweetly.

"In truth, I've been thinking a lot lately about you and your brother and Elmwood," he confessed.

Still holding his hand, she came around to his side and knelt at his feet.

"About what is to become of you all if this war cannot be stopped—and I fear it cannot." He took her hands between his.

She gazed up into his eyes, which were the color of her own. "What do you mean? What about Elmwood?"

He rose and lifted her to her feet. "That's enough of such serious talk for tonight. I've given myself a headache. Now, don't worry that pretty little head of yours," he said, leaning to kiss her forehead. "Go to bed. We've a lot to do in the next week if we're to host a ball."

Cameron wanted to press him, but she decided that for once she would behave herself. "All right, Papa," she said, forcing herself to push aside her concerns. "But you must go to bed, too. Promise me. You look so tired."

He kissed her hands and released them. "Good night, Cameron, love. Sweet dreams."

She gave a little wave as she left him in his study. *Sweet dreams,* she thought. *They will be if I can just keep that blasted Jackson Logan from them.*

5

"Oh, I couldn't possibly try on one of your gowns," Taye said breathlessly, pressing her hands to her flushed cheeks. "It wouldn't be fitting."

Cameron, laced tightly in stays and layers of starched petticoats, stood in the middle of her bedchamber surrounded by the rainbow-colored sea of lace, silk and tulle of the ball gowns Taye had laid out for her to choose from.

After a moment of indecision, Cameron climbed over a stool they had placed in the center of the room for her to stand on and show off each gown. She dragged a salmon ball gown behind her, one of six draped over chairs in the room. "Why don't you try this one, Taye? Just so I can see how it looks on you."

Taye giggled. "I couldn't possibly. Mama would have my hide if she knew I was putting on your ball gowns."

"Oh, please, just for fun?" Cameron fanned herself with her hand. It was so hot in the upstairs room that the idea of going downstairs in her underwear was beginning to sound appealing. She didn't know if she could possibly stand yet another layer of smothering fabric.

"Tell me you wouldn't like to try it on," Cameron continued. "Taye, this gown would really be far prettier with your complexion than it ever was with mine."

Taye smiled shyly, her lips pressed together in indecision, her beautiful eyes shining with longing.

Cameron knew Taye wanted to try on the gown; she just wasn't sure how to convince her to be so daring. Then an idea popped into her head. A terribly, sneaky idea. And it just might work.

Cameron narrowed her amber eyes as she dropped the lovely gown carelessly to the floor. "Do you really think I should wear the green-and-yellow tarlatan with the double skirts?"

"Absolutely." Taye began to pick up the other gowns to hang them in the large armoire. "I told you, the green is perfect with your hair and eyes. I've never seen you look more fetching. And so ladylike. No one will recognize the hoyden they've seen all week jumping fences that are far too high for her to be jumping."

Cameron settled one hand on her slender hip. "I'll make you a bargain, then. I'll wear the gown if you'll just *try* on the pink one."

Taye's blue-eyed gaze widened. "That is near to coercion. You ought to be ashamed of yourself, Miss Cameron Campbell!"

Cameron lifted the discarded salmon ball gown on the end of her finger. "Just try it on," she wheedled. "Please, Taye, for me? For Cameron, your best friend in the whole wide world?"

With a sigh of resignation, Taye set a blue organza gown aside and began to unfasten the hooks of the unadorned, simply cut cambric day dress she wore. "I don't know why I allow you to talk me into these things," she argued good-naturedly. "I should learn to resist you better."

Cameron slipped a linen dressing gown over her undergarments and tied the ribbons that closed it over her abundant petticoats. "Because you love me," she said triumphantly. "That's why you let me talk you into these things." She waggled a finger. "And because you know I'm right."

Taye slipped out of her dress and allowed Cameron to pull the salmon ball gown over her head. There were so many yards of crackling fabric and lace that it seemed for a moment as if Taye would be lost in the gown, but at last her head emerged from the neckline and Cameron smoothed it over her tiny waist and rounded hips.

"Oh," Cameron breathed as she turned Taye around to address the minute buttons of the gown up the back. "It's beautiful. *You* are so beautiful!"

"Please," Taye murmured. "You'll embarrass me."

Cameron gave the V bodice of the ball gown a tug to better show off Taye's youthful, pert breasts, as was the evening fashion. "It's perfect." She snapped her fingers. "But wait. I do believe something is missing." Her face lit up. "That's right, there were tiny bows that were pinned to each puffed sleeve. I know right where they are—in a trunk in one of the guest rooms." She held up her finger. "Don't go anywhere. And don't you dare take that gown off. Find the white crinoline that fits you. I'll be right back."

In stockinged feet, Cameron hurried down the hallway. She really didn't have time to search for the bows. The guests would be arriving soon. Sukey had already knocked on the door twice, warning Cameron that she needed to join her father so that they could receive the guests upon their arrival.

All day Cameron had been thinking what a pity it was that Taye would not attend the ball. What if this was Elmwood's very last ball? There was no telling what would become of them all if war came. There was no telling what would become of her beloved Elmwood if soldiers marched through her fields and forests. Didn't Taye deserve to attend at least one ball in the only place she had ever known as home? Cameron realized there was no reason Taye couldn't attend the ball. What did she care about the silly mores of the day? It was *her* ball and she was the hostess. Taye could come as her guest and no one could say a word about it. The trick, of course, was to get Taye dressed properly. From there, Cameron thought, it would be easy to inveigle her into joining the festivities.

Cameron hurried down the hall, vaguely aware of the sound of hushed voices coming from the east wing. The guest rooms were off that hallway. She was certain she would find the ribbons there in a striped trunk in the yellow room. She turned the corner and stopped short.

At the end of the hall, near the room that had been made up for Captain Logan, she saw him. He stood with his back against a closed door, his arms around the slave woman, Naomi. She had draped herself provocatively over him and was caressing his arm through the starched white linen of his pressed shirt. Her face was only inches from his, her lips moving as she spoke seductively. Naomi's sultry voice was too low for Cameron to hear, but it was obvious what the two were about from the way their limbs were entwined. They were so engrossed in their lewd tête-à-têtc that they had not heard Cameron come down the hall.

Cameron swallowed hard as Naomi drew a dark hand up Jackson's pant leg and inward toward only heaven knew where. Cameron knew she should turn and run. She was shocked beyond words, horrified at this obscene behavior. Yet she could not turn her eyes away. She felt a strange heat creep up her limbs. How dare they! How dare *he* carry on like this in her home?

Jackson said something to Naomi in a hushed, lazy tone, and his husky words, though Cameron could not make them out, rendered her nerves raw.

Cameron still considered herself a relative innocent in the ways of men and women, but she had bred horses. She knew enough to realize that what was going on between Jackson and the housemaid was the overture before the physical act of mating. She was disgusted by their open behavior…yet maddeningly found it erotically fascinating. Naomi did not appear to be a woman being taken advantage of; she seemed to be enjoying the love play with the senator's guest. Had Naomi come to Jackson because he had requested her, or was the slave woman giving herself of her own free will?

Cameron was stunned, yet captivated at the same time. She bit down on her lower lip, her breath coming in funny little, short gasps. She simply could not take her eyes off Naomi and Jackson.

The beautiful Naomi tipped back her head and laughed deep in her throat. Jackson leaned forward to whisper in her ear, his lips nearly brushing her ebony skin. There was no doubt where Naomi was touching the captain. Cameron felt a sizzling flame radiating out from the pit of her stomach. Perspiration trickled between her breasts and her limbs seemed heavy and unresponsive. She knew she was blushing because she could feel her cheeks burning. Moistening her dry lips with the tip of her tongue, she drew in a strangled breath and forced herself to turn away.

As she hurried down the hall, without the ribbons she had sought, she pushed aside a nagging feeling of jealousy. Could she be jealous of Naomi? She hated Jackson. He was the last thing on earth she wanted. Wanton Naomi could have him!

Trembling, Cameron pushed through her bedchamber door and went directly to the curtained four-poster bed to lay down. She felt faint, light-headed.

"Cameron, are you all right?" Taye murmured, hurrying to her, immediately concerned for her well-being. "What's the matter?"

Cameron closed her eyes for a moment, wiping the beads of sweat from her upper lip. She was so embarrassed by her body's reaction to what she had seen that she couldn't bring herself to tell Taye. "I—I couldn't find the ribbons. I'm sorry."

"Dear, that's all right," Taye murmured, pressing her hand to Cameron's cheek. "Oh, my, you're overheated. Let me get a cool rag for your forehead." She rushed off for the porcelain water basin on a wash table on the far wall. "I told you, you were doing too much and that you would run yourself ragged before the guests even arrived," she chastised like a mother hen with a wayward chick.

Cameron closed her eyes, forcing herself to breathe evenly, forcing herself not to think about where Naomi's hand had been. "I'll be all right in just a moment."

Before Taye made it back with the wet cloth, Cameron sat up, feeling more like her old self already. "I'm all right, really. Don't trouble yourself. It was just very hot in the spare room," she lied as she rose from the bed. "Now let me try and find the slippers that go with that gown of yours."

* * *

"Why, Masta Captain," Naomi murmured, her voice as smooth and silky as the best Scotch in his grandfather's homeland. "I believe you are happy to see Naomi." The slave woman's voice was thick with an island accent he recognized from his travels in the Caribbean Islands, and she smelled of a heady mixture of spice and a night-blooming flower that reminded him of a wildflower he had never seen growing anywhere but in Haiti.

Jackson chuckled. "Where are you from, my lovely? Haiti?"

The slave woman blinked, her dark eyes widening with surprise. Something told him it was not easy to surprise Naomi. Though she was young, no more than seventeen or eighteen, she had the eyes of a woman much older, much wiser.

"How did ya know, Masta Captain?" she breathed. "Haiti was the land of my mother."

He brushed his hand against her cheek. Naomi was a pretty piece, her dark skin healthy and gleaming. She had a way with her voice, her hands.

He smiled to himself. She would probably be a nice roll. A little something to ease the tensions of the evening before he joined the senator and his spoiled daughter for the ball.

But as Jackson allowed the slave woman to run her experienced hand over the bulge in his trousers, his thoughts settled on Cameron. All week he had avoided her as if she were the black plague, and still he could not get her out of his head. Even now with this lovely lady administering to him. He kept thinking about his and Cameron's encounter in the barn the day he'd arrived at Elmwood. He kept remembering the way her tawny cat eyes had practically shot sparks at him. She had been so furious with him, and rightfully so. She had been so utterly warm and sweet and full of fire at the same time that he had been unable to resist taking her into his arms and kissing her the way she deserved to be kissed.

Jackson was not usually so forceful with women; he didn't have to be. He had not meant to push Cameron against the barn wall the way he had. He certainly had not intended to tear her gown. He truly regretted those actions. But she had made him so angry, the way she had brandished the pitchfork so precariously close to the end of his nose, and so sexually charged at the same time. He had wanted nothing but the taste of her mouth on his and he had been rewarded with a pureness he had not expected.

His thoughts turned back to the pliable, ample-breasted woman in his arms. It would be so easy to lead the willing Naomi into the privacy of his room. He could be done and out before the first guests arrived here at Elmwood.

Naomi laughed, her voice rich and husky and tempting…her knowing eyes promising the secrets of ancient feminine wisdom.

And yet, as her silken lips brushed his collarbone and her moist tongue rasped against his skin, he realized Naomi was not who he wanted, not who he ached for, no matter how willing and succulent.

Jackson gently, but firmly pressed his hands to Naomi's hips and extricated himself from her arms. "I thank you for the offer," he said kindly, meaning it. "But I am expected by the senator below stairs momentarily. Though I would love to get to know you better, my dearest, it would be rude for me to miss my own party." He pressed a kiss to her forehead and a gold coin into her warm hand. "For you," he said. "Share it with no one else."

"Thank you, Masta Captain," she purred.

As he walked back into his room to retrieve his cravat and coat, she called after him.

"Maybe later, Masta Captain?"

He winked at her. To him, all women were a delight—young, old, black, white. He genuinely loved them all. "Perhaps."

She rewarded him with a flash of white, even teeth and a sultry, come-hither glance before disappearing down the hall.

"This coat or this one? What do you think, lovely?" the senator asked, holding up a rich green frock coat and another of a deep burgundy hue.

Sukey rose from the edge of the bed she and David shared.

Ordinarily, she would not have entered his bedchamber and closed the door this way; it would not be fitting in the light of day. But he had insisted he needed her help and assured her that the entire house was in such an uproar in last-minute preparations for the ball that no one would even notice where she'd gone.

Sukey smiled lovingly. "I adore the burgundy on you, but my guess is that Miss Cameron will wear the green-and-yellow gown you like on her so much." She took the green coat from him and smoothed the rich fabric. "The two of you would look charming on the front porch matching so nicely."

The senator smiled absentmindedly. "Sukey, I've been thinking. Do you think I made a mistake in inviting Captain Logan to remain here at Elmwood?"

"Whatever would make you say such a thing?"

"I like Jackson a great deal. He is an excellent businessman, perhaps better than his father had been. And Jackson is hell at a poker table." The senator chuckled. "But I know the good captain's foibles, too. He's arrogant and self-involved and a womanizer to which the likes of Mississippi does not often see." He scowled. "Whoever had coined the phrase 'a woman in every port' was most likely speaking of Captain Jackson Logan."

Sukey gazed up at him. "Ah, you are concerned for Cameron."

"You should see the way he looks at her." He rested his hand on Sukey's shoulder, the burgundy coat flung over one shoulder. "You know, I always suspected she was smitten with him years back when she was just into her first lady's corset, but I never got the impression that the feeling was mutual. She was nothing but a child then and Jackson was nearly thirty. But now…" He paused. "I've seen the way he looks at her with his granite eyes—the way a shark devours its prey. I wouldn't want Jackson to attempt to take advantage of Cameron."

"I have an idea, my love, that Cameron can take care of herself. She would knock the captain down a notch if he or any man tried to take advantage of her."

The senator sighed, gazing into Sukey's dark eyes. "You're right, of course. You always are."

He tossed the burgundy coat onto the bed. "And you're right about the coat, too. Now don't you see why I need you here? I hate it when I have to go to Washington and leave you behind. I can barely dress myself. Only last week Thomas had to go back to my hotel room for my cravat. I had completely forgotten it."

Sukey helped him into the green coat she held out for him. "I hate it when you go to Washington, too, but not so I can dress you," she teased.

He leaned over and pressed his lips to hers. Sukey closed her eyes, enjoying the familiar feel and taste of his mouth on hers. They had been lovers for so many years that they knew each other better than they knew themselves. Theirs was an enduring relationship that most women only ever dreamed of. Sukey knew how fortunate she was to have David and she thanked God above for him each and every day.

"Well, perhaps this inconvenience of my being in Washington while you are here can soon be set right."

Sukey took a step back, her eyebrows furrowing. "Whatever are you talking about?" She pushed his hands aside and began to tie his cravat properly.

"I'm talking about taking you to Washington with me when we are forced to leave Elmwood. You may go with the girls to New York if you like—you'll be welcome at the Stuarts, of course—but I'd like you at my side, lovely. Considering the gale winds that will soon blow, I fear I will need your gentle kindness and practicality to keep me steady."

She shook her head. "You mustn't speak of such matters. You will bring bad luck down upon us all." She made a sign that had been passed down by generations in her mother's homeland of Africa to ward off evil spirits.

"Now who is being impractical? The war is coming, lovely, and neither you nor I can stop it. I am seriously considering Seward's offer to serve the president. If I return to Washington, I will take you with me." He lifted a dark brow. "Unless you do not want to go with me."

She took his big, strong hand between her smaller ones and gazed into his eyes, now glowing with his love for her. Though less than ten years older than she, he seemed to have aged so greatly in the last year. She knew it was this terrible discord over slavery that had taken years from his life and for that she would always be sorry. But Sukey was proud of her man, proud that he was willing to stand up for what he knew, in his heart, was right.

She pressed his hand to her cheek, closing her eyes. "I will go wherever you ask me to go. My heart will be your heart. My heart has always been your heart. You know that. Taye is a full-grown woman now, and she'll soon be off on her own life's adventures. I belong with you, my beloved."

He caught her chin between his thumb and forefinger and lifted it. She opened her eyes to gaze adoringly into his. "Things are going to be different than they have been, Sukey. Different for you, different for Taye. A war will take a terrible toll, but I would fight every battle myself if it would mean freedom for you and for Taye."

"We already have our freedom," she said smiling sadly. "Don't you remember? You gave it to us years ago."

"That isn't what I mean and you know it. I want you to have the freedom, the acceptance, to walk into a room on my arm. In any state in this Union, North or South. I want Taye to have the right to travel in whatever social circles please her, to marry whomever she pleases."

"You make it sound so easy." Sukey shook her head. "You make it sound so easy that I sometimes think you are as naive as my Taye." She lifted up on her toes and he still had to lean over to meet her lips. "But that is one of the reasons I love you so," she whispered.

"What would I do without you?" the senator asked.

Sukey stepped back to straighten his coat. "You would not look nearly so handsome at your ball. Now go. I think I hear carriages out front."

He grabbed her around the waist and lifted her off her feet the way he had years ago when they were both young. She squealed with laugher. "Put me down before you put out your back."

"I wish I did not have to leave you," he said playfully. "Instead of talking with my neighbors and sharing cigars, I wish I could climb back into that bed with you and…" He whispered in her ear.

She laughed, her cheeks burning with embarrassment. "Put me down, and put me down now," she chastised.

Reluctantly, the senator planted one last kiss on her lips and lowered her to the floor.

"Go on with you," she shooed. "I've a million things to do. I'll be waiting here tonight when you retire."

He blew her a kiss and walked out of his bedchamber. Sukey had to retrieve her handkerchief from her sleeve to blot her foolish tears of happiness.

6

"No, no I can't," Taye argued as Cameron tugged insistently on her hand, luring her down the candlelit hallway. "It wouldn't be appropriate."

Cameron had donned the lovely green-and-yellow ball gown Taye had suggested, and when she was completely dressed, she had to admit that her companion had chosen well. The tarlatan gown had a tight waist that dropped to a V in the front, a fashionable bateau neckline and puffed, banded sleeves that reached to her elbows. She wore her auburn hair swept in an elaborate coiffure of curls with tiny green bows nestled in her glossy locks rather than the typical headdress.

"Please, Taye, please come to the ball. If you don't, I shall not be able to enjoy myself. How could I possibly dance every dance with you sitting up here, mending my torn riding breeches?"

Taye's face reflected a mask of conflicting emotions. Cameron knew that the seventeen-year-old wanted desperately to attend the ball, to see the beautiful gowns and handsome men, to hear the music that would waft through the ballroom. What young woman wouldn't? The elegant balls held at Elmwood were always the talk of the county for weeks afterward. He was known for his fine hospitality, superior musicians and exquisite banquet fare.

Cameron knew that Taye was torn between her desire to attend the ball and the desire to please her mother. Sukey would mostly definitely not approve of Taye's attendance. Though the housekeeper considered herself and Taye part of the Campbell family, she had very strict definitions of what that entailed and attending balls was definitely not among them. If, however, Cameron could just get Taye downstairs in the salmon ball gown, Sukey wouldn't dare go against Cameron's wishes and send her daughter upstairs again. Cameron knew it was a deceitful ploy, one she would surely hear about from Sukey later, but she didn't care. Something inside her told her this would be the very last ball she and her father would ever host here at Elmwood, and it was important to her that Taye enjoy the revels.

Taye loosened her death grip on Cameron's gloved hand. Cameron knew her beloved friend was vacillating and seized the moment. "Please," Cameron begged. "You don't have to come right into the ball room if you don't want to. You can hear the music from the hall or even from the library." She lifted Taye's hand outward to get a better look at her. "You're so beautiful in this gown that it seems a pity no one but me will see you in it." She narrowed her cat eyes slyly. "Mr. Burl will be here. I think he would like to see you in this gown."

Taye twisted her delicate fingers and gazed longingly down the curved grand staircase that had been polished until it shone.

"Please," Cameron begged.

Taye inhaled sharply, her gaze darting to meet Cameron's. "I absolutely will not receive your guests in the receiving line."

"Of course not," Cameron agreed quickly. "I never expected that. It wouldn't do. Papa and I and Grant, should he bother, will receive our guests. You can go to the library and have some punch and perhaps a little something to eat. There are already tables of canapés set up."

"I could make sure everything is the way the senator would want it," Taye said, following Cameron's lead.

"Like any other considerate hostess would," Cameron encouraged. "Not like a servant."

Taye grimaced, still undecided. "You know very well that Mama would never approve." She lifted her blue-eyed gaze and a furtive smile played on her lovely lips that Cameron had darkened with rouge. "It would be very mischievous of me to go against her wishes."

Cameron reached out and took Taye's hand again, squeezing it reassuringly. "But she would understand. And you could blame me completely. She knows that I always lead you into mischief." She took one step down and was relieved to have Taye follow. "You could tell her I was being my insufferable self and I forced you to come to the ball."

"I won't stay long," Taye said, taking another graceful step down the staircase. "I'll just stay in the shadows and watch."

In the ballroom Cameron could already hear the musicians setting up their instruments. A slave girl dressed in white hurried through the hall below with a tray of sweets in each hand. The senator called for Cameron from somewhere below.

"Cameron? Cameron Elise, where have you gotten to, young lady? Our guests are arriving!"

"I have to go," Cameron whispered. "Please say you're coming."

Taye flashed a beguiling smile and lifted her starched petticoat to follow. "I'm coming. I'll do it." She halted, frowning suddenly with concern. "But you're sure I look all right? Not too much rouge?" She patted her cheeks. "Mama would never forgive me if I appeared looking like a painted lady."

Cameron giggled at the thought. "You look beautiful."

"Well, so do you." Taye reached out and smoothed a pin curl near Cameron's ear. "The captain will be awestruck."

"The captain? What do I care what he thinks about anything?" Cameron lifted her crinoline and started down the grand staircase, almost at a run, calling over her shoulder. "I don't give a fig for that man or anything he thinks."

Downstairs, Cameron found her father sampling the Scotch Jackson had brought him, shipped from their homeland. After telling his daughter repeatedly how lovely she was, he escorted her on his arm to the front hallway to meet the guests who were just beginning to arrive. For the next hour, Cameron stood at her father's side and smiled, accepting kisses and compliments from their friends and neighbors. Several times she looked for Grant. It was only polite that he be there to receive Elmwood's guests, too. After all, he was the heir to his father's land and fortune. But Grant was nowhere to be seen, which was typical. He had never been dependable, never would be. Sometimes she couldn't believe that the two of them had been born from the same parents.

The number of guests who came on such short notice pleasantly surprised Cameron. It seemed as if her father had invited everyone in Mississippi to Elmwood this evening. She greeted so many familiar faces, and many unfamiliar ones, that eventually the names all began to swirl in her head. At last, at her father's insistence, Cameron excused herself to go to the library and have a drink of cold punch. She had talked so much that her mouth was quite dry.

As she passed the ballroom where the musicians were now warming up, she spotted Captain Logan. He was dressed impeccably tonight in white breeches so tight that he might have been poured into them, a sparkling white linen shirt and cravat, and the most beautiful dark teal coat she believed she had ever seen. It fit his muscular form so well that she knew it had to be custom made, and not anywhere in this vicinity. Jackson stood in the arched doorway to the ballroom, flocked by young women in pastel gowns who chattered and cooed like brightly colored birds. There were women everywhere—blondes, brunettes, young women and those whose beauty was beginning to fade. Why, there were so many that they stood around him two deep, utterly enthralled by whatever honeyed nonsense he was feeding them.

As she passed the group, Cameron heard Jackson say something about the force of the gale winds as they rounded the horn. The braggart! He was no doubt spinning some yarn in which he would, of course, be the hero, the dashing captain of the ship who saved the day. She tried to slip by without his taking notice of her, but just as she thought she had made it safely through the hall, he caught her eye. There was no denying he was watching her. He lifted a brow as if to invite her to join him and his flock.

Out of habit, she offered a small, polite curtsy to Elmwood's guest of honor, then stiffened her back, raised her chin and hurried for the library. As she made her escape she could have sworn she heard a mocking chuckle. Laugh at her, would he? The nerve of that man!

Cameron was so distracted by Jackson that she nearly ran right into her brother. "Oh, Grant. Sorry." She put out her hand to keep from bumping into him and took a step back.

Despite their father's wealth and the fabrics and tailors at his disposal, Grant did not have a great deal of fashion sense. He was dressed tonight in a gaudy silver coat with lapels that were entirely too wide. He wore his still-damp hair combed back in such a manner as to make him appear almost sinister. But it was not his dress that made him unappealing, Cameron realized as she studied him. It was the air about him. Grant always seemed to be carrying a chip on his shoulder, anticipating the smallest slight from those around him, real or imagined.

He gazed over her shoulder in the direction of the ballroom. "I see that Papa's pirate captain has been introduced to our neighbors."

"I doubt he's a pirate," Cameron said tartly. "Insufferable rogue, perhaps, but I don't think pirating is as profitable these days as simply taking advantage of the current market and good men's hard-earned dollars."

Grant scowled.

Cameron could smell whiskey on his breath. Papa had partaken of a token drink before the ball, but she guessed that her brother had sampled more than one.

"I believe it is time we break up the captain's little party, don't you?" Grant said, already walking away. "I'll tell the musicians to begin playing at once."

Cameron watched as her brother limped off and then she continued to the library. Quenching her thirst with a silver cup of fruit punch, she bumped into a friend from a plantation down the river, Marie DuBois. After making polite conversation and inquiring as to the health of the new baby boy and heir to Wide Acres Plantation, she excused herself to find Taye. She hoped her friend hadn't retreated upstairs already, not when the music was just beginning.

As she glanced around the large library, its walls lined with shelves and towers of books, her attention came to rest on the portrait that had been commissioned the summer Cameron was thirteen and Grant fourteen. It had been painted by a traveling artist who had arrived on a steamy afternoon and begged to be permitted to paint the brother and sister, only accepting payment if her father approved of the completed portrait. The artist had been extremely talented and had captured the exact hue of the blue gown Cameron had worn and her impish smile. More amazingly, he had captured her brother's sour character, while still painting a smile on his face. The most fascinating aspect of the Campbell children's portrait, however, was that, if one looked closely, one could see a younger girl painted in the background in shadows. It was Taye.

The day the portrait was completed, and the senator ordered that it be hung above the marble fireplace in the library, was the only time Cameron remembered hearing her father and Sukey exchange cross words. Cameron wasn't supposed to be listening from behind the stairwell, of course. She remembered their argument, as if it had only been this morning. For some reason Sukey had not wanted the portrait hung in such a public place. Her father had been adamant. Sukey had said the portrait did not belong in the family library, that it wasn't proper. Her father had said it was the most proper place to hang it in all of Elmwood. The argument had ended with Sukey lowering her gaze submissively, saying that Elmwood was the senator's home and that he could certainly hang a portrait of his children anywhere he pleased.

"There you are," the senator said, snatching Cameron from her reverie as he came through the library door. "The first waltz is about to begin." He bowed formally and offered his arm to her. "Will you do me the honor of allowing me to dance with the most beautiful young woman in all of Mississippi?"

She curtsied deeply. "It would be my pleasure, Papa."

Out on the dance floor, they drifted with the divine music. After beginning the first waltz as host and hostess, others joined them, and for a few minutes Cameron was lost in the dazzling lamplight and the glorious strain of the violins that could bring a tear to her eyes. The enormous floor-to-ceiling windows of the vaulted ballroom had been thrown open to let what cool April breezes remained sweep through the brightly lit room. On the gentle wind she could smell the scents of early crepe jasmine blooming. As the waltz ended and her father again bowed, Cameron closed her eyes, trying to capture the scents and sounds, wanting to etch this precious memory to her mind forever.

"You don't mind if I borrow your father for just one dance, do you, dear?" Mrs. Fitzhugh, a widow who had been after her father for years like a cat on cream, curtsied before Cameron and then the senator.

She was wearing her blond hair arranged in an enormous headdress with peacock feathers protruding in every direction and Cameron had to bite down on her lower lip to keep from laughing. "He is all yours, madam," she said, winking at her father.

As Cameron walked off the dance floor, she caught sight of Taye standing alone outside the ballroom in the shadows of the hallway. Cameron was relieved to see she was still here. Now her next task was to get her friend actually into the ballroom where she could justly enjoy the music.

"Not so fast."

Cameron felt a hand close over her arm. "I believe it is the custom here in Mississippi that the guest of honor dances with the hostess," Jackson drawled.

"I don't want to dance with you." Cameron's amber eyes sparked with annoyance.

At the sound of her raised voice, a group of ladies and gentlemen standing nearby glanced at her and Captain Logan with interest.

"Let go of my arm," Cameron demanded, lowering her voice.

He tightened his fingers around the bare skin of her forearm, scorching her flesh, sending rivulets of fire dancing down her spine. "Now, Miss Cameron, you certainly couldn't mean you would forgo such tradition. You would be the talk of the county for weeks. They would speak of that spoiled brat of a girl, Cameron Campbell, who has no appreciation for everything her father provides her with, no respect for her position in Southern society. Why, everyone in the county would be shocked."

"They'll be more shocked, sir," she hissed under her breath, "if I bring my fist up to your face and give you a bloody nose."

To her surprise, he tipped back his head and laughed, his rich, deep voice echoing off the high ceiling above them. "My goodness, we are full of spit and fire this evening, aren't we, Miss Cameron? Just the way I like you."

She tried to pull her arm free from his iron grasp, while not bringing any attention to herself. She recalled how she had seen him and Naomi in the hallway. A sheen of perspiration beaded across her upper lip. All she could think of was where she had seen Naomi place her hand on Jackson and how it had made heat flash under her skin.

"Let me go."

"Dance with me this one obligatory dance and I swear I will set you free." His steely gaze met hers and he lowered his head so that only she could hear what he said. "Unless you are afraid to get too close to me. Afraid you will not be able to control your desire for me, *again*."

Cameron sucked in her breath, her ire flaming like a freshly lit torch. "One dance," she muttered. "And then you will stay out of my way."

He smiled handsomely and held out his arm in the formal position, his elbow bent. "Shall we go, my dear? I believe they are playing our song."

Cameron walked to the dance floor, the belled skirt of her ball gown swaying slightly, feeling as if her feet were stuck in Mississippi clay. Everyone was looking at her, looking at them. Whispering. She knew what they were saying. They were remarking how handsome Captain Logan was, how lovely the senator's daughter looked on his arm.

Cameron smiled as her eyes met those of the guests, but her mind raced. She knew she should not have agreed to dance with him. Proper Southern etiquette be damned; she should have just taken her leave. But the idea that he thought she could not trust herself with him made her so angry that she couldn't bring herself to refuse him. It would be like surrendering to him.

They reached the center of the ballroom and turned to one another. Cameron allowed Jackson to clasp her hand. She felt his other hand slide possessively to the back of her waist and she placed the other gloved hand on his shoulder as the music enveloped them. As they danced, she focused her gaze over Jackson's shoulder, holding her body stiff and erect, mindful not to touch him any more than necessary.

Even from this distance, the hem of her bell-shaped gown barely brushing his polished shoes, she could smell his skin, his hair, that masculine scent that clung to him and haunted her dreams. He kept his gaze fixed on her, his mouth upturned in a half smile. He was taunting her, the cad. The blackguard. Grant was right. He probably was a pirate, as well.

"Lovely ball," Jackson said, leaning close so he could whisper in her ear. The warmth of his breath on her already prickly hot skin made her dizzy.

"We are dancing, sir," she said, afraid to meet his gaze. "We are not conversing."

Out of the corner of her eye she saw his face grow serious. "Didn't you hear what I said in the barn? What do I have to say...do...to convince you how sorry I am about the way I behaved that day? Damn it, that was six years ago!"

She tried hard to focus on a shimmering green moth that had found its way into the ballroom, and not on Jackson's deep, rumbling voice. The ethereal creature fluttered around oil lamps hoisted high above the dance floor and cast a shadow from the vaulted ceiling onto the dancers below.

"I never meant to hurt you, Cam," she heard Jackson continue. "You must believe me when I say that." He was silent a moment and then spoke again. "I haven't been able to forget you."

Cameron thought of him and Naomi in the hallway. Not forgotten her? He seemed to be trying rather hard, to her.

"Cameron, please, talk to me. Tell me what you're thinking, at least. I swear, I take pride in thinking I know women pretty well, but I have no idea what goes on in that beautiful, stubborn head of yours."

When she did not respond, he clasped her chin between his thumb and forefinger and forced her to turn her head and meet his gaze.

She fought tears that burned in the back of her eyelids. Why was he doing this? She had been so careful to construct a wall around her heart to protect it from him. But the words she had just heard came dangerously close to taking a chink out of that wall, to crumbling the brick to dust.

"Someone is going to see you," she whispered. "Please don't touch me like this." She meant, of course, that she did not want him to touch her face, but she meant her heart as well. *Don't touch my heart this way, don't make me think there could be something left between us,* she prayed silently.

He surprised her by immediately dropping his hand and taking hers again as they made a turn in the ballroom, continuing to waltz. She would almost have preferred he hadn't met her request because that was what she expected. The man was such an enigma. She thought she knew him, knew him all too well, yet did she?

"You know, I came here to Elmwood to apologize," Jackson said. "I've been meaning to for years."

She frowned. Surely he didn't think she would believe his lies so easily. In the last six years he had had plenty of opportunities to come to Elmwood and apologize. On more than one occasion she had even been in Washington, a stone's throw from his family home near Baltimore.

"Please, Jackson," she said drolly. "You came here because you had a message for my father. You were asked to come."

He nodded slightly. "I did come because I was asked to

bring your father that message. But I could have simply said I wouldn't be traveling this way. Cameron, if war comes, and your father believes it will, I—'' He halted and then started again.

Cameron was so fascinated by what sounded like emotion in his throat that she lifted her head to look at him. For just a moment she allowed herself to look into those gray eyes of his where she knew she would be lost.

"I wanted to make my apologies," he said. "I would not want to go to my grave owing you that apology. I have done many things in my life that I am not particularly proud of, but what I did to you— It was inexcusable."

"Setting our affairs in order, are we?" She lifted a feathery brow. "A waste of breath I should think. From what you have said, I doubt you are in any danger of being killed in battle, sir. Unless you are caught blockade-running and hanged by your neck."

The dance fortuitously ended at that moment, and Cameron removed her hands from him. She turned around and strode off without another word, praying he wouldn't follow.

And a part of her hoping he would…

7

Taye hovered in the hall, gazing pensively into the ballroom. She had never remembered the music from Elmwood's ballroom being so exquisite. Perhaps that was the difference between listening to an orchestra from one's bedroom and hearing it, feeling it, in person. The waltzes were so beautiful that Taye had to fight to keep her feet still beneath the yards of Cameron's petticoats that she wore. Though she had never waltzed in public, she felt she knew the steps as well as any belle sweeping across the floor. Cameron had taught her how to waltz and they had spent hours locked in her bedchamber practicing. She also knew a number of lively country dances and she adored reels. Cameron had been an excellent instructor.

Taye realized that she had toyed with danger long enough. She had sampled the punch and nibbled delicious canapés. She had listened to the music and watched elegant dancers glide across the waxed hardwood floor in dashing frock coats and extravagant ball gowns. A perfect memory etched in her mind forever. She needed to excuse herself before her mother, who was busy ordering servants in the kitchen, caught her.

"What do ya think yer doin', Miss Highty Mighty?"

Startled, Taye turned to see Naomi in the shadows of the hall. She wore a simple white dress with a blue-and-white-checked turban wound around her head, and she was carrying silver trays.

"Ya hear me, Missy?" Naomi hissed, her black eyes smoldering with accusation. "Ya'd best get yerself out of that fancy gown an' in the kitchen before your mama catch ya. Look at ya, all dressed like a pretty bird. 'Cept ya know the truth inside." She tapped her voluptuous left breast. "In here ya know what ya is, no matter how Missy Cameron dress ya up."

Tears sprang in Taye's eyes and she dashed at them, angry with herself for letting Naomi upset her. "Leave me alone," she whispered, her heart hammering. "Go about your business. You know you don't belong in this hall. Use the servant's hallway the way your mama tells you to."

"I ain't sayin' this to be mean, girl, but ya can stand there and pretend ya's one of them," Naomi continued, beneath her breath. "But ya never will be. Ya'll never be nothin' but half of what they is. The other half of ya's always gonna be what we is. That's slave, girl."

"Hush your mouth," Taye whispered, boldly giving Naomi a push. "Go to the kitchen before someone sees you and you get yourself into trouble."

Naomi took a step back, surprised by Taye's passion. Maybe more of Miss Cameron's confidence was rubbing off on Taye than either girl realized.

Naomi made a clicking sound with her tongue, shaking her head as she hurried off. "Times gonna be rough for that yella gal. Don't need the bones to tell me that."

Taye turned, gazing into the ballroom again through teary eyes. Suddenly the candle and lamplight didn't glow so brilliantly. The music was not so melodious, though the orchestra was playing a Virginia reel. Dancers were laughing and whirling around the dance floor, but even the ladies' gowns no longer seemed so brightly painted against the floral-papered walls of Elmwood's enormous ballroom.

Taye whipped around to make her escape.

"Not so fast, my little rosebud."

She felt a man's hand catch hers and turned in shock. No one else had spoken to her all evening.

"I was wondering if I could have the next dance," Captain Logan drawled, smiling warmly.

Taye lowered her lashes, unable to help but be flattered. "I couldn't," she murmured.

He held her hand in his warm one, his touch strangely reassuring. "Oh, come, Miss Taye. Just one dance is all I'm asking. Not for your hand in marriage."

She couldn't resist a shy giggle. "Captain, you say the most ridiculous things."

"That may be true, but what I request is certainly not ridiculous. You are absolutely breathtaking tonight, my dear. Should you agree to be my partner, just for this one dance, I would have the most beautiful woman in the ballroom on my arm."

Taye dared to glance up at the captain through her thick lashes. "And what of Cameron, sir? Would you not say *she* is the most beautiful woman?"

He tipped his head back and laughed. "How clever you are, Miss Taye."

"And clever you are, sir, not to answer such a question put to you by a lady."

"Just one dance, please," he cajoled. "And then I swear, I will set you free."

Taye gazed longingly into the ballroom. She wanted so desperately to dance. Just one waltz! One waltz in Elmwood's ballroom would surely last her a lifetime. "You know I can't," she said.

"You can if you wish it."

"I shouldn't, Captain. You know I shouldn't. My mother would be appalled."

He clasped his hand over hers. "I am the senator's guest of honor. I would think she would be appalled to learn that her daughter had denied a guest of honor's simple request."

She flashed him a shy smile. He was so handsome, Cameron's Captain Logan, and so hard to resist. He had a charm about him that made every girl feel special. "All right," she conceded. "If you are certain it would not be—" Before she could finish her sentence he pulled her through the doorway and into the ballroom. Taye barely caught her breath before she found herself wrapped in Captain Logan's strong arms, dancing her very first waltz.

Grant stood near the open window of the ballroom and took a sip of whiskey from a silver flask he kept in the breast pocket of his coat. Out of the corner of his eye he caught a glimpse of a young woman in a pink ball gown walk out onto the dance floor on Captain Logan's arm.

"Son of a bitch." Grant stiffened with anger, but even as he did he could not help noticing how beautiful Taye was. Breathtaking. So sweet and innocent. She danced by, not seeing him, and his ire increased. How dare she? How dare he! What the hell did that pirate think he was doing dancing with Taye? With *his* Taye?

Grant had known the mulatto girl his whole life. Had loved her, it seemed, since the first day she came toddling out of Cameron's nursery. She was so stunning, so sweet, unlike his sister who was nothing but snarls and claws.

Grant ached for Taye. He ached to hold her in his arms. He ached to see her naked, to touch her creamy cocoa skin. He wanted her to beg him, wanted her to want him to take her. He scowled and took another pull of the flask as he saw her laugh at something Logan said. He didn't like the way she smiled at that devious bastard. No one deserved those smiles but him. Grant didn't just want to possess Taye sexually, he wanted...he wanted her to love him, the way she loved Cameron.

Cameron, the greedy bitch. She took everything. Taye's love. Papa's love. Everyone always liked her better than him. Even the slaves. When he spoke to the slaves they barely acknowledged him. They followed his orders because they had to, but they dragged their feet. They followed his wishes only out of fear for the beating they would receive if they didn't. But Cameron... If Cameron said something, they jumped. "Yes, Miss Cameron," this, "Yes, Miss Cameron," that. They ran at her beck and call, grinning, white teeth bared like the simpletons that they were. It made him sick to his stomach. Even Naomi, who gave her body freely to him, didn't respect him. Not really. He saw it in her dark eyes. He sensed it in the way she looked at him through those inky, fringed lashes.

And why? Why? Because of Cameron and Taye, of course. Because of what they did to him the summer he was fourteen. No one respected him because he had been labeled a coward by his father in front of everyone—and those two had caused it. In Mississippi, there was nothing worse that could be said about a man than labeling him a coward. No matter what a man did, he could never escape such an accusation. Never prove himself a real man again.

Grant tipped back the silver flask and sucked the last drop of the biting whiskey from it. That damned Logan had no right to be dancing with Taye. A darky, for God's sake. As he glanced around, he could see the guests were beginning to stare at the couple, murmuring quietly. Damn it, if his father didn't have enough sense to stop this absurd display of bad manners, he would do it.

Taye was breathless. Captain Logan was an exceptional dancer, light on his feet despite his size, moving easily to the rhythm of the music. She felt as if she were dreaming, whirling round and round in a beautiful gown on slippered feet that barely touched the floor.

After another turn around the ballroom, she sensed that people were watching them. She glanced over the captain's shoulder to see disapproval etched on their faces. The women opened their fans and tittered behind them.

"Captain," Taye whispered, her heart hammering with fear. "We must stop. They're staring at us."

"They are not," he murmured gallantly.

"I told you I shouldn't have come in here with you." She lowered her gaze to the buttons of his waistcoat, her chin quivering.

"Lift your chin, Taye. Don't do this. Don't give them what they want."

"You don't understand," she murmured. "I should never have entered the ballroom."

"You have as much right to dance in this ballroom as any

woman here," he said fiercely. "More than some, probably. And don't let anyone tell you any differently."

She lifted her head to look into his gray eyes, eyes burning with self-confidence. "You are very kind, sir," she said weakly.

"No, I'm not. I'm a selfish bastard most of the time." He studied her with those intense gray eyes of his again. "But I truly believe what I have just said. Cameron believes it. The senator believes, and so must you."

As his words sunk in, Taye's spirits lifted. He was right, she thought, stiffening her spine. She did have a right to dance, didn't she? To look pretty, to enjoy the music the same as the whites?

Out of the corner of Taye's eye she caught sight of Grant heading straight toward them. "Oh, no," she groaned.

Logan spotted Grant and tightened his grip on her, refusing to allow her to escape.

Grant followed them as they whirled in a circle to the waltz still playing. "Excuse me, Captain Logan, but do you realize that you are dancing with one of my servants?" he ground out.

"Back off, boy," the captain ordered from between clenched teeth. "You don't *ever* want to tangle with me...and you know it."

"Is that a threat, sir?" Grant's voice trembled as he attempted to feign bravado.

"A promise."

Grant turned and hurried off the dance floor as fast as his limp would allow.

"Oh, Captain Logan" Taye breathed. "You've made him very angry."

"I don't care." The captain whirled her around, holding her tightly. "I'm not putting up with his bullshit. Pardon my language, ma'am. He's a spineless little whining bully and a disgrace to the Campbell name."

"You don't understand," Taye whispered. "He *is* weak, but he is the senator's son and he uses his power in dreadful ways." She lowered her gaze, frightened to her very bones, not only for herself but for the other young women of Elm-wood. "He takes out his vengeance on the innocent in such terrible ways," she murmured, too embarrassed to go on.

The waltz came to an end and Taye tried to pull away from the captain. "Wait," he said, refusing to release her. "Listen to me, Taye. If that bastard ever, *ever* tries to harm you, you tell me. I don't care where I am or what I'm doing. You get word to me and I'll take care of him. I mean it."

She forced a smile. "Thank you, Captain," she whispered. "For everything." Then, head held high, she walked out of the ballroom as gracefully as Cameron Campbell would have.

Cameron stepped off the lower veranda into the house, pat-ting her cheeks. She had just needed a little air. She felt better now, stronger. Her dance with Jackson had affected her more than she wanted to admit. She walked down the lamp-lit hall-way toward the sounds of the music and the guests.

"There you are," Letty Havingston said coming from the parlor.

Letty's cheeks were pink with excitement and little beads of perspiration clung to her temples. Her yellow watered-silk gown was frilled, pleated, netted and fringed. She looked to Cameron much like an overly decorated, thickly frosted lemon birthday cake.

Letty paused breathlessly to fan herself before continuing. "I knew you weren't nearby, else you would have stopped them."

Cameron frowned. Letty wasn't one of her favorite people and she certainly wasn't a woman who looked her best in yellow. She had grown up on a plantation down the river a short distance from Elmwood and had recently married one of the neighbors. At her wedding last fall she, who was three years younger than Cameron, had made a comment about it still not being too late for Cameron to catch a husband. Cam-eron had never had much in common with Letty, who only cared about her gowns and who had called on her that week, but she cared for her even less after her comment at the wedding.

"What are you talking about, Letty?" Cameron rested her hands on her hips. She wasn't in the mood to even pretend she liked her neighbor.

"You haven't heard?" She brought a gloved hand to her cheek.

"Heard what? Come, come, I haven't time to play guessing games, Letty."

The young woman's eyes were as round as Caroline Campbell's Irish porcelain dinner plates. "Why, that dear Captain Logan has just scandalized your family." She lowered her lashes. "He is a finely handsome man, but I hear there are some families that do not *receive* him in Mississippi."

"Letty." Cameron reached out impatiently and tugged on the lace of the woman's bodice.

"Oh!" Letty cried.

"Get to the point!"

"Why, he danced with your mulatto. The pretty one. What's her name? Taye, is it?" Letty's sides heaved with exertion, straining the seams of the watered silk.

Cameron's eyes widened nearly as large as Letty's. "Danced with her where?"

"In the ballroom, of course. Right in front of everyone." Letty tapped a kid-skin slipper in obvious disapproval. "I saw her in the library earlier. I assumed you had put her in the gown so she could serve guests in the library and not be an eyesore. As for Captain Logan," she whispered conspiratorially. "I cannot imagine what got into him. Your brother tried to stop him, but— Oh!" She opened her fan and began to wave it in front of her face. "We were all shocked. We couldn't help but be!"

Cameron fought to restrain the grin about to break over her face. How brave of Jackson Logan. How brave of Taye!

Cameron turned and walked away from Letty without another word. She had to find Taye at once and hear what had happened. How had Jackson convinced her to step out into the light of the ballroom and dance? Of course, Letty had said that Grant tried to point out to Jackson his faux pas. God above, Grant had to be hopping mad. Taye would barely speak

to him, and yet she had danced with Jackson. She had to find
Taye immediately.

"There you are. Good, I won't have to come looking for
you." The senator stepped out of his private study, into the
hall waylaying Cameron.

"Papa, can it wait?" She laid a hand on his coat lapel. He
looked tired. No, more than tired, worried. Upset. She wondered if he was feeling poorly. "Papa, are you all right?"

"Yes. No." He took her by her wrist and pulled her into
the study.

"Papa, can't this wait? I have to find Taye. Apparently she
danced with Jackson and the guests are in an uproar."

Her father walked behind his desk and picked up a heavy
crystal glass half filled with Scotch. There were only a few
candles lit in the study and the light was dim, the room shadowy. "I saw her dancing," he said quietly. "She was so beautiful," he continued slowly. "She knew they were talking
about her and she danced anyway. She walked off that ballroom floor with her head held high." He looked to Cameron.
"The way any female Campbell would have."

"Papa, what's wrong? Why are you talking like this?" She
closed the door behind her, not wanting any of the guests to
see her father this way. "Why isn't there more light in here?
Papa, you're scaring me. Tell me what's wrong."

He turned his back to her to look out the open window. A
breeze off the Pearl River ruffled the silk drapes, bringing with
it the rich scent of the riverbank and the perfumed night.

"Papa," Cameron breathed, truly frightened now. "Tell
me."

"A messenger just rode in. He has brought news." He
turned slowly to face her, almost like a wraith in the semi-
darkness. Suddenly he seemed decades older; his skin was
chalk, his cheeks gaunt. "The war has begun, Cameron. Very
early this morning, Confederates under the command of a
General Pierre Beauregard opened fire with fifty cannons upon
Fort Sumter in Charleston, South Carolina. The war has
begun."

Cameron lifted her skirts and darted around the desk. She

threw her arms around her father. "Oh, Papa," she whispered. "I am so sorry."

He didn't hug her back. He just stood there, his arms at his sides as if immobilized by the tragic news.

"It's time, my love. Time I declare which side I am on."

She took a step back. "The North?" she whispered, feeling suddenly numb. It had been so easy to discuss these issues at the dining table and over cards in the library. It had always sounded so noble, freeing all slaves, even if it meant war. But now Cameron realized with abrupt clarity what war would mean personally to her father. He could not declare himself for the North and represent Mississippi in any way.

"We—we won't be able to stay at Elmwood," she managed, her voice cracking.

He shook his head slowly, lifting the amber-colored Scotch to his lips. "No. Once our neighbors and my constituents here in Mississippi get word, I'll be considered a traitor. It will not be safe for us to continue to live here." He gave a small laugh that was without humor. "You know what kind of hotheads we Southerners can be. Ah, Cameron. How I prayed this day would never come."

Cameron thought her heart would break. Leave Elmwood? How could she? She lifted her lashes to look at him, refusing to cry. There would be plenty of time for tears later. "What will we do with the slaves, Papa?"

"Give them all their freedom, of course. I've already set a plan into motion. I will have to hurry those plans along now. Mr. Burl has been working on the details for some weeks." He turned to look out the window again, but didn't really seem to be looking at anything. "I knew this was coming, Cameron. I prayed it wouldn't, but now it's here."

"You said it would not be safe for us to stay here, Papa. Where will we go?"

"That's really why I called you in here, dearest. You and Taye must pack your belongings. I have been asked to serve as an advisor to President Lincoln in Washington so I will be traveling there. I'll be sending you north to stay with the Stuarts in New York."

Cameron bit down on her lower lip. She wanted to protest, but she was so shocked by the reality of what was happening that she could only nod.

"I will have your horses shipped for you as soon as I can make the arrangements. I imagine transportation north will be difficult soon, so I will do it as quickly as possible."

"And Grant and Sukey?" She yanked off her white silk gloves and tossed them on his desk. No young Southern woman would be seen at a ball without gloves, but they seemed absurd now, considering the circumstances.

"I do not know what your brother will do. I have yet to speak with him. I wanted to tell you first. As for Sukey—" He took a breath, hesitating.

Cameron waited. She knew that Sukey went to her father's bed at night. She knew that many masters warmed their beds with servants. It was not a practice that she liked to dwell on or question. But it was not until this very moment that she realized there must be something more to Sukey and her father's relationship. There was something now, something in his eyes that made her suddenly realize that.

"I will be going back to Washington and Sukey has agreed to accompany me."

Stunned, almost speechless, she stared at him. The way the senator kept eye contact with her made her proud. He gave no explanation of his relationship with the woman who had once been a slave, but for a Southern gentleman to even insinuate such a relationship made her father an even more remarkable man to her than he had been a moment before.

"Grant is going to be very angry," she said, finding her voice and deciding to change the subject. Perhaps she and her father would be able to talk about Sukey some time, but she sensed this was not it.

The senator gazed into his glass, swirled the liquid and watched it slosh up the sides of the cut crystal. "I have some difficult decisions to make concerning your brother and you." He paused. "But I don't want you to worry about that. Not now. Now I want you to go out and enjoy what remains of the ball. Then you'll need to pack. You and Taye will be leaving at first light, accompanied by Mr. Burl.''

"But what of the Stuarts?" Although she knew the family only slightly, she liked Regina and Robert, a childless couple who had always been kind to her. "We should send word we're coming."

"They have been expecting you, Cameron. I have corresponded with them over the past months and they knew that when the war finally began, you'd be coming right away.''

"Oh, Papa…" She lowered her gaze. Again, her father made her feel like a child. So many things had gone on here at Elmwood that she hadn't been aware of.

"I need you to be my brave girl, now, Cameron. Do you understand that?"

She nodded, afraid to speak for fear he would hear her trepidation in her voice.

"Now go on. The guests will be departing soon." He shooed her with a big hand. "I will talk with you later tonight before you go to bed. I need to speak with Mr. Burl and then with your brother."

Wanting to be the good girl for once, she walked to the study door. "You're sure you don't want me to stay with you?"

He offered a sad smile. "Off with you."

"All right," she agreed, forcing a smile. "But I'll be back. I love you, Papa."

"I love you, too, dear daughter."

Cameron walked out of the study and closed the paneled door behind her. She leaned against it, trying to catch her breath.

Oh, heaven above. War? They were at war? She stumbled down the hallway and when she saw the grand staircase, she started up the stairs. She had to find Taye. She had to be sure Taye was all right and tell her what was happening. Taye needed to know.

But Taye was nowhere to be found upstairs. She was not in Cameron's room or in the smaller one that was hers at the end of the hall. Cameron heard a door close down the guest hallway. Could that be Taye? What on earth was she doing down there?

As Cameron walked down the hall, lit only by the occasional wall sconce, she focused on placing one foot in front of the other so she wouldn't fall. She felt as if she were sleepwalking. Leave Elmwood? How could she leave Elmwood?

At the sound of footsteps she lifted her head. It wasn't Taye, but Jackson. She whirled around, intent on getting away from him. He was the last person she wanted to see right now.

"Cameron, what's wrong?" He came up behind her quickly, catching her around her waist as she swayed.

"Cameron, are you all right?" He sounded so concerned for her well-being. So sincere.

She turned in his arms to look up into his eyes. She had no intention of confiding in him, but the words just tumbled out. "War," she whispered. "God help us, Jackson, we're at war."

8

"**I** know," Jackson murmured in her ear, his arms securely around her waist.

"You know?" He sounded far away and yet she could feel the heat of his body so near to hers. She could feel his hands on her, steadying her so she didn't tumble. Even her own voice sounded strange in her ears. She felt detached from the world around her, as if she were floating above it all. Nothing seemed real, not the papered walls of the hallway with the entwined magnolia leaves, or the heart-pine plank flooring beneath her dance slippers. Not even Jackson and the strength of his arms around her felt quite genuine. It seemed as though it were all a dream, a dream that she would soon wake from and find everything forever changed.

"I was with your father when the messenger came." He spoke slowly, seeming to sense her bewilderment. "Honestly, Cam, we were anticipating it. Sumter was a bomb waiting to go off. It has been since January when that merchant ship was driven back by Carolina forces. When your father heard, he and I—" he paused "—had matters to discuss."

She didn't understand what he meant. What matters did he and her father have to discuss? Jackson had already said he would have no part of the war, take no side. What could the firing on Fort Sumter possibly mean to him, except another opportunity to make money?

But she was too upset to question him. It was all too much

to take in and make any sense of right now. "Papa says I have to leave Elmwood," she whispered, pressing her palms against his white shirt. He wasn't wearing his coat any longer, and his Irish lace cravat was untied and hung loosely around his neck. "Taye and I are leaving tomorrow for New York to stay with the Stuarts."

"I know." Jackson brushed the hair off her damp forehead.

She was hot and sticky and her dress was scratchy against her skin. The thought of lying naked between the cool sheets drifted through her head. Maybe she just needed to take off some of these damned layers of clothes. Maybe if she could breathe, she could think more clearly.

"I know how much you love it here," Jackson continued, "but your father is right. It won't be safe here for you. Not when your neighbors discover that your father will be serving on the president's war council. These damned Southerners can scare up a lynch mob faster than a horse race."

"War council? Is that what he'll be doing in Washington?" She smoothed his pressed shirt, shivering as she felt the ripples of his muscular chest beneath her fingertips. "I didn't know. He only said that he would be going there—he and Sukey." Her legs felt weak and she swayed a little.

"Do you think you need to lie down, Cameron?" Jackson steadied her. "I could take you to your room and find Taye for you."

She looked up suddenly, panic leaping in her chest. She slid her hands up over his shoulders and clung to him. "No. No, don't leave me alone. Please, Jackson." She didn't know what had come over her. She wasn't a coward, wasn't afraid to stand up for her convictions. But suddenly it was all too overwhelming. War between the states. Leaving Elmwood. Being separated from her father.

He closed his arms around her and held her tightly as if she were that young, innocent girl again. "It's all right, Cameron," Jackson soothed, pulling her against his chest. "It's all right. You'll be safe in New York. The Stuarts are fine people. Robert will keep you from harm."

"No, it's not that. It's not that I'm afraid for myself."

Clutching his shoulders she fixed her gaze on his gray eyes. "But so many people will die, Jackson. Don't they understand that war brings death and destruction?"

"Aw, Cam, you're too young to have to think about this." He ran his hand across her cheek in a gentle caress. "You're too beautiful to have to face the ugliness that will come."

Cameron didn't realize Jackson intended to kiss her until she felt his warm breath on her face an instant before his mouth found hers. She knew she ought to resist, and she even went so far as to push against his shoulders with her hands. But he gave no regard for her effort to fend him off, and her hands fell uselessly to his shoulders.

"Jackson..." she murmured against his lips. She wanted to stop him, to fight. Resisting him was the only way to protect herself from him. It was the only way to protect her heart. But he had her pinned so tightly and she just didn't have the strength to fight him.

At first his kiss was gentle. He brushed his warm mouth against hers, his lips as light as a moth's wings. But then she felt his body tighten, as if he struggled against himself. He seemed to attempt to resist his own temptation, but failed. He pulled her harder against him, crushing her mouth with his. She couldn't breathe. She was suddenly dizzy and the world seemed to be spinning around her. She tried to struggle as his tongue invaded her quivering mouth.

No, no, she wanted to say. But something deep inside her could not defy the burning heat, the taste, the feel of his tongue inside her mouth. Instead of pulling away, Cameron was mortified to find herself molding her body to his. She pressed her groin to his and felt the hardness and heat of his desire for her.

When at last she tore her mouth from his, gasping for breath, she heard herself mutter his name. "Jackson." It was as much an endearment as a curse.

His gray-eyed gaze met hers and what he saw in her own amber orbs must have said what she could not bring herself to utter. He swept her into his arms and hurried back down the hallway toward the guest bedroom he occupied.

As Jackson made the distance to the door, Cameron thought of a million reasons she must not cross that threshold with him. This far away from the rest of the household and guests, no one would even be able to hear her if she cried out. What if she changed her mind and he tried to force her?

But Cameron did not protest. She only looped her arms around Jackson's neck, closed her eyes and pressed her tear-dampened cheek to his broad shoulder. She couldn't be alone right now and it seemed that only Jackson would be able to understand that.

He practically kicked down the raised-panel door to get inside the guest room. He closed it with the slam of his foot and, without even jostling her, threw the bolt on the lock. They were alone now; no one could happen upon them. The room was dark save for the moonlight that poured in through the open windows and she could hear the slow, rhythmic beat of the slaves' drums in the distance.

"Jackson—"

He pressed his fingers to her lips as he pushed through the filmy netting that hung from the bedposts and lowered her to the rumpled tester. "Shh," he whispered. "Don't talk. For once, Cam, don't say a word."

She opened her mouth to protest, but he sank down on the bed beside her and enveloped her in his arms, taking her mouth with his again. She was overwhelmed by his size, his power, and the desire for him that licked like flames at her limbs.

"Don't speak," he insisted, covering her cheek, her neck with soft, fleeting kisses. "Don't think. Just feel. For once, Cam, put your mind aside and just let your body take over." He drew his lips to the hollow of her throat as he brought his hand up beneath her breast.

Against her will, she heard herself moan with pleasure. *I have to stop him,* she thought wildly. *I have to stop myself.* But as he pulled the bateau neckline of her ball gown down off one pale shoulder to reveal the swell of her breasts, she was powerless to resist. One brush of his fingertips and she ached for his touch.

"So beautiful," Jackson murmured, as he squeezed her breast gently. One kiss turned into a barrage of kisses as he explored her parted lips, her cheeks, her earlobes, until he found her mouth again, first lightly, then so demanding that he left her breathless and weak.

Cameron ran her fingers through his thick, silky hair. Without realizing what she did, she guided his mouth lower—first to the pulse of her throat, then down her chest to her hardening nipple. Even through the layers of the fabric of her chemise and camisole, she felt his mouth hot and wet on her burning flesh.

"Not a girl anymore. A woman…" Jackson rolled over in the bed, taking her with him. He pulled down the layers of her tarlatan gown and broke the strap of her chemise. She didn't care. Nothing mattered but his hands, his mouth and her need to be suckled.

He yanked on the ribbon of her corset and at last freed her aching breasts. Cameron's sharp intake of breath startled her as he clamped his mouth, at last, over a rosy nipple. She had forgotten how glorious this felt. Apparently, she had pushed the memories of the night before Jackson had left her so far from her mind that they had nearly vanished.

Nearly.

Jackson stroked and kneaded her breasts, suckled her nipples, until she writhed in his arms, hot and sweaty and aching all over—for what she didn't know. All of her strength seemed to be so sapped from her that when he slid lower on the bed, dragging his warm lips over her bare belly, she couldn't fight him.

Didn't want to.

There were yards of petticoats and taffeta between them, but he didn't seem to notice. He stretched out beside her and, cradling her in one arm, brushed his lips to hers. At the same moment he slipped his hand beneath her skirt, up her stocking-covered calf to her bare thigh. It had been too hot to wear drawers.

Cameron tried weakly to protest, but he silenced her with his kisses. There was no need to fight him, she thought. She couldn't win. She had let him go too far. She had let herself go too far. And his strokes felt so good, so right that she relaxed again and left her body to float in the sensations his fingertips were creating.

At the first brush of his hand against her most intimate place, she half rose off the bed. Years before, he had touched her breasts, but he had gone no farther. Not down *there.*

Cameron's breath caught in her throat. If she was going to stop him, she had to do it now, before it was truly too late. She had felt his hardness beneath his breeches. She knew what he was going to do to her if she didn't escape.

"Jackson," she managed to squeak.

"Shh," he hushed. "Relax. Leave the world for a moment and just be with me."

He continued to stroke with his fingertips, light at first, then with more pressure. Cameron was drowning, drowning in sensation, drowning in fear, drowning in anger with herself for not being able—no, for not wanting to stop him.

When he parted her tender flesh, she moaned, past the point of giving any thought to putting an end to his assault. Nothing existed now but his mouth on hers, the taste of him and the feel of his hand between her trembling thighs. His hand kept moving rhythmically; her legs were now hot and wet. She did not anticipate the violation of his fingers. Worse, she did not anticipate her reaction. Instead of crying out in shock, in protest, she parted her legs, wanting nothing more than for him to drive farther home. He kissed her deeply, his tongue moving inside her mouth to match the rhythm of his fingers, stroking, pressing deeper.

Taye stumbled on a tread on the servant's back staircase and grabbed the railing to keep from tumbling. She cried out in frustration, fearful she would fall. Tears blinded her vision so that she could barely see where she was going.

They had finally done it. She'd just heard word from one of the kitchen slaves, who had overheard the senator talking to the messenger. Some fort had been fired upon. The South had declared war against the North and nothing would ever

ever be the same again. A sob rose in Taye's throat and she fought against it. Her beloved Elmwood would be changed forever. And what would become of her? Where would she go? What would she do? She could not imagine life without Cameron and yet they could be separated now.

Taye bit back another sob and started up the stairs again. She had to find Cameron. Cameron would know what was going on. She would know what was going to happen to them.

"Miss Taye, is that you?" a male voice called from the bottom of the dark stairwell.

She half turned, in her confusion not knowing who it was until she brushed at her wet eyes and the figure at the bottom of the stairs came into focus. It was her beloved. Still dressed in his dark coat and a starched white cravat, he did not seem as neat as he had been when she had seen him from afar at the ball.

"Mr. Burl," she breathed. She wiped hastily at her eyes again, not wanting him to see her like this.

He came up the steps, and as he grew closer she realized that his coat and shirt were disheveled, as if he had been running. "Have you heard?" he asked, his voice thick with emotion.

She gripped the railing with both hands, for fear of tumbling against him, and nodded.

"War," he breathed, glancing away. "The senator said it would come and yet I was a fool. I believed we could all sit down together as honorable men and work this out. I believed we could free those enslaved and still preserve the South." He shook his head as if ashamed.

Taye longed to reach out and touch him, to try to comfort him, but she kept her hands pressed to her sides. "It isn't your fault, Mr. Burl. I know you have done everything you possibly could. I know how hard you have worked for the senator's cause. Your cause," she whispered.

"I am so sorry this has happened, Miss Taye," he breathed, looking up at her through the darkness. "I am sorry we could not prevent it, but do not worry about your own safety. Not for a moment. The senator says he will send you and Miss Cameron north where you'll be safe.''

Another sob caught in Taye's throat, and before she knew what had happened, Mr. Burl came up the last few steps. He took her by her arm to steady her. ''It's all right,'' he whispered in her ear. ''Just stay here a moment until you catch your breath.''

She sank to her knees as much disoriented by Mr. Burl's nearness as by word of the war. She clutched the stair rail, then sat down upon a step. He sank down beside her, the step so narrow that they brushed hip to hip. She turned away, looking down into the darkness, embarrassed by their closeness. ''I feel silly. I don't know what's wrong with me.'' She pressed her palms to her cheeks.

''It's a shock to all of us,'' he assured her. ''Please don't be upset with yourself. I—I couldn't bear the thought.''

She turned to face him as she realized he still held her arm with a trembling hand.

''Mr. Burl—''

''Miss Taye, please, I only have a moment. The senator has a great deal for me to accomplish. I have mountains of documents which must be—'' He halted and then went on faster than before, tripping over his words. ''Forgive me for babbling on. Only…only I could not forgive myself if I did not speak to you before I left.''

He lowered his head and she studied him in confusion. What was Mr. Burl—*Thomas*—trying to say to her?

''Miss Taye.'' He took her hand between his. ''I want you to know how greatly I respect you and how much I like you. How I wish—'' He groaned. ''Heavens be, I am making a mess of this.''

Taye's heart pounded in her chest. She was afraid to believe what she thought Thomas was trying to say to her. Did he really have feelings for her? It was too much to hope for.

''Thomas,'' she breathed, daring to bring her face closer to his. Even in the darkness of the stairwell, she could see his dark-eyed gaze fixed on hers.

''I know I have no right to say this but what I am trying to express, Miss Taye, is that…that I would like to court you once this has passed. It cannot possibly last long. When the South realizes its terrible error in judgment and surrenders, I should like to officially court you, and should you find us compatible, I should like to ask for your hand,'' he finished timidly.

Taye suddenly felt so light-headed that she closed her eyes for a moment. Her heart leaped, but then it fell. What was Thomas saying? What was he thinking? The war would not end quickly. And even if it did, what made him think anything would be any different then? He would still be a white man and she would still be half-African slave. She and her girlish fantasies!

Taye stiffened, pulling her hand from his. ''Mr. Burl, please, listen to me. I know that the senator wants you to marry Cameron and I think you should do it.'' She stiffened her spine and sharpened her voice. ''Right away.''

''But I don't love her,'' he sputtered. ''It is you I—''

Taye rose, gathering her skirts. She would not let him go any further. To do so would only break her heart, which was already splintered in a hundred pieces. There could never be anything between them. It had only been a childish dream of hers that she had allowed Cameron to encourage. Any lingering hope she held for the future had been crushed tonight in the ballroom when she had danced with the captain.

''You are not in love with her, Mr. Burl?'' she said, harshly, rushing up the steps. ''What does that have to do with anything, in this world that we live?''

Taye thought she heard Thomas call her name, but she didn't turn back. She kept running until she found the door of Cameron's bedchamber. She flung herself into the room and onto the bed, then covered her head with a pillow so that no one would hear the sounds of her sobs.

Cameron felt as if she were caught in a tide. Thick, heavy, all-encompassing waves of pleasure washed over her. She had no choice, no way to fight the strength of them. All she could do was ride one wave after another as the sea of sensation lifted her higher, faster—to where she did not know.

Jackson was kissing her, murmuring endearments in her ear. All she could do was cling to him, kiss and be kissed. His touch was torture. It was ecstasy.

Suddenly, Cameron felt every muscle in her body contract. She was overwhelmed by a shocking wave of such intense rapture that she pulled her mouth from Jackson's, sucking in a great breath of air as her body convulsed in shimmering ripples of gratification.

"Oh, oh," she breathed, shocked and embarrassed and amazed, all at the same time, by what he had done to her.

Jackson slipped his fingers from her and let his hand rest on the mound of fiery curls between her legs.

"Oh, what have I done?" she moaned, rolling against him so that she could hide her face.

"It's all right," he whispered with amusement as he kissed the top of her head.

"No. No, it isn't all right." She shook her head, her face still buried in the folds of his damp, wrinkled shirt. "I cannot believe I have—" She lifted her head suddenly. "But you didn't—" She didn't know what to say, how to say it, but she could still feel the hardness of his manhood against her leg. The act was not yet complete—was it?

She could hear Jackson smiling. If he laughed, God knew she would kill him.

"It's all right, Cam, just lay still for a moment. Bask in the warmth of the pleasure."

She rolled her head, burying her face in his shirt again, still mortified. Slowly, as her breathing became more normal, she became aware of the room around her, of the softness of the feather tick and the feel of his hard, lean body still pressed so intimately to hers. She heard his breathing and the sound of the slave drums outside her window again.

"Cameron," he said after a few minutes of almost comfortable silence. "I don't want to do this to you, but I must go. Someone..." He paused as if searching for the right words. "Someone waits outside to speak with me and I must not delay that meeting any longer."

"Someone?" she murmured, gazing up at him through her lashes. "I don't understand. Who waits to speak with you? And why?"

He pressed his sensuous lips together. "Who or why doesn't concern you."

She sat up, pushing him away from her, angered by his sudden coldness. She tugged at her corset, trying to pull it up, but it would never work sitting. She would have to stand up. She yanked at the ribbon crossly anyway. She was more angry with herself for what she had done, but it was so much easier to be angry with him.

"I wish that I could lie here with you and—"

"Please." She held up one hand, unable to meet his gaze. "Stop before you make me start hating you again."

"Cameron—"

"Just go," she ordered. "Go see to your messenger. I'll go to my room on my own without letting anyone see me like this...see my shame."

He started to say something more, then exhaled impatiently and rolled away from her. She laid back and closed her eyes, waiting for him to go. Only after he had closed the door quietly behind him did she allow a single tear to slip down her cheek. She wondered why she cried. She knew it was out of loss but loss of what? Did she cry because her beloved Mississippi had gone to war and she would have to leave Elmwood? Did she cry for her father, the proud, ambitious senator who would leave his home, his life, his world, to stand up for what he believed in. Or did she cry for herself and her heart that she feared she would lose again to a man who could never love her?

9

Cameron eased open the door and cautiously gazed out into the dark hallway. She had to be certain that no one saw her leave the guest chamber Captain Logan was occupying. Such gossip would be scandalous. It could ruin her father's political career. At that thought, she laughed aloud and then choked on her laughter that came out near to a sob. Ruin his career? What career? Her father, the senator from Mississippi, a state that had seceded from the union months before, would be setting his slaves free and declaring himself a Yankee.

Still, she didn't want anyone to see her leaving Jackson's room. If nothing else, it was a matter of pride now; she wanted her name in no way connected to his.

Taking care that the hall was empty and silent, she slipped down the corridor. With her corset unlaced she couldn't pull up the bodice of her gown properly, so she held her hands over her breasts, trying to shield herself from anyone she might accidentally run into. Luckily, the upstairs passageway seemed deserted. She could still hear strains of music drifting from the ballroom, but the hour was late and guests were departing. Voices floated upward in the high-ceilinged central hall as men and women left for their elegant coaches that had been brought around front by Elmwood's slaves, dressed in spotless white garments.

Cameron supposed someone from the Campbell family should be at the door to wish their guests farewell, but in light of her father's news, such a social faux pas seemed inconsequential. Her father obviously had a great deal to accomplish in the hours between now and dawn, and he certainly wasn't fit to be seen in public anyway. Not with those haunted eyes. When the neighbors discovered that the senator had freed all his slaves and was preparing to move north to serve under President Lincoln, they would certainly have more than just cause enough to gossip. Hell, there could be a lynch mob, she thought, dangerously near to tears again.

Cameron pressed her naked back to the wall, took a quick peak around the corner and saw that the family hallway was deserted. All she had to do now was make a run for her bedchamber, her haven. Just a few more steps and she would be safe in the rose-colored room she had slept in since she had left her mammy's nursery. She groaned and closed her eyes, leaning her head on her mother's imported magnolia wallpaper. Cameron could not believe she had let Jackson lure her into his room. She couldn't believe she had let him make love to her.

That is what they had done, hadn't they? Even though there had been no actual consummation, she *had* had sex with him, hadn't she? Though maybe it depended on one's definition. After all, she was still a virgin, *technically*.

God above, she couldn't think about this now or she would surely go mad.

She took a deep breath and raced for the sanctuary of her bedchamber as quickly and quietly as possible. Inside, she threw the door shut and leaned against it, heaving a sigh of relief. She had to get a hold on herself. Her father needed her. She couldn't think about her own predicament right now. She needed to change her clothes, run a brush through her hair and find her father. She didn't have time to agonize over what she had done with Jackson or what had possessed her to do such a thing. Not when her father's life was falling apart. She would have plenty of time later to punish herself over Jackson. Right now she had to push the whole matter aside. Forget it ever happened. If she was lucky, she would never lay eyes on the man again. If she was very lucky, he'd be hanged as a pirate by the first blockade set in American waters.

Cameron took another breath, her heart beginning to settle to a normal pace. There was something about being in her own room that gave her strength. As she began to feel like her old self again, her disorientation turned to anger. How could Jackson have taken advantage of her this way? He knew she was overwrought by news of the war, knew she was vulnerable. Damn him and his blackguard heart!

Now, if she could just hold on to this anger, everything would be so much easier. If she could forget about the way he had made her feel inside, and remember how angry he made her, she would be all right. She needed to focus on the thought that she and her father were now committed to the North. Captain Logan, as he had said himself, was committed to his own cause. If she could keep all this in mind, while forgetting the treacherous response of her own body to his seduction, she could get through this.

A noise from the far side of the room startled Cameron and she instinctively gathered the bodice of her gown to try to cover herself. Who could be in her room? The sound came from the wispy shadows of the netting of her bed. Someone was weeping.

"Taye?" Cameron whispered.

Through the darkness, Cameron saw a silhouette that could only be Taye's rise to a sitting position in her great four-poster rice bed.

"Cameron?"

Taye was terribly upset; Cameron could hear it in her voice. Heavens, in all the confusion, Cameron had completely forgotten about Taye dancing in the ballroom. And she had surely heard about the war by now. Guilt washed over Cameron and she rushed to the bed. "Taye, what's wrong?"

"Haven't you heard?"

Forgetting about her shocking state of disarray, she dropped on the bed, reaching out to hug Taye. "The firing on Fort Sumter. Yes, Papa told me. But, please don't cry, puss. It's going to be all right. This is no more than what has been expected for weeks."

"But this means war, Cam."

Cameron took a deep breath, trying to keep her own fears at bay. "Yes, theoretically. But it will all be over in no time. You'll see. Papa says the South can't possibly expect to win and they will soon surrender. After all, we have no munitions factories, no way to arm and clothe and feed an army." She took both of Taye's trembling hands in hers. "And Papa says you and I will go north and stay with the Stuarts a while. Won't that be fun?" She spoke to Taye as if they were little girls and Grant had been picking on Taye again. Cameron always came to Taye's rescue. She always would. Their bond of friendship was one of spirit, much stronger than a bond of blood could ever be. "I was thinking we could take some of my horses. I've been promising to help you improve your seat. I should think—"

"Cameron, don't treat me like a child," Taye interrupted, bringing her tear-streaked face close to her friend's. "War, we're at *war*. Over me. Over Mama and Naomi and Uncle Jessie and the others."

Cameron shook her head. "We are not at war over you or your mother. You are already free. We are at war over the issue of slavery. We will fight to free all of your mother's people, give them all the rights they deserve."

Taye choked on grim laughter. "You accuse me of being innocent of the ways of the world, but sometimes I think it is you who are the child, Cam." She lifted Cameron's hands and kissed them. "You are so idealistic sometimes, so unrealistic." She shook her head sadly. "This war will not be a quick affair. The South will not surrender easily, for though they may not have weapons, they have their honor and their pride. This fight will be long and drawn out and bloody beyond what either of us can even fathom right now. The South, men like Grant—" she spit his name as if he were some disease "—will not capitulate easily. They will die in their cotton fields with their slaves beneath a yoke before they will surrender their way of life. Before they'll admit that a man or a woman with black skin is as precious in God's eyes as they are.''

Fresh tears ran down Taye's cheeks, bringing tears to Cameron's own eyes. She squeezed Taye's hands. Was Taye right? She couldn't consider the possibility. Not now. "Stop this. Stop it right now," she insisted firmly. "I will not hear of this kind of talk. Papa will not hear of it. What he is doing, what he *will* do is what is right.''

Taye brushed a lock of hair off Cameron's cheek. The beautiful coiffure Taye had created for the evening's festivities was in ruins, but Taye didn't seem to take notice of her friend's dishevelment. She was too upset. "I am not saying it is not morally right. I am only saying how costly it will be. And that cost frightens me, Cam.''

Cameron threw her arms around Taye and squeezed her tightly for she needed the hug as much as she thought her friend did. "Oh, sweetheart, as long as you and I stick together, we'll get through, all right?''

Taye nodded. "All right.''

Cameron rested her head on Taye's shoulder. A part of her needed to share with someone what had happened between her and Jackson, but she decided against saying anything. Taye was already upset enough; there was no need for Cameron to transfer another burden to her companion's shoulders. "Now I need you to help me get changed into something more suitable for packing and preparing to go. I want to go back to Papa and talk to him.'' She rose, turning her back to Taye. "I've already started undressing,'' she lied, taking a chance that Taye had been lying facedown on the bed crying and hadn't seen Cameron enter the room in this state. "But I need your help.'' She pulled down the bodice of her gown and fumbled with the ribbons of her corset, pretending to loosen the stays that Jackson had previously loosened. "I was so hot I couldn't breathe in this thing anyway. I'll have to have something less constricting if I'm to do Papa any good. I imagine he will want the valuables moved to the cellar to be locked up until they can be transported.''

"Let me get a light for the room from outside the hall.''

Taye grabbed a broom straw from a vase on the fireplace. "And I'll be right back."

Cameron watched Taye slip out of the room and she heaved a sigh of relief. Taye didn't suspect a thing. She had no idea that only half an hour before Cameron had wantonly lain almost naked in Captain Logan's arms.

"Listen to me," David barked at his son. "I do not have time to go round and round on this issue. None of this should come of any surprise to you, Grant. You have known for quite some time where I stand."

The senator had retired upstairs to his room where he had sent for his son. Captain Logan was to be up in half an hour's time. Just as soon as he sent a message to his ship in Baton Rouge, he promised he would be in. David hoped he could get this ugly business with his son over with and get him out of here before Jackson returned.

"Absurd talk around a dining table over a cigar, is one thing," Grant ranted, helping himself to the Scotch David had brought up from his study. "But *this,* this is reprehensible. The Campbells of Mississippi cannot suddenly declare themselves Northerners!" He gestured woodenly. "We are as Southern as yonder river that flows through Elmwood."

David rubbed his temples, trying to think how to best deal with his son. He knew the boy would be angry, disappointed, frightened even, but he did not have time for one of Grant's temper tantrums. There was too much to accomplish before dawn. First he needed to be certain he could get Cameron and Taye safely out of here, then he needed to tackle the formal emancipation papers that would have to be completed to set his slaves free. If he were to release his people without those legal manumission contracts, they would be hunted like animals and sold into slavery again.

"I told you," David said slowly as if Grant were a little boy again. "I must make a stand. This event at Sumter demands action and I cannot continue to support slavery any longer."

"Cannot *continue* to support slavery?" Grant threw back a

swallow of Scotch, his tone thick with cruel sarcasm. "You seemed happy enough to *continue* to support slavery when we planted cotton this spring. You seemed willing to *continue* to support slavery when we began clearing that land down by the river and you spoke of the profit Elmwood would reap!" Grant was so angry that as he spoke droplets of spittle and Scotch sprayed from his mouth.

"I must ask you to lower your voice," David said, his own ire beginning to rise. He had known his son would not understand this difficult choice he had made. He was foolish to have ever thought the boy could. But he loved him so much that he had hoped that, even if Grant had no sympathy or tolerance for his father's cause, he would at least have sympathy and tolerance for the man who had given him life and everything he possessed. After all, despite his law degree, Grant had never worked a day in his life.

As the senator stared at Grant, he felt as if his son were suddenly coming into focus for the very first time. A sense of dread crept over him as he stared back into the eyes of the angry young man. Had he been making excuses for Grant all these years as Cameron had so often tried to point out? Did he love the boy so much that he had excused behavior that should never have been excused? Had he glossed over basic personality traits in his son that were unpardonable to him? The possibility disturbed him a great deal.

"All right," Grant seethed. "Let us say for a moment that Senator Campbell does declare himself a northern sympathizer. What then?" He went on without giving his father a chance to respond. "You won't be safe south of the Mason-Dixon line," Grant scoffed as he walked to the side table to pour himself another Scotch. He was drinking too much too fast, and that worried David. His son had never been a solicitous drunk.

"You will have to run for your life," Grant went on in that same sour, biting tone. "I find it hard to believe you would be willing to simply abandon your much loved Elmwood and become a Yankee. Leave all your precious slaves behind."

"I will not simply leave my people behind," David said

firmly as he removed his cravat and tossed it onto the bed he and Sukey shared. How he looked forward to climbing into that bed tonight and holding his beloved in his arms, if only for a few moments. Sukey was who he needed right now, Sukey and her quiet gentle, steely strength.

The senator met his son's sullen gaze. He had spent enough time trying to coddle the boy. Grant needed to hear the truth and then they both needed to move on. "I am setting the slaves free. All of them. I am shuttering Elmwood for the duration of the war and going north where I can be of assistance to my nation's government."

"Setting them free!" Grant raged. "Are you mad?"

David had seen his son angry many times. As a child he had thrown loud, kicking, biting temper tantrums. As he had grown older, those outbursts had become less frequent but no less inappropriate and unbecoming of a Campbell man. It seemed that, when angered, Grant lost his ability to think clearly about anyone but himself. *Was* he just a bad seed?

"You cannot set those darkies free. They belong to Elmwood. They belong to me!" Grant reached for the bottle of Scotch. It was almost empty now and the seal had not been broke until sunset, just before the ball began. "If you're going to run away from your responsibilities and leave me to do the work, how am I supposed to run Elmwood without the slaves?"

"Elmwood will cease to produce," David said coldly. His justification of his son's behavior due to his disability was fast waning. He had just told his son that the United States was going to war, brother against brother, and all Grant could think of was his own purse. "The slaves will be set free and I will live on the money I have saved. You may go to our town house in Baton Rouge. You will have an allowance, but you may have to seek work in a law office and put that expensive education I paid for to use."

That said, David opened the doors to the veranda. The warm, humid night air hit him in the face and cleared his head almost immediately. It felt good to speak to Grant this way, to tell him how things would be. He should have done it years ago. He should have listened better to what Cameron had been trying to tell him. He was tired of his son's complaining, his failings, the excuses. It was time Grant pulled his own weight. And it was time, David decided resolutely, that he be completely honest with his son. What did he have to lose? As angry as Grant was, he doubted he could make him angrier.

"Don't you walk away from me, Papa," Grant ground out. "This conversation is not over."

"You are right, it is not over." He turned, resolutely to face his son. "I must also inform you that I have decided to leave Elmwood to Cameron." He continued without preamble. He had babied the boy for too long; he would not be gentle now. That was the thing about war. It had a way of maturing everyone in its path—a cruel but necessary fact. "You have never loved Elmwood the way we love her. Frankly, you don't deserve her. Now, I am not saying that I am disinheriting you. I will give you the house in Baton Rouge and your portion of my wealth, should there be anything left when I die."

"Leave Elmwood to Cameron?" Grant demanded, almost dazed by the news. "That is ridiculous. She is a woman!"

"And a fine young woman she is. She could run this plantation with her eyes closed. After the war, things will be different, but I have faith in her. I know that, if I am gone, she will be able to protect what I and my father before me have built. Perhaps she will even have the foresight to take this place in a direction never considered before the war." He smiled at the thought, though he somehow sensed he would not be around to see it.

"This is ridiculous, insanity, all of it!" Grant paced back and forth inside the bedchamber, dragging his bad leg behind him. When he drank too much his limp became exaggerated, and it was difficult for him navigate across the room without moving grotesquely. "You don't know what you are saying. You are disturbed by the news of Fort Sumter. Out of your head with shock."

"I am most certainly disturbed by the news," David agreed. "I am greatly disturbed by the thought that brother will fight brother on this soil I so love. I had prayed we would not come to this. But I am not in the least bit mentally incapacitated. I know exactly what I am doing. I am changing my will. I have been a fool in the past concerning you, Grant, but no longer.'' He made a fist. ''I am leaving Elmwood to Cameron and I am going to make certain my other daughter is well cared for.'' David didn't know what made him say that. It hadn't even been on his mind to tell Grant. It had just slipped out, as if his subconscious had spoken without his conscious mind being made aware.

Grant halted in the middle of the room and his head snapped up. ''Other daughter?'' His face had suddenly grown pale, his thin lips drawn back, almost in fright.

David looked his son straight in the eye. ''Born out of wedlock seventeen years ago.''

Grant frowned in confusion. It was obvious he still did not know who David spoke of. ''A bastard child?'' he muttered. ''You, *Saint David,* had a bastard?''

The remark hurt, but David was beyond hurt now. ''Taye,'' he said simply. ''Taye is my daughter. Mine and Sukey's. I married your mother because it was expected of me, and I respected her greatly, but it is Sukey I have always loved.''

A look washed over Grant's face that, at first perplexed, then frightened David. It was hatred he saw in Grant's eyes. Something even worse than hatred, if such an emotion was possible. But maybe he was misinterpreting. Of course such news was a shock. It would be a shock to Cameron as well when he confessed to her.

David wondered now, however, if he should not have waited to speak of Taye. Perhaps this was too much for his son's weak disposition, undermined by strong drink.

''Taye is your daughter?'' Grant said stiffly.

David stood in the doorway to the veranda, his back to a giant elm tree that grew along the house's east side. The bedroom was so well lit with lamplight that he could not misinterpret the look on his son's face. Shock. Horror. Hatred.

''Your daughter,'' Grant murmured, his voice so quiet now that it was more disturbing than the previous shouts of rage.

''I am sorry for deceiving you all these years. I should have been more of a man and confessed long ago, but I was selfish, I suppose. My career, my position in the state." He shrugged. "You and I both know such liaisons are commonplace in the South. We just don't talk about them."

Grant brought his hand to his chest, certain his heart was going to leap from his breast. Taye was his father's child? That meant she was his half sister. A feeling of disgust washed over him, but it was a repugnance colored with an inkling of excitement. His sister? Taye was his sister? His father's bastard darky child? A chill passed over him.

Slowly, he lifted his gaze. As the shock of all his father had said settled in his mind, he met the taller man eye-to-eye. He could feel his heart twisting, shriveling. All he had ever wanted was his father's approval. He was not a coward. All he had ever wanted since he was fourteen was to hear Senator David Campbell take those once hastily spoken words back.

A lump rose in Grant's throat as he came to the realization that he would never gain that respect from his father. He took a step toward him, feeling as if he walked in a dream.

He could not allow his father to do this, of course. Free the darkies, make Cameron Elmwood's heir. He couldn't let Taye go either. He just couldn't. He loved her. Hated her. Grant took another step.

Dark hazel eyes met dark hazel eyes. Grant's father was taller than he was, though not as stocky. He had a trim waistline for a man his age. He had an air about him that seemed regal.

He would miss him.

"Grant," David said quietly. "I think you need to retire to your room and get some sleep. I'll wake you in a few hours and we can talk."

"I don't want to talk." Grant spoke through clenched teeth. The rage inside him simply bubbled up and exploded. "There will be no more talking."

He threw himself forward, ramming his shoulder into his father's stomach. Taken by surprise, the senator grunted and doubled over in pain. The impact of Grant's heavier body hitting his sent him hurling backward.

"No, no, no, this is not how it will be," Grant muttered. He took a step back and hit his father again. They fell back, striking the veranda rail with such force that it jarred his teeth. There was a sharp crack, then the rail fell free and the senator tumbled backward into the darkness.

Grant shifted his weight to keep from falling with his father and dropped to the floor. He heard his father utter a cry that was more of a gasp than a call for help. Then he heard the terrible thump of a body striking the hard ground two stories below.

Panting, Grant crawled across the floor of the veranda to the edge and peered over the side. Even in the darkness he could see his father's still body and the odd angle at which his head lay. Bile rose in his throat and he sat back, clutching his head. His mind was swimming. He was going to be sick. He'd had too much Scotch and heard too many confessions. A spasm gripped his stomach and he leaned over the railing to vomit. When the spasms subsided, Grant sat back on the floor, gripped his middle and rocked back and forth slowly.

"Goodbye, Papa," he whispered, wiping the sour bile from his mouth with the back of his hand. "Goodbye and good riddance."

10

A loud knock on the bedchamber door made both Cameron and Taye turn from the mirror. Taye had just pulled Cameron's hair back in a modest chignon so that Cameron could join her father. Cameron had dressed in a simple white muslin bodice and gray skirt that would be suitable to wear to pack her belongings, to attend to her horses and travel in if necessary. Her green ball gown now lay discarded carelessly on the floor, as forgotten as the dance slippers she'd kicked off.

"Yes?" Cameron called at the sound. "Come in."

Naomi entered the room, still dressed in her white serving clothes, her hair tied up in a turban. The expressionless look on her face alerted Cameron at once to the fact that something was terribly wrong.

"What is it, Naomi?" Cameron half rose from the bench in front of the rosewood dressing table mirror that had once been her mother's.

"Masta Grant says ya have to come quick. The senator, he taken a tumble." Naomi's voice was as devoid of emotion as her smooth brown features.

"Oh, heavens! Papa?" Cameron sprang off the bench and hurried for the door. "Is he hurt? Where is he?"

Naomi stepped out of Cameron's way as she rushed through the doorway into the hall. "Masta Grant's in the senator's bedchamber."

Taye started following Cameron, but Naomi caught her arm.

"Not you," Cameron heard Naomi say. "Masta Grant say just his sister."

Cameron raced to the end of the hall in the family living quarters and pushed open her father's bedroom door. Grant was seated on the edge of their father's great bed, his head in his hands.

"Where is he?" Cameron demanded, glancing wildly about. "Naomi said the senator was in his bedchamber! Grant!" Cameron shouted when her brother made no immediate response. "Where is he?"

Without lifting his head, Grant pointed to the open veranda doors.

Cameron was utterly bewildered. "Why aren't you with him? Why are there no lamps out there? Why isn't anyone here to help him?"

She raced toward the open doors of the second story veranda. As a child she had played here while her father worked on hot summer afternoons. She had used the railing to line up toy wooden horses her father had brought to her from his travels.

"Papa!" Cameron called. He wasn't there. He wasn't anywhere! Panic leaped in her chest and a sense of sinking dread she could not control washed over her.

"Grant, where—" She halted in midsentence at the sight of the broken rail. "No," she whispered. "No." Like a sleepwalker, she approached the splintered railing, forcing herself to lift one foot and then the other. "No, no," she kept repeating in a whisper. But even before she made herself gaze over the edge to the ground below, she knew what she would see.

Cameron gathered her courage and made herself look. She pushed the toe of her sturdy kidskin boot to the edge of the flooring and leaned over. Far below, her father lay in the grass. Sukey sat with him, his head cradled in her lap. She was leaning over him, rocking, crying. Cameron knew from the angle at which his body lay that she would see the mask of death on his face when she peered into his eyes again. "Papa... Papa..."

If Sukey heard her or sensed her presence, she gave no indication.

"I knew he had had too much to drink." Grant appeared behind Cameron, startling her.

Cameron flinched. She hadn't realized her brother had stepped onto the balcony. She instinctively took a step away from the edge and put distance between her and Grant, who was holding up an oil lamp. "What happened?" she whispered, in too great a shock to trust her voice.

"It was the Scotch that bastard Captain Logan brought. From *home,* from the Highlands," he scoffed bitterly.

Tears ran unchecked down Cameron's cheeks, but she cried silently as she attempted to fathom what her brother was saying.

"He was upset about Fort Sumter. I told him to ease back on the strong drink, but he wouldn't listen."

She studied Grant in the yellow lamplight, trying to read his facial expression, which seemed at this moment to be smooth and hard. "You were here with him when it happened?"

"I took him out onto the veranda thinking the fresh air would do him good. But he was so upset. He was ranting about the war and how terrible it would be for Elmwood. You know how he can get, Cameron." Her brother's icy gaze bored into her.

She took another step back. "But Papa never drinks too much. I don't think I've seen him drunk since the Christmas I was seventeen and he tasted all of the brandy he had been given as gifts. Even then—" She turned away. How could this have happened? When she saw her father in his study, yes, he had been drinking Scotch, but he had by no means been intoxicated. She looked to Grant again. "He...he just fell?"

"He tripped." Grant shrugged. "A terrible accident. Tragic." He shook his head looking down into the darkness. "But just an accident."

There was something about the way Grant said those words that sent a chill of fear through her bones. She stared hard at her brother. *Had* this been just an accident? She took a step toward him, studying his face until he looked away, made uncomfortable by her staring.

"Grant," she murmured. "You haven't shed a tear for him?"

He glanced up quickly at her and then strode back into the bedchamber, leaving her to stand alone on the veranda. "Tears?" he mocked. "What good would tears do any of us? He would still be dead. Now come on. Let's get some darkies down there and have him carried into the front parlor. We certainly cannot let a senator from Mississippi lie in state on the front yard."

Thomas stood in the velvet darkness of the hallway outside the senator's study and listened to Grant Campbell and Captain Logan argue. He couldn't make out what they were saying, but both men were obviously very angry. While Grant ranted and raved, so intoxicated now that he slurred his words, the captain spoke quietly, slowly, his voice deep and razor edged.

It was close to dawn and it seemed that Elmwood's household had finally settled down to sleep a few hours. That or collapsed the way a family eventually does after a tragedy such as this. Thomas pressed his back to the wall. He was tired, tired to the bone. And afraid. He didn't know what to do now, where to turn. This had been the worst night of his life. First there had been word that war had been declared. The senator had called him into his study and told him, his voice cracking when he spoke the words. Right after that, Thomas had tried to talk with Taye and she had spurned him. Nearly broken his heart.

Then there was the senator's tragic accident. A lump rose in Thomas's throat. He had so admired and loved the senator. And now he was dead. Grant said he'd fallen from the balcony, and Thomas wanted to believe him. Had to believe him. With the coming of war there were things the family had to do. Things the senator would want accomplished. The question now was, how did Thomas approach the senator's son? He needed to tell him about the documents already drawn up. Grant needed to understand that it was imperative the papers be signed immediately. It was the only legal way to free Elmwood's slaves as the senator had wanted.

Thomas heard an angry burst of words from inside the study and the door banged open. He instinctively shrank back against the wall as Grant limped out and slammed the door behind him.

"Thomas!" Grant grunted. "There you are, you little weasel! What do you think you're doing, lurking in the hall?"

"I was waiting to speak with you...Mr. Campbell."

Grant grabbed Thomas by the coat sleeve and led him to the dark, cloistered servant's stairwell. Thomas didn't like Grant, never had. But the senator had loved his only son so greatly that Thomas had tried to tolerate him.

"What is it? I have no time for you!" Grant grumbled. "I am sure you know by now that my father fell to his death from the veranda tonight.

"Doesn't matter." Grant waved a hand. "I wanted to speak with you anyway. With my father dead, the family will no longer require your services."

"I understand," Thomas murmured.

"So I want you to go."

"I— Certainly. After the funeral..."

"Now," Grant ground out.

Thomas lifted his gaze to meet Grant's rheumy hazel eyes. "Sir?"

"What part of that statement did you not understand, you little ninny? You heard me. I want you to leave Elmwood. Now."

Something in Grant's tone made the hair on the back of Thomas's neck rise up, and it took every bit of gall he had to speak again. "I would like to remain for the senator's funeral, sir. And—and there are some matters you and I must discuss. Matters you may not have been aware of that the senator would want you to attend to."

"Matters my father would want me to take care of?" Grant mocked. "Who are you, Mr. Burl, to tell me what *my father* would want?" He pressed his face close and his sour breath struck Thomas in the face. Again, Thomas tried to move back, but this time Grant held him firmly.

"I do not mean to presume, sir." Thomas halted, took a breath and started again. He was a loyal man, and though Grant frightened him, he knew he had to fulfill his duties, to stand up for the senator's wishes. "There is an issue with the slaves, sir. Your father, the senator—"

"Are you not listening to me, you little pus pocket?" Grant grabbed Thomas by the coat lapels and forced him backward so hard that his head struck the wall.

"Sir," Thomas protested in shock, suddenly dizzy and sick to his stomach. "I know you are overwrought, but you have no right to handle me this way."

"Shut up and listen to me," Grant growled, still holding tightly to Thomas's coat. "I'm giving you one chance and one chance only. You get yourself on that horse and ride the hell out of here now, without so much as a word of this to anyone, or you will find yourself with a gunshot through the chest or a knife in your belly before you can say 'Pay the invoice,'" he hissed. "Am I making myself clear?"

Thomas trembled all over, but he stiffened his spine. "I will not go anywhere until I discuss this matter of the slaves with you. And if you will not listen to me, I will see Miss Cameron."

Grant sunk his fist into Thomas's stomach, and Thomas doubled over in a grunt of shock and pain.

Grant brought his mouth close to Thomas's ear. "If you don't get on that horse, you are not the only one who could meet an ill fate. I see the way you look at Taye. I see it if no one else does, you despicable negra lover."

Thomas managed to straighten enough to look into Grant's evil eyes. "Surely," he gasped, "you would not—"

Grant's face was hard, without any compassion whatsoever. "You have had your warning. Now you either tuck your coat-tails between your legs and head north to join your negra-loving Yankee dogs, or you and little Miss Taye will not live to see the outcome of this ridiculous squabble between the states."

Thomas's lower lip trembled as he fought back tears. "You bastard," he whispered.

Grant jerked his hands off Thomas and took a step back. "Goodbye, Mr. Burl." He headed for the study. "A pity we will never cross paths again."

Thomas stood for a moment in the dark hallway trying to consider his options. He was not a hasty or thoughtless man. It was not in his character to act before thinking or permit himself to be cowed by threats of violence. If he could get to Miss Cameron, or better yet Captain Logan, perhaps someone could help him. He owed that much to the senator. His life was worth his loyalty to Senator David Campbell who had been like a father to him. But then he thought of Taye and of the terrible power Grant held over her. Grant would carry through on his threat. He would harm her; Thomas knew it.

He saw clearly the most rational decision, the realization of what he had to do.

Quietly, quickly, Thomas slipped down the passageway toward the door. He would have his horse saddled and be off Elmwood in ten minutes' time. He hated to do it, but the thought of risking Taye's life was more than he could stand. Even after what she had said tonight, the way she had refused his attentions, Thomas couldn't risk harm to her.

He couldn't because he loved her.

Jackson stood by the roadside not a mile from Elmwood, watching as Thomas rode by, hell bent for God knew where. He had wanted to reveal himself, to speak to the young man, but he couldn't for fear Thomas would inquire as to why Jackson was out here in the middle of the night. He'd dispatch someone tomorrow to track the lawyer. He didn't blame Thomas for making a hasty retreat. No doubt Grant was responsible. But Thomas was a good man, a man Jackson might be able to use elsewhere.

Jackson had just met with a dark-cloaked stranger who would arrange his contacts in Jackson, then later in Baton Rouge. It had all been laid out weeks before, back in Washington, but now the game was on.

Jackson sucked on a thin cigar and the end lit up in a glow of red. He did not smoke often, didn't particularly care for the taste. Right now what he really wanted was a stiff drink, but he needed to keep a clear head about him.

God damn Grant! Jackson knew as sure as he knew his own name that the coward had something to do with the senator's death tonight. But there was nothing he could do about it. He had no proof; Grant certainly was not about to make a confession. And Jackson, as much as he hated to concede, could not remain here at Elmwood. Not to get to the bottom of the senator's death. Not to comfort Cameron, even if she would take the shoulder he was willing to offer. Jackson had to move on; his country needed him.

He dropped the cigar to the hard-packed dirt road and ground it out with his boot. He could hear the senator's voice in his head as he stepped into the woods to grasp the reins of the mount hidden behind a clutch of stunted pines. "Nothing to be done here, Jackson," he heard David Campbell say in his elegant southern drawl. "Better to go where you can do some good. We need you, Jackson."

He leaped onto the horse and grasped the reins tightly. So he would do what the senator ordered. Tomorrow, after the funeral, he would be on his way. He had a secret meeting tomorrow midnight in a hotel room in town, anyway. He would follow the instructions given, go where he was told to go. In the end, it would be better this way. The farther from Cameron Campbell he got, the better off he'd be.

He sank his heels into the horse's sides and the skittish animal bolted. Jackson would fulfill his duty as expected, but there was one thing here he still had to do.

He urged the horse into a canter and headed back up the road toward Elmwood.

"Cameron, please, open the door," Jackson urged from the hallway. When she didn't respond, he banged the wood panel with his fist again with annoyance. "Cameron!"

"Go away," she called. She sat on the edge of her bed, in the darkness, dressed in her nightclothes. Once her father's body had been moved to the library and left in Sukey's care, Taye had insisted that Cameron come to her room, change into her bedclothes and lie down, even if she couldn't sleep. That was more than two hours ago; it had to be close to dawn by now. Though the draperies were drawn against the rising sun, she knew it was there just on the horizon.

Cameron's gaze fluttered to the door as Jackson pounded, heavy-fisted again.

Taye covered Cameron's hand with her smaller one. "What does he want?" she whispered, her voice filled with concern. She stared at the door through the darkness, her eyes wide with fear. "He shouldn't be at your door this time of night. It isn't fitting to be so near to a lady in her nightclothes. Surely he realizes you can't receive him in such a state."

Cameron patted Taye's hand to comfort her. "It's all right, puss. Don't be afraid. He's harmless enough. It's just his way to bluster about. He has no ill intentions. He is just annoyed that I will not speak to him," Cameron said, her gaze still fixed on the door.

"Cameron, please," Jackson said again, lowering his voice. Surely he realized that if he continued to carry on this way, someone in the household would hear him. He turned the doorknob, and she was thankful she had locked it. "Let me in or at least come out. I need to talk to you privately."

Cameron rose and walked toward the door in her filmy nightdress, feeling mysteriously drawn by his persistent voice. She had no intentions of letting him in, of course, but she could not remain on the bed with him so near.

Taye rose to her knees, clutching her hands to her breasts. "Cameron, don't," she whispered.

Cameron halted at the door, but she did not reach for the knob. "Go away," she told Jackson in a whisper. She was so numb with shock and grief that she felt disconnected from her body. It was as if the bare feet that carried her across the thick floral carpet and then smooth hardwood were not her own. Even her voice sounded foreign to her ears. "Go away, Jackson," she breathed. At the door, she pressed her hand to a wooden panel. It was cool and smooth beneath her palm.

"Cameron, I am so sorry for your loss." She could hear him breathing. She could almost feel the warmth of his body through the oak panels.

He seemed so genuinely concerned.

But Cameron couldn't talk to him, couldn't see him. Not now. She was too overwhelmed, too lost. It would be too easy to lose herself in that deep voice, those strong arms.

"I thought you were leaving Elmwood." She pressed her hand to the wood panel.

"I am. I have business elsewhere, but I won't depart before the funeral."

Cameron closed her eyes, the passing of her father still such a fresh wound. With the spring heat of Mississippi already bearing down on them, her father's burial in the family plot on the edge of Elmwood's property must be less than twenty-four hours after his death.

"And then it will be on to your ship, I suppose?" she questioned, surprised by the agitation in her tone. She thought that she was too exhausted, too spent for any emotion. "I suppose there is a great deal for a *merchant* such as you to do, in the face of war."

"Cameron, you don't understand. You think you do, but you don't." He rattled the doorknob again. "Open this damned door!"

A part of her wanted to open the door, yearned for any comfort he could offer. But she had to be strong.

"Go away, Jackson," she said firmly. "I do not want to speak with you."

"Cameron, it isn't just your father I want to talk to you about. I want to tell you—"

"Jackson. Forget about it. Forget it ever happened. Now go, or I will call one of the houseboys to have you physically removed from my doorway."

She heard a sound at the door, as if he had brought his fist to the panel once more, but this time with far less force. She leaned her head against the door, fighting the urge to open it.

He sighed. "All right. Try to get some sleep. But I will talk to you before I go, even if I have to break down this damned door,'' he finished gruffly. ''Do you understand me? I won't be put aside.''

She squeezed her eyes shut, biting down on her lower lip. ''Cameron!''

''All right,'' she whispered. ''But don't come to my room again. I'll see you in my father's study.'' She swallowed a lump that rose threateningly in her throat. ''After the funeral.''

He paused on the far side of the door for a moment as if he intended to say something more. Then she heard him turn and walk away, his boot heels striking hard on the floor as he retreated down the hall toward his own chambers.

When he was gone, Cameron stood a moment longer, her cheek pressed to the cool wood.

''Is he gone?'' Taye whispered, still fearful.

Cameron choked back a sob. ''He's gone.''

''Just lift your arm. There you go, my love,'' Sukey murmured tenderly. She dipped the linen washrag in a basin of warm, soapy water and drew it along David's lifeless forearm.

Such a beautiful arm.

David was already clean, she knew. He'd had a bath only late yesterday afternoon in preparation for the ball. David had always been fastidious with his cleanliness, both with himself and his clothing. Just the same, she wanted to bathe his body, needed to do this for him, before she dressed him for laying out.

Sukey had already picked out breeches, a starched shirt and coat for him. She would bury him in his favorite green coat. It was old and a little threadbare, really too tattered to dress a United States senator in, but he had loved it dearly. It was a coat Cameron bought him a few years ago when they had all traveled to Baton Rouge to shop. She had bought herself a gown to match, but then outgrew it as her body had blossomed from a child's figure to that of a woman's.

Yes, the green bombazine coat would be perfect. It was his shoes she could not decide upon. The coat was cut for afternoon or evening wear so she knew she should put on a pair of polished shoes.

Sukey dipped the rag in the water and again wrung it out and began to wash his hand, one long finger at a time.

So, did she put the shoes that matched the coat on his feet, or did she dress him in his tall, worn riding boots he was most often seen in at Elmwood? Sukey wished she had someone to ask. Cameron perhaps could be consulted, but hopefully the poor dear was sleeping. No, she couldn't bother Cam. Asking Grant was out of the question. After meeting briefly with Captain Logan in the study, he had locked himself in his bedchamber. He had called for Naomi and a bottle of whiskey, and no one had heard from him since. He had not even bothered to be present when his father's body was carried into the library.

The little, sniveling—

No. Sukey would not allow herself to think bad thoughts. Not now. It was ill luck. As she prepared David's body for the meeting with his Maker, she must think only good thoughts. She carefully washed each fingertip with the washrag, and when she came to a small ink stain on his thumb, she rubbed harder. Her thoughts must only be of the goodness of this man, she reminded herself. Not of others' failings. Not even of her own inconceivable loss.

When David's hand was finally clean, Sukey laid it gently at his side and drew back the sheet. She smiled down at his angled face. Lying here on this table, his eyes peacefully closed, he appeared as if he were merely sleeping. He didn't look dead. Not gone from her life.

Sukey's lower lip trembled as she fought the tears that stung the backs of her eyes. She didn't have time for this. There would be plenty of time for tears later. Right now she had to keep a clear head. There was so much to do, and as Elmwood's housekeeper, it was her duty to see the tasks completed. David's body had to be prepared for burial. Two young slaves were building a coffin in the woodshed, but others would have to be roused from their beds and sent to the family burial plot to dig the grave. Due to the heat, the funeral could not wait. Messengers would have to be dispatched to the neighboring plantations to notify friends of the senator's accidental death as soon as the hour was decent. And though the notice was short, there would still be many here at Elmwood by noon. Even considering his opposition to slavery, Senator David Campbell had been a man well respected by others. Food would have to be prepared for the guests who would attend the funeral. The festivities of last night's ball would have to be cleaned up and black mourning crepe draped about the house.

Sukey made a clicking sound between her teeth. "So much to do, my love." She dipped the rag in the basin again and pulled the sheet back farther to bare his broad chest. How many years had she laid her head upon this chest?

They had fallen in love when David was only seventeen and she fourteen. A year later, they had consummated their love. Though in the years when he had been married to Caroline, they had not seen each other alone as often as before, David had never made her feel less loved. The night his wife Caroline died, she had held him in her arms and comforted him. A few short years later, he had remained at her side while she gave birth to their daughter.

Sukey brushed her fingertips over David's chest of springy, graying hair. His body was cool now, his limbs growing stiff. She needed to finish up. It would be dawn soon and Elmwood would come alive. David needed her to fulfill her tasks. To be strong.

A sob caught in Sukey's throat and rose up until she released it as a wail. She fell to her knees, lowering her head to David's lifeless body. The washrag fell from her hand, forgotten, to the floor. "Do not leave me, my love," she moaned, rocking back and forth. "Please do not leave me. Take me with you," she sobbed. "I would rather be dead than without you. I *am* dead without you."

11

Cameron stood near her father's open grave, Taye's fine-boned hand clasped tightly in hers. A clergyman, hastily summoned from the local Episcopal Church the Campells attended regularly, droned on, pontificating at length on the boundless rewards of heaven. She gave the minister's eulogy scant attention. Right now she did not care what the Bible said of the greater glory of the hereafter. All she cared about was that her father was dead, and life as she knew it was crumbling to her feet.

Cameron and Taye were both garbed in navy-blue gowns with black lace veils draped over their heads. Because of their tender ages and the lack of previous tragedy in their lives, they had no proper mourning attire, and there had been no time to purchase black gowns. Sukey had finally given in this morning and agreed that "her girls" would wear the navy winter gowns found in the back of a chiffonier.

Still holding tightly to Taye's trembling hand, Cameron slid her other hand up under the veil and tugged at the confining neckline of her gown. It was one o'clock in the afternoon and the April Mississippi sun beat down on their backs. The gown she wore was tight-fitting and itchy. She could not fathom wearing the garment the rest of the day as she moved through the crowd of neighbors and friends gathered at Elmwood and accepted their condolences. Her gaze shifted over the crowd of mourners as she tried to ease the neckband's smothering constriction. Despite the suddenness of her father's death, there were many gathered at the family gravesite to pay their last respects to Senator David Campbell. There were many faces she recognized as guests from last night's ball. It was difficult to believe that less than twenty-four hours ago they were all blithely garbed in ball gowns and frock coats dancing the waltz. Now they were garbed in black, shedding tears for their lost friend.

Cameron's cheeks, however, were dry. She could not cry today. The pain of her father's death was too great. She feared that if she allowed herself to weep, she would never be able to stop the flow of tears.

As she looked out at the sea of black mourning clothes, she noted that Thomas Burl was noticeably absent. In the confusion of last night, no one knew what had happened to him. It wasn't until this morning that Cameron realized he was gone. When she checked with the stable, she discovered that he had departed before dawn, carrying nothing but a knapsack, "Ridin' like hell, Missy Cameron," the groom had said. Cameron wondered why Thomas had left so hastily and without so much as a goodbye to her. It was so unlike him.

Surrendering her battle with the abrasive neckline, she let her hand fall. Someone on the far side of the grave pit caught her attention, and Cameron lifted her gaze beneath the black veil. *Jackson.* He was not even pretending to listen to the minister. He was staring at her, doing everything to get her attention but jump up and down waving his arms.

She stared back from behind the black lace that she hoped obscured his view of her face. She couldn't think about Jackson now, about these emotions that kept churning inside her, feelings that she continued to suppress. He said he would be leaving after the funeral. Good riddance, she thought. Out of sight, out of mind. If he left, if he simply disappeared from her life, she wouldn't have to deal with the things she was feeling. If he left now, she could forget about what had happened last night in his room. She could well pretend it had never happened at all.

Jackson continued to stare at her with those penetrating gray eyes.

Cameron must have squeezed Taye's hand in reaction, for Taye, her beautiful face streaked with tears, turned immediately to Cameron. "Are you all right?" she whispered.

Cameron nodded, this time gripping her friend's hand in reassurance.

Thankfully, the minister was finally winding down. Cameron made a conscious effort not to meet Jackson's gaze again as the coffin was lowered into the ground. She stepped forward and picked up a handful of fresh-turned Elmwood soil and tossed it into the grave. The dirt made a resounding thud as it hit the coffin that still smelled of new-cut loblolly pine, and she had to fight the nausea that rose in her throat. "Goodbye, Papa," she whispered. "Goodbye."

Lowering her head, ignoring those who were trying to speak with her, she headed for the house. Taye grabbed her arm. "Where are you going?"

"To see Grant. It is ridiculous that he missed his father's funeral. And now he is going to leave me with these people all day," she spat. "Consumed with grief, my rosy buttocks. He's hung over. That, or still drunk. That's why he couldn't come down from his bedchamber today."

Taye clasped Cameron's hand, looking into her eyes "You mustn't upset yourself like this. Maybe it's better if you let him be. Not all of us are as strong as you are, Cam. Not all of us can face our fears and misfortunes so boldly." She pressed her rosebud lips together. "It's not possible for us to understand another's grief."

Cameron studied Taye's blue eyes and remembered that Sukey had not been present at the funeral either. "I didn't mean your mother," she said quickly. "I was talking about my worthless brother, puss. Not dear Sukey."

Sukey had made all of the funeral preparations, had the house cleaned, and was at this moment overseeing food that was being prepared in Elmwood's great kitchen. She had not attended the burial because she said she had too much to do. Cameron had a feeling that her father's death hurt Sukey so greatly that she could not bear to see him interred beneath the soil he had so loved. But, not knowing just how much Taye knew of their parents' relationship, she said nothing of it.

"Your mother is doing what is expected of her. What Papa would have expected of her." Cameron ran her hand along Taye's sleeve. "Now go see if you can help her. These people can find their way to the ballroom on their own, don't you think?"

Taye nodded and let go of Cameron's arm so that she could hurry off.

Instead of taking the front hall entrance that the others were using, Cameron headed for the back of the house. She was just crossing the lower veranda when she heard a voice behind her.

"Where do you think you're going?" Jackson grabbed her arm, preventing her from going any farther.

She spun around, instantly angry with him. It seemed to be the only emotion she could handle when dealing with Captain Logan. "Checking on my brother."

"Cameron, I told you I had to go." He frowned at the veil that covered her face. "Get this damned thing off so I can see you!" He reached out with his free hand and jerked the black veil back off her face, letting it rest on the back of her head. "I must speak with you."

She tried to jerk her arm from his iron grip, but to no avail. "You're hurting me," she ground out between clenched teeth.

"So stop struggling."

She gave one hard jerk and then relaxed the muscles of her arm. It was no use. He was too strong to fight. "I don't have time to talk to you. Grant has himself locked up in his room with Naomi. You saw. He didn't even come down for the funeral."

Jackson's steely-eyed gaze locked with hers. "And you think he'll come out for you?"

"He's overcome with grief."

"That or guilt."

Without considering the consequences, Cameron drew back

her hand and smacked Jackson hard across the face. The slap sounded as loud as cannon fire in her ear and stung her hand.

He didn't even flinch. "You don't want to get into a slapping contest with me," he threatened hoarsely, "because I guarantee you will not win."

"You would strike a lady?"

"What lady would strike a gentleman?"

"You're insufferable."

"Do you take no responsibility for your own behavior?"

She lowered her gaze, ashamed of herself, but too proud to say she was sorry. Somewhere in the back of her mind the question of how great a role her brother had played in her father's fall had arisen, but the thought was just too difficult to consider. Now, feeling pain and despair greater than she had ever known, she couldn't face the possibility that Grant could have committed the ultimate crime of patricide. And she could not forgive Jackson for thrusting the unthinkable on her.

"Five minutes," she said.

"What?"

She lifted her head to meet his gaze, setting her jaw. "I'll give you five minutes of my time. In the library." She jerked her arm again and this time he let go of her. "Let me go in first," she said walking away. "You follow a few minutes later. I don't want anyone to see us together."

She walked away, and he let her go.

Cameron did not go to Grant's room, but went directly to the library. She needed a moment to collect her thoughts before she talked to Jackson again. She couldn't believe she had struck him. After what she had let him do to her body last night...after the intimate way she had touched his body... Her cheeks blossomed with heat as she forced herself to push those memories aside.

Once inside the library, she closed both doors that led from the hallway inside. She walked to a side table, poured herself a small dose of brandy and raised it to her lips. The liquor burned a fiery path down her throat, but she welcomed the pain. She would have to wash out her mouth with toilet water before she greeted the mourners, else everyone in the county would be liking her to her brother. But it was after noon and the day of her father's funeral. As far as she was concerned, if anyone deserved a drink, she did.

She had just walked to the open window with her glass when she heard the door open. Someone slipped in and closed the door behind him. She didn't need to look to see who it was; she could sense Jackson's presence.

Her throat constricted, and she raised the glass again, taking a deep swallow to give herself courage. "No one saw you, did they?" she murmured, not turning to look at him.

"I don't think so. I came in through a window in the cellar, crawled along the servant's hallway and flattened myself out so I could slip under the door unnoticed."

She spun around to face him, the cut crystal brandy glass still in her hand. "That isn't funny."

He gave her a boyish half smile. "I'm sorry. You're right. It isn't. It's just that you weren't terribly concerned with what anyone thought when you let me carry you to my room last night."

If her amber eyes were daggers, she could have cut him down from ten feet away. "You are no gentleman to remind of *that*."

"May I remind you that I was no gentleman to begin with, and you knew it." He walked to the side table and poured himself a far more generous portion of the senator's brandy. "A refill?" He lifted the crystal decanter.

Cameron looked down at her empty glass. The alcohol was already making her empty stomach do flip-flops and she felt light-headed. "I haven't had that much," she defended.

"I didn't say you had." He walked to a leather-upholstered chair and sat down, stretching out his long legs. He was dressed in black riding breeches and a bleached linen shirt and cravat. He had left the black coat he had worn to the funeral elsewhere. In any other circumstances, she might have thought he made quite a fetching sight.

She eyed him coldly. "I am not my brother to drown my sorrows in drink."

"I know that."

His tone was so smug, so damned...arrogant. He made her want to slap him again. She walked over to the side table and brought the glass down hard on the polished wood, marring the finish. "All right, what do you want?" she demanded. "Tell me and get out."

"Cameron, Cameron," he shook his head, remaining infuriatingly calm. "Come sit and talk to me. I'd take you in my arms and try to comfort right now, but I know better. You're liable to tear me from limb to limb if I try."

"It's a good thing you realize that," she answered, reluctantly taking a seat on the settee across from him. She sat not because he wanted her to but because she was feeling dizzy from lack of sleep and the potency of her father's brandy. "Now tell me what is so important that you must see me now when fifty people wait in the ballroom to pay their respects to my family."

"I want to make arrangements for you to leave here. Today."

Her brow furrowed. "*You* want *me* to leave *my* home and you think I will go?" A black vortex spun and buzzed in her head.

"You have no idea the turmoil that will come of the firing on Fort Sumter, Cameron. I don't think you truly understand what war means. Now, I know your father was intending to send you north to New York. He told me so himself last night."

She crossed her arms over her chest and rested her head on the backrest of the brocaded blue silk settee. "I'm not going anywhere. I am in mourning, in case you have forgotten. My father just died."

"All the more reason why you must go today. If you leave with me, I can escort you and Taye to the train station. There's no telling how long the trains will continue to travel north. After that, you would have to travel by horseback."

"I am not leaving Elmwood!" The black lace veil felt itchy against the back of her neck, and she scratched irritably. "My brother is now the heir to my father's lands, to the men and women who work these lands. Do you have any idea what a mess he will make of this plantation?''

''That is exactly why you must go.''

''My father intended to free his slaves, you know.'' She lifted her shoulder. ''Not that you would understand that.''

''I know he had intended to free them.'' He lifted a leg to prop his boot on his knee and leisurely sipped his brandy. ''But my guess is that your brother will have other ideas.''

''Then I will just have to change his mind, won't I?'' She grabbed the offending veil and ripped it off her head. She gave it a toss and the lace floated to the Turkish carpet like a black apparition on a moonless night.

''Cameron, stop being such a child and listen to me.'' Jackson jerked his boot off his knee and brought it down with a loud stomp. ''It could be dangerous for you here. Don't you hear what I'm saying? Your *life* could be in danger.''

''And you think the lives of those men and women out there are not in danger?'' She pointed in the direction of the slave quarters. ''I must convince Grant to set them free. That or…or I'll set them free myself!''

''You have no legal right to do that. You have no legal rights whatsoever over this plantation.''

Cameron leaned over and covered her face with her hands. ''Is this all you wanted to talk to me about? About leaving my home? Because if it is, I think you should go.''

He stood, leaving his empty glass on a small rosewood table beside the chair. As he came slowly toward her, she tried to map out her best escape. ''No, that wasn't all I wanted to talk to you about,'' he said gently, in a voice that made her warm and shivery.

But she couldn't listen. Not now. Not to that voice. She wanted to cover her ears with her hands, but instead she just tightened her jaw and steeled herself.

''I wanted to talk to you about last night.'' He sat beside her on the settee, his leg brushing against hers. Even through the fabric of his breeches and the layers of petticoats, she could feel his heat.

She shook her head. ''It was a mistake.''

He drew back. "A mistake?"

She made herself look him in the eye. It was the only way to make him believe that what she said was true. "I—I was upset and I needed comfort. It was nothing more." She swallowed the lie that was a lump in her throat. "Nothing more than what I would have sought from another man." She lifted her shoulder in a shrug. "You just happened to be available."

His eyes narrowed dangerously. "Nothing more?"

He slid his hand over the brocade of the settee and she leaped up before he touched her. She couldn't stand the thought of him touching her right now. What if she shattered?

"Look," she said, trying to think quickly. "We were all upset last night. You didn't mean for it to happen. I didn't mean for it to happen. And nothing really did happen, did it? It's all forgotten and done with."

He rose from the settee, his voice hard edged when he spoke again. "I see."

"So you can go about your merry way, pirating or whatever it is you intend to do."

"And you will not consider leaving Elmwood with me now?" He glanced at the portrait of her and Grant with the shadowy figure in the background. "Not even for Taye's sake."

"You let me worry about Taye." She tucked her hands behind her back. "Thank you for staying long enough for the funeral. My father liked you. I'm sure he would have appreciated knowing you were here."

Jackson stood near the door. "Cameron..."

"Please," she said firmly. "It really would be better if you left now. I have my brother to deal with, and Taye, and Sukey. I'm so worried about Sukey. She is acting so strong, but I fear she's going collapse. And the slaves—" She cut herself off. Self-pity would not do anyone any good. "I have a great deal to do," she finished.

"I'll try to get back as soon as I can to check on you. I'm not sure how close my ship is to being seaworthy."

"You don't need to come back." She gave a wave of her hand, dismissing him. "Have a good war."

He paused, his hand on the doorknob, as if he wanted to say something more. Then he just walked out and slammed the door behind him.

A part of Cameron wanted to call out, "No, stop. Wait, don't leave like this. Don't leave me this way." But she would not allow herself to do it. She would not allow herself to cry, either.

"There you are," Taye said, walking out onto the lower veranda. "I looked everywhere for you."

Cameron stood at the rail, gazing out into the darkness in the direction of the slave cabins. Firelight flickered in the distance and she could hear the sounds of the slaves' drums. She could hear their voices as they sang their haunting, rhythmic songs of mourning. With the coffin buried, the guests departed and the food cleared away, there was no evidence left of her father's burial except for the drapes of black crepe over the mirrors. In the slave community, however, Taye had explained to her that they would mourn for days. They would follow their call to work each morning as expected, but they would pay respects to this lost master by night.

The slaves' religious practices were so foreign to Cameron that they often frightened her. But tonight she decided that she liked the thought that those men and women out there would mourn her father in the coming nights. While everyone here in the household seemed to be trying to pretend her father's death—his life—had never taken place, she was thankful for the mournful songs that reverberated through the night air.

Cameron leaned on the veranda rail, so tired she feared she was near to collapse. "What are they saying?" she whispered.

Taye came to stand quietly beside Cameron. "I am not good with my mother's native tongue, I fear." She was quiet for a moment as she listened. "They speak to the mother goddess of the earth and ask her to protect their fallen brother."

Cameron smiled a sad smile. She liked the thought that the slaves of Elmwood considered her father a brother. He would have liked that.

"Where is your mother?" Cameron asked, turning away from the sound of the drums and twinkling night fires.

"She is sleeping with Naomi's mother tonight."

"Not in her room, here where we can keep an eye on her?"

Taye pressed her lips together. "She says she cannot bear the thought of sleeping beneath the roof without him."

Taye sounded confused, frightened. Cameron wanted to tell her friend that she knew there was more between them than either she or Taye had realized, but the time, once again, did not seem right. Taye was tired and upset and Cameron had no desire to upset her any more.

Cameron looped her arm through Taye's and led her off the veranda into the quiet house. "I think that is where both of us should go. To bed. Perhaps things will not look so dismal in the morning," she said optimistically.

Taye nodded, but made no move toward the grand staircase. "I saw him ride off this afternoon." Her blue-eyed gaze searched Cameron's. "I'm sorry."

Cameron knew who she meant of course. Jackson. "Don't be," she said. "It's better this way."

Taye reached out and grabbed Cameron's hand in her smaller one. "Do you mean that?"

Cameron didn't have the courage to meet her gaze. "I don't know what I mean. I'm too tired to think." She looked back at Taye. "But what I do know is that there must have been some reason Thomas left so hastily."

It was Taye's turn to look away as she withdrew her hand from Cameron's.

"Perhaps my father had sent him on some urgent business and he decided he had better go."

"He would have said goodbye to you," she said softly, her eyes filling with tears.

"What he should have done," Cameron replied, "was said goodbye to you. In the light of everything that's happened, he should have gotten up the nerve to speak to you."

Taye's lower lip trembled. "We did talk earlier. Before the senator—" She cut herself off, took a breath and started again. "I think we said goodbye then."

Cameron's brow furrowed. She didn't quite understand what Taye was saying, but she had a feeling there was more to this than Taye was letting on. "You don't have to tell me now," she said, taking her companion's arm and tucking it under hers to lead her up the steps. "But you are going to tell me. Every word. Now come on." They started up the polished steps, arm in arm. "Get your nightclothes and come to my room."

"You want me to sleep in your room?" Taye murmured, seeming so young and childlike.

"I know one thing tonight," Cameron said, gazing into the darkness as she tried not to think of Jackson. "I know I can't sleep alone."

PART TWO

12

Cameron pounded on her brother's bedchamber door. "Grant! Grant, do you hear me? You can't stay locked up in there forever," she shouted. "Now come out—" her voice cracked "—or at least let me come in. I need to talk to you."

A full week had gone by since their father's death, and Grant still remained cloistered. He had allowed no one inside but Naomi, and Cameron had lost patience with her brother days ago. She was completely overwhelmed by all that was happening, not just on Elmwood, but in Mississippi and the United States.

Three days after the Confederate army had fired upon Fort Sumter, President Lincoln, having only been sworn in a month before, issued a proclamation. He had called for seventy-five thousand militiamen, and summoned a special session of Congress for early July. It seemed that his response to the South's attack would be swift and potent. To further embroil the matter, Robert E. Lee, a Virginian and former superintendent of West Point, had been offered command of the Union army and declined. Word was, he would command the Confederates.

Cameron couldn't cope with everything alone. She needed Grant's help. *Someone's* help. She pounded on the door again. "Grant! Listen to me, damn it! It's time you got yourself sober and met your responsibilities. I'm trying to do what's best, but you have to help me with some of these decisions." She sighed, closed her eyes for a moment and leaned her forehead on the paneled door. "Grant," she said softly. "Grant, aren't you listening?" She pressed her hand to the smooth wood, fighting a sense of ragged despair. "Isn't anyone listening to me?"

"I don't know that you should be doing these things," Sukey said, entering the senator's study.

Cameron glanced up from her father's massive desk, pen poised. Despite the open window and the steady breeze, she was hot and tired and it was only midafternoon. She'd been here since early morning working on Elmwood's accounts, trying to take a full inventory. Virginia had seceded from the Union with Arkansas, Tennessee and North Carolina expected to fall in behind. As troops were beginning to rally and more Southern men were joining the army daily, Cameron was scrambling to set the plantation accounts in order. She had begun to make arrangements to sell off plows, farm wagons, a carriage and livestock, as well as some household items. She had to raise enough cash to keep the plantation running and be able to give the slaves coin in their pockets when they were set free.

Meanwhile, she was also making those plans to set the slaves free. In the two weeks since her father's death, she had been into Jackson twice to speak with an old lawyer friend of her father's. Mr. Joseph, the executor of her father's will, had been hesitant to help her. Though he knew of her father's distaste for slavery, it quickly became apparent to Cameron that he didn't know the depth of the senator's convictions. Mr. Joseph was unaware that her father had intended to side with the North, and she saw no reason to tell him now. Despite the lawyer's misgivings and his questions about the legality of such actions, when she called for the favor in the name of her father, he relented. He promised to begin the necessary paperwork to emancipate Elmwood's slaves, but insisted that as soon as Grant was back on his feet, he would have to speak personally to him, since Grant was the sole heir.

Cameron gazed wearily at Sukey. She had not been herself since the senator's death, and Cameron and Taye were both worried. While Sukey was making a halfhearted attempt to continue her duties in the household, she wasn't the same person. Her hair and her clothing were not as well kept as they had once been, and she tired easily. Cameron had gone so far as to have the doctor come out to the house to examine her, but he could find nothing wrong. It seemed that Sukey had lost her will to live.

"Sukey, I understand your concerns," Cameron said gently, "but—"

"The senator would not approve of you working so hard," Sukey replied in a soft, dreamy voice. As she spoke, she drifted across the polished floor of the study, running her fingertips over the belongings that had once been David Campbell's. She touched a leather-embossed cigar table, a walnut clock on a shelf, the half-filled brandy decanter Cameron could not bear to put away. "As master of the house, your brother should be consulted in these matters."

The room still smelled of the senator. Maybe that was why Cameron herself had spent so much time here since his death. She could still smell the faint scent of his favorite cigar and the aroma of his brandy. If she concentrated, she could almost hear the rustle of his coattails as he settled in his chair to read the *Biloxi Times* and point out articles of interest to her. When she closed her eyes, she imagined she could feel his great presence.

Cameron opened her eyes, fearing she was becoming as faint-witted as Sukey. "Grant *should* be consulted," she said, her tone sharper than she had intended. She took a deep breath, forcibly gentling her tone. There was no need to take her frustrations out on Sukey. Sukey was not the one who had created these troubles. "I would love to consult my dear brother." She gazed upward at the tin-paneled ceiling. "If he would come out of his bedchamber!" she shouted, as if he could hear her.

"Now, now," Sukey said, drifting toward the door. "A woman of your station mustn't raise her voice so. It's unladylike. What will the neighbor's think?"

"A woman of my station shouldn't have to go to her neighbors' homes and offer to sell her livestock at half the price they're worth either, but I will do what I have to, to preserve Elmwood.''

If Sukey heard Cameron, she gave no indication. "I think I will make some lemonade. Lemonade is soothing on such a hot day. It will make you feel better." She patted her pasty forehead with a plain white handkerchief. Since the senator's death, she had lost weight and now looked pale and gaunt. "Would you like to join Taye on the veranda for some lemonade, Miss Cameron?"

Cameron sighed. Lemonade on the veranda was the last thing she wanted right now, but Sukey looked so hopeful. "Certainly," Cameron said, relenting. "I can take a break for something co— For something to drink." She'd almost said *cold* but remembered that the last of the ice packed in straw deep in the bowels of the ice house was gone. There'd be no more ice until winter when flatboats brought shipments downriver from the North. She chuckled wryly. With war looming, who would worry about ice? That, and a hundred other luxuries she'd come to think of as commonplace, had evaporated into smoke—perhaps forever.

"I'll tell Taye that you're coming," Sukey said, wandering out of the study. "I'll ask Cook for some ginger cakes to go with the lemonade. Your father loves ginger cakes." Her dark intelligent eyes focused on Cameron and then clouded. "Be sure to change out of that riding habit into something more suitable. The yellow morning dress would be lovely. It's one of the senator's favorites."

Cameron glanced at the dusty tartan riding habit she had worn to the stable this morning. The yellow morning gown *would* be lovely. What would be lovelier was some device to turn back time. If only she could go back one month; there would be so many changes she would make. She would save her father, stop the war and make sure that that conniving bastard Jackson Logan never set foot on Elmwood.

Cameron had heard nothing from the captain since the day of her father's funeral when he had left her once again. Oh, he let on that he cared what happened to her, to Elmwood, but if he had truly cared, wouldn't he have stayed to help her through this? If he was so worried about her safety, wouldn't he have at least sent a letter in the last two weeks?

Cameron set down her pen and rose from behind her father's desk. At the window, she pressed her hand to her back that ached from being seated in the chair so long. "Damn you, Jackson," she whispered. "How did I let you do this to me again?"

She gazed out into the field beyond the house. The cotton had been planted before the war began, but she had no idea how she would harvest it. If she had her way, the slaves would be gone in another fortnight, all headed north with the money she was gathering from the sale of Elmwood's belongings in their pockets. The trick now was to get Grant to agree to freeing them according to Papa's instructions. After all, it was inevitable, wasn't it? But without her brother's signature, Elmwood's people could never be legally set free. She had faith in Grant but knew that she needed to find the right moment to discuss the matter with him.

However, with each passing day that Grant spent locked in his chambers Cameron became less confident that he would let the slaves go. Taye thought Cameron was a fool if she believed she could convince her brother that setting them free was best for Elmwood, for all of them. So Cameron had come up with an alternative plan, just in case Grant could not be convinced. She had discreetly inquired about the Underground Railroad, a series of safe houses along the route north which would provide shelter for slaves traveling to freedom. Next week she and Grant would attend a party in Jackson. It would be their first public appearance since their father's death. The party was being given by one of her father's loyal constituents, and only because he was one of Grant's comrades at the card table, Grant had agreed to escort Cameron. He had agreed through his closed door, and she worried he may have forgotten their conversation. While she had no desire to socialize, she had been told there would be a man there who could give her information on the Underground Railroad. She was merely to show up and a man named James would find her.

"There you are." Taye walked into the study. Cameron turned to face her friend, who looked as worn and tired as the rest of them.

"Mama was looking for you. She said you asked for lemonade on the veranda, but you never came for it."

Cameron frowned. "Actually, I didn't ask for lemonade. Sukey told me it would be served on the veranda and that I should come and have some."

Taye approached Cameron and reached out to stroke her arm. "She seems confused, doesn't she?"

"I think you need to seriously consider my suggestion," Cameron said. "A change of scenery might do her good. There's no reason why you and your mother cannot go to the Stuarts now. I can join you once matters here are taken care of," she said meaningfully. She didn't dare speak aloud of freeing the slaves for fear the walls had ears. "Once Elmwood is shuttered, I'll be in New York in no time."

Taye shook her head obstinately. "I am not leaving here without you." She lowered her voice. "I am not leaving you with *him*." She glanced upward. "Besides, you forget that Elmwood is my home, too. I will see this through with you, and then we will travel north together."

Cameron couldn't resist a sad smile as she wrapped her arm around Taye's delicate shoulders, and the two women walked out of the study. "I would rather you went," she said, "but I am glad you are staying." She gave her a squeeze. "Now let's have our lemonade, and then if you don't mind, we need to find something for me to wear to the Hitches' party next Saturday."

Taye halted. "And you are certain this isn't dangerous?" she whispered.

Cameron shook her head. "Hardly. All I am doing is gaining some information in case we need it."

Taye again glanced upward in the direction of Grant's bedchambers. "I am hoping for the best," she said softly, "but I fear he will not sign the release papers, Cam."

"Then we'll do this without him," she said confidently.

* * *

Cameron sat across from her brother in the carriage and smiled, trying her best to be congenial. She had dressed carefully in a jewel blue organza gown that featured a low-cut bodice and tiny, corseted waist. She could barely breathe, Taye had laced her so tightly, but she had learned long ago that her brother, like most men, could be manipulated by a woman with a sweet voice wearing a fetching gown.

"I am glad to see you are feeling better, Grant" she said. "Taye and I have been worried about you."

His gaze fell on her with interest. "Taye said she was worried about me?"

She nodded, seeing no need to tell him that Taye had actually said she was concerned for his soul, concerned he was going to burn in everlasting hell for his debauchery. Since their father's death, Cameron and Taye had learned that Grant had not only brought Naomi into his bedchamber, but sneaked other young slave girls into the house. There was no way for Cameron and Taye to stop him. He was the master of the plantation, but it sickened both women.

"We have missed you at the supper table," she lied. "And there are so many matters concerning Elmwood that we need to discuss."

"I don't know what you mean. Elmwood will continue on as she always has, only with me in charge instead of Papa."

Cameron glanced at the bright lantern swinging at the coach's door. "Grant, you really don't believe that, do you? The South is at war with the North. Soldiers could overrun us. Do you know what hungry, sick soldiers will do to a plantation like Elmwood? Soldiers from either side?"

He gave a laugh as he adjusted his cravat. He was wearing a puce coat tonight that did nothing for his already pale complexion. "Now, now, no need to worry your pretty little head, sister dear. Have no fear, your brother has a plan to protect our interests."

Cameron sighed and glanced out the window at the setting sun. This was not the direction she was hoping the conversation would take. They were running out of time. She had to get Grant to agree to sign those papers emancipating the slaves. "Grant," she said, forcing herself to go on. "We need to talk about something. About Papa's wishes."

He flicked a speck of dust from his pant leg. "What wishes?"

She met his gaze. "Concerning the slaves. Grant, we have to set them free as Papa intended."

To her surprise, he did not explode in anger, but burst into laughter. "Set the darkies free? You jest?"

She slid across the carriage seat to sit beside her brother. "Grant, you know that was what he intended to do. If we could find Mr. Burl, he could confirm it. He might even know where the papers are that I suspect Papa had begun working on."

"Set the darkies free?" Grant repeated. "I don't know what you're talking about. Papa had no intention of doing anything of the kind."

Cameron stared at him, thinking what an inveterate liar he was. "Grant, how can you say such a thing? You were at the same dining table I was. You heard the things Papa said. You know how he came to feel about slavery."

Grant gave a wave of his hand. "That was nothing but political pot stirring. It is what politicians do best, and our father was an expert." He crossed his arms over his chest and sat back. "You know Senator David Campbell always sided with the underdog. It made for good supper conversation. He always said that heated discussion was good for digestion."

Cameron stared at her brother in disbelief. "Grant, surely you are not serious?" She pulled away from him, sick to her stomach. "I had thought you were only hiding these last weeks, drowning yourself in whiskey and women, but now I wonder if you are not seriously ill."

Grant's eyes narrowed dangerously. "That will be enough, Cameron. I told you, I have everything under control. Now, if you cannot hold your tongue, we will turn this carriage around and go home."

Cameron felt a flutter of panic in her chest. Instinctively, she knew that her plan to legally emancipate the slaves was not going to work. Taye had been right and she had been wrong. Grant would never set the slaves free, not even if the South came tumbling down around them.

She forced herself to lower her gaze contritely. "No, please, Grant, I want to go to the Hitches'. It's been so long since I've worn a pretty gown out," she managed weakly. "I'm sorry. I didn't mean to quarrel with you."

"There, there, now." Grant patted her shoulder, taking on the role of the gallant brother. "Don't cry, dear. Let us forget this conversation ever took place. I know you are overwrought about Papa's death. I should not have taken so much time to mourn him." He gave his coat a tug. They had reached the Hitch mansion and were rounding the opulent circular drive. "But I am feeling better now, stronger. I'm prepared to accept my duties as the heir of Elmwood. Ready to make decisions that must be made."

Cameron kept her gaze lowered, fearful her brother would see the contempt in her eyes if she looked at him. She was so angry, so disgusted that she could barely think. But she could act. She was becoming a better actress every day. "Whatever you say, brother. I'll do what I can to help you."

He patted her gloved hand. "I'm certain you will. In fact, I know you will." The carriage came to a halt and one of the Hitches' footmen opened the door. Grant stepped out of the carriage and offered his hand. "All is forgiven. Now come, dear sister, let's enjoy an evening out. I think we both deserve it, don't you?"

It was all Cameron could do to make herself accept Grant's hand.

Once received by the host and hostess, Grant left Cameron's side, his eye on the card tables already set up in a study for the male guests. Cameron accepted a cup of punch from a young black boy wearing gold rings in his ears, a feathered turban and matching red-and-white jacket and trousers before wandering from one group of women to another. She accepted condolences on her father's passing, forced a smile and pretended to listen to the women's chatter of the war and their brave husbands who were enlisting. As she nodded, smiled prettily and fluttered her fan with the other women, she kept an eye out for the mysterious James who would speak to her about the Underground Railroad. She had no idea how old he was, what he looked like or why he was here. It was Naomi who had given her the name. Cameron tried not to think about how Naomi had known who to contact. She had bigger problems to worry about right now.

After Cameron's discussion with Grant in the carriage tonight, she retained little hope she could set Elmwood's slaves free legally. Now she would have to take the more dangerous route of simply setting them free with money in their pockets and a map to direct them north along the "railroad." It would be dangerous for both her and her family, as well as the slaves, but she saw no other choice.

She smiled prettily and moved to another group of women. If she was going to find this James, she had to be seen.

Jackson stepped out of the cloakroom, slipped his arm around the officer's neck and jerked him backward into the darkness before he ever knew what hit him.

The uniformed lieutenant opened his mouth to protest and Jackson stuffed a handkerchief into it. Nothing came out of his throat but a guttural cry of protest.

"What do you think you're doing following me?" Jackson whispered hoarsely in the man's ear.

The man, no more than twenty-five, shook his head frantically, mumbling.

Jackson slipped a long-bladed knife from his polished boot and pressed the tip to the soldier's pale neck.

"You've got thirty seconds or I slit your jugular. You'll be dead in less than a minute and this fine new gray uniform of yours will be a bloody mess."

The officer stiffened against Jackson. Though he could not speak, his body language told Jackson all he needed to hear. "That's better," Jackson muttered. "Now, remember, I can slit your throat with or without the handkerchief."

The man nodded and Jackson yanked the cloth from his

mouth and threw it to the floor. He kept the knife point at his throat. "Who are you and why are you following me?"

"A message," the man croaked. He sucked in a great breath. He smelled as if he had pissed himself. "From…from Smitty."

Jackson lifted an eyebrow curiously. He hadn't expected to hear from his informant until later in the week. "Smitty sent you?"

The man tried to nod but flinched when he felt the tip of the knife sink into the flesh of his neck. "Aye. Smitty sent me. I've got word on what you've been waiting to hear."

Jackson lowered the knife and spun him around. "So why the hell didn't you tell me that in the first place?" he said with a grin. "Why don't you get a drink and slip out onto the veranda? I'll follow shortly and we can talk there."

In the mansion's ballroom, Cameron heard the host's booming voice as he made a patriotic speech of the honor of the South and how gentlemen would defend that honor. While others cheered, Cameron was sickened by such declarations. Hoping no one would notice her, she slipped down a dark hallway. She had been here for hours, and so far, still no luck with the mysterious James. She needed to sit down for a moment and catch her breath, needed to get away from her Confederate "brothers and sisters" and their unrealistic view of what the next months, perhaps years, would bring. Cameron knew there was a lady's retiring room set aside for guests where they might sit and rest and adjust their clothes, but she had no desire for company. What she needed was a quiet, dark study or library.

Glancing over her shoulder to be sure no one saw her enter the hall, she collided with a tall male figure.

"Oh, goodness. I'm so sorry, sir," she said in the voice she knew men appreciated. She gave a little laugh as she glanced up. "Silly me, I—" Halting midsentence, she stared at the face of the man she had collided with. "You!" She reached out and smacked Jackson hard with her painted fan that matched her jewel-blue ball gown. "What are you doing here, you worthless cad?"

He gave her a lazy smile as his iron fingers closed over her wrist. "Good to see you too, Cameron, dear." He pulled on her wrist and started back the way he had come down the hall.

"Let go of me!"

"Shh, someone will hear you."

"I don't care! I'm not going with you," she sputtered as he dragged her away from the sounds of the party. "Jackson—"

He opened a door and pulled her inside. The room was small and paneled in dark wainscoting. It smelled heavily of cigar smoke and leather and was probably the host's private smoking lounge. Jackson shut the door with his foot and pushed her against it.

She could barely see his face in the darkness. There was only a narrow beam of moonlight that fell through an open window. She heard a dog bark, but it seemed far away. "Jackson, what do you think you're—"

Without a word, he covered her mouth with his.

Cameron was shocked by the unexpected assault. God help her, she couldn't breathe! Between her too tight stays and his mouth on hers, she feared she would faint. She struggled, infuriated with him. She beat his back with her fists and then, when that didn't work, she yanked on the lapel of his fine gray jacket. Still he didn't relent. He slipped his tongue into her mouth and though she resisted, there was some part of her deep inside that wanted his mouth on hers, wanted the taste of him.

Cameron groaned. If he didn't release her, she knew she really would faint from lack of air. She went limp in his arms but her mouth responded to his, against her will.

When Jackson finally pulled his mouth away, still holding her tightly, she closed her eyes, panting. She made no attempt to escape him; she was still too weak-kneed. Too shocked by his attack and by seeing him here. "What are you doing here?" she muttered when she could find her voice.

"I was going to ask you the same."

She lifted her lashes to meet his gray-eyed gaze. "I am a guest, my brother and I. Mr. Hitch and my father were old friends."

"Guests, are you? Then why are you creeping about the house, glancing over your shoulder as if you're looking to lift the silver?"

She turned her head, unable to stand his penetrating gaze. "What, now you're spying on me?"

"You should be with the other women, listening to the patriotic speeches." He was mocking her now.

She lifted an eyebrow. "And *you* shouldn't be?"

He gave her that dashing devil-may-care smile. "Cam, you know my feelings on politics."

"Far too well," she said tartly.

"Seriously, you shouldn't be here in this house." He loosened his grip around her waist, but only to move his hands to the door so that she was trapped between his arms. "Surely you realize you're in a nest of flaming Confederates. They catch wind of your opinions on this war and you're liable to be stripped and tarred."

She batted her lashes. "Not with Grant here. He's thick with these men. Mr. Hitch was anxious to have him here tonight. Grant owes him money for gambling, probably."

"That doesn't tell me why *you're* here."

Without giving him warning and a chance to catch her, she ducked under his arm, making her escape. "It's none of your business why I'm here." She walked around a small leather settee, putting the piece of furniture between them. Her eyes had adjusted to the darkness and she could better see him.

He grinned. "I'm glad to hear you talking that way. It sounds as if you're all right. Since your father's death, I mean."

She had to concentrate not to react. Who was he kidding? If he truly cared how she was taking her father's death, he wouldn't have left the day of the funeral, would he? "I thought you went to your boat in Baton Rouge."

"My *ship* is not quite ready. I'm headed there within the

next few days. I had some…*business* to attend to here in Jackson first.''

She lifted an eyebrow, trying to ignore the sting of his mouth she could still feel on her lips. She tried to pay no heed to the burning ache in the pit of her stomach and farther below. ''I'd just as soon not know what that business is, sir,'' she said haughtily, trying to cover for the mixture of emotions that were racing through her.

Again, the boyish grin. ''That's good, because I'd just as soon not tell you.''

She stared at him over the back of the leather settee, feeling as if they had just reached a stalemate.

''So, how are you?'' When he spoke again, his tone was gentle.

To Cameron's amazement, she felt the backs of her eyelids grow scratchy. No one but Taye had cared how she was since her father had died. ''It's been hard,'' she said simply. ''Grant stays locked in his chambers most of the time, and I'm trying to do what I think Papa would want us to do.'' She lifted her hands and then let them fall, feeling the utter futility of what she was attempting to accomplish. What if she couldn't find this James tonight? What if she couldn't get information about the Underground Railroad? Mississippi was already calling for donations of slaves to help with the labor of the army. So far, Cameron had been able to hold out, pleading mourning, but soon the Confederates would not take no for an answer.

Jackson came around the settee toward her, and though she wanted to move away, her legs would not carry her. He sat down on the settee and patted the place beside him. ''You look like you need to sit down.''

She glanced at the closed door. What she needed to do was make herself visible at the party. What if James was looking for her now? She had studied the face of every male she met tonight wondering if he might be James. Was he the elderly gentleman with the handlebar mustache, or perhaps the tall slender young man in the black-and-gray coat?

''Come now, just for a moment,'' Jackson cajoled. ''And then I'll set you free.''

She lifted her petticoats and sat beside him. "You say that as if you hold me prisoner." She lifted her chin a notch. "I can walk out that door at any moment I care to."

He brought his face close to hers, and she smelled his clean shaving soap and the hint of tobacco smoke on his collar. The man was utterly hateful, and yet insanely intoxicating.

This time, when he leaned toward her, she made no attempt to escape his touch.

13

Cameron pressed her hand to Jackson's hard, muscular chest and lifted her chin to meet his kiss. She could not help herself, could not resist the draw of his warmth, his overwhelming masculinity. A heavy glorious aching pulsed through her body as he parted her lips to kiss her more deeply. Jackson slid his hand to the nape of her neck and his caress sent a trill of shivers through her.

"Damn but I've missed you, Cam. Tell me you've missed me," he whispered, pulling her onto his lap.

She could not keep her gaze from his. She tried to read his face as she searched his gray eyes. Not breaking eye contact, he clasped her hand and slowly, deliberately, removed her white glove. As he plucked each finger of the lace glove, Cameron felt her breath come in little gasps. It was such a simple gesture, and yet intensely intimate.

"Admit it," he cajoled. "You've been thinking about me. Thinking about that night in my room. In my arms."

She felt the warmth of embarrassment scald her cheeks as she tried *not* to think of that night in his room. The man was a blackguard to remind her. No Southern gentleman with a decent upbringing would be so discourteous as to remind a lady of such an impropriety.

She stubbornly remained silent as he tossed the lacey glove over his shoulder and took her other hand in his. He removed the second glove and then traced the lines of her bare palm with his finger. Little thrills of pleasure ran from her fingertips up her arms and outward throughout her body to lap against her most intimate places. She had never realized a hand could be so sensitive.

When he moved to kiss her again, she looped her hands around his neck, her fingers catching in his dark, silky hair. She allowed him to press a trail of warm kisses across her chest above the bodice of her ball gown. "Say it," he murmured.

She wouldn't say it. She wouldn't tell him she had missed him. She might be a wanton, but she was no fool. It was bad enough that she could not resist his sinful temptations, but to confess that she feared she might feel more for him than pure lust would be madness. She would not, *could* not, let him break her heart again. It was already too brittle. She feared she'd not survive such a calamity again, not now after the devastating loss of her father.

"I have to confess," he whispered, his breath hot in her ear. "I came here tonight because you were on the guest list. I didn't actually even receive an official invitation from the host."

"You're nothing but a rogue," she accused, her voice husky and unfamiliar to her ears.

"I think we've already established that."

She lifted her lashes to meet his gaze. His gray eyes were dark and pooling, hooded with desire for her. He was so blessedly handsome. And he manipulated her so easily. Who was she fooling? Nothing had changed between them since she was that silly, seventeen-year-old girl. She knew he brought her into the darkness here for this, and yet she had been unable to resist him.

Jackson laid her back gently on the settee so that her head rested on the floral, padded arm. Her petticoats rustled and crackled as he pressed her into the silken fabric. She parted her lips, accepting his tongue into her mouth, straining against him.

He slid his hand beneath her skirts, over her stockinged calf. Sensations of pleasure coursed up her leg to the place that seemed to be the center of her desire. Already she could feel the dampness there.

Cameron wanted to cry out and stop him, but she couldn't. It felt too good. The weight of his body over hers, the taste of him—it was all too powerful. She was overwhelmed by the sound of his murmurs, the scent of his clean skin and shaving cologne and the masterful way he seemed to instinctively know how to touch her—and where. It was not just in those most intimate parts, it was her entire body that seemed aflame for him.

Jackson slid his hand over her silk-stockinged calf as he buried his face in the swell of her breasts.

"All right, so don't say it, you little witch," he murmured, half angry, half amused. "You don't have to say what your body says for you."

Cameron fully intended to protest, but he managed to pull down the low neckline of her gown to reveal one full, aching breast. She bit down on her lip to keep from crying out as he caught her nipple between his teeth and tugged gently.

She moaned and, without intending to, guided his hand farther up her leg, over her lace garter…higher.

Jackson's fingertips on her inner thigh seemed cool and fiery at the same time. She could already feel herself aching, throbbing for that touch that she had only known once, but that she now craved above all else. She had read recently about women with opium addictions. Was this what it was like? This desire that could not be overcome?

"You are so beautiful," Jackson murmured, his voice rumbling with desire for her. "You were made for loving, Cameron. This body of yours was made for loving."

To Cameron's surprise, he slid off the settee, going to his knees on the floor.

She lifted eyelids that seemed so heavy she could barely keep them open. What was he doing? She heard the rustle of her petticoats and felt his warm hand on her thigh. She struggled to sit up, but his powerful grip held her on the settee as he pulled down the waistband of her pantalets.

Cameron gasped, mortified as Jackson lowered his head until it disappeared into the sea of petticoats. The first touch of his mouth *there* made her cry out in disbelief. She raised a hand to push him away, but instead found herself biting down on the soft flesh of her hand between her thumb and forefinger to stifle the groans of pleasure that issued from her throat. Against her will, she lifted up so that he could pull her pantalets farther down.

No, no, she wanted to cry out. Instead, she moaned...*yes.*

Jackson's assault with his mouth was gentle, rhythmic. He probed with a finger as he lapped with his tongue. Cameron writhed on the settee. Every part of her being knew she must stop him, stop herself, and yet she couldn't. Already she could feel her body tensing, her muscles contracting and then relaxing in delicious anticipation of that which she knew was not far off.

A sob of frustration slipped from where she muffled her own sounds with her hand. She lifted her hips to meet his touch, at last surrendering. Cameron felt as if her entire body were molten fire, pulsing, aching. She wanted him. She didn't care what that made her, a wanton...a whore. She wanted to feel him inside her. She wanted to experience for herself that age-old rite of coupling between a man and a woman. She wanted to experience that with Jackson, here, now.

Another wave of indescribable pleasure washed over her and her release was sudden and powerful. She cried out, no longer caring if anyone heard her.

"Jackson," she panted.

He rose from the floor to sit on the settee beside her and gathered her in his arms.

She felt as if she were weightless, floating on the last little surges of ecstasy.

"I want you, Cam," he whispered in her ear, kissing her cheek. "I cannot tell you how badly I want you. And not like this." He kissed her temple. "I want all of you."

"Not here," she managed. "Someone will come."

"I know." He lifted his head, drinking in her gaze. There

was something more on his face now than desire, something gentler, but what it was she didn't know. "Come with me. Now," he said. "We'll go to my hotel."

She wanted to. She wanted to go with him to his hotel and take off all her clothes. She wanted to see him take off his. She wanted to make love with him before the war parted them forever. With everything going so badly in her life right now, perhaps this one thing could sustain her. She knew there was no future with a rogue like Jackson Logan, but a part of her was just as certain she would never feel this way again about a man.

She wanted to go with him. With every fiber of her being she wanted to be a part of him for just this one night.

Then Cameron thought of Elmwood. Of the slaves. She was not here tonight to play at love games with Jackson. She was here to meet with a representative of the Underground Railroad. She could *not* do this.

She pushed Jackson back with the heels of both hands. "Jackson, please. Let me go."

Sensing the sudden change in her manner, he sat up, helping her to sit up beside him. He ran his hand through his disheveled hair, the spell seemingly broken. "Cameron—"

She put up a hand to stop him from speaking. If he said anything more, she was certain she would walk out of this room hand in hand with him. She shoveled down the layers of rumpled petticoats, still smelling the raw scent of her pleasure thick in the warm night air. She wondered where her gloves had gotten to and how she was going to gracefully pull up her pantalets. "Don't say anything more. Please," she insisted. "I'm sorry. I cannot go with you. I should never have come in here with you." She lifted her gaze to look at him from beneath her lashes.

His gray eyes narrowed critically. "You are nothing but a tease, Cameron Campbell," Jackson accused.

She pressed her lips together, getting off the settee. She pulled up her undergarments through the layers of gown and petticoats, beyond all thoughts of decorum. "That wasn't my intention. It truly wasn't.'' Spotting one of her gloves on the floor behind the settee, she retrieved it. "I'm sorry, Jackson.''

He lifted his leg to rest it on his knee and pushed back a lock of his hair, smoothing it. "Probably not as sorry as I am.'' He shook his head. "You know what I ought to do. I ought to lock that damned door and rip off your clothes and do to you what needs to be done.''

She trembled as a shiver of fear passed through her and warily took a step back.

"Please,'' he growled. "You insult me. I'm not going to hurt you. I said it is what I *ought* to do. What I half think you *want* me to do. My little spoiled senator's daughter cannot seem to accept that she has grown into a desirable woman. A woman who also desires. I think you would rather I took you by force than come by your own free will.'' He scowled and looked away. "But I won't. I'll not give you the pleasure. You want me, then you'll have to come to me next time.''

She gasped. Come to him? She'd sooner throw herself into Satan's bed.

"What you don't realize, however, is that if you will not come to my bed willingly, Cam, there are others who will.''

She grabbed her other glove, refusing to listen to Jackson and his foul talk any longer. Nothing he was saying was making any sense. He was just angry he had not gotten what he wanted. Of course she did not want him to take her by force. She didn't want him at all. She was just upset, by her father's death, her brother's behavior. She was confused and not herself. And he had taken advantage of her weakness in the foulest manner possible. He had assaulted her body, her senses, and made her almost believe that it was her choice…her wish.

She patted her coiffure, praying it wasn't too mussed. She had to get back out to the other guests. It wouldn't do for her to return to the party looking as if she had been tumbling in the hay with a field hand, though. She decided to change the conversation entirely.

"I have to go before someone comes in search of me.''

"By all means, go.'' He indicated the door.

She sighed, fighting the waves of emotion that suddenly rose in her throat. "Jackson, we—" She took a breath as she slid her hand into one of the gloves. She hoped the glove would insulate the sensations that still pulsed through her body. If she could just remove the memory of his touch from her mind, maybe she would be all right. "We probably will not see each other again. Not with the war and all. You know that."

He watched her carefully, his handsome face still twisted in an angry frown. "So you have finally come to your senses. You're going to New York to stay with the Stuarts."

"I'll have you know that I never lost my senses," she said tartly. "I only mean that I will be busy setting my father's affairs straight. And you with your business." She lifted her shoulder. "We will not likely cross paths again."

He came off the settee like a rabbit out of a hole, but all long legs and a shaking fist. "You little fool. Setting your father's affairs straight, my ass. You've come up with some kind of scheme, haven't you?"

Cameron quivered as he stepped closer, leaning over her. "It's not really your affair, is it, Captain Logan?"

"This has something to do with the slaves, doesn't it?" He glanced over her shoulder toward the door. "Something your brother knows nothing of."

She yanked on the second glove and gave it an angry tug. "I have no idea what you're talking about. Now if you'll excuse me..." She flounced her petticoats for good measure. "I'd like to join the party." She spun on her heels and charged for the door.

"Do you have any idea what kind of danger you could be putting yourself in? You get yourself into trouble and there will be no one to get you out, Cameron. Do you hear me?" he shouted after her. "There's no Papa the senator to help you now."

"Good evening, Captain." She opened the door and slipped out, closing it firmly behind her before she had a chance to hear his final words.

* * *

"Son of a bitch," Jackson muttered as he brought his fist down on an inlaid mahogany table. He hit it so hard that a small porcelain dish on the table rattled and threatened to clatter to the floor. As he placed his hand on the delicate dish to steady it, he glared at the door. His first impulse was to go after Cameron and drag her back. Perhaps there was some way he could convince her how dangerous it was for her to remain in Mississippi. Surely there was some way to get that silly woman to realize that whatever she was playing at, it was no game. He knew she had no idea the enemies her father had made in Congress, and how those enemies would not hesitate to hurt her now if they could. If only he could get it through that stubborn head of hers and make her understand.

Jackson groaned aloud. He could still smell the scent of her desire in the room…on his hand. He breathed deeply. He didn't just want to knock a candy dish off a table. He wanted to put his fist through a wall.

Had he lost whatever reason he possessed? This was not the kind of baggage to carry, entering a war. What business was Cameron of his? She was nothing but an old friend's daughter. An old *dead* friend. She was a lush and desirable woman, but as common in Mississippi as full houses in high-stakes poker games.

"Liar," he accused himself. "Of such as Cameron Campbell, there's but one, praise God."

He walked to a desk and helped himself to a glass of his host's brandy. As he poured, his mind drifted, against his will, to thoughts of the senator. A strange sense of nostalgia— something rare for him—washed over him. He missed his old friend more than he had thought possible. There was something about knowing Senator David Campbell was always out there that Jackson had relied on. Over the years, he and the senator had crossed paths regularly. They had both done each other favors, but there had been a bond between them that went deeper than two men who could use each other. He just wasn't certain what that bond was.

He sipped the brandy as he tried to bundle his emotions and

tuck them neatly away. This ineffectual sentiment wouldn't do. Christ, he was getting soft. He had a mission to accomplish and emotion would be nothing but a detriment to him. He didn't have time to worry about Miss Cameron Campbell and her slaves. He didn't have time to think about her sweet mouth and how she set him mad with desire every time he saw her. His country had just been plunged into war and he had a job to do. When he'd left Washington D.C. a month ago, his instructions had been clear. There had been no mention of falling for honey-lipped women, or favors to old friends.

Jackson set the brandy down, not wanting it now. He glanced at the door again. Where had Cameron gone? Why had she suddenly been in such a hurry to get away from him when she had seemed so willing, at first, to come into his arms?

He wondered if there was another man. Had someone caught her fancy? Times like these, a woman needed a protector. To be unmarried, without a father or another male relative who gave a damn—he thought of Grant with disgust— could be dangerous for a young woman. Yes, a man in her life was just what she needed.

The thought that he could be her man flashed through his head but he shoved it aside. He had a job to do. He couldn't be burdened by a wife. He laughed aloud. Wife? What would make him think Cameron would be his wife, even if circumstances were different? She loathed him for what he had done to her that summer she was seventeen. And he deserved that hatred.

He settled on the arm of the settee and ran a hand through his hair to smooth it. He needed to collect his thoughts and get out on the veranda where the soldier would be waiting for him with the message from Smitty. But still, he couldn't get thoughts of Cameron out of his head.

Yes, a man was just what she needed.

So why did the thought of her with someone else put such a burning ache in his belly?

*   *   *

Cameron cradled her cup of punch in her shaking hand as she watched the dancers whirl in a circle to a familiar Virginia reel. Everyone had been at the party long enough to relax, to drink a little more than perhaps they should have, and the atmosphere was gay. Women were laughing, flirting openly as they tapped gentlemen with their fans. There were bewhiskered men and lads too young to shave strutting about in bright new Confederate uniforms, their chests thrown out like banty roosters.

Cameron sighed. She was tired and upset and she wanted to go home, but James still had not contacted her. She watched unfamiliar men dance by, and she wondered if one of them might be her James.

As the reel came to an end and another began, she walked into the study to refill her glass. It wasn't so much that she was thirsty as she needed something to do, something to keep her from thinking about Jackson. The blackguard! How could she have allowed him to lure her into that dark study like that? How could she have let him kiss her again? She was ashamed of her unbridled licentious behavior and knew for certain she was going to burn in hell for her impure thoughts.

And to think Jackson had been so close all these weeks and not come to call. Not once had he come to Elmwood to see how she was doing, or how Elmwood was faring with her father gone. He was probably too busy making arrangements for transporting goods illegally. Things were already becoming difficult to get, simple objects like cloth, glassware and, of course, ammunition. Soon the only way the South would be able to get such goods would be by dealing with rogue blockade-runners like Captain Logan. Well, she'd go hungry before she'd purchase anything from him, or any man like him!

"Miss Campbell?"

She turned in surprise when a soft male voice whispered her name. No one had approached the punch table. There was no one in the room, in fact, but a servant dressed in a white coat who was adding precious ice to the punch bowl.

She stared at the old black man for a moment. He lowered

his gaze subserviently, but then his lips moved. She had to listen carefully to catch what he said.

"Ya is Miss Campbell, ain't ya?"

She nodded.

"Please turn away, Missy. The likes of you ain't supposed to be talkin' to the likes of me. Someone'll be gettin' all 'spicious-like on us."

She turned away immediately, lifting her glass to her lips to pretend to drink. "I'm listening."

"I understand ya needs some names. Some places."

"That's correct."

He chuckled. "My mama always said wasn't no good whitey but a dead whitey, but I always said she was wrong." He cackled again. "I thinks I can help ya, little lady. Old Jamie thinks he can."

"Naomi!"

Naomi turned in the darkness, gut-wrenching relief washing over her as she recognized the familiar voice.

Her bare-chested man, his skin as black as the night, stepped into the thin thread of moonlight from behind a hanging cypress tree and opened his arms to her.

"Manu!" Naomi ran barefoot through the grass and leaves of the swamp and leaped into the air with utter confidence. Her Manu caught her in arms that were as massive as a bull's legs and drew her to his chest.

"By Krobo's mist! I thought the dogs had got ya for sure." She covered his face that was damp from sweat with kisses. "I been waitin' half the night, man."

"I'm sorry. Sorry, suga'." He pressed his warm, familiar mouth to the pulse of her throat and caught her lower lip with his tongue.

Still in his arms, her feet dangling off the ground, Naomi threw back her head and let the warmth of his kiss erase the cold memory of the master's mouth from her flesh.

"How fast ya think this boy can run?" Manu asked, lowering her until her bare feet hit the soft humus, but still holding her against his bare chest. "Ya know it got to be seven mile upriver from Atkin's Way here to Elmwood."

Naomi took his huge hand in hers and led him to the holey wool blanket she had spread out for them beneath the bows of a drooping cypress tree. This tree had become her home away from home since meeting Manu more than a year ago.

Manu was her heart-love. Her one true love. They had both known it the day they first laid eyes on each other in Elmwood's horse barn. Manu had been sent to fetch his master's wagon and Naomi had just happened by the barn. Ever since, they had been meeting here several nights a week. If Naomi was caught wandering in the darkness, she knew she would take a lashing from Master Grant himself for straying too far from the house. If Manu was caught leaving Atkin's Way, his master would not be so kind. He'd be beaten, maybe sold if he was lucky. If his master decided to make an example of him, he would be flogged to death in front of the plantation's entire slave population.

More than once Naomi had suggested to Manu that he stop coming, or at least not come so often, but he refused. Without his "life's heart" he said, he had no reason to go on living. Naomi was afraid for him, but so thankful to have him, especially now with the old master gone. Master Grant was a revolting little toad of a man and more than once she had considered putting a curse on his puny rod so that he would not trouble her any further. The only reason she didn't was because she knew so long as she rode him and kept him happy, she had power over him. It was that woman's power that could get her things like medicine and clothing needed among her people. Naomi had learned that truth of life younger than many. She'd not yet met her twelfth year cotton picking when she'd met up with Master Grant in the corn shed, but she had learned quick enough. And now, with the war and the life of so many of her people uncertain, it was even more important that she keep a good hold on Master Grant. A good hold on his pitiful excuse for a man-rod, that was.

Manu pushed Naomi down onto the blanket and she

laughed, thrusting her arms out to him. "Ya bin waitin' long?" he asked.

"Hours. The masta and Miss Cameron gone out fer the evenin'. I finished my chores early and come right away."

"Masta Grant," he growled, nuzzling her ear. "I could rip that man's heart out with my bare hands."

"Manu."

He clenched a mighty fist. "Ya know I could."

She brushed his square jaw with her hand. "I know. I know it," she whispered soothingly. "But don't ya worry yer head over Masta Grant. I got him wrapped 'round my finger."

"Got him wrapped 'round yer titty, ya mean."

Naomi let her hand fall from his face and she stared up into Manu's black eyes, a canopy of twinkling stars above them. Against her will, her own eyes filled with tears. "Ya know ya hurt me when ya say them things. Hurt me here, bad." She pressed his hand to the place above her left breast where her heart beat for him.

"I'm sorry. I'm sorry." Manu wrapped his strong arms around her again and hugged her tight. "Ya know it just makes me crazy thinkin' of that white son'a'bitch touchin' my sweet dreams." He cradled her in his arms as if she were a baby, and she rested her head on his bare, muscular chest. He smelled so good to her. He smelled of sweat, the rich Mississippi soil, the quiet night and hope. Manu was her hope.

She ran a hand over his smooth dark skin, lingered over his nipple. "Ain't no need to go over and over this, Manu, and ya know it. I do what I got to do. I was straight wi' ya about that white devil and the masta's guests from the first time we met under this tree."

"I know." He kissed her forehead.

"'Sides, now more than ever I needs 'im. *We* needs 'im. I got to keep him happy so he don't take no notice of what Miss Cameron tryin' to do."

He smoothed her coarse, dark hair that she wore pulled back in a tight knot at the nape of her neck. "That whole thing, it still worries Manu, ya know," he said. "Ya sure she can be trusted? She got such an uppity nose and that hair, it ain't the color hair oughta be.''

She smiled up at Manu, drinking in the love that shined in his black eyes for her. She wanted to have Manu's baby someday, that was how sure she was of their love. Not now, of course. Now, she took care with her monthly potions to be sure she didn't conceive. But the day would come when she and her man would walk out of here hand in hand to a new land where blacks were free to love and live where they pleased. It was good white folks like Miss Cameron who were going to help her and Manu see that dream.

''I tol' ya before,'' Naomi assured him, running her hand over his bare chest and then lower to the hard muscles that ridged his stomach. ''Like her uppity ways or not, she always been honest with me, even since she was a girl. I believe her when she say she gonna set us free one way or t'other no matter what Masta Short Pizzle say.'' She tucked her finger in the waistband of his ragged pants.

He shook his head. ''I just worry 'bout us given up James's name. What if she tell someone that shouldn't be tol'?''

''She won't. I tol' ya. She one of the smartest white folk I ever known.'' She slid her hand down over the massive bulge, evidence of his love for her. This was what she fantasized about when Masta Grant was doing his grunting.

''She got a good heart, too,'' Naomi murmured. ''Ya know Naomi can see right into a man's heart. See the color of it.''

Manu pressed his lips to hers as he loosened the button of his breeches and sprang out hot and hard for her. ''Shush about that crazy business. Ya know it scare Manu.''

''Ah,'' Naomi murmured. She yanked off the cutoff breeches and threw them into the bushes. She rolled him onto his back and climbed astride his hips.

She sat feeling the length and width of him against her damp nest. Slowly, tantalizingly, she lifted the threadbare cotton feedsack dress over her head to reveal her nakedness beneath.

"Don't nothin' scare my man," she teased proudly, stroking him with her hand.

He reached out to gently squeeze one full breast. "Nothin' but you," he chuckled, guiding her breast to his open mouth. "Now come here and give Manu some of that suga'...."

14

"There you are, Taye. Surely you haven't been hiding from me," Grant said, limping toward her.

Taye cringed inwardly, but she refused to show Grant just how fearful she was of him, or how much she despised him. She stepped aside and studied the toes of her slippers peeking from beneath the pale-yellow sprigged gown she wore, hoping he was only passing.

Grant stopped directly in front of her. She pressed her back to the wall, still not lifting her dark lashes to meet his gaze. *"What?"* he said softly in the same tone he had used once upon a time when teasing small animals with a stick. "Nothing to say this morning, dear Taye?"

She lifted her gaze, gritting her teeth. "You'll have to excuse me. I've household duties to attend. My mother is not feeling well."

He scowled as he pressed his hand to the wall beside her head, blocking her escape. "They say she hasn't been out of bed in days. She got some kind of fever?"

Taye shook her head. Grant's hazel eyes were as cold as a snake's. No, not a snake, a snake was a living creature. Grant's eyes were as lifeless and hard as glass. "She— I think she has been working too hard. She tires easily."

"If she can't work, I'll not have her on this plantation. My father was too lenient with his darkies. He'd accept any excuse for a day off."

Taye's lower lip trembled. She knew she should just keep quiet. It was always the quickest way to get rid of Grant, but for once she couldn't bite her tongue. "You forget, sir, that my mother is an emancipated woman. She worked for the senator as the housekeeper for wages."

"Worked for the senator, my lily-white ass, except maybe flat on her back!"

Without thinking of the ramifications of her actions, Taye drew back her hand and slapped Grant in the face.

He grunted as he jerked in surprise, then pulled back his hand and struck her across the cheek with his open palm. The slap smarted, but not as greatly as his remark about her mother.

"Who the god-damned hell do you think you are?" Grant growled as he clasped both her shoulders and shoved her against the wall. "Who do you think is in charge around here?"

Tears filled her clear blue eyes. "You are, sir."

"That's right. I am. I am the master of Elmwood Plantation. Do you realize you could be flogged, a negra such as yourself striking the master? Hell—" he spit "—I've seen your kind hanged for a lesser offense."

He loosened his hold on her shoulders, but still he didn't let her go. Taye turned her head aside and prayed Cameron would come along. Someone, anyone, even Naomi—someone to diffuse the situation. She didn't speak for fear of what she might say. At this moment she hated Grant Campbell more than she had ever hated anyone in her life. It was a raw, ugly rage that radiated from her belly outward to her limbs, making her numb and blind.

He thrust his face into hers. "Look at me when I speak to you! Things are going to change around here, do you hear me?"

Taye slowly turned her head to stare into his reptile eyes and nodded.

"Now, we can do this hard, or we can do this easy." He removed his hand from her shoulder and to her shock brought it roughly under her breast. "We can do it *my* way or the hard way. And you know what it is I want, so don't play all innocent.''

He pinched her breast cruelly and Taye gave a little cry.

With his other hand he quickly covered her mouth and nose. Taye's eyes widened with fear as he cut off her air supply. She ceased struggling immediately for the sake of self-preservation.

''Shh,'' he whispered. ''That's right. I'm not going to hurt you.'' He adjusted his hand so that she could catch her breath as he looked each way down the hall, then back at her again. ''Just no need to call in the troops, is there? No need to call that bitch of a sister of mine to your rescue.'' He drew his face closer to hers, his face contorting with sudden blind anger.

Now Taye was truly frightened, for there was something in his eyes that was far less than human. Tears ran down her cheeks as she wondered how he could hate her so much. Why? She had never done anything to him.

''That's what she always does, doesn't she?'' he intoned. ''Always has.''

''I don't know what you mean,'' Taye managed to gasp from beneath his hand.

''Don't know what I mean?'' he barked. Again he looked both ways down the hall. ''Surely you remember that day at the mill?''

She shook her head, fighting her tears, but unable to stop them. Heavenly Father above, where was Cameron?

''Well, let me refresh your memory.''

Before Taye could escape, he grabbed her around the waist and dragged her down the hall. It occurred to her that if she screamed someone would surely come, but before she could gather the courage, he pressed his lips to her ear. ''You make a sound and you will wish you hadn't,'' he threatened cruelly. ''I'll humiliate you in front of them all.''

Taye clamped her mouth shut.

Slowly Grant made his way down the hall, dragging his bad leg. One would have thought it would be a burden to take her with him, but she was so small that his gait seemed to barely be affected.

Inside the study, he closed the door and, without letting go of her, lifted her up and pushed her down hard in a chair. "You don't remember that day at the mill?"

She shook her head. She did remember an incident at the mill when she about eight, but only vaguely, as if it had happened to someone else. She had fallen in the millpond and hadn't been able to swim. But she wasn't even certain he spoke of the same incident.

"Well, let me remind you," he sneered. "It was a sunny July afternoon. Hot. You remember those days when we were children. Flies buzzed and the air was so thick with the smell of rotting river vegetation that it seemed coddled."

Taye closed her eyes. Against her will, memories of childhood summer days at Elmwood fluttered through her head.

"My sister and I were walking along the road that led to the grist mill where Elmwood use to grind its own flour. We were going to go wading there along the shore. Skip stones. The great senator had his house in a flurry preparing for one of his famous balls. It would be hours before we were missed and dragged home." Grant loomed over Taye, his focus growing distant as he continued. "As usual, Cameron's little darky *companion* was tagging along. My sister refused to leave her behind, always letting her follow wherever she went like a pet lap dog."

To Taye, Grant's words were like another slap on her face. She made a move to get out of the chair. She would not sit here and listen this! But he grabbed her by the shoulders and shoved her so hard that the back of her head hit the chair and jarred her teeth.

"You'll listen," he growled.

Her gaze locked on his, she could do nothing but nod and pray Cameron would come looking for her when she was done at the barn.

"As I was saying," Grant continued, calmer now. "Little Taye was following behind as always, and having a hard time keeping up. She was only, I don't know, seven, maybe eight."

Oddly enough, he smiled at the memory. "So petite, so pretty with her cocoa-and-milk skin, uncommon pale-blue eyes and pink little rosebud lips."

Taye's stomach roiled as she listened to Grant describe how he had seen her, even as a child. She had always sensed he had some unnatural desire for her, but this was almost too much to bear.

"I was fourteen and had begun to stretch my legs a little. Beginning to feel like a man. My father had given me duties on the plantation, put his trust in me. But this wasn't one of those days. This was one of those days when I was still a child."

"Cam! Cam, wait for me," petite Taye called, running barefoot down the middle of the dirt road.

Cameron glanced over her shoulder and slowed. "Come on, Taye." She waved a hand. "We'll wait."

"I don't know why you don't leave that little darky in her room when you go out," Grant complained. "She's a nuisance."

Cameron halted, threw back her mane of tangled red hair and planted one hand on her hip. "If you're in such a hurry, go on without us."

Grant stopped and gave a stone in the road a good kick. He watched as it hurled through the air and hit a tree with a pleasant thud. "You said it was going to be a contest. You promised you'd challenge me to a game a skipping stones."

"I don't know why you want to. I'm better at it than you are anyway," Cameron answered, her tone saucy and defiant.

"Are not."

"Am, too."

He gave her a little shove for good measure. "Are not."

"You better stop," Cameron said, giving him that evil eye. "Or Taye and I will go home and then you'll have to play by yourself."

Grant scowled and started down the road again, wishing his mother had given birth to a boy instead of a girl before she'd up and bled to death with some woman's ailment the next time she got pregnant. He had always wanted a brother. If he had a brother they could be best friends. A little brother would be nice to him. A little brother would admire and respect him. Not like *her*. Cameron thought she was better than he was. She was always running to Papa telling him when Grant cut her apron strings or hid her inkwell when she was supposed to be practicing her handwriting.

"Fine," Grant snapped. "I'll meet you at the mill. You just better hurry up." Not waiting for his sister and the mulatto girl, he went on ahead. A few minutes later, after he had settled himself on the bridge above the spillway, Taye wandered over and sat down beside him.

Grant watched as her short brown legs dangled above the water that rushed beneath the bridge, driven by the gristmill's wheel. "Where's Cam?" he asked, not bothering to look her in the eye. A white man didn't look a darky in the face. There was no need to.

"Gone to make a wee in the woods," Taye said in her pretty, singsong voice.

Grant glanced sideways at the girl. He hated her. He hated the way Cameron fussed over her and the way she was allowed to come and go in the house, like she was one of the senator's children instead of just his negra whore's daughter.

But secretly, Grant liked her, too. He liked the color of her skin, like his Papa's morning coffee with just a tiny bit of cream. He liked the sound of her voice, liquidy and smooth. And he liked her pale-blue eyes. He knew they were freakish for a darky, but he liked them anyway.

Sometimes, when no one was around, Grant liked to watch Taye. He thought she had the prettiest lips and he wondered what it would be like to kiss them. He wondered what it would be like to stick his tongue in her mouth. He'd done that with women already. Once with Anne Cally at a spring ball. A couple of times with some of the slave girls, when he could catch them in a barn and wrestle them to the ground.

Grant glanced at Taye sideways and laid a cautious hand on her knee.

Taye looked at him, her brow furrowed. "Get off." She gave his hand a smack and knocked it off her knee.

He put his hand back possessively again. He was the master's son. He could do what he damned well pleased and no one but his father could stop him. No one would dare.

Taye kicked her little legs in the air above the water. "Stop it," she said, thrusting out one of those pretty pink lips. "I'm gonna tell Cameron and then she's gonna punch you in the nose."

"I'm going to tell Cameron," Grant mimicked, but he didn't move his hand off her bony knee. Her skin was warm and she smelled like the flowers in the meadow near the stable.

Grant glanced over his shoulder. No one was in sight. He could hear the voices of the darkies who worked the mill, but they seemed a good distance away. Cameron had to still be in the woods. He met Taye's blue-eyed gaze and held it as he slid his hand up her skinny leg. He was curious as to whether she would be afraid or whether she would like it.

"Stop," Taye said as she grabbed his hand and tried to move it. "Stop it, Grant." Her first words were defiant, but then she whimpered. "I'm going to tell."

He slid his hand farther up her leg and tucked it beneath the hem of the flowered dress that was so pretty on her.

Grant didn't know what happened next. One minute Taye was sitting beside him on the bridge and then suddenly she threw up both arms to hit him. He felt one small fist connect with his chin and then she tumbled down. He called out, lunging forward to grab her, but he couldn't reach her fast enough.

Taye screamed as she fell. Grant heard another scream. His own?

It seemed as if it took forever for the girl to hit the water. He heard the splash.

Grant leaped up, waving his arms. He didn't know what to do. She had to be twelve, maybe fifteen feet below him. She was flapping her arms, crying out now. She couldn't swim— most of the darkies couldn't. He watched her go under and then pop up again.

"Oh, God. God damn," he muttered. He didn't know what

to do. He couldn't jump. It was too far down. He would hurt himself. He looked around, but he didn't see anyone. Where were the slaves working at the mill? Did he cry for help? Could anyone get here in time?

They would blame him, of course. They would say it was his fault she drowned.

Tears blinded Grant's eyes as he took off down the road for home. He couldn't stand to hear Taye crying out. He just wanted to go home. To go home and crawl into his bed.

Then he heard someone running.

"What happened?" Cameron screamed.

Grant looked up to see his sister racing toward him. He didn't know what to say. He pointed, so scared he thought he was going to piss his pants. He didn't mean to knock her off the bridge. He just wanted to touch her. He just wanted to love her.

"Taye?" she screamed in his face. "Taye?"

All he could do was nod.

Cameron raced across the rickety bridge to the place where Taye had fallen in. As Grant turned, he saw her jump fearlessly into the pool of water far below. As she disappeared from sight, he wondered if she might break her neck in the fall.

He heard the splash, Cameron calling to Taye, and then thankfully the sobbing voice of the little dark girl he loved. Hated.

By the time he made himself turn around and go back to the bridge, Cameron had fished Taye out of the water. She dragged the sputtering little girl up the grassy bank.

"What goin' on here?" One of the slaves who worked at the mill appeared out of nowhere. Suddenly Grant found himself surrounded by black faces.

"What ya young'uns up to?" another said.

"Look like Sukey's girl done taken a tumble into da drink."

"Look like she all wet, but all right 'nough."

Grant felt as if the world were spinning around him. All he wanted to do was run.

"What's wrong with you?" Cameron shouted at him as she

stepped back onto the road with Taye in one arm. "Were you just going to let her drown?"

Some of the darkies left Grant to go to the girls. Others just stood there and stared at him. None of them actually accused him of anything. They wouldn't dare. But they didn't have to. He knew what they were thinking. He could see it in their condemning black eyes.

The pounding of hoofs sounded on the road and Grant looked up to see his father riding toward them like some dark-haired Roman God bursting out of the clouds. "What's going on here?" the senator demanded as he dismounted. He was dressed impeccably as always in pale-blue breeches and matching coat.

One of the slave women pointed. "Sukey's girl done taken a tumble off'en the bridge, Masta. She lookin' all right, though."

"Yeah," Cameron spat. "No thanks to him!" She left Taye, who was now crying softly, in the care of one of the slave women and walked over to stand in front of her brother. Right there, in front of their father, she gave him a shove. "I asked you a question, you worm. What were you going to do? Just let her drown?"

Grant gave her a shove back.

"Hey! How dare you touch a woman like that," the senator exploded. "How dare you lay a hand on your sister." He stepped between them. "And you, Missy," he addressed Cameron. "Keep your hands to yourself. I will have no violence in my family." He turned back to Grant.

Papa was a lot taller than Grant, even though Grant had grown a lot this last year. But now he seemed even taller. A giant. "Well?" their father demanded.

"Tell him!" Cameron shouted. "Go ahead and tell him what you did when Taye fell off the bridge into the water!"

Grant felt sick to his stomach. He didn't know what to say, but it didn't matter because he couldn't speak. The darkies were closing in on them, listening, whispering.

"Well, I'll tell you," Cameron went on. "Nothing. That's what he did. He would have let her drown."

Grant felt his father's eyes bore into him. He had never been so ashamed, so mortified, in his life.

"You made no attempt to save Taye?" the senator asked, his voice deathly soft.

"Missy Cameron done jumped in after the girl," one of the bolder slaves offered.

"Son?" the senator said. "I'm asking you a question."

Grant couldn't look him in the eye. Couldn't speak.

"You'd let a little girl drown when you can swim?" he asked in disgust.

"She…she fell from the bridge," Grant sputtered. He didn't know how to make him understand. It wasn't that he *wanted* anything to happen to Taye. He loved Taye. "It…it was a long way down."

"So my son is a coward. Is that what you're saying?"

"Papa…" Grant sobbed, trying hard not to cry. In his father's eyes, in the eyes of a true Southern gentleman, there was no greater crime than to be a coward.

"Is that what you're saying, Son?" Papa shouted.

All those black faces staring at him. Calling him coward, whispering the word. The world seemed to spin around Grant as his father's voice echoed in his head. He wasn't a coward! He just wasn't a damned fool like his sister! She risked her life to save that little pickaninny.

"Get out of my sight," the senator spat in disgust. "You're not fit to be a Campbell."

Then he turned away. Grant's papa just turned away from him. He reached out, picked up Taye and he set her on his horse. Then he took his dripping wet, red-haired daughter by the hand and walked away, leading the horse behind him.

"But I'm not a coward," Grant now shouted, spittle flying into Taye's face. "And I'm going to prove it to you. I'm going to prove it to you all!"

"Taye said you wanted to see me." Cameron walked into her father's study. Taye had been disturbed when she found Cameron in the barn after a ride on Roxy. Cameron had questioned her as to why she was upset but she wouldn't budge.

She just said that Grant wanted her and that she would see her in the morning, if that was all right. She was going to stay with her mother in the slave quarters for the night.

Grant looked like he had been drinking. His face was bright red and puffy. He had taken off his coat and loosened his cravat.

"That's right, I did want to see you. Wanted to talk to you." He walked to the window and pushed it open so that she could see out into the fields beyond the house. "It's time I put my mourning for our father aside and meet my responsibilities."

Cameron didn't know if drinking and whoring day and night fell into the category of mourning, but she was willing to give some leeway. At least he was dressed, up and about and trying to think of Elmwood.

"I could definitely use some help," she said cautiously. "You know the president issued a proclamation of blockade against the Southern states. We will receive no more shipments of any kind from the North. Not legally, at least. We'll begin to run low on necessary supplies very soon. I know you would like to think this war will not be long but I fear we have to prepare for the worst."

He nodded. "I see from the bookkeeping—" he indicated the open leather-bound journal on their father's desk "—that you have started selling off Elmwood's possessions."

She watched him carefully, unable to tell if he was upset with her for selling the farm vehicles or not. "I had a buyer. I thought it was wise to sell while I had the chance."

"No, no, it's all right." He turned to her, raising his hand. "If this war is going to be long, we need to collect what cash we can."

He walked to the antique writing desk that had been their grandmother Campbell's and ran his hand over it. It was where her father kept his most important papers and possession—the family Bible, the deed to Elmwood, his will, the ownership rights of Elmwood's slaves. There was even a secret compartment built into the lid of the desk that she had played with as a child.

Cameron watched her brother as he picked up a book of
documents and flipped through the pages. Those documents
contained the names of the slaves here on Elmwood. Was it
too much to hope that he had decided to honor his father's
wish and emancipate the slaves? Was that what he wanted to
talk to her about?

"I will need money because it is going to be in short supply
for all us Southern gentlemen. Unable to sell our cotton and
sugar cane, it's going to be difficult to maintain the lifestyle
we are accustomed to. I'll need money if I am going to shutter
Elmwood and go to the house in Baton Rouge." He slammed
the book shut. "But that's not why I called you here. Elmwood is my responsibility now. Papa's money is my responsibility now. I want to talk to you about your plans."

She moistened her dry lips, trying hard to read her brother's
face. "My plans?"

"Cameron, it's time you stopped getting your own way.
Papa spoiled you and we both know it. It's time you got married and stopped being a burden to the Campbell name."

15

Cameron stared at her brother. The room suddenly felt stifling, as if it were many degrees hotter than it had been only a moment before. She felt dizzy, as if she had just taken a tumble from one of her Arabians. She knew it was just the heat of the day, a lack of sleep and the fact that she was trying to eat as little as possible to be certain everyone else was well fed. She rested her hand on the back of her father's leather chair to steady herself. "Did you say married?"

Grant's brow furrowed. He had put on weight in the last weeks from his heavy drinking and the added poundage was none too becoming. He reminded her of a hog fattened for butchering, with wrinkles of flesh around his jaw and across his broad forehead. Yes, definitely a hog, ready to set to spit over a bed of hickory-wood coals. All Grant needed now was an apple stuffed in his mouth.

"Did I stutter?" He took a seat behind her father's desk as if it were his own and always had been. "You heard me. I said it's time you married."

"Surely you jest?" she sputtered, pushing a lock of hair off her damp face. She had been riding and had come straight in from the barn. "Grant, have you lost your mind? Our father is dead. We are about to lose our livelihood. Elmwood is going to suffer terribly in this war. The South, our lives, are crumbling around us and you want to talk about me getting married?"

"Surely you realized you would have to marry some day,"
he scoffed, propping a boot on the edge of the desk. She saw
that there was dry grass and horse manure stuck to the sole.
David Campbell would never have entered the house with
soiled boots.

She walked to her father's bookcase and stared, but did not
see the leather tomes. The truth was, she had seriously considered never marrying. With her horses, she could probably
make enough money eventually to support herself. What did
she need a man for? They were all alike, untrustworthy cads
like Captain Logan. But she knew there was no need to go
into that with Grant. Now, she just had to reason with him.

Suddenly a horrifying thought occurred to her, and she
whipped around. "You haven't offered my hand in marriage
to anyone, have you?"

He scowled. "Christ, no. Don't you think I have better
things to do than play matchmaker to my little spoiled brat of
a sister?"

She walked to her father's leather chair and sat on the edge
of it, unable to resist a sigh of relief. She didn't care what he
called her, so long as he had not promised her to some middle-
aged Confederate officer with a handlebar mustache and sour
breath. "Then even if I did agree to be wed, which I will
not," she said tiredly, "who in sweet heaven's name would I
marry? One does not locate a husband the way one finds a
new hat or a riding coat. Me, marry?"

Inexplicably, an image of Jackson flashed through her
head—gray eyes that really were quite wicked, sensuous lips
turned in a mocking smile, dark, silky hair, broad shoulders
and a lazy grace that was almost beautiful on a man his size.
That was when she laughed out loud. What had made her think
of that hell-rake? She and Jackson married? They were as ill
suited as a hawk and a swan.

Grant gave a queer look in response to her inappropriate
laughter and then lifted one shoulder in a shrug. "I honestly
don't give a fat fuck who you marry. But you need a man to
keep you. It is the fate women were born into. Eve and the
apple and all of that sin bullshit." He flicked something that

had fallen from his boot off the desk. Manure? "I can take a look next time I'm in Jackson and see if any of Papa's friends' sons are looking for a wife."

That was it! It was all Cameron could stand. She shot out of the leather chair that still smelled of her father's tobacco. "Grant Campbell, I will not be sold off like a carriage or a horse you have tired of! This is not what Papa would have wanted and you know it."

"You're right, this *is* all Papa's fault," he retorted. "He spoiled you. He let you run about the county on those horses that were as wild as you were. You should have been married two or three years ago and dropping babies by now like the rest of the girls your age." He pursed his lips in disgust. "I mean, look at you. You don't even know how to dress like a civilized woman. You're clothed no better than a field hand."

She crossed her arms stubbornly over her chest. She had been riding in a pair of Grant's old breeches and a white lawn shirt that had long ago been her father's. Grant detested it when she wore men's clothing, even to ride in private or muck a horse stall. "I am not marrying."

Grant lowered his leg from the desk and came out of the chair, his cold eyes narrowing. "Then you will take the few coins I throw you and you'll *walk* out of here." He pointed toward the road. "Because that is your only due. Elmwood will no longer be able to support both of us, and I am the heir. Whatever she has left to offer is mine."

Cameron was most undoubtedly not going to marry to put a roof over her head, but she had to be careful how she responded to his preposterous proposition. She had to have *some* money. The Stuarts would take her in if need be, but she couldn't arrive empty-handed. The family was financially comfortable, but by no means wealthy. She could not take advantage of her father's friends that way, especially not when she would be taking Sukey and Taye with her. Besides, the longer she stayed here at Elmwood, the more she realized she didn't want to go north. She didn't care if her father thought she would be safer there. She belonged here at Elmwood, now more than ever. Sukey and Taye needed to go because they would be safe there, but she wanted to stay here. Here at home on Elmwood. Grant could go to Baton Rouge and she could stay here and look after the place.

"I have my horses," she said softly. "I can raise them and support myself."

"No, you won't."

She strode toward the desk and leaned on it to thrust her face into her brother's. Again, she had to fight the threat of tears. "They are *my* horses. Papa gave them to me."

"They are *Elmwood's* horses and therefore mine," he shouted in her face, his breath as bitter as his disposition. "They've already been sold. The buyer will be here in the morning to take every Arabian on this place."

Cameron drew back, fighting the sudden, overwhelming sense of defeat. Not her beloved Arabians. Not Roxy. But Grant was right. Legally he had a right to do this, all of it. "I will not marry for the sake of filling my belly," she maintained stubbornly. "You can take my horses, you can send me packing from my childhood home, but you cannot force me to marry."

He eased back into the senator's chair. "Suit yourself. Of course, I must warn you, you're making a mistake. If you marry a wealthy neighbor on his way to war, you'll most likely quickly become a widow. It would cost you nothing but a futter or two."

Cameron could not believe the language Grant was using in front of her. He had never talked that way when their father was alive.

"You could turn a healthy profit," Grant continued, "if you played that game several times."

She took a breath, trying to calm herself. She was so angry that she felt as if she were going to jump out of her skin. She glanced up at him again. "I will not sell my body for the sake of putting food in my stomach."

"Fine. I suppose you can take the jewels Mama left you. They're mostly paste anyway. I'll give you a few coins and you can go to the Stuarts. I am sure they will spoil you the way Papa did."

"I don't want to marry, and I don't wish to live with the Stuarts."

He sighed, sitting again. "Your only other choice is to live off my goodwill." He lifted his hands as if giving in to her. "I would never see my dear sister go hungry, but I can tell you things will be different. You can go with me to Baton Rouge if you must, but there will be new rules. Your outrageous behavior must be curtailed before you do something stupid and disgrace the family name."

Cameron felt her cheeks grow warm, and she turned away as she recalled the Hitches' ball. She thought of Jackson yet again, this time of what he had done to her. Against her will she felt heat diffuse through her cheeks and warm every fiber of her being. Had she and Jackson been elsewhere, would they have stopped where they had? Or would she have *done something stupid,* like succumbing to the passion of the moment and making wild love with him on the floor of the study? She could not lie to herself and say she would not have done that. The truth was, she didn't know. She had become as much a stranger to herself as her brother had.

"Well, think that matter over. There are going to be other changes around here." He flitted his fingers at her. "You're the least of my worries, if you want to know the truth."

The hair stood up on the back of Cameron's neck and she met her brother's gaze. What did he mean by that? "What other changes do you intend to make?"

"That is none of your concern. You're dismissed."

Dismissed? He thought he could dismiss her like one of the servants? "You despicable son of—"

"I think that will be enough," Grant said in the same tone he had used to bully her and Taye when they were children. The trouble was, he actually was in control now. In control of all of their lives.

"Go to your room." Grant rose out of the chair and pointed to the door.

She came around the desk. "You can't do this!" she shouted at him. "Tell me what *matters* you refer to. Papa would have wanted you to consult me. *He* consulted me before making important decisions concerning Elmwood.''

Grant's hand shot out and he caught a thick lock of her bright hair.

Against her will, she cried out. ''Grant,'' she said, covering his hand with hers to try to ease the burning pain. ''You're hurting me.''

''Go,'' he ordered, slowly releasing his hold on her hair. ''Go before this truly becomes ugly. I will not expect your company at supper. You are to remain in your room and contemplate the ill way you have spoken to me today.''

Cameron turned away from Grant. Her eyes stung with tears. Her heart was shattering and her head smarted. But it wasn't her own discomfort, heartfelt or otherwise, that worried her. If Grant thought he could get rid of her by marrying her off, what else did he think he could do? Cameron couldn't be concerned for herself right now because there was an entire population on the plantation he could harm far greater than he could hurt her.

She walked out of the study and closed the door quietly behind her. She would have to talk to Naomi. Naomi would have to talk to their contact. The slaves had to go and take their chances on the Underground Railroad before it was too late.

Naomi walked into Master David's study, a pitcher in hand to water the fresh lilies she had left here yesterday. Miss Cameron liked fresh flowers, whether she would admit it or not, and she spent so much time in this room these days looking at Elmwood's papers that Naomi liked the idea that she might make Miss Cameron smile.

Master Grant sat at the big desk, like a frog on a log, staring, his face without expression. He had been arguing with Miss Cameron. They had been locked up in here a long time and when Miss Cameron left the study she had been crying. Naomi didn't know that she had ever seen Miss Cameron cry. Not when she was a girl. Not when her father died. Not in front f anyone at least. Naomi had a feeling they were more alike han she had ever thought. Naomi only cried alone.

In the past Naomi had never liked Cameron much. She had o many possessions—the dresses, the horses. She was too poiled by her father, Taye and even Sukey for Naomi to like er. But in the weeks since the senator's death, Naomi had acquired a new-found respect for the young white woman. She vas tough, and she stood up for what she thought was right. Besides, any woman who was going to try to free Naomi's people was a woman she had to respect.

"Afta'noon, Masta," Naomi said, taking care to sound sexy and sweet at the same time. That was the way he liked it. All innocent and "Oh, please, Grant, don' do sech things to me." That was the only time she was permitted to use his Christian ame. If that wasn't repulsive enough, he always called her Faye. Master Grant had a thing for the yellow girl.

Grant didn't bother to look at her and she fought the urge o grab him by his starched cravat and make him do so.

"What are you doing?" he snapped. "I'll be expecting my supper soon. Don't you have duties to attend to in the kitchen?"

"I ain't no kitchen cookin' girl. I serve the masta and his house." She walked behind the desk to water the lilies. "But, lon' ya be worryin' 'bout yer supper, Masta. Ida whipped up a nice pork roast with berry stuffin'." She set down the pitcher, laid a hand on each of his shoulders and began to knead with her fingers.

He gave a little sigh and relaxed beneath her capable hands.

"There ya go, Masta Grant. You just got yerself all worked up, that's all. Ain't no need to get yerself in a steam."

"You're right. I don't know why I let that bitch of a sister of mine get me so upset. I am the master of this household now."

He brought his fist down hard on the desk and Naomi jumped in reaction to his show of brute strength, just as she knew he would want her to.

"That's right. That's right," she mumbled. "A girl got to now her place."

He glanced over his shoulder at her and smiled. She had to swallow hard to fight the urge to gag on her own rising bile. How she hated Grant.

"At least some girls know their place," he said as he grabbed her and swung her into his lap.

Naomi wiggled her buttocks against the rise in his breeches, puny as it was. Grant thought he was a man, but he had no idea what a man truly was. Now her man Manu—*there* was a man. A man who could fill a girl up and still have a little something left over. She smiled to herself thinking of Manu. Tonight they would meet in their special place and he would wipe away all memory of Master Grant and his rough hands that now squeezed her breasts viciously.

"What's say you and I go upstairs for a little presupper relaxation?"

Naomi gave a little wiggle and rose off his lap. She wouldn't dare deny him. She had a sick mother on bed rest in the cabin where she and her mother and her six younger brothers and sisters lived. Two years before her father had died of a fever he got from a cut. What Naomi did here at the big house with Grant, with Elmwood's guests, permitted her mother to lie in bed when the rest of the slaves left for the fields each morning. It was because of what Naomi did on her back that her mother got extra food, medicines and warm blankets for when the breezes turned chilly. For the most part the old master of Elmwood had always been good to his slaves. They always had enough to eat and a decent roof over their heads. But to an old woman like Naomi's mother, there was nothing better than a special treat from the big house once in a while. If she knew what her daughter did to procure those indulgences, she never mentioned it.

"Ya want me to meet ya upstairs?" Naomi murmured huskily, giving him the eye over her shoulder as she glided away.

"Wait for me there." He winked. "And put the dress on I like you in the dress."

"Yessah," Naomi responded as she walked out of the study. As she took the polished stairs one at a time, she tried not to think about what she would have to do upstairs, but

rather of Manu and her dream of having a family someday.
Because without a dream, a girl didn't have a reason to keep
living.

"You lookin' fer me, Miss Cameron?" Naomi called in the
twilight.

Cameron sat on a small stone bench in her mother's flower
garden. The sun had set, but there was still a red haze of light
from the burning ball that had slipped beyond the horizon.

The garden was probably not as lovely or as fragrant as it
had been in the days when her mother and a dozen gardeners
had tended it, but Cameron still thought it was pretty. As a
little girl she often sat at her father's feet on his second-story
veranda and watched her mother in the flower garden.

"Thank you for coming," Cameron said softly. "You
brought the flower basket and a knife?"

Naomi nodded. She hoped this would not take long. She
wanted to go back to her cabin, check on her mother and then
wash off before she went into the swamp to meet Manu. She
did not want to go to her man still smelling of the master's
stench.

"Ya want me to cut ya flowers now?" she asked, wrinkling
her nose. It was strange request, this time of day, but not any
stranger than some of the other things white folks asked her
to do.

"I want to talk to you, but I want you to kneel there and
cut flowers in case anyone sees us." She looked at her meaningfully. "We don't want anyone to be suspicious."

Naomi nodded and dropped to her bare knees. "I'm
listenin'."

"I need you to make contact with whomever it is you've
been talking to. We need to get the boats we discussed to get
everyone across the river. Tomorrow night if it's at all
possible."

Naomi glanced up, her heart leaping in her chest. "But ya
said ya wasn't ready, Miss Cameron. Ya said things wasn't in
place yet."

Cameron ran a hand through her hair. She had changed into

a pale-green sprigged gown and forgone most of her petticoats. It was a warm night but there was a breeze coming off the Pearl River that almost felt cool. "Naomi, please just do as I ask."

"Might take me awhile," she said, averting her gaze. "Not sure if I head out now that I can get back by dawn." She knew she couldn't be back if she spent the night with Manu in the swamp first.

"I'll cover for you in the house in the morning. I'll tell Sukey I sent you on an early-morning errand."

Naomi nodded her head. "All right then, Miss Cameron. I'll see what I can do. 'Course ya never know with this bunch. They don't 'zackly take to changes in plans. They won't like the idea of hurryin' up. That's when things goes wrong."

Cameron rose without looking down at Naomi. She thought she had seen something or someone move in the shadows of her father's veranda. Was Grant watching her?

"Stay here and finish cutting the flowers. Leave them in the kitchen and be on your way. I left a coin for you under the boot scrape near the back kitchen door."

Naomi didn't look up. "Thank ya, Missy Cameron."

Cameron walked away, smiling sadly. "No, Naomi. Thank you."

16

Cameron heard her name being called. *"Cameron... Cameron...* She snuggled deeper into the smooth, cool sheets.

It was him. Jackson.

She recognized his sensuous tenor voice and the edge of defiance that was always underlying in his tone. He was a rogue and no gentleman, a man without honor. She knew it, but it didn't seem to matter. Not here, not now.

"Jackson," she murmured. She rolled over languidly and smiled. When she opened her eyes, he was there sitting, on the edge of her rice bed. The sun was just rising, but the drapes were drawn and it was still cool in the room. The pale mosquito netting that hung from the canopy swayed in the morning breeze like a lover's caress.

"Cameron," he teased as he leaned over to kiss her cheek. "Wake up, sleepyhead."

She turned her face to brush his mouth with hers and reached out to touch him. He was naked, all long arms and legs, sinew and muscle.

She stretched like a cat as he leaned over her. He whispered in her ear but she didn't really hear what he was saying. It didn't matter. Nothing mattered but this exquisite togetherness. She stroked his bare chest and teased his nipple with her index figure. In retaliation, he leaned over and touched the tip of her breast with his warm, wet tongue.

She laughed and he grabbed the light sheet and pulled it off her. She was not at all surprised to find that she, too, was naked beneath the bedcovers.

With one broad, experienced hand, he caressed her breast. He rolled her nipple between his thumb and forefinger and she moaned with delicious pleasure.

She slid over to make room for him and he stretched out beside her, cradling her in one arm.

She ran her finger over his muscular chest and lower, over his flat stomach. There was a trail of dark hair that led from his navel downward. She lifted her chin to look into his gray eyes as she slid her hand down until she clasped him in her hand.

"Cameron," Jackson breathed huskily.

"Cameron! Cameron!"

She woke with a start to her name being called from the hallway. This time, the sound was no caress.

"Cameron! Cameron, you have to come quickly!"

She sat straight up in bed, all sweaty, her heart pounding, her pulse throbbing. Her nightgown was twisted around her legs and felt itchy and hot against her skin. She licked her dry lips as she thought of the feel of Jackson's most intimate part in her hand. She was shocked that she would dream such a thing.

"Cameron!" Taye's desperate voice sent fantasies of Jackson skittering from her mind.

"Taye!" Cameron had barely thrown her feet over the side of the bed when Taye came bursting into her bedchamber. She was dressed much like a housemaid in a calf-length white linen dress with her hair tied up in a turban. She must have been helping in the kitchen because she smelled of flour and sweet molasses. Taye was an excellent cook, but mostly she just made cakes and pastries.

"Taye, what's wrong?" Cameron met her halfway across her bedchamber and put out her arms to catch her.

Taye grasped Cameron's shoulders, her blue eyes bright with tears. "It's Grant. He's just come from town with armed men. They're ordering all of the slaves back into their cabins."

"Ordering them into the cabins? What does he think he's doing?" Cameron let go of Taye and grabbed the first piece of clothing she could find. It was the dirty breeches and shirt she had worn riding the day before, left carelessly on the floor.

"I don't know." Taye wrung her hands. "But they're locking them in."

"Locking them?" Cameron thought aloud as she yanked her sleeping gown over her head.

Seeing she was completely naked beneath the filmy gown, Taye turned around in embarrassment.

Cameron ignored her as she hopped on one foot and then the other to pull on the breeches. "How is Grant locking them up? There are no locks on the cabins."

"Sliding boards across the doors. Nailing the windows shut, too." Taye's voice trembled as she hugged herself, her back still to her dear friend. "Cam, I'm scared. I don't mean to say anything bad about Grant, I know he's your brother, but he's been acting a little—"

"Crazy?" Cameron said pulling on the lawn shirt without so much as a camisole beneath it. "You're not insulting me. I think there's a distinct possibility he's gone quite mad."

Still not turning to look at her, Taye scooped up a pair of stockings and Cameron's riding boots.

"No time for those." Cameron grabbed the worsted stockings from her and tossed them over her shoulder to the floor. "Let's go. I'll pull my boots on on the way downstairs."

Cameron left the bedchamber with Taye right behind her. By the time they reached the front porch, Cameron had wiggled into her boots and broken into a run.

Taye hiked up her skirts and ran after her. "I have to check on my mother and be certain she's all right," she told Cameron. "She stayed with Naomi's mother again last night."

Even before Cameron reached the shaded hollow where the slave cabins were located, she heard the frightened wails of women and children as they were being herded into the cabins. At the slave quarters' clearing, Taye separated from Cameron and hurried off to Naomi's cabin.

Slaves passed Cameron, plodding double file. They did not

look at her as they were ushered by. One of the field hands, Josiah, tried to pull away from an armed ruffian and the man struck him in the back of the head with the butt of his rifle. Josiah went down on one knee, and dark blood welled from the wound in his close-cropped hair.

"That will be enough of that," Cameron barked, sprinting toward them.

"Get up," the ruffian ordered Josiah, ignoring Cameron.

Josiah struggled to his feet and staggered toward the cabin where the other men were being herded. They were separating the slaves, sending women and children to some cabins, men to others.

"Did you hear me?" Cameron snapped. She laid a hand on the armed man's shoulder, and he jerked around to look at her.

"What the Christ?" He broke into a crooked grin. "Well, hello there, little lady." He looked her up and down as if she were some tart on a street corner in New Orleans. "You one of the stable boys? 'Cause if you is, Elmwood got some *fine* stable boys. They don't make no stable boys with tips down southern *Mississip* way."

Cameron tossed back her bright hair that tumbled over her shoulders, unbrushed. "What do you think you're doing with my slaves?" she demanded.

"Your slaves?" The ruffian had a ragged beard and foul breath that smelled of rotting teeth. "These is Mr. Campbell's slaves. I just signed on to help him round 'em up. Beats diggin' trenches fer the army." He reached out to touch her neck with a dirty palm, and she slapped it away.

"Leave her alone, you dumb ass," she heard Grant bellow. "That's my sister. Can you not tell the difference between negra slaves and white women?"

The ruffian took one look at Grant who was striding toward them and he nodded to Cameron. "Mighty sorry, Miss. My mistake."

Cameron turned to Grant who strode down the grassy knoll, straw hat on his head, a cigar protruding from his mouth. He was dressed smartly this morning in a pale-blue coat and white breeches, looking every bit the planter. "What are you doing?" she demanded incredulously. "These men and women should be in the fields at work."

"No work today." He halted in front of her. "Change of plans. I told you there would be a lot of changes here at Elmwood."

Now that Grant was close, she could smell liquor on his breath. Heavens, it was only nine in the morning and he was drunk or getting that way. "Out early or getting in late?" she questioned caustically.

"I should slap your face for that." He smiled. "But I am in too good a mood to cause such an ugly scene. Now go back to the house, and please put on something decent." He glanced at her breeches and beat-up boots with repugnance. "Christ, I'm going to have those clothes burned."

A slave woman and her two small children were escorted by them. The little girl was crying softly while her mother tried to soothe her.

Cameron watched them go by. "What the hell are you doing, Grant?"

"I'm warning you." He grabbed her arm. "You embarrass me in front of these darkies and I swear to God I'll have you flogged for insolence."

Cameron eyed him for a moment, then decided that he was just drunk enough, or just angry enough with her, to do it. "Please, tell me what you're doing," she said quietly. "I have a right to know."

"You do not have a right to know." He strode away, headed toward the house. "Jenkins, see they're all locked up securely, take a count and report to me."

"Aye, sir," another rough-looking man carrying a rifle said.

Cameron stood for a moment in indecision, watching as the slaves were forced into their cabins. Alone, she could do nothing. There were too many of these armed guards, who were obviously being paid by Grant to do his dirty work. She ran after Grant. "Tell me what you are doing with our slaves," she repeated, trying hard not to panic.

He glanced at her from beneath the wide-brimmed hat he

wore, lifting one eyebrow. "Dress as a young woman of your station should, tame that wild mane of yours and join me on the lower veranda. Breakfast will be served. We can talk there."

She wanted to tell him she would do no such thing. How could he expect her to think of dressing properly, of having breakfast, at a time like this? But Taye was right. Grant was crazy. It would be faster to change clothes than to argue with a madman. In the front hall, they parted and she ran up the grand staircase. "I'll be right down," she called to him. "And you'd better have a good explanation for this."

Less than half an hour later, Cameron walked out on the veranda in a lavender morning gown, sprigged with green blossoms. She had secured her mane of wild red hair back in a neat chignon and added a straw bonnet with a wide-brimmed lavender ribbon to the ensemble. In light of the morning's events, taking such care with her dress seemed beyond the absurd. But she sensed she was on dangerous ground with her brother and had to take every advantage she could seize. If using her feminine wiles would give her any lead, she was going to take it.

"There you are." Grant, always mannerly when it suited him, rose out of his chair at a table set for two. He grinned. "I must say, you do paint a pretty picture when you put forth a little effort." He leaned to kiss her and she offered her cheek.

She forced a grateful smile and allowed him to help her into her chair across from him. She placed her yellow napkin in her lap as he was seated again.

"Coffee?" he asked congenially.

She preferred tea to his dark roast coffee but she accepted with a nod. How could Grant be behaving this way, as if this were any other morning and they were merely having breakfast on the veranda? He had just ordered all their slaves to be locked up.

He waved to a kitchen girl standing nearby who carried a tray to the table and began to set out serving platters of eggs, sweet sausage and hotcakes.

Cameron's stomach groaned at the thought of food. It was all she could do to sit here and watch Grant spoon soft scrambled eggs onto his plate when she knew what was happening down at the cabins.

"Excellent," he told the young serving girl. "Thank you. Now join the other house servants by reporting to the cabins, please."

"Our house servants, too?" Cameron muttered in disbelief.

"Shh," Grant hissed under his breath. "Not in front of them. I will no longer allow you or anyone else to embarrass me in front of them."

Cameron stared at her brother, having no idea what he was talking about. What did he mean he wouldn't allow anyone to embarrass him in front of *them?*

Cameron watched the servant go. "Enough," she said throwing down her napkin. "What is going on here? Why are you locking our slaves up? What are you doing with the house servants?"

He crammed a forkful of eggs into his mouth and reached for the pot of honey. "Won't be needing them. I'm leaving for Baton Rouge in two days."

"That doesn't answer my question. What are you doing with our slaves?"

"Selling them."

"Selling them? What...what do you mean you're selling Elmwood's slaves?"

Grant's brow furrowed as he drizzled honey on his hotcakes and the eggs. "What part of 'I am selling the slaves' did you not understand, Cameron?" He feigned patience. "The part where I said *I* meaning, I, Grant David Campbell, master of this plantation, or *will be selling the slaves,* meaning I will take money in exchange for allowing someone to haul their black asses off this plantation and be responsible for feeding and clothing them?"

Cameron's lower lip trembled and for an instant she feared she would cry. Fortunately she was too livid for ineffectual tears. "You cannot sell Elmwood's slaves! Many of the men and women were born here. They—" She was so distraught that she could not find the right words to express herself. "Grant, these men, women and children are not property to be sold like a carriage or a plow. They are people like you and me who have families—mothers, fathers, children. Many have never known any other home but Elmwood."

"Then I suppose they will have to adjust," he retorted not unlike an intolerant child. "Pass the sausage. You should try some. It's really quite tasty. I fear such delicacies will soon become scarce."

Cameron made herself pass him the warm dish as she tried to decide the best way to deal with him. If reasoning wouldn't work, maybe bullying would. Grant had always been of weak resolve, his self-esteem low. "Grant, you listen to me," she said harshly, rising out of her chair. "You cannot do this."

He stabbed a piece of sausage off the serving platter and hurled it onto his plate. Eggs leaped off their mother's morning china onto the white linen tablecloth. "What do you mean I *can't* do this?" He went on faster than before. "I am the master of this plantation and owner of everything the prodigious Senator Campbell once owned. The will has been legally read and probated. It's really all quite official. I spoke to the attorney, Mr. Joseph, only yesterday." He set down his fork and shook a finger at her.

Cameron instinctively slid her chair back, not liking the sudden change in his voice. She had never been fearful of Grant, but there was something about his tone that sounded dangerous. And now...now the senator was no longer here.

"You have been a very naughty girl, Cameron, going behind my back the way you did, talking to Mr. Joseph about matters that don't concern you. Thank goodness I recovered and was able to go to town myself and straighten this matter out. Thank goodness no real harm was done." He laughed but without mirth. "Emancipate the slaves, indeed." He brushed back a wisp of sandy blond hair that fell over one eye. "Oh, don't worry. Mr. Joseph does not think ill of you. I explained how you have not been yourself, what with the death of our father, the war and all. It's really too much for a well-bred, genteel young woman such as yourself to cope with, don't you think?''

Cameron opened her mouth to speak, to disagree—for she was coping far better than she would have thought possible—but then pressed her lips together in silence. She could see that she would be wasting her time trying to rationalize with Grant. What she needed to do now was not panic.

She pressed her hand to her chest in an attempt to slow her pounding heart, struggling to keep her breath even. She didn't want Grant to know just how upset she was. Somehow, she didn't know how, she was going to set them free before they were sold. She needed to get away from this table and Grant as quickly and as cleanly as possible. There was a lot to do if she was going to get the slaves off Elmwood quickly. All she could think of was thank God, and thank Naomi, that she had begun to collect information on the Underground Railroad. She didn't have information on the whole trek north, but she knew the first stop the slaves would have to make along the northern Mississippi border. That would be enough to get them safely out of Grant's hands.

She thought suddenly of Naomi. She had not seen the girl this morning. Had she not returned to Elmwood yet? Cameron only prayed Naomi would realize something wasn't right when she approached Elmwood and not allow the armed men to capture her.

Cameron had to find Naomi. She had to get someone to help her. But who? Who could help her? Memories of her dream tumbled through her head. Jackson. Could Jackson help her? Would he? She would have to find him. Send someone for him. But what if he had left for Baton Rouge by now? She shoved that thought aside as well. One thing at a time.

Cameron lowered her gaze submissively as she turned her attention back to her brother, knowing intuitively how she must play him. ''When?'' she asked.

''When?'' He lifted an eyebrow as he set down his fork.

''When will they go?''

''Why do you ask?''

''I—'' she had to think quickly ''—I wondered how much

longer I would have the house slaves available. I've done a lot, but more will have to be done to fully prepare the house to be shuttered. Furniture must be covered. Paintings taken down and locked in the cellars.'' She gazed up at him from beneath her lashes. ''I should think it will take a few weeks. You'll have to find buyers, give them time to make financial arrangements. Elmwood's slaves must be worth a great deal.''

''No, you don't understand. I'm not going to sell them. I am auctioning them off. The day after tomorrow the auctioneer will arrive, as will the buyers. Each darky will be set on the auction block and sold to the highest bidder. The sale has been posted in all the neighboring counties. I understand there's a buyer coming from Louisiana who is interested in an entire wagon load of men to cut new fields.''

''Grant!'' she gasped. ''If you auction them, women will be separated from their husbands, their children even.'' She had not intended to argue, but she couldn't help herself. What kind of man would separate families?

What had happened to Grant to make him so malevolent? He had never been a kind man, or even a fair one, but Cameron would never have suspected this of him. Something had happened, but what? Had Grant sold his soul to the devil? Was that what he had been doing all those days and nights locked up in his bedchamber, after their father's death?

The thought was absurd, of course, but was it any more incongruous than the idea of Grant auctioning Elmwood's slaves off one by one like cattle?

''As I told you yesterday, I'll be shuttering Elmwood, and I'll be moving to Baton Rouge to stay in our town house until the war is over. I will not need these slaves in Baton Rouge. Better to sell them now while I can make a decent profit.'' He smiled. ''And I'll take only gold in payment, no promissory notes or paper money that may lose value in the coming turmoil.''

Cameron could tell by the look on his face that he was entirely serious. She felt as if she were living a nightmare, only she knew better than to think she would awake in her gossamer-curtained bed to find that none of it was true. ''I understand selling the men, we'll not be able to plant another season, but what about the women?''

"Ah, the women. The auctioneer says the women don't sell for much in this kind of situation. Buyers are looking for hard labor. They put the negras in the fields without feeding them much and let them work until they die in their traces.'' He wrinkled his thin nose with distaste. "Women don't last long enough to make it worthwhile.''

"Then what are you going to do with our women? Are you going to let them stay here?'' she asked hopefully. "Take them with you?''

"Oh, I'm going to sell them, too.'' He smirked. "To the best place for women like them—a whorehouse in Baton Rouge.''

She rose out of her chair, flinging her straw bonnet. "You can't do this!'' she shouted at him. "Grant, you can't sell our women to be...to be used as...''

"Whores?'' He laughed. "Oh, but I can. It's all perfectly legal.''

Cameron had to bite her tongue to keep from letting out a string of expletives. Sell the slaves, sell her horses and make the slave women whores? Never in her wildest dreams could she have thought her brother would stoop to such a debase level of humanity.

Papa had always made excuses for Grant. He had always made Grant out to be a better person that he was, but how could he have been so wrong? How could they both have so misjudged Grant? What had happened these last few weeks to turn Grant so utterly against her, against all of Elmwood?

Cameron lowered her gaze to meet her brother's. He was picking his teeth with a gold toothpick. "Grant,'' she said, quietly. "We must discuss this. You cannot—''

A scream rent the air and Cameron and Grant both turned toward the open doorway that led into the house.

"Help me!'' Taye screamed as she burst onto the veranda.

One of the armed men Grant had hired followed a step behind. He reached out and grabbed Taye, lifting her off her feet.

"Leave her alone!" Cameron shouted.

Grant rose out of his chair, dropping his napkin onto the table. "How dare you disturb my breakfast," he snarled at the man.

"Sorry, Mr. Campbell. This one tried to run away. Hit one of my boys with a branch." He slung her into his other arm. "'Course didn't take much to catch her. She ain't nothing but a little sprite of a thing."

"Cameron," Taye sobbed. "Please. He…he thinks I'm one of the slaves. He won't listen to me."

Cameron spun around to face her brother. Dressed in a white kitchen dress and turban, Cameron understood how someone could mistake Taye for a slave. Without her expensive gowns and coiffured hair, she was nothing but a mulatto slave in the eyes of these Southerners. The thought infuriated her. Of course the man would not listen to her anymore than he had listened to Taye. Only Grant could stop this. "Tell him to release her at once," Cameron ground out under her breath.

Grant stared at Taye for a moment as if in indecision. Their gazes met and Cameron sensed a battle of wills between them.

"My way?" Grant asked Taye directly.

Taye drew her pretty mouth back in a tight frown, her pale-blue eyes filling with obstinance. "I would rather die," she whispered.

Grant seemed to flinch inwardly, but then his demeanor changed. He smiled that infuriating, fake smile of his. "Oh, Taye dear, you are so young. What you do not realize is that there are many things far worse than death." He gave a flip of his hand and turned away. "Lock her up with the other negras."

"Lock her up!" Cameron shouted. "You can't lock her up. She is a free woman and you know it."

"And you have the documents?"

"Papa must have—" Cameron cut herself off, realizing the futility of this conversation. Either Grant had the official documents in his possession or, God forbid, had destroyed them. The truth of the matter was that, without documentation, here in Mississippi Taye was nothing but another slave woman.

"Dear Miss Taye doesn't accept my *hospitality* when it is offered," Grant scoffed, "so she can just join the others." He waved a ringed hand. "Lock her up with the other female house slaves." He took his seat again.

Cameron made a move toward Taye as the ruffian tucked her under his arm to carry her off. Taye put out her hand to Cameron, tears running down her face.

"You take one more step toward that little ungrateful bitch," Grant ground out, "and I will have you locked up with the rest of the whores."

Cameron froze, her head spinning. Whores? Who was he calling a whore? Why was he pretending Taye was a slave? It was almost too much for her to absorb, but she had to stay strong. She had to remain strong for Taye and the others. She had to use her head. If Grant locked her up, she wouldn't be able to do anything to help them. Tears glistened in her eyes as she kissed her fingers and offered her hand to her dear friend. "I'll come for you," she mouthed.

Taye pressed her lips together and nodded bravely.

Cameron watched in disbelief as the man carried her dearest friend away. Only when they were gone did she finally turn to her brother. Taking a moment to collect her thoughts and weigh her options, Cameron walked over to the edge of the veranda and picked up the hat she had tossed.

Grant had taken his seat at the table and was ladling jam onto a biscuit. "Will you join me to finish breakfast?" he asked as if none of that had occurred.

"No, I think not," she said softly.

"Then go to your room. Begin packing your belongings. You will either catch the train north day after tomorrow or you will accompany me to Baton Rouge. No unwed sister of mine will remain behind, alone, without an escort."

"Grant—"

"Another word," he said sharply, "and I'll nail your door shut as well." He held up his fork. "Not another word."

Cameron pressed her lips together and nodded solemnly.

She left the veranda and headed for her bedchamber. She had a lot to do if she was going to get the slaves off Elmwood tonight.

"So what you make of it?" Naomi asked Manu softly. They stood in the cover of trees behind Elmwood's slave quarters staring at the doors and windows that had been boarded up. She could hear the frightened murmuring from inside the cabins.

"I don' know, sweetness. All I know is I got to get my black hide back to da plantation before I's missed." He rested a hand on her shoulder. "And if ya had any sense, ya'd be high-tailin' it out of here. Ya know the train path. Ya know where the stops is." He clasped her hand and gazed lovingly into her eyes. "This is you' chance, Naomi. Yer chance for freedom. Y'd best take it."

She squeezed his big hand with both of hers. "Yer right. I got to do somethin', but not without ya. I ain't goin' nowhere without my man, and ya know it." She searched the dark eyes she had so come to love. "I think this is a chance fer both us. Ya ain't goin' back to Atkin's Way."

His brow furrowed. "I ain't?"

She shook her head. "My guess is that Masta Grant has done decided to sell his darkies. How long before ya think yer masta will be doin' the same?"

Manu nodded. "Guess yer right. Ya always been real smart, Naomi girl."

"Guess I am. But it don't take much smarts or entrail readin' to figure this one out."

"So we just wait 'til dark and head off?" he asked.

She gazed back at the cabins. "I can't just go off and leave 'em. Not my mama."

He glanced at the barred cabins and grimaced. "I's afraid ya was gonna say that, sweetness." With a look of resignation, he turned back to her. "So just tell this boy what he's gonna do and be done with it."

She rubbed his strong, hard shoulder. "You're goin' to go back into the swamp and gather whatever we have hidden there. The blanket, the pack, the little bit of food and the coin I got buried.''

He nodded. ''Then what?''

''Then you wait for me. I have a feelin' we're gonna be high-tailin' it out of here, one way or another.'' She lifted up on her toes and kissed him soundly on the lips. ''Now go on with ya.''

''But what about you? Where ya goin'?''

Naomi gazed through the trees in the direction of Elmwood's big house. ''Why I'm goin' up to the house to see Miss Cameron and find out what by Krobo is happenin' here.''

17

Cameron paced her bedchamber, kicking her infuriating petticoats in front of her as she tried to think. Her brother was insane. Unequivocally mad. Sell the slaves! Send the women to a whorehouse!

Damn! She had to stop him. But how?

A soft tap on the door startled Cameron and she spun around to stare in the direction of the source, half fearing it was Grant. He had herded all the house servants to the slave quarters as well. Who else was left in the house?

She walked to the door and hesitantly placed one hand on the smooth paneled wood, remembering who had been on the other side the night her father had died. Sweet heaven, what she wouldn't give to have Jackson's strength here now, a bulwark against the terror that surrounded her.

"Who is it?" Cameron whispered.

"President Lincoln," a soft voice replied. "By Lumusi's swelling belly, Miss Cameron, it's Naomi. Can I come in?"

Cameron jerked open the door and flung her arms around Naomi, dragging her inside. "Oh, thank goodness you're safe. I was afraid you'd be locked up the moment you set foot on the property." Cameron squeezed the slave woman tight. "Thank God I sent you to town last night!"

Naomi took a step back, smoothing her dress, obviously not sure what to make of Cameron's welcome. Never, in all the years they had known each other, had Cameron hugged her.

"'Course I didn't let 'em lock me up," Naomi scoffed, proudly. "I could smell that filthy white trash and their guns soon as I crossed the Pearl."

Cameron gestured with both hands. "We have to do something, Naomi. Quickly. Grant is selling all the slaves. House and field hands. Everyone."

"Sellin' 'em?"

Cameron nodded. She saw no need to tell Naomi the entire sordid truth. This was enough for the young girl now. "I have to get them out of here. We've got to have help."

"Seen it," Naomi whispered hoarsely.

Cameron stepped back and looked into the black woman's eyes, eyes that seemed to take on a haunted gleam. Suddenly chilled, Cameron rubbed her bare arms as gooseflesh rose on her skin.

"Seen it in the entrails. Seen it in the flames and the twistin' smoke. Didn't know what it 'twas. Couldn't see 'zackly what was comin'. Knowed it was bad, but not this bad." Naomi blinked and refocused. "Oh, ya tell me what to do, Miss Cameron, and Naomi, she'll do her best. Me and Manu, we'll do our best."

"Who's Manu?"

Naomi smiled the prettiest smile. "He's my man. Me and Manu, we gonna get married and get us a little house once we're free." She swayed slightly in her clean but worn housedress. "Maybe have us a baby."

Cameron couldn't resist a smile. Right now, the thought of a cozy home, a husband and a baby almost sounded good to her. "He'll help us?"

"He'll do whatever he's told." She grinned with a chuckle. "Least whatever I tell him to do."

Cameron smiled again, then frowned. "But Manu isn't one of our slaves, is he?"

She shook her head. "Nope. He's not from Elmwood, but it's best ya not know what plantation he come from. Let's say he ain't goin' back."

A runaway slave, Cameron thought. How dangerous. But soon all of her slaves would be considered runaways if she had anything to do with it. She grabbed Naomi's hand and led her to the bed. The two women sat side by side, black and white, as if a bottomless chasm of laws and customs didn't divide them, as if they had been best friends their entire lives. "Listen," Cameron said. "I think I have an idea, but you have to be brave, Naomi. This could be very dangerous."

"I ain't scared," Naomi answered. "Got my spirits with me, right here." She ran slender fingers over a little bag she wore around her neck on a leather thong. "Old Africa spirits, powerful they are. They keep me safe."

Cameron wondered just what was inside the bag, but she wasn't sure she really wanted to know. She gazed into Naomi's dark eyes. "I need you to go back to town as quickly as possible. Steal one of our horses if you can manage."

Naomi gave a little half smile. "Been done 'afore. Can be done again."

"But those men are armed out there, Naomi." She rested a hand on the girl's thin shoulder. "You have to be careful."

"And just what is this runaway darky girl gonna do in town, Missy?"

Cameron took a deep breath. She knew that once she voiced her wishes aloud, she would be committed. It was difficult for her to ask for Jackson's help, especially after he left her the way he did, but she had no other choice. "You're going to find Captain Logan. He can't be too hard to locate. Try all the hotels."

Naomi crossed her arms over her breasts. "I thought the captain done gone to Baton Rouge fer his boat. He tol' me he was goin' straight there after the senator done passed."

Cameron wondered when Naomi had had the opportunity to talk to Jackson alone. A thorn of jealousy surprisingly poked her brittle emotions. But this was no time for hurt feelings. This wasn't a time for self-centeredness or selfishness. "Last weekend he was still in Jackson at some hotel." She did not meet the young slave woman's penetrating gaze. She knew it was ridiculous, but she felt as if Naomi knew more about her and Jackson than she possibly could.

"I saw him at Mr. Hitch's ball but that was only two weeks

ago. He said he was leaving for Baton Rouge soon. Hopefully he hasn't left yet. Go to him, Naomi. Tell him that Grant is going to sell our slaves and tell him I need his help. Now.''

Naomi listened patiently, nodding.

"If you can't find him—" Cameron lifted her hands, fighting the oppressive feeling of helplessness again "—I don't know what other choice we have." She said that, but already her mind was churning. She needed Jackson, *wanted* Jackson here, but she had to accept the fact that he might not be willing to help her even if Naomi was able to find him.

Cameron rose off the bed and walked to the window. She parted the drapes and gazed out over Elmwood's land, her attention settling on the slave quarters in the distance. "You said your man was here, hiding. Will he help us or do you think he'll want to head north right away?"

"I can't go without knowin' my mama is safe. Ya know how she's been feelin' poorly." Naomi came to stand beside Cameron at the window, but took care to remain behind the cover of the drapes. "What ya want Manu to do?"

Cameron turned to her. "What did you find out last night about the boats?"

"It's bein' worked on. I'm tol' it can get done with a couple more dollars."

"Good, because we'll have to get everyone across the river immediately."

"'Mediately when?"

"It will have to be tomorrow night."

"Don' know 'bout that, Miss. The man I been talkin' to said he could get 'em, but I'm not sure he can get 'em that quick."

"Naomi, we have no choice. The water's still too high this time of year to wade across. It's boats for Elmwood's slaves or they swim across the Pearl. The auctioneer comes in two days' time."

"Auctioneer is it?"

Naomi said something beneath her breath that sounded like a voodoo curse, and Cameron's insides clenched. Taking a deep breath, she went on. "Hopefully you'll bring back Jackson and together we can stop my brother. But if something happens, I'll just have to give the slaves what information I have on the Underground Railroad. They'll have to head for the first house, and take their chances.''

Naomi raised hard eyes to meet Cameron's. "Chances," Naomi echoed. "Yea-ah. Take they chances."

Cameron walked to her bedside and took a small purse from a drawer. She gave Naomi several bills and some coins from the stash she was hiding to give the slaves when they left. "Take some of this and give it to Manu. Send him after the boats. The rest may help you find the captain.''

Naomi studied the money in her hand, probably more than she had seen in a lifetime. Would she be tempted to take it and head north to freedom with her man? Cameron realized it was a risk she'd have to take.

"Do you understand what you need to do?" Cameron asked gently.

"Yes, Miss Cameron. Naomi will do what she can."

"But don't you risk your own life. You can't be caught, Naomi. You have to understand that. If you are caught, I don't know that I can protect you from Grant.''

"This girl understands what ya be sayin'." She shook her head. "That Masta Grant, he got some powerful bad magic in his pocket." Then one corner of her mouth turned up slyly in a half smile. "But Naomi…Naomi got ways to protect herself, old ways, ways no white lady best know about.''

"He's sick, but he's my brother, Naomi. I don't want him dead.'' If anyone killed him, it would be her. "I just want to stop him.''

"Yes'm, I reckon that's fair 'nough. But Masta Grant, he gone too far, he playin' wit' fire. Sometimes, sometimes fire burn. Do he raise the old bad ones, ain't nothin' and nobody goin' to protect him. It ain't me you got to worry about, Miss Cameron. It's that dark fire.''

"Be careful." Cameron gave Naomi a quick hug. "I'll see you soon. All right?" She gazed into the young woman's eyes.

Naomi offered a quick smile. "See you soon. My man's waitin' for me." She opened the door.

"But how will you get out of the house?" Cameron asked. Naomi winked. "Same way I done got in. Magic."

Before Cameron could answer, the girl slipped out and disappeared silently down the hall in the direction of the guest wing.

"What do you mean there's one missing?" Grant demanded angrily.

The bearded man stared at the front porch step, not making eye contact. "We took a count the way you said. One wench is missing 'ccording to how many darkies you said you ought to have. We talked to your overseer and he says a house slave by the name of Naomi is missing."

"That little slut," Grant muttered. His eyes widened with fury. "So have you looked for her?"

"Checked the fields, the barns. No one has seen her."

"I'll kill her," Grant muttered, flexing his fingers as if he had Naomi by the throat. "I swear I'll kill her. After all I've done for her." He glanced around. "Keep looking for her! The little negra has got to be here somewhere!"

Grant turned away, so angry that he couldn't see straight. How dare that little bitch hide instead of joining the other slaves who allowed themselves to be herded in like a bunch of sheep? How dare she! Who did she think she was? Did she think she was better than the others? Than him?

He walked into the house, cursing his crooked leg that slowed him down. Nothing was going right. Nothing was going the way he had planned. Why hadn't Taye begged for his help? How could she have preferred to be locked up in that filth when she could have remained with him? Did she understand that he loved her? That all she had to do was be nice to him and he would take care of her.

She was another uppity bitch, just like Naomi. She thought she was better than she was. So what if her mother had slept with a white man? Taye was still born negra, wasn't she?

Grant remembered what his father had said about Taye being his daughter. The idea disgusted him...and yet in a way it excited him. Did that make her his half sister? Would sleeping with her be incest? he wondered, growing warm around his collar.

Not really. Not in the biblical sense, he reasoned as he walked up the grand staircase toward his sister's room. Not when her mother had been a black slave. Not when she was only half human. He licked his dry lips thinking of her, thinking of what she would look like naked in his arms, what she would feel like.

Grant had pretended she was in his arms many times. Naomi would dress up in the gown he had stolen from Taye's room, and she would say what Grant told her to say. But it never quite rang true. Taye was well educated, soft-spoken. Naomi was nothing but a whore who did what he asked for the coin she knew he would give her when he was done.

Of course all women were really whores, weren't they?

Well, he'd give Taye one more chance this afternoon, after she'd had time to contemplate her fate in one of those hot cabins. If she wouldn't come willingly to him tonight, he'd…he'd take what he wanted, he decided angrily, and then he'd sell her along with all the other whores!

Grant slammed his fist against Cameron's door and then didn't wait for her to answer. He strode in and she whipped around from where she stood at the window. Her eyes were red as if she had been crying. His sister never cried. Somehow it gave him a certain pleasure to think he might have initiated this response.

"My horses," she said softly. "You really did sell off all of my horses?"

He couldn't resist a smile as he walked to the windows and drew back the drapes. Far below and to the west, several men were leading his sister's precious Arabians one by one from the stables to be tied behind a wagon. "No woman should be riding blooded animals like those. They're dangerous."

"Dangerous?"

"Papa should have sold that first one," he snapped, letting the drape fall as he limped away. "If he had, I wouldn't be a cripple today."

"If you hadn't been so mean," she challenged, "and whipped that mare, she wouldn't have thrown you."

He whirled around to face her. "Shut up before I shut you up," he snapped. "Now tell me where that little black bitch is."

"I don't know what you're talking about."

"Naomi! They say she isn't with the others. She's missing!"

Cameron folded her hands demurely. "Why, you sent all the house slaves to the cabins. You and I are quite alone here in the house."

"I know where I sent them, damn it! But I'm telling you, she's not there."

"I'm sure she'll turn up. They probably miscounted. There are so many crowded into those cabins."

He scowled. She was possibly right. He wiped his mouth with the back of his hand. "I'm hungry," he grumbled.

"Would you like me to order you something to eat? I could have it served to you on Papa's veranda." She paused. "Oh, that's right. There's no one to cook, and I'm afraid I'm quite helpless when it comes to a kitchen." She sighed. "If only Taye was here. She cooks."

"She does?"

Cameron nodded. "Quite well."

Grant thought for a moment. He had wondered how he was going to get her back in the house without losing face. This was the perfect excuse. He would send for her to serve him and his sister. She could cook for them and tonight she could join them. They could play music in the parlor the way they used to, and dine together by candlelight. It would be such fun, like the old days. If Taye could see what fun he could be, she might realize that she belonged with him. Belonged to him. She would see the error of her ways and come willingly to his bed. Once she realized how good they could be together, she would accept her fate. She could be his mistress in Baton Rouge. The war would be so much easier to ride out with sweet Taye at his side. Even if he had to put up with his damned sister, Taye would sweeten the pot.

"All right," Grant grumbled, pretending she had persuaded him. "I'll write a note, and you may go down and deliver it to the guard called Jack. I'll instruct him that the mulatto wench is to be sent to the house. But no one else is to be let out." He shook his finger. "And no tricks, sister mine, or you'll both regret it. Taye will have to manage in the kitchen alone."

"Oh, thank you!" Cameron declared. Then she ran past him and out into the hallway. "I'll get her now."

"I don't understand," Taye said, running along beside Cameron. "Why did he change his mind?"

The two women ran through the garden behind the house toward the kitchen. "I don't know. It was too easy." Cameron halted at the back door, panting from the exertion of the run. But she felt good, strong. Now she had a plan. She was going to get these men and women safely out of here, she just knew it.

"But what's important is that we're together." Cameron laid her hand on her friend's that was sticky with perspiration. It had been incredibly hot in the cabins, so hot that Cameron had insisted all the armed men haul drinking water to the cabins. She had told them no one would buy slaves that had died of thirst.

"We're together," Cameron said. "And together we're going to free our slaves before Grant auctions them off."

"Auction them off?" Taye's eyes filled with tears. "But…but Mama is in a cabin. She's a free woman. Surely he does not think—"

Cameron clasped Taye's hands tightly in hers. "Look at me," she said urgently, cutting off Taye's words. There was a slight, hot breeze and she could smell the crepe jasmine on the air. "I've sent Naomi for Captain Logan."

Taye grew wide-eyed. "Naomi?"

"And there's a man trying to get boats for us on the river. I plan to send the slaves north tonight one way or another."

"Oh, Captain Logan," Taye breathed. "He's going to help

us? That's wonderful, Cam. Captain Logan will know what to do. He'll know how to handle Grant. Grant is afraid of him."

Cameron fought the irritation she felt. She didn't know why Taye like Jackson so much. Didn't she realize that he was not the gentleman he pretended to be? "I don't even know if the captain is still in the state," Cameron said, not meaning to snap. She took a breath. "Either way, we're setting the slaves free tonight. I have what money I could get to give them and directions on how to reach a house on the Underground Railroad north of here."

Taye threw her arms around Cameron and gave her a quick squeeze. "I told Mama that everything would be all right," she said with a newfound hope in her voice. "I told her not to worry, that you would make everything all right again."

Cameron stepped out of Taye's arms and into the main kitchen feeling far less confident of her abilities than Taye sounded.

"She serving our supper?" Grant asked. He stood in the window of the dining room smoking a cigar when Cameron entered. Her father would never have smoked in the dining room.

"It will be ready shortly."

He smiled in a way that frightened her. "Excellent," he murmured, an almost sinister tone to his voice.

Cameron walked up to her brother. She had changed into a pale-yellow gown that was tight waisted with elbow-length sleeves and a low décolleté. She dressed this way to placate her brother, not because she wanted to. "Why do you say that?" She tugged on the sleeve of his pale-green coat. "Grant, I don't care how angry you are with Taye or why. You cannot sell her as a slave."

"I can do what I want with her," he snapped. "And it's high time all of you ladies realized that." He sounded like a spoiled child. "I can do whatever I want and no one can stop me."

Cameron felt dizzy with fear for Taye. "So you're going to

sell her as a common slave, knowing Papa freed her and Sukey years ago?''

He lifted one shoulder. ''Perhaps. Perhaps not.'' He strode away, flicking cigar ashes on the polished floor as he walked. ''What I have decided to do is put an end to that girl's teasing.''

Cameron felt sick in the pit of her stomach. ''I don't know what you mean,'' she said, fearing she did.

''Of course you do! You all do it. She twitches her ass and bats her lashes and she pretends she wants it, but then when a man tries to take what's offered, she rebukes him!''

''Grant—''

''It's time Taye gave up that virginal walk of hers, with her nose in the air as if she thinks she's better than others. I plan to initiate her into the world of carnal matters. If she pleases me, maybe I'll take her with me to Baton Rouge. If she doesn't, she'll be sold with the rest of the whores! It's time you women knew who wears the pants in this family.''

''No,'' Cameron murmured, staring at him in disbelief. If Grant raped Taye it would be her fault. She was the one who had convinced Grant to let her out of the cabins. She fought the suffocating sense of panic in her chest. Sweet Lord, if she had left matters alone, Taye might still be locked safely in the cabin with her mother.

No, not safely. Lord, what was she thinking? Was she as mad as Grant? Her brother had just threatened to sell Taye to a house of ill repute—sweet, innocent Taye, the friend who was closer to her than anyone in the world. Had the whole world gone crazy? Panic seized her, but she pushed it down resolutely. She had to hold Grant off until Jackson could get here. But if he didn't— No, she couldn't think of that. She wouldn't.

Trembling, Cameron lowered her gaze, pretending to demur. ''Grant, you know I can't agree with such behavior, but—'' she grit her teeth to make herself say it ''—you are the master of this plantation now. Naturally, the decisions are yours.''

He smirked. "It's good to see you are finally realizing that."

She glanced at the glass he had left in the windowsill and tried to recall something Naomi had once told her about making droughts of laudanum and henbane that induced both sleep and amnesia. How much would disable a man without harming him, she wondered, wishing frantically that she had paid more heed to the woman's words. "Would you like me to get you another drink?"

He smiled. "I would. Why, thank you, dear sister."

"Send her up," Grant said, staggering up the stairs, a glass in his hand. It was the third drink Cameron had made her brother and he was barely able to propel himself forward under the mixture of the alcohol and the drug.

"Oh, I will," she said from the hallway. It was long after dark. Naomi had not returned, and Cameron had a sinking feeling that she had not been able to locate the captain. Either she hadn't been able to locate him, or she had taken the money and headed north with her Manu. If she had, Cameron couldn't blame her. What were the chances she would be able to save these slaves anyway? Perhaps Naomi had the good sense to recognize when self-preservation was called for. Perhaps Cameron should be as wise, but she wasn't. She knew what her father's wishes had been. And no matter how Grant denied it, had Senator David Campbell been alive today, Elmwood's slaves would be free.

Cameron made herself smile prettily at her brother who was now hugging the gleaming banister. "I'll find Taye and order her upstairs."

"Damn straight," Grant murmured, talking to himself as much as to Cameron. He attempted to make a fist and swing it in the air in a gesture of manliness but he couldn't hold himself up. "Show her who's in charge."

Cameron stood at the bottom of the stairs for a full ten minutes before she crept up and into her brother's room. Just as she suspected, he lay unconscious on the bed, fully clothed, his shoes still on his feet. She hoped she hadn't given him too much of the mixture in his drink but when she heard him snoring, she knew he was in no danger. If he hadn't drunk so much in an attempt to bolster his courage to seduce Taye, or worse, perhaps he wouldn't be unconscious now. Looking down at him, she couldn't resist a smile at the thought of outsmarting the sick son of a bitch.

Grant Campbell would not be initiating anyone into the world of carnal knowledge tonight.

18

"You want me to dress, *monsieur? Oui?*"

Jackson lay stretched out naked on a four-poster bed in an expensive hotel in Baton Rouge, staring at the ceiling elaborately painted with dancing cherubs, moons and stars. He barely glanced at the naked blonde who strutted in front of him, in a pair of black-netted stockings and a red garter belt. Her accent was light, but she was most definitely French Cajun.

"*Oui.* You heard me, get dressed," he grumbled in ill humor. He reached for a cigar in a small mahogany humidor beside the bed.

Cerese was at his side in a moment to light his smoke with a small oil lamp from the bedside. As she leaned over him, her large, pendulous breasts swung in front of his face. Her areolas were dark, her nipples large. She smelled of good French perfume with a hint of milled soap. Jackson liked his whores squeaky clean and he paid well for that guarantee. Cerese was usually just his type, lusty and experienced without being crude.

But this lady of the evening didn't smell of the Mississippi soil, or fresh air or moonlit nights on the Pearl River, and she was not a redhead. Her eyes were faded blue, not the tawny shade of a cat's. Her purring voice was too soft, too fawning.

Jackson cursed beneath his breath and waved her away. Once upon a time he would have spent a full night with this flash piece. He'd have taught her tricks of her trade no one else had taught her. He would have brought Cerese to cries of pleasure more times in one night than any other man had before.

But it just didn't seem right to Jackson—not having the woman he wanted here. Not holding her in his arms. When he had attempted to kiss Cerese's painted mouth, he'd actually felt sick. He was as disgusted with himself as he was by her. How had he let this happen? "Didn't I tell you to get dressed?" he demanded.

"If *monsieur* is having difficulty—" She dropped to her knees beside the bed and clasped his flaccid member in her cool hand. "Cerese could—"

"Did you hear me?" he grunted, waving her away. "I said get dressed." He scowled. He wasn't embarrassed, just annoyed, and he wanted her the hell out of here. "Don't worry, you'll be paid." He rose from the bed, and without bothering to put on his silk night robe, he strode naked to the curtained balcony to gaze out.

The street below was well lit and a barrage of sounds assaulted him the moment he pulled back the fine brocaded silk drapes. Carriages rolled past pulled by prancing horses with gay feathered headdresses, and the street was as busy as midday though it had to be after midnight. Jackson heard the sound of husky female laughter that reminded him of another woman's laughter, and he looked down, half hoping to see Cameron Campbell appear by magic. But Cam wasn't there, of course. A man and a woman, linked arm in arm, passed below on the walk. Somewhere farther down the street a banjo played and he recognized the Cajun tune.

Christ, he was getting soft. He wished his ship were ready to sail tonight. He already had some of the cargo loaded—turpentine. He had made several good contacts and his mission was well laid out. He had his orders from Washington. He needed to get out on the open sea. Perhaps the brisk breezes and salt air would wash that red-haired woman from his veins.

Half a block down, a man leaning on a lamppost caught Jackson's eye. He knew the man. Tonight he was dressed like a gambler, in a cheap suit, and was sipping from a liquor bottle he had pulled from inside his coat. Other times he had been a soldier, a wealthy businessman, a common working man, even a lamplighter.

"Hell," Jackson muttered under his breath. And he had been hoping to turn in early tonight. Now he would have to dress and go to one of the designated meeting places. From there he would be given instructions as to where the true meeting place would be. He waited until the gambler caught sight of him on the balcony and gave a half salute.

"Monsieur?"

He turned to find Cerese dressed. Except for the bright-red lips and cheeks, she was so respectfully gowned that no one would have known she was a whore.

"Money is in the top drawer." He turned his back to her again. He would wait until she was gone and then he would dress. He would make his meeting and be back in his room within two hours' time if he was lucky.

He heard footsteps, the drawer open and the shuffle of money as she counted the bills. At last the hotel room door opened and then closed. He had given her genuine Yankee bills. He knew better than to think the Confederate paper that was being printed would be worth more than the ink it was printed with in a few months' time.

Jackson blew a smoke ring and stared into the darkness wondering what Cameron was doing tonight. Dancing at some Confederate ball? Laughing, tossing those dark-red curls that smelled of sunshine and sassy smiles?

Cameron crawled on her belly along the grass between the barn and the corn crib. The scent of rich, dark Mississippi soil, still warm from the day, filled her nostrils. A mist lay thick on the ground. She heard the sound of nocturnal creatures—frogs, insects and the long, drawn-out hooting cry of a great horned owl—far in the distance. Shapeless things flitted through the air overhead, and her stomach clenched as images of bats rose in her mind. She despised bats, but she couldn't let herself be distracted by foolish fears. There was too much at stake to allow her own weaknesses to keep her from doing what must be done.

The moon and stars were shrouded by thick clouds, but she hadn't dared bring a lamp for fear the armed men who stood around the cabins might see her. Several of the men had bedded down along the edge of the woods, but Cameron and Taye had counted three armed guards walking the perimeter. She crawled for fear of being spotted walking out in the open. Close to the ground like this, she was almost invisible, protected by the shadows of the outbuildings and the shifting fog.

She laid her cheek on the ground and glanced behind her. Although she couldn't see Taye, Cameron sensed her friend following in determined silence. She, too, was dressed in breeches and a white shirt, but they'd tied a scarf around her waist to keep the pants up. Cameron was completely comfortable in the male clothing, but Taye had looked so uneasy when they'd dressed in her room that it had actually made Cameron laugh.

She paused and waited for Taye to creep up beside her.

"You sure this is going to work?" Taye whispered.

Cameron knew she had to make herself sound confident. Too many people, including Taye, were counting on her. "It's more than a quarter of a mile from the slaves' quarters to this corncrib." She indicated the building ahead of them with two fingers, like a soldier pointing out the enemy. "Surely the men will come to see what's on fire. Once they get there, they'll try to put it out."

"And that will give you time to set the slaves free?"

Cameron nodded. "And run. Now as soon as you set the fire, I want you to go the long way around the barn, through the grove of apple trees, down to the river. There's just the one boat, but it's a good size. We'll make as many trips across the river as we have to."

Cameron gazed at the corncrib built of vertical slats with spaces between them and gauged the distance from here to there. She sat up on her knees and handed Taye the tinderbox she had brought. "Be sure to have a good-size pile of husks. We want a big fire."

Taye nodded, pressing her lips together in an obvious attempt to be brave. "I'll see you by the river."

"See you by the river," Cameron whispered, lowering herself to her hands and knees. Once she reached the tree line she would be safe to get to her feet and run.

Cameron safely reached the grove of gum and hickory trees behind the slave cabins and there she waited in the darkness for Taye's fire. Knitting her hands together, she prayed silently that her plan would work. After she had found her brother unconscious on his bed, she had slipped down to the river. There she had found the single boat, a crudely made flat-bottomed vessel that was more like a raft, but it would work. All she needed to do was get everyone across the river. Then they would break into groups and head north toward the first stop on the Underground Railroad on the border between Mississippi and Tennessee. There had been no sign of Naomi or Manu. Cameron sighed, accepting the fact that the young girl was gone and that Jackson was not coming to her rescue. She was going to have to do this on her own.

Cameron smelled the smoke from the fire before she saw the flames. It was the biting acrid scent of a fire started from dry material that burned hot and fast. Just as the first flames shot into the air, Cameron heard one of the guards cry out.

"Fire!"

"Fire? Ya see it?"

"Jimmy D.," Jenkins called.

Cameron saw the men sleeping on the ground bolt to their feet, rifles in hand.

"Ya stay here," the leader told a man in a cap. "Keep yer eye on the negras whilst we see what's on fire."

Cameron had hoped all of the men would go, but she knew they could deal with one guard if they had to. She sprinted around the first cabin, still keeping to the shadows. The guards had made makeshift locks of wood that slid into panels so she didn't have to use the crow bar she had hidden in the woods.

Keeping one eye on Jimmy D., she lifted the timber that barred the door of the first cabin. "Shh," she whispered as she swung the door open, praying it didn't have rusty hinges.

She met with wide eyes huddled in the darkness.

"Missy Cameron," one of the men whispered. "It's Missy Cameron."

She recognized the face. "Bay, listen to me. The corncrib is on fire." She glanced behind her to see Jimmy D., his back to them, staring in the direction of the corncrib. "There's just one guard. Do what you have to, but don't kill him. He's got a rifle."

Bay, a strapping man in his early twenties, nodded solemnly. "What then, Missy?"

"Get everyone out and down to the river. There's a boat that will take you across. It's going to take more than one trip because one boat was all I could get. I have money for all of you, and several maps. There are people who can help you farther north."

"Da railroad," he murmured solemnly as if uttering the name of God.

She nodded, stepping out of his way.

While several men slipped into the darkness to subdue the guard, Cameron went to the next cabin. Other men she had released fanned out to open each door that housed the men, women and children. Fortunately they had been crowded together in only a few cabins. It would be faster getting them out this way.

As Cameron eased the door open and murmured a warning of silence, she met with Sukey's wide-eyed face. "Sukey," she whispered, reaching out to touch the hand that had soothed her when she had a fever and bandaged her scraped knees and burned fingers.

Sukey blinked. There was barely any recognition in her eyes. She looked tired and dirty. "Miss Cameron," she breathed.

Cameron gave the women the same instructions. When she heard a shuffle, she turned to see three men wrestling the guard to the ground. Not a word was uttered, and thankfully his weapon was not fired. "You must keep the children quiet," Cameron urged, stepping back to let the women pass. "Down to the river. Everyone has to get down to the river quickly."

The clearing between the cabins was suddenly a jumble of dark figures. The slaves moved almost silently out of the clearing, but Cameron could feel their fear. She could taste it on her tongue like the ashes that were beginning to filter through the air.

The clouds shifted in the sky and a beam of moonlight fell suddenly in the clearing. It was only then that Cameron spotted the lone woman left behind. She ran up behind Sukey and pulled her into the cover of darkness in the woods. "Sukey, come, we have to hurry," Cameron whispered urgently.

"My daughter," Sukey murmured. "Where is Taye?" She halted and her wrinkled brow furrowed. "Is she with her father?"

Cameron gave Sukey a little push. She had no idea who Sukey was talking about. No one had ever said who Taye's father was, but this was not the time or the place to discuss it. "Down by the river," she said. "Taye is waiting for us down by the river." She took her hand and began to run, forcing Sukey to run with her.

By the time Cameron reached the water's edge, another cloud had thankfully covered the quarter moon. It was so dark here in the woods that she could barely make out the dark forms of the slaves climbing onto the raft. She was amazed how quiet the children were, their hands held by parents, grandparents. Babies clung to their mothers' breasts, their eyes white and round in the darkness, but their mouth pursed in silence.

"Can't take no more," she heard one of the men say as two other men used a pole to push off in the lapping water. "Be back fer ya."

Cameron waited by the water's edge with the others, her hands clasped, her heart beating as hard as she knew the woman's next to her was.

"Cam," she heard someone call. She turned to the woods to see Taye running toward her. "My mother."

Cameron grabbed Taye's hand. "You mother is here, waiting for the boat to come back," she whispered. She met her friend's gaze, hating the thought of parting, but knowing that for Taye's own safety, she had to go. "You must go with her on the next boat."

Taye shook her head, clasping Cameron's hand tightly. "I won't leave you."

Cameron didn't want to tell Taye about Grant's plans for her. She didn't want to frighten her any more than she was already frightened. "You're in danger here," she whispered. "You must listen to me. You have to go north."

"We'll find the papers that freed me," she insisted. "With my papers, not even Grant can send me away. I know where they are, I think. The senator kept them in the secret compartment in his mother's writing desk."

Tears scratched the backs of Cameron's eyelids, but she didn't dare unleash them for fear that once she weakened they would never cease. She could hear the men and women clambering out of the boat on the far side of the river. Fortunately it was narrow here, and the boat would return in a moment to retrieve the others. Two more trips and they would all be safely across.

"Listen to me," Cameron said, squeezing both of Taye's hands in hers. "That is not the danger I speak of."

"Then what?" Taye looked into her eyes with such innocence that Cameron could barely bring herself to speak again.

"Grant," she breathed.

"Grant?"

Cameron lowered her gaze. "He fancies himself…attracted to you. If you will not submit, I am afraid—"

Taye pulled free and covered Cameron's mouth with her slender fingers. "It's all right," she whispered. "Don't make yourself say it. I know what he desires."

"You do?"

"For a long time now he has tried to bully me, bribe me into it." Taye's voice was low, quiet, but amazingly brave.

"I have been such an idiot," Cameron said louder than she intended. Several slaves glanced her way and she lowered her voice. "How could I have— I've seen the way he looks at you, but I honestly never thought he would dare—"

"Enough," Taye said. "Don't torture yourself this way."

"So you'll go north?"

"I'll take my mother and go, but only if you'll do the same."

"I can't leave Elmwood!"

"Why not? What's here now without the people we love? Nothing but shadows of what was." Taye's voice was amazingly steady now, and she sounded far wiser than her seventeen years. "There is nothing here now, Cam, but echoes of what will never be again."

Cameron stared in the direction of the house, wondering if Taye was right.

"We'll travel north together," Taye said quickly. "We'll go to the Stuarts. We'll all be safe there, you and me and Mama. We'll be safe from the slave hunters. Safe from Grant."

Cameron knew that by the time the war passed through Mississippi, little would be left of Elmwood. What her brother did not sell or take with him now would be stolen, and with no workers to plant and tend the soil, the fields would grow fallow and barren. Without the many men and women who cared for it, the house would soon fall into a pitiful state of disrepair. How could she live here alone? she wondered. Eventually what little coin she had left, after giving everything she could get her hands on to the slaves, would be gone, too. Why would she remain at Elmwood if her father was gone, her horses were gone, Taye and Sukey were gone?

And then she thought of Jackson. Images of his face spun in her head. The sound of his teasing male laughter tickled her senses…and then filled her with a strange warmth. Jackson was here somewhere now. Here in the South. If she went so far north, she would doubtless never see him again.

Was it Jackson Logan who still held her here? She was fascinated by that thought, but too overwhelmed by everything around her to really contemplate it.

The boat landed and more men and women hurried to board. They were growing anxious now, glancing over their shoulders, their hushed whispers growing louder, more frantic. A baby began to cry softly and it was quieted by its mother's breast.

In less than two minutes the boat was off again. One more load and all of the slaves would be across. She could still smell the thick smoke of the burning corncrib and prayed that Taye had built a big enough fire.

On the far side of the Pearl River, Cameron could already see two of the men passing out the maps and coins she had given them to the families. Small groups were fanning out, running into the woods. It would be easier for them to travel undetected to the closest stop on the Underground Railroad with fewer people.

Taye released Cameron to seek her mother who was standing at the river's edge clutching a simple cotton wrap the senator had given to her years ago. "Mama, we must go across. On the next boat."

"I don't want to leave my home."

Cameron watched sadly as Sukey, her own eyes cloudy with confusion, looked into Taye's eyes.

"I must remain here with your father," she said.

Taye looked to Cameron as if to say "she doesn't know what she speaks of."

"No, you have to come with me," Taye repeated gently but firmly. "You have to help me, Mama."

When Sukey made no response, Taye looked to Cameron. "I don't know what's wrong with her. She gets confused like this sometimes now, doesn't make any sense. Naomi could find no illness." Taye let her words fade into silence and into the darkness.

Taye gathered Sukey in one arm and gently steered her back toward the river. "There, there, Mama." She led her mother closer to the place where the boat would return for them.

"You don't understand," Sukey said in her familiar silky voice. "He will be so perturbed with me."

Cameron's head snapped around when Sukey uttered those last words. *"Be so perturbed with me."* God in heaven, that was what Sukey had always said about Cameron's father when Cameron had tried to convince Sukey to let her and Taye do something the senator wouldn't approve of.

"He will be so perturbed with me." The words rang in Cameron's head.

Could Taye possibly be the senator's daughter? Her father's child? Could Taye be her sister?

Shots rang out in the woods behind them and someone screamed. The clouds shifted again, as if by command of some ill being, and light suddenly flooded the spot where the last group of slaves stood waiting their turn.

"This way!" a man's voice shouted from the commotion of the woods.

Taye turned to Cameron, more frightened than Cameron had ever seen her in her life. Several of the slaves dove into the water and began to swim for the far side. A man and his wife scooped up their two children and ran along the bank.

"Halt and ye won't be shot," the voice shouted as a man broke through the woods into the clearing, swinging a rifle. More of the guards poured out of the woods.

"Get'm!" a man shouted, releasing the dogs.

"You there!" Jenkins shouted to the man and his family running along the bank. "Ya take another step, and I shoot the little 'ens first."

The family halted where they were.

Cameron took her eye off Taye and Sukey for no more than an instant, but when she turned back to them, Sukey was gone.

"Mama!" Taye shouted and started after her.

Cameron grabbed Taye's arm. "Stand still," she whispered harshly. "They won't dare shoot me." She took off after Sukey who seemed to be headed not for the water, not to escape, but back toward the house.

The single shot rang out. The sound of the baying dogs, even the insects in the forest, faded. Taye's cry barely registered. Cameron thought she felt the bullet in her own chest as it struck Sukey in the back.

"No!" Cameron screamed as she lurched forward, the only one who dared move. She caught Sukey as she fell, and as the two tumbled to the ground, it registered in Cameron's mind how much weight Sukey had lost. She had never been a big woman, but she weighed barely a feather now.

Rolling up and out of the leaves, Cameron slid her hand under Sukey's body and turned her over to look into her eyes. They were closed, but Cameron knew that even if they were open, they would be sightless. She had died before she hit the ground.

Taye crumpled to her knees where she stood, sobs racking her body.

Cameron kissed Sukey's warm forehead, then gently lowered her to the grass. The moonlight spilled onto them, and as Cameron withdrew, she realized that the strain she had seen on Sukey's face since the senator's death was at last erased. It tore Cameron's heart to think it, but Sukey seemed relieved, at peace.

Cameron strode toward Jenkins. "Pull the trigger again," she said softly, thrusting her face into his, "and I will kill you myself if it's the last thing I do on this earth."

Jenkins blinked. He said nothing, but Cameron sensed he was just a little afraid. "Round 'em up!" he shouted. "And find a way to get across that dammed river and get the rest of them. Mr. Campbell is going to have my ass for this, boys."

On the far side, the abandoned boat was beginning to drift downriver. Cameron prayed it would not come ashore on this side; it would give the others on the far side a better chance of getting away.

Cameron slowly walked to Taye and knelt in front of her, taking her in her arms as if she were a child. They did not speak, but clung to each other. Taye wept for the loss of her mother. Cameron wept because she did not know how she would protect her dear friend from her brother now.

19

It was midmorning the next day before Grant *escorted* Cameron to her bedchamber. He had been awakened by Jenkins at dawn and told of the slave rebellion and his sister's assistance. The slaves that could be caught had been rounded up and locked in the cabins, this time under more careful watch. Men with dogs were still searching for those slaves who had slipped into the night. Jenkins had locked Cameron up in one of the cabins with Taye and the slave women who had been recaptured. It was not until a fuming Grant appeared in the slave quarters in the morning, bleary eyed, that Cameron had been released from her prison.

No matter how Cameron had begged, Grant had not allowed her and Taye to bury Sukey in the family graveyard on the hill beyond the big house. Cameron had been forced, instead, to bury the beloved woman who had been like a mother to her, in the slave graveyard just beyond the slave quarters. Grant had allowed her only two men to dig the grave, and they had been chained at the ankles. When the terrible task was done, and Taye and Cameron had laid Sukey to rest without so much as a wooden marker, Grant had locked Taye in the slave cabin again. This time if anything caught on fire, or anything else suspicious happened, Grant had ordered that the guards could just set the cabins on fire and send them all to burning hell at once.

Cameron stepped into her bedchamber, exhausted and forlorn, and crumpled to her bed.

"You leave this room without my permission and I start killing negras, you understand me?" Grant demanded, scratching at a red welt on his cheek.

She covered her eyes with her forearm, fighting the tears she had been wrestling since Sukey's death. She realized that if she started to cry now, she would surely flood the Mississippi.

"You hear me?" Grant barked.

Cameron nodded. "What are you going to do?" she whispered. The room was overly warm, but she didn't dare open the drapes to open the windows. The beating sun would only make it hotter.

"What do you mean, what am I going to do? I'm going to sell them at auction tomorrow just as I said before you pulled your stunt and caused me to lose a great deal of money."

"Are you going to auction all of them?" she asked shakily, afraid to mention his previous intentions for the younger women, afraid to speak Taye's name.

"All of them."

Cameron was so tired that she could not think clearly. As her thoughts drifted, she wondered if perhaps Taye would be better to be sold as a slave. At least then she would be safe from Grant. Then, perhaps, Cameron could track her down later and prove she was a free woman, or merely help her escape.

Right now it was so hard to preserve any hope.

"Get some sleep," Grant ordered. "You look like hell. The auction is in the morning and we will be leaving immediately afterward. Jenkins and his men have agreed to stay here and see that the house is secured and everything else I've sold is picked up. We'll take a carriage to the Mississippi River where I've booked passage to Baton Rouge on a riverboat."

Cameron could not bring herself to ask who would accompany them or why. Amazingly, more than half the slaves had gotten away and scattered in the woods, but the others had been brought back to be sold. To be sold at auction and be separated from their husbands, perhaps even their children, was bad enough, but to degrade the women by selling them to a whorehouse was beyond her understanding. What had made Grant such an evil man? Why did he hate so much?

For the first time since her father's death, she was almost thankful he was gone. At least he could not see his son shame the family this way.

"So I will accompany you to Baton Rouge?" She was too drained for any emotion.

"I think it's best," he answered coldly. "At least for now. You and your actions are, after all, my responsibility."

She lifted her arm to glance at her brother from across the room. Even in the dim light of the shaded bedchamber she could see that he looked terrible, perhaps even worse than she. His eyes were bloodshot and his face was puffy, his mouth twisted in a frown. The welt on his cheek was swollen and angry.

It occurred to her that she should feel guilty for drugging him, but she didn't. She had saved Taye from his pawing, hadn't she? At least last night she had, she thought, her misery rising up in her throat to choke her.

"Can I not just stay here at Elmwood?" she asked despairingly.

"Not hardly." He rubbed his cheek again. "From your night's activities, it's quite obvious that you need stringent supervision. Of course, if our father had not allowed you to run so wild and unmannered," he continued with contempt, "you might not be such a burden to me now."

He backed out of the room, pressing his hand to his head. Cameron hoped he had one hell of a headache.

"I'll bring you something to eat later. Just remember, you dare step foot outside this door and Jenkins shoots a darky in the head. If he has to kill one, it will be your fault because I warned you. Do you understand me?"

She covered her eyes with her forearm and nodded.

"Do you understand me?" he ground out again, louder this time. "I didn't hear you."

"I understand," she said softly without opening her eyes.

Grant walked out of the room and closed the door, leaving her alone in her torment.

"What ya doin'?" Manu stood near the small fire he had built to cook the stolen potatoes. He watched Naomi closely, but she could tell he feared getting too near to her.

Naomi muttered under her breath in her mother's tongue and swept the sweet-smelling smoke she had made from a pinch of herbs toward her. Her voice was low, reverent of the gods who she knew drew near. "I'm callin' my magic," she said.

Manu took another step back, seeming to jump in his sweaty skin. "God a'mighty, woman! Ya know that mess, it scares me."

She breathed in the pungent smoke and smiled dreamily. That was one of the reasons she loved Manu so much. He was big and powerful; he could kill a man with his bare hands. Had. And yet he could admit that something frightened him.

Naomi reached into her sack and pulled out a gourd rattle. She shook it to a rhythm she heard only in her mind.

"What'cha doin' now?" Manu whispered.

"Callin' 'em. Ya hear 'em, Manu? Ya feel 'em drawin' near?"

Manu stared into the darkness as if he feared wolves. From where they camped, they could hear the steamers crawling down the Mississippi River. They could smell the mud of her steep banks and taste her waters.

"I don' hear nothin' drawin' near," Manu said throwing back his shoulders. "Don' hear nuthin' but my big ole belly rumblin' out a hunger."

She laughed softly and closed her eyes. She could feel them now, near her, guiding her. Manu went on talking. He spoke of how bad things had turned at Elmwood and that he wondered how soon before the same happened at Atkin's Way, but she barely heard him. As Naomi breathed in the smoke and opened her mind to the powers of life around her, she felt herself enfolded in the mighty arms of her mother's gods.

When she heard the voice she awaited, she lowered her head

in reverence. She shook her rattle and rocked on the heels of her bare feet. She parted her lips and sang words she did not understand…did not need to understand. The voice, a female voice, told her where she must go, what she must do. It did not matter what she wanted, all that mattered was the voice. You had to follow the voice.

She would have to follow the river….

The voice faded, the smoke drifted away. She silenced her rattle.

Naomi rose from the squatting position, not sure how much time had passed. Manu was digging the potatoes out of the coals.

"Eatin' time," he said with a wide, toothy grin.

She grinned back, pleased. She knew what she had to do now and that knowledge gave a girl power. "Eatin' time," she told Manu as she tucked her rattle away. "Then lovin' time." She brushed her hand across his face. "Then time for Naomi to fly."

The broad smile fell from his face. "What ya sayin', suga'?"

"I have to go to Baton Rouge." She pronounced it the way the voice had. She could speak a little French, taught to her by her mother.

"I don' know what yer talkin' 'bout. Manu ain' going to Baton Rouge. He ain' goin' nowhere but north."

She slid her hands over his bare chest, feeling the silken iron beneath her fingertips. "That's right. Yer goin' north to make sure my mama gets to the Tennessee line safely. Gets herself underground with the others."

His dark face fell as he realized what she meant. "But ya ain' goin'."

She shook her head. "Not yet. Soon, but not yet." She drew closer to him, pressing her body to his, letting his warmth and strength seep into her very bones. What she was about to undertake was dangerous, dangerous but had to be done. When she couldn't find the captain in Jackson, she'd come straight home to Elmwood. But she met Shem and some of the others in the night and they told her what had happened. Naomi hadn't known what she should do next. That was when she turned to the gods. But now she knew.

"Tell me what yer aimin' to do," Manu said, staring at her with big black eyes that were filled with love for her.

"I'm goin' on a little journey," she said. "Won' be gone but a few days. Then ole Naomi will just hike herself north and meet up with her man."

He shook his head. "I don' like it. Don' like it one bit."

She smoothed his cheek. "Didn' no one say any of us had to like it." She lifted on her toes and still he had to lean over to meet her lips. "Just sayin' it has to be done."

"I'll jest wait here for ya then," he whispered against her lips, seeming to know he would not be able to change her mind.

She shook her head. "Too dangerous. Slave hunters'll be crawling all over these woods soon. Ya gotta go north with the others."

Manu pulled her tightly against him and rested his head on her breast. His deep, manly voice cracked when he spoke again. "Thing is, suga', I don' know if I *can* go without ya."

Cameron slept until late afternoon and roused herself long enough to eat a little cold meat on bread that Grant brought her. After sponging some of the mud and grime of the night before off herself, and climbing into a nightgown, she slept again. Her dreams were fitful. Over and over she heard the gun blast and Taye's scream as Sukey fell. She heard the slave's baby cry before it was soothed by her mother. But mostly, she saw Jackson laughing, mocking her.

Why hadn't he come? she asked herself again and again, waking and then falling back into sleep. Why hadn't Jackson come to help her?

Cameron was so exhausted, so defeated, that she slept the night through. At dawn, she bathed with the rest of the water Grant had left her and dressed carefully. She wore a traveling gown of pale blue that was covered in soft ruffles and crisp ribbon. She donned a wide-brimmed straw hat with a matching blue ribbon, and found a parasol. By the time Grant knocked on her door, her trunk was packed and she was waiting by the window for him.

"Come in," Cameron called almost before she heard his knock. She had recognized his footsteps because of his limp. Besides, who else could it be? They were quite alone in the house, she and her monster of a brother.

Grant stepped into her room dressed smartly in gray pants and a matching coat. His waistcoat was pink and he was carrying a fashionable bowler hat beneath his arm. "Ah, I see you're ready. How good of you." He opened his arms. "And what a fetching sight you are, my dear sister."

He spoke as if none of the past had occurred, as if Papa were still alive, Fort Sumter had not been fired upon and the South was not going to fall. "I thought you could accompany me to the auction and then we would go. I'm anxious to see Baton Rouge again and be reacquainted with our Louisiana friends, aren't you?"

She glanced out the open window. In the distance, she could see the slave quarters. Jenkins and his men had herded the slaves out and chained the men together. The women and children stood in a huddle near one of the cabins, out of the sun. Among them she spotted dear Taye, still in Grant's breeches, moving from one woman to the next, comforting them.

"You will not reconsider?" Cameron asked.

"I will not." He fussed with the welt on his cheek that appeared even angrier this morning. "Now, you can come along and behave yourself, or you can wait for me until I am ready to leave."

Cameron met her brother's cold gaze. She was not a coward. She would watch the slave auction. She might not be able to prevent it, but at least she could stand there and bear witness to the injustice of it all. And she would be there for Taye. No matter what Grant did, she had to be there for Taye.

Grant picked up the parasol Cameron had left near the window and handed it to her, offering his arm as if they were on a morning outing.

"Shall we go, sister?" he asked cheerfully.

She snatched the parasol from him and walked out the door.

* * *

Taye stood in the shadow of the cabin, resting her hand on her forehead to protect her eyes from the sun. It was only June, but the sun seemed brutal. Life seemed brutal.

As Taye stood with her arm around one of the frightened slave girls, she watched Jenkins and his men. Nothing seemed quite real as she watched them line the male slaves up and then chain them to each other with leg irons.

Nothing seemed real as she gazed in the direction of the slave cemetery and saw the mound of fresh dirt from yesterday's burial. Taye did not allow herself to cry as she thought of her mother. Perhaps Sukey was better off, for if there was a heaven, surely the senator was there, surely her mother was at his side, smiling. Thinking back, Taye knew in her heart that, though she had always given her mother pleasure, it was the senator who had really brought out that radiant smile of Sukey's.

The young woman Taye held against her whimpered as one of Jenkins' men walked by them and made some crude remark. Taye tried to soothe her with soft words of encouragement, but what could she say that would give any genuine comfort?

The lower barnyard was filling with men in wagons and a few in carriages who had arrived for the auction. She had heard someone say that the auctioneer was already here and preparing to begin. Mr. Campbell had a riverboat waiting for him.

Taye watched, dull-eyed like the others, as the male slaves were ordered to march toward the stable where a makeshift platform had been built this morning to display them for sale. Behind the men, the women were herded and Taye followed, too stunned to do anything else. As she passed through the barnyard, she looked up at the big house that had once been her beloved home.

Was Cameron all right? Grant had been furious when he discovered that she and Taye had set the fire and freed the slaves.

She prayed he had not hit Cameron, had not hurt her. This wasn't her fault. None of it was. Cameron had only been trying to fulfill her father's wishes. She had only been trying to help those whom she saw as less fortunate than herself.

Taye, along with the other women, was ordered to stand to the left of the platform. The men were auctioned off first. She watched, her mind barely registering, as one familiar man after another was bid on and quickly sold. As she observed the sickening event, her mind drifted.

She remembered her mother laughing and dancing. She thought of Cameron on horseback, flying over a fence, her red hair whipping behind her, a grin on her face as if she could conquer the world.

Taye even allowed herself to think of Mr. Burl. Sweet, gentle Thomas. In the near two months since the senator's death and Thomas's disappearance, Taye had not allowed herself the liberty of thinking about him much. What good would it do her? For whatever reason, he was gone. She remembered how sincere he had been that night on the stairs when he confessed he had feelings for her. How could she have been so foolish as to rebuff him the way she had? Even knowing realistically they could never be together, why hadn't she been kinder? Why hadn't she told him how she felt about him when she had the chance? Now she would never have that chance.

It was not until the women started walking onto the platform that Taye spotted Cameron and shook herself from her dream state. Cameron was standing near a carriage beside Grant, her parasol over her head. She was wearing the pale-blue traveling gown that she was always trying to get Taye to try on. She had always said the blue would go so well with Taye's eyes.

Cameron stared intently at Taye. She did not speak, of course, but there was something in her eyes. Something beyond the sorrow. Was it hope? Was Cameron trying to tell her something? Was she trying to say that no matter where Taye was sent, she would come for her?

Taye dared a brave smile.

The young girl Taye had been trying to quiet had to be physically removed from Taye's arms when it came her time to be sold. Taye watched as she was led off, sobbing, to a waiting wagon.

Taye squared her shoulders. She would walk up onto the platform with her head held high. She would not cry. She would not show weakness, which she knew delighted these men. She would pretend to be Cameron Campbell.

Taye started up the rickety steps.

"Christ, not that one," Grant shouted from where he stood at the carriage.

The auctioneer glanced up, tipping his straw hat to see through the glare. Taye watched, oddly mesmerized by the sweat that trickled down from his temples over his wrinkled jowls. "What's that?"

"Her." Grant pointed impatiently with a walking cane. "The yellow. Get her off the auction block. She's not up for auction. She's mine and I'm taking her with me."

Taye did not know she had fainted until much later.

20

Midmorning the following day, Cameron found herself sitting on the edge of a low platform bed in a private berth, bathing Taye's face in cool water. The riverboat rocked gently, moving south down the Mississippi toward Baton Rouge, as if rocking the two women in its arms. Despite all Cameron's prayers for salvation of any sort, they would reach their destination tonight in time to disembark in the morning.

After Taye fainted on the auction block at Elmwood, Grant had ordered her loaded unceremoniously into the carriage. The three departed for the riverboat landing before the slave auction was over, before Cameron got to truly say goodbye to her beloved Elmwood and the people who had worked it so faithfully.

But Cameron had greater things to worry about than her own sentiments, which, in the light of recent events, seemed childish and self-centered. When Taye did not regain consciousness immediately after fainting, Cameron feared she had suffered some kind of head injury or that some terrible, life-threatening illness gripped her. Cameron had sat in the carriage as far from her brother as possible and cradled Taye in her arms. Eventually Taye woke, spoke sleepily to Cameron, then slipped into a deep sleep again.

As Cameron bathed Taye's forehead now, she realized that the poor girl was simply exhausted. She fainted in fear of Grant, or perhaps in relief of not being sold as a common slave. Once she was in the relative safety of Cameron's arms, she simply could not wake because she was so tired. That, added to the trauma of her mother's death, it was a miracle she was not seriously ill.

Taye's dark lashes fluttered and opened to reveal her pale, clear-blue eyes. "Cameron," she whispered.

Cameron smiled, relieved to see Taye at last fully awake. "Morning, sleepyhead."

Taye's gaze drifted across the small berth they shared. The room was small, no more than eight by six with a bed only a single pallet wide that they had had to share last night. But at least it was private. Not only had they not had to share the lodging with any other female passenger, but Grant had not entered the room either. He had spent the night in the captain's quarters drinking and gambling and would no doubt continue throughout the day and tonight.

Taye pushed her elbows back and sat up a little. "Where are we?" she murmured, still trying to acclimate herself. She sounded dreamy, as if her mind was still far away.

"The riverboat, puss. We're headed for Baton Rouge."

Taye's blue-eyed gaze met Cameron's, and she pressed her lips together. The tone of her voice had none of the life in it that Cameron knew so well. "I thought he was going to sell me there on the block, Cam. Odd thing is, I didn't really care all that much."

Cameron grasped Taye's slender shoulders and pushed her gently into the bed again. "Hush. I'll not hear such things out of your mouth."

Taye obeyed like a young child chastised by her mother and lay back on the pillow. She reached out with one hand and brushed Cameron's cheek with her fingertips. Her blue eyes were so poignant, so filled with sadness, that it made Cameron's heart ache.

"I wasn't completely asleep in the carriage," Taye whispered. "I heard what Grant said. What he was going to do. I heard you arguing."

Cameron's stomach fell. She had been trying to deal with one matter at a time, and the first had been to get some rest for Taye and to get her awake and eating, drinking something. Cameron hadn't allowed herself to contemplate Grant's evil intentions. The fact was that he intended to carry out his plans to sell Taye's virginity to the highest bidder at a notorious bordello in Baton Rouge known as the *Juchoir,* which meant The Chicken Coop in the language of the Creole. Apparently he had already sent word to the owner of the establishment, Peppin Toussant. The highest bidder would win Taye for the night, and then she would join the other ladies of the house to work nightly for the proprietor as his property. Grant had commented to Cameron with delight that Peppin thought a blue-eyed mulatto girl's virginity would fetch a handsome price. The proprietor insisted that Grant Campbell would be the talk of the town for providing such exciting entertainment as a virgin auction.

"I'll stop him, Taye. I swear I'll stop him. I won't let him sell you or your virginity in some whorehouse."

"It doesn't really matter," Taye murmured as if she were talking about someone else. "Mama is gone. Elmwood is gone." She smiled dreamily. "And my Mr. Burl is gone as well. No castles in the sky left now."

Cameron grabbed Taye's shoulders again and gave her a shake. "You listen to me," she said fiercely. "You must not give up. You have to fight. We cannot let him get away with this."

"It's his right, Cameron."

"It is not his right. Damn it, Taye!"

Taye cringed as if she feared Cameron might hit her and Cameron was instantly repentant for her outburst. Taye was like a small child right now, or an injured animal. She had to care for her gently and give her time to recover. When Cameron spoke again it was with the soft, reassuring voice she had used with her beloved Arabians or with a slave child.

"You are a free woman," Cameron said. "Grant has no right to sell you. Even if you were not free, he would have no right to sell what is only yours to give."

"I have no proof I am free." She lifted her lashes. "Unless

you had a chance to..." She let her voice and her hope fade when she saw Cameron's face.

They had never found the emancipation papers, but Cameron had found no opportunity to look for them again. "He wouldn't let me go into Papa's study before we left. I was hoping I could find your papers."

Taye rolled onto her side, presenting her back to Cameron. "It doesn't matter. None of it matters." Her voice was ethereal and haunting, a sound Cameron knew would take many years, if not a lifetime, to forget. In Taye's voice Cameron could detect the measure of each of her own failures. She could hear each like the singular, reverberating notes of a bittersweet Brahms composition.

But she would not fail this time. She might not have been able to stop the war or her father's death or the sale of Elmwood's slaves, but she would not see Taye sacrificed to Grant's twisted desire for revenge. And that's all it was, Cameron realized on the journey here. Grant was a miserable man who wanted what he could never have, what he could never be—and that was goodness. He could never have or be Taye, so he would ruin her, humiliate her, tear her down to his own level.

In the carriage yesterday Grant had ranted and raved. He talked of past slights made by Cameron, Taye, his father, even servants. Some Cameron recalled to have some truth to them, but others seemed entirely manufactured of petty jealousy and spite. She remembered clearly the day Taye had fallen into the millpond and she had rescued her. Cameron remembered her father shouting at Grant, but she remembered no lasting repercussions. The senator had recovered from his anger, which mostly stemmed from his fear of losing the little girl. But after that, Grant had never been the same. In the days that followed, at every turn her brother had imagined that others felt differently about him. He imagined that he was a coward, a man unworthy of respect, and it became a self-fulfilling prophecy.

Cameron got off the bed to fetch some bread and cheese and a little cool milk she had brought from the boat's kitchen.

Hoping to ply Taye, who was already too thin, with a little nourishment, she let the entire subject of Grant and what was to come in Baton Rouge go. Cameron would think of a way to save Taye from this fate.

Or she would give her life trying.

Baton Rouge seemed brighter, louder and more vibrant than Cameron remembered, though it had only been a year since she last traveled here with her father. The changes did not seem for the better to her, though. The streets, the passersby, even the shop windows, seemed gaudy and intemperate in the face of the onrushing tides of war. As the hired carriage carried her, a listless Taye and Grant toward their elegant town house on an exclusive tree-lined street, Cameron watched out the window.

Did no one here realize that men were fighting in the north? Did they not realize that men were dying in order to preserve the way of life Southerners had grown accustomed to, while others were dying to extend the right of freedom to all men and women?

Cameron rested her cheek on the windowpane, feeling as detached from the world as Taye looked. All day and all night she had racked her brain trying to figure out how she was going to get Taye out of this mess. She had still not come up with a viable solution, but she was putting together a plan to at least be there. Once in the whorehouse, she surmised there would be opportunities to escape. She would make an opportunity if she had to. Grant had already said the two women would be separated once they reached the town house and would not be permitted to leave their rooms. As such, they would not have the opportunity to confer and come up with any more fanatical attempts to escape him or his plans.

Cameron glanced at Taye who sat beside her, eyes open but seemingly unseeing. She reminded Cameron of Sukey in the days following the senator's death. Now that Cameron suspected that Taye might be her father's child, and therefore her sister, Sukey's behavior made even more sense. She had lost the man she had loved, the man who had fathered her beloved child.

Cameron patted Taye's hand. Taye was in no shape to hear of Cameron's suspicions, now. Even if she was, Cameron had decided to keep those thoughts to herself until she could further investigate them. There was a chance she would never know the truth. After all, the only two people who could really shed light on the matter, Sukey and the senator, were both dead.

Cameron squeezed Taye's hand bringing herself back to the problems at hand. Her half sister or not, Cameron loved Taye and she would not allow her to be sacrificed this way. As for Sukey's slow descent from depression to what seemed like near madness, Cameron simply would not allow Taye to surrnder to such a fate. She would get Taye out of this mess, out of Baton Rouge and north to safety. She didn't know how, but she would do it.

"Ah, here we are," Grant said, smiling as if they had just been on a Sunday carriage ride. "Home, sweet home." He glanced at Cameron, his tone cooling. He scratched at the welt on his cheek that now seemed to be festering. Wounds did that sometimes in the summertime.

"Upon our arrival," he continued, "you will go immediately to your room. She—" he indicated Taye "—will be cared for and prepared for her debut." Cameron ached to slap his detestable smile off his face.

But she had learned the hard way that the best way to control her brother was with honey and not venom—at least most of the time—so she nodded subserviently. "Whatever you think best," she said, hating the words as they came out of her mouth, but knowing they were necessary. She looked away to prevent Grant from seeing the loathing reflected in her eyes. "Whatever you want for now," she whispered to herself. "But our time will come."

For the next week, Cameron remained in her small but comfortable room in her father's elegant town house in Baton Rouge. She was all but cut off from the rest of the world, not seeing anyone but Grant and the house servants who were loyal only to him. She was busy scheming. Each night Grant invited her to supper in the parlor. She dressed carefully and attended him, pretending to be the sister he wanted her to be. Cameron did not see Taye, but she heard the hustle and bustle in the hall as a dressmaker and her attendants came and went.

Grant made no further attempt to seduce Taye, and for that she was thankful. In the state she had last left Taye, she feared her friend would not have the capacity, mentally or physically, to fight him off. Cameron had no choice but to bide her time and wait.

Just when she feared she would shatter for the waiting and worrying, Grant made an appearance at her door one afternoon a week after they had arrived. "I will not be available for supper tonight," he told her. He was dressed in a gaudy, expensive silk shantung coat of teal with breeches. His waistcoat was pink and his shirt and cravat lily white and overly ruffled.

Cameron's heart leaped in her chest but she kept her eyes averted for fear her brother would be suspicious. "And why is that? You do not usually go out until later in the evening, Grant."

He broke into a grin. "Tonight is our big night. Mine and Taye's."

Cameron's heart plummeted. "You know that I don't want you to do this," she said, fighting to keep her tone even.

"And you know I don't care what you think," he snarled. "She didn't want me, would not accept my genuine offer of *protection,* and it is now time the little negra gets her comeuppance." He self-consciously rubbed at the sore on his cheek. The whole side of his cheek was red and raw and the spot in the center was oozing. "It's time she be humiliated the way she has humiliated me."

"Could I say goodbye to Taye?" she asked quietly.

When he did not answer, she looked up. He seemed to wrestle with a response. She guessed he did not want to take the chance she and Taye would outsmart him again, but she also sensed that he wanted to share Taye's humiliation with as many people as possible. He wanted Cameron to feel Taye's degradation, wanted her to share in part of it.

"You can come down when I call you," he said finally. "Give me your opinion on the virgin dress I had made."

"All right," she said.

"And then you'll return to your room. You continue to behave as well as you have since we left Elmwood and perhaps I will take you out next week. To see a show, to dine. Would you like that?"

What I would like, she thought, would be to see you three feet underground. She nodded. "I would. I tire of being alone when I can hear so much around me."

He turned away and strode down the hall. "I'll call you down at seven."

All too soon the small case clock in Cameron's bedchamber struck seven in the evening and a maid rapped on her door. "Master Grant wants you," she said. "Downstairs in the parlor."

When Cameron stepped out into the hallway she saw a thin man dressed in working man's clothes sitting on the floor. He was trimming his nails with a large knife and at his belt, a nickel-plated revolver gleamed. Cameron didn't have to ask why he was there. She passed him without making eye contact. He had been there, of course, to protect Grant's *property*— her and Taye.

When Cameron walked into the parlor, Taye was already there. She stood with her back to the door, her hands at her sides. She was dressed in a beautiful pale-blue gown with a bandeau neckline and elbow-length puffed sleeves. White petticoats peeked from beneath the hem of the gown as did white ruffles at the edge of the sleeves and bodice. Her dark, glossy hair had been done up in a mass of tiny ringlets and even from across the room Cameron could smell the light scent of lilac perfume.

"Taye?" Cameron said, trying hard to keep her voice steady.

Grant sat on the settee, drink in hand, watching the inter-action between the two women with a detestable delight.

"Turn around, Taye," he snapped. "You'd better learn to obey your betters."

She obeyed without hesitation.

Much to Cameron's dismay, Taye appeared even more glassy-eyed than when she had last seen her the week before. She looked at Cameron, but she did not appear to see her.

"What do you think?" Grant asked, sipping his whiskey. "Quite fetching, isn't she? Peppin will be running the auction tonight. Did I tell you he says we'll get top dollar for her? A blue-eyed virgin mulatto doesn't come his way often, he says." Grant chuckled with delight.

She was indeed fetching, quite beautiful, in fact. The gown was a masterpiece of pale-blue satin and crisp white trim. She appeared virginal, indeed, and so young that it frightened Cameron.

Cameron rushed forward to put out her arms to Taye. She hugged her tightly, but Taye made no attempt to return the embrace. "Don't worry, I won't let this happen. Just be ready to run," she whispered quickly in her ear, hoping that her brother was too occupied with his delight to realize she had spoken to the girl.

Cameron stepped back, and as she did, she thought she caught a glimmer of recognition in Taye's eyes.

"So what do you think?" Grant said, draining his glass as he rose. "The gown, will it do?"

"It will do," Cameron answered, trying hard not to think of the ultimate purpose—to entice a man to bid and then rape Taye.

"Well, we're off. I've several places to stop before we make our debut at the *Juchoir*." He indicated that Taye should walk before him out into the front hall and she obeyed. "Now, none of your shenanigans," Grant warned, waggling a finger at his sister as he followed toward the front door. "Return to your room so Jules can keep an eye on you, and if you're a good girl we will go for a ride in the carriage tomorrow."

It was all Cameron could do to allow Grant to lead Taye

out the door and to the waiting carriage. But, filled with resolve, she turned on her heels and went up the steps.

It was amazingly simple for Cameron to slip out the window, over the small kitchen roof and into the alley without
the guard ever knowing she was gone. Thank goodness Grant
had insisted years before, when her father bought the town
house, on taking the room with the nicer view. With windows
on the main street, Cameron would never have been able to
escape the house without being seen.

Dressed in the breeches and shirt that she had hidden in the
bottom of her traveling trunk, and a pair of heeled slippers,
she followed the main street by way of the alley. It was almost
sunset and the humid Louisiana evening assaulted her nostrils
with a myriad of smells—rotting vegetation, mud from the
street, unwashed bodies. It was a heady perfume that seemed
to scent the entire town. Familiar with the streets of Baton
Rouge, she walked through the elegant neighborhood and into
the seedier side of town. In less than an hour she located what
she was looking for. After all, every day was wash day somewhere, wasn't it?

Cameron tried not to think about what she was doing, or
the risks, as she dressed in the stolen clothing in a woodshed,
taking care not to muss her elaborate hair creation or smear
the rice powder, rouge and eye color she had carefully applied
to her face before sneaking out her bedchamber window.
Without a mirror, she could not see herself, but she prayed
she looked the part she aspired to. With red petticoats and a
cheap showy lavender gown, the bodice pulled impossibly low
so that her breasts almost poured from the top, she prayed that
a country girl from Mississippi would blend in at the *Juchoir*.

Cameron had seen that kind of woman before. They were
everywhere on the streets here in Baton Rouge after dark, even
hanging out windows calling to the men who passed by below.
The trick was the attitude, though. She could dress the part,
but would she immediately be spotted for what she was, a rich
virginal Papa's girl who was used to fine gowns and bone
china?

Sticking to the alleyways as best she could, Cameron hurried to the street where the *Juchoir* was nestled among a row of bordellos. Here, men came to play cards, eat, drink and have their pick of women. Just the thought of Taye being brought here, being forced to do what these men would force her to do if Cameron did not succeed, made her sick to her stomach.

Taking a deep breath, telling herself she could play the part, Cameron walked out of the alley and onto the plank sidewalk. She practiced swinging her hips. She eyed each man as she passed him, throwing every ounce of proper street decorum she had learned out the window. She had not walked ten feet when a man passed and whistled under his breath. Before she reached Toussant's back door, two intoxicated men made her an offer if she would go back to the room with the both of them. Smiling to herself, she slipped into the rear door and found herself in the kitchen. At least she had managed the walk.

"God-a-sakes! What ya doin' back here, suga-pie?" A large black woman with a gleaming gold tooth peered around a great black stove. "Mr. Toussant find ya back here lazin' about, shirkin' ya duties and you'll be out on that pretty tail of yours."

Cameron blinked, stalled, trying to accept the part she was playing, not sure how such a woman would respond. She came around the stove. "He can toss me out on my tail for all I care," she said saucily, trying to sound as if she hadn't had the years of education her father had provided. "I been thinkin' 'bout goin' out on my own, anyway."

The black woman lifted a bushy eyebrow. "Well, ain't ya the little high missy. Now get out of my kitchen and get to work." She gave Cameron a push toward a door on the far side of the warm room, but the push was gentle and her voice was filled with compassion.

Cameron flashed her a sassy smile and walked through the door as if she were a tart every night of the week.

It didn't take Cameron long to find the main parlor. The moment she entered the wallpapered hall, she heard female laughter so light it sounded like glasses clinking together. She smelled cigar smoke and whiskey and ladies' perfume.

She slipped into the great room and a bearded blond man turned to her, his face lighting up. "Well, hello there, lovey." He brushed his lips across her painted cheek and she pretended to play coy. "And Toussant said he didn't have any real redheads here tonight. Christ a God, I'm going to have his ass. You're the cutest thing I believe I've seen this week. George Atwall of Biloxi, Miss, glad to make your acquaintance."

As she smiled, she turned her head to gaze into the room. She had not seen the new carriage Grant had purchased outside, but she wanted to be sure she knew the moment he arrived. She had overheard him bragging to Jules in the hall. The auction was to begin at ten but she was afraid he would arrive early to "show off" the prize of the night.

"Now what's your name, lovey?" the man with his arm around Cameron asked.

"Why, it's Tawny," she said in a silky voice as she ran her hand down his coat lapel.

"Tawny? Isn't that the sweetest name? You know I do believe I once knew a girl…"

Cameron ignored George as she gazed out over the smoky room. Grant and Taye were not here yet, which was good. She would have a little time to check the place out and make possible plans to escape.

While smiling flirtatiously, she counted the number of entrances and eyed the staircase. As she combed the room, she was suddenly startled. It couldn't be. She inhaled sharply, blinked, unsure she could trust her eyes.

Slowly her gaze narrowed and anger bubbled up inside her. That son of a bitch. Jackson Logan.

21

Cameron turned away quickly, feigning interest in the man beside her. Suddenly her heart was pounding, and she nearly laughed aloud at the absurdity of it all. She had climbed out a window, stolen clothes, and now pretended to be a whore, but it was the sight of Jackson Logan that set her adrenaline racing.

George went on talking about his business in Baton Rouge, and Cameron stole a glance in Jackson's direction. He was talking to two painted trollops, one a blonde, the other's hair an unnatural shade of black. He had not seen her—too busy with his ladies of ill repute, she thought with great annoyance.

Of course what business was it of hers who he kept company with? This was certainly no epiphany to her. Cameron knew very well what kind of man Jackson was—the kind that didn't deserve a decent woman and wouldn't recognize one if he came face-to-face with her.

The question was, now what did she do? She already knew she would have to keep well hidden from her brother. Could she avoid Jackson, too?

The smart thing would be to ask for his help. She hated the thought of it, especially when he hadn't come after she had sent Naomi for him. If only he had answered her plea at Elm-wood, none of this would have happened.

George leaned close and whispered something lascivious in Cameron's ear. A few weeks ago she would have been shocked, but now she just laughed huskily, paying no mind to his words whatsoever. Just play the part, she told herself. Consider your options carefully.

If Cameron was honest with herself, fair with Jackson, she could not hold the fact that he had not come to Elmwood against him. Cameron had no way of knowing for sure if Naomi actually had tried to find him in Mississippi. Even if she had, perhaps he had already come here.

She glanced at Jackson again. The blond tart had cozied up to him and was handing him a drink. She wore a black-and-pink lace dress that nearly bared her nipples, and her face was heavily made up with rouge and dark kohl eye pencil. Her hair was a mass of yellow-blond tight curls, decorated with a small black feather headdress. Why, the little floozy! Cameron couldn't help but see the way she looked at Jackson with those big brown eyes of hers, enticing him to join her upstairs.

Cameron glanced at the winding staircase that men and women, linked arm and arm, ascended. She knew what went on in those rooms, and she could imagine the lascivious and carnal acts that must imprint the very walls of this den of iniquity. Of course she couldn't help but see the way Jackson looked at the blonde, either, all princely smiles and gallant flirtation. He was a libertine, a blackguard of the worst sort, treating these shameless strumpets as if they were gentlewomen at a respectable ball rather than sluts in the parlor of a bordello!

As Cameron watched Jackson out of the corner of her eye, she couldn't keep herself from contemplating why he came to places like this. Against her will she felt a prickle of sorrow. Why couldn't Jackson be satisfied with a decent woman from a respectable family? Why could he never be satisfied with her?

Cameron turned to George from Biloxi, who was now trying to kiss her in earnest. "Excuse me, fella," she said with a come-hither smile. "I think I hear someone calling me, but I'll be right back, I warrant you." She patted his chest and then smoothly slipped out of his arms.

"Wait!" The man stumbled after her, but thankfully, a tart

dressed in peach and cream grasped his arm and spun him around. ''Where you think you're goin', mister?'' she purred.

As Cameron sashayed across the crowded parlor that smelled of cigar smoke and sexual tension, she told herself that she could not allow her own resentful feelings for Jackson to get in the way of saving Taye tonight. If there was any way this hell-rake could assist her, she had to humble herself before him and ask for that help. She would give him a piece of her mind for being in a disgusting place like this later, when she and Taye were free from Grant.

The question was, how did she get him alone to talk to him? The answer was obvious. *Play the part.*

Cameron strutted toward Jackson and his attendants swaying her hips seductively. He was seated in a chair of brocaded blue silk that sported wide arms. The blonde sat on one arm while the dark-haired woman sat on a stool at his feet, her dress pulled up so high it was a wonder her nether parts weren't chilly. Cameron eyed the black lace stockings as she slid onto the arm of the chair opposite the blonde.

''Hello, handsome,'' she said huskily, giving Jackson a gentle nudge with her bare shoulder.

''Well, hello to you, sweetheart. I don't believe I've had the pleasure—'' As he turned his head to look into her eyes, she saw the shock of recognition register and she wondered for a frightened moment if he would give her away.

Then, thankfully, infuriatingly, his facial expression changed to one of amusement. ''Of making your acquaintance,'' he finished lazily.

She was relieved that Jackson had the good sense to realize he mustn't let anyone know who she was or that she didn't belong here. She knew in her heart that he might toy with her a bit, but he would not put her in any danger.

Cameron couldn't believe she was really here, really doing this. Thank goodness her father was not alive to see it.

She tried to smile seductively, lowering her lashes the way she had watched some of the other women do. She thrust out her lower lip slightly in a pout, knowing others were watching her, too. She couldn't rouse any suspicion. "Well, we'll just have to right that wrong, won't we, luv?"

The blonde frowned. "Who are you? I haven't seen you here before."

Cameron fought a sense of panic in her chest. She lifted a brow, thinking quickly. "Tawny. Why, who are you?" she asked equally antagonistic.

"Well, I'm Lacey, Lacey Silk, of course. Everyone knows Lacey."

Cameron slid her arm over Jackson's broad shoulder, her motion slow and, she prayed, seductive. She had to get him alone and tell him what was happening. She had to get him to help her. "Well, everyone will soon know Tawny, too," she challenged.

"You've got that right, sister," Jackson quipped, enjoying this exchange between Cameron and the tart entirely too much.

Cameron slid her hand behind his neck to the soft place beneath where he tied his hair in a queue as if in a caress...then she pinched him.

He gave a little start and she lowered her head to gaze into his gray eyes. She had to fight the impulse to snicker. "What's say we go elsewhere?" Cameron purred. She fingered his neat queue, trying hard not to take any pleasure in the feel of his silky hair or the scent of his clean skin...trying to deny the thrill of danger that made her feel more alive than she'd ever felt before.

He lifted a dark brow. "A place where we can be alone?" his husky voice teased. "Where we can get reacquainted, you mean, *Tawny*."

Jackson had drawn so near that if she leaned a fraction of an inch, she could brush her lips to his. Heavens, what she would give to taste that mouth on hers right now. She knew it was absurd, but it was an absurd moment in life, wasn't it?

"That's what I was thinking," she breathed, unable to tear her gaze from his.

"Hey, hey, wait a minute." Lacey leaped up from the arm of the chair. The black-haired woman got to her feet, backing out of her companion's way.

"I don't know who you are or what you think you're doing, but I got dibs on this one, sister." She hooked her thumb, looking more like a cattle driver than a whore now. "So you had best move your light skirts along," she threatened.

Cameron's breath caught in her throat and she glanced quickly at Jackson. He still sat in the chair, his arms now crossed over his chest.

"So who says you got dibs?" Cameron asked, settling one arm on her hip.

"Who says? Says me!" Lacey took a step forward and gave Cameron a shove.

There was a murmur of interest in the room. Cameron could see that she and Lacey were drawing the attention of the other patrons and working girls, now. But what choice did she have? She didn't have time to wait while Jackson rolled with a whore. She had to get him upstairs and speak with him alone right away.

Cameron gave a push in return, and the moment Lacey moved, Cameron reacted. Lacy threw herself at Cameron, but Cameron sidestepped her just in time to make the girl miss and tumble to the fringed Turkish carpet.

Lacey gave a screech, rolled and scrambled to her feet in a flurry of pink petticoats and foul curses. "Why you uppity bitch! I'll show you!"

Cameron balled her hands into tight fists, and prepared to defend herself while the onlookers howled and stamped the floor.

"Hey, hey, hey, what's going on here?" A thunderous man in a red silk dressing gown with an embroidered dragon across the front came huffing over. A fat cigar protruded from his mouth that oddly looked to Cameron as if it had been painted with rouge.

"Peppin, my friend." Jackson shot out of his comfortable seat, seeming to realize he had better put an end to this now before Cameron caused a real scene.

Peppin Toussant, the proprietor, broke into a grin. Yes, his lips were most definitely rouged.

"Why, Capitaine Logan, I did not know you had arrived."

The giant of a man spoke with a French accent that was heavily accentuated by local dialect. He offered his hand warmly as Jackson stepped between Cameron and the furious, panting Lacey.

"Good to see you again, Peppin."

"And what do we have here?" Peppin asked, looking from Lacey to Cameron. When he saw Cameron, his gaze registered that he didn't recognize her. "Just hired by Matty?" he asked.

Thankful for the pretext, Cameron nodded.

"The bitch is tryin' to steal my john!" Lacey said.

Peppin silenced her with a look, then returned his attention to Jackson, smoke from his cigar curling around his balding head. "My girls fighting over you again, eh?"

Lacey's eyes bulged, and her face reddened to an angry brick color. "He was mine first and then that red-haired bitch came along!" she insisted.

"Now, now, Lacey, *mon amour.*" Peppin held up a meaty hand and the girl was immediately quiet. "I am quite certain we can settle this amicably, can't we, Capitaine Logan, *mon ami?*"

"*Oui,* absolutely," Jackson said. He reached out with both arms to pull Cameron and Lacy toward him. "I'll take both."

The room burst into cheers and ribald laughter, and men and women began to turn away, returning to their drinks, conversations and flirtations.

Peppin lifted an eyebrow that, upon closer inspection, also appeared to be painted. "Your shipping business must be doing well."

"And I anticipate it will do better with the war." Jackson winked. "So if you'll excuse us." He started to turn toward the staircase, leading both the whore and Cameron with him.

Cameron tried to pull away. She'd be damned if she was going upstairs with them! But Jackson grabbed her wrist and gave a tug that told her he would not release her and that she was going up the stairs one way or another.

"Take me to your room," Jackson told Lacey quietly. "You'll be paid well."

The blonde pulled away from Jackson and flounced up the

staircase ahead of him. "I'd best be, for doublin' with that bitch."

Cameron's eyes widened with anger and Jackson tugged on her arm again. "Let's go, shall we, *Tawny?*" he said under his breath. "Before you bring any more attention to yourself."

Cameron didn't want to go upstairs with them, but she knew she had no choice. Time was running out. According to the china case clock on the mantel in the parlor below, they had little more than an hour before Taye's auction would begin.

Cameron and Jackson followed Lacey down a long hallway that was lined with closed doors. As she hurried to keep up, she tried not to hear the giggles, the deep rumbling male voices or what sounded distinctly like bouncing bedsprings. Sweat beaded above her upper lip. If she had the time to contemplate the sounds, she'd be mortified.

"This way." Lacey pushed open a door at the end of the hall near a back stairway.

Jackson let Cameron enter first. The room looked much like Lacey's gown, all black-and-pink ruffles that Cameron found suffocating in the small room. The window was closed and draped with black velvet, the smell of the cheap rose toilet water almost more than she could bear.

Jackson closed the door with Lacey inside and reached into his coat for his money clip. "Thank you so much, sweetheart, but what I need you to do now is make yourself scarce for a while." He began to pluck bills from the wad of cash he held.

Lacey arched a plucked brow with immediate interest. "Ya don't want me to…you know." She indicated the bed.

"Not tonight, sweetheart." He continued to pull out bills. "Honestly, Tawny and I have known each other a long time and we still have a little…*unfinished business,* shall I say?"

"So ya don't want me, but you want to pay me?" She stared at the bills in her hand and then wrinkled her powdered nose. "Ye ain't going to kill her and make a mess in my room, are you?"

He glanced at Cameron as if the thought had crossed his mind. If she had had anything to throw at him, she would have.

"I'm paying you to keep your sweet mouth shut," Jackson said, "and to make yourself scarce for the next hour or so."

"Ahh." She nodded in understanding.

"Can you do that?"

Lacey grinned slyly. "For another bill or two, I think I can find myself a cup of coffee down in the kitchen and get off my feet."

He added three more bills to the pile and she slipped out the door. "Good night," he called, still playing the gallant.

"Night, sweety," she said all honey and sugar now.

The moment she was out in the hall, Jackson closed the door and threw the bolt.

Cameron lowered herself to the edge of the bed in relief. "Oh, thank God you're here, Jackson." She covered her face with her hands.

"What the hell are you doing here? Another one of your games, Cameron? Dressed like a whore?" He walked to a table covered in a large pink lace doily and poured himself some brandy Lacey kept for customers.

Cameron lowered her hands to look at him. All at once she was intensely aware of how tiny the ruffled, velvet wallpapered bedchamber was, and how close to her Jackson stood. She was intently aware of all the emotions she had kept locked up inside her these last few weeks.

"Oh, Jackson," she cried out suddenly. "So much has happened, such terrible—"

Cameron didn't know if she flung herself into his arms or he grabbed her. She didn't know if she lifted her chin to kiss him or if he crushed his mouth to hers. It didn't matter. The only thing that mattered now was Jackson's mouth, his touch. She had been so lonely, so lost, that she craved the human contact. She craved the taste of him, the feel of him.

"Jackson," Cameron moaned, parting her lips to welcome his tongue.

He kissed her roughly, deeply, turning her so that they fell onto the lace-covered bed.

"Mother of God, I've tried to forget you," he muttered,

running his hand through her hair and covering her mouth with his again.

Cameron was suddenly in a frenzy to be kissed and to kiss. She ran her hand over the back of his head, yanking out the small ribbon that kept his hair neatly tied back. It fell in a dark, silken curtain almost to his shoulders and she threaded her fingers through his hair, pulling him closer.

Jackson pressed his lips to the pulse of her throat and lifted his hand beneath one breast.

Cameron moaned and covered his hand with hers, guiding him. Her breasts ached to be touched, her nipples straining against the fabric of her undergarments.

Jackson sat up for a moment and yanked off his coat, flinging it across the room. Cameron grabbed his shoulders, lifting up on the bed to meet his mouth again.

Covering her face with fleeting kisses, he pulled on the low neckline of her gown and it fell easily over her shoulders.

"I can't tell you how many times I've dreamed of this," he whispered huskily. His mouth drew a damp, hot trail over the swell of her breast and she thrust her chest outward until her hard, pink nipple brushed his lips.

Jackson caught her nipple between his teeth and gently tugged. She moaned, shocked by the guttural sound of her own voice. Shocked by her desire for him. Her heart was pounding, her pulse racing. All the blood from her head seemed to be draining lower, until it pulsed between her legs.

Somehow Jackson managed to pull her dress over her head. She jerked off his cravat, his shirt, and dropped them to the pile of discarded clothing on the floor. He yanked off her corset cover. Her fingers found the laces of the corset and both fumbled with the ribbons, fingers tangling as they tried to bare her naked flesh.

Cameron laughed, so desperate for his touch that tears welled in her eyes. He gently kissed the flesh above the ruffle of the corset and removed the last of the fabric between them. In the flurried passion of the moment, it was the sweetest thing he could have done.

"Cameron, Cameron," he murmured, his voice husky with desire for her, warm in her ear.

She looped her arms around his neck and lay back on the plump lace pillow. She wore nothing but stockings and pantalets, and he nothing but his tan breeches. She ran her hands over his bare, muscular chest in awe of the hard, firm flesh of a man's body. Of his body. How many times had she dreamed of this moment, tossing restlessly in her sleep, imagining these moments?

Jackson suckled one nipple after the other, and then dragged his hot mouth across her bare belly. As she lay back on the pillow, lifting her arms to grasp the headboard, she knew she would not stop him this time. Since that day years ago when they had first met on the elm drive outside her father's home, she and Jackson had been destined for this. Destined for this since time began.

Jackson grabbed the waistband of her pantalets and she lifted her bottom off the bed, wiggling out of them. The last rays of sunset had fallen beneath the rooflines of Baton Rouge but Cameron could still see Jackson in the dim light that came before true darkness. She opened her eyes to watch as his hair fell around his face as he lowered his mouth, blazing a trail of burning kisses over her navel and lower to the triangle of bright curls.

Cameron let her eyes drift shut and swung her head to the side. A moan of anticipation escaped her lips as his thumb and fingers found the source of her pleasure. She lifted her hips to meet his touch. He circled her, entered her for moisture and then circled again. His pressure was light and steady. When he lowered his head again, she couldn't tell what was his mouth and what were his fingers. It didn't matter, nothing mattered but the pleasure that coursed through her and filled a desperate void in her heart.

Cameron heard herself cry out with pleasure. He halted his motion and rested his cheek on the mound of curls. Cameron reached down and ran her hand over his head in a caress of thanksgiving. Then, to her surprise, to her delight, he began to touch her again. She thought the waves of joy had crashed around her and drifted to sea again, but it was only an ebb in the tide.

He stroked he, teased her until she was once again on the edge of the precipice. Only then did Jackson slip out of his breeches and cover her body with his. Cameron was beyond thought, beyond reason. She felt his rigid member against her leg and was shocked by its size. Still…hesitantly…she parted her thighs, the need inside her more overwhelming than her timidity.

He slipped inside her and she cried out in joyous discovery. So it was for this that men and women died and wars were fought and civilizations crumbled.

He began to move inside her and she easily picked up the rhythm that now seemed to be their own. She drew her nails down his back, fearing she scratched him, but unable to help herself.

He whispered her name in her ear and his breathlessness sent trills of pleasure through her. He wanted her, he needed her. Could he possibly love her?

Cameron wanted it to go on forever. She wanted the world and all of her troubles to end here. But she could prolong her own peak no longer and the moment she cried out, clutching Jackson in ecstasy, he gave a moan. He thrust one last time and then was still.

Cameron couldn't open her eyes. She was overwhelmed by the ripples of pleasure that still washed over her. She was even more overwhelmed by the emotion Jackson had filled her with with each thrust. Again, the word *love* came into her head. Heaven help her, she was in love with him…still.

Jackson rolled onto his side on the soft bed and pulled her into his arms. She moved to get up but he caught her by the waist and dragged her back, squirming naked in his arms. "Just one moment longer," he whispered in her ear, his eyes half shut. "Let me hold you another moment before all hell breaks loose." He rolled onto his back, settling her head on his chest. "Which I know it will," he teased before she could protest. "It always does when the two of us are in the same room together for more than five minutes."

Cameron wanted to jump, to get dressed. She didn't know how much time had passed. She needed to think of Taye, needed to get Jackson to help her come up with a plan to save her friend.

Later, when she had the time, she would try to sort out what she had done here on this bed and what she had felt...still felt, if she was willing to admit it.

Cameron gave a sigh as she relaxed. She could feel his heart pounding, his heavy breathing, but both were slowing now.

He kissed her forehead and the gesture seemed amazingly tender. If only this could last forever.

But it could not.

Cameron drew her palm over the flat of his stomach, fascinated by the feel of his muscular flesh. "I need your help, Jackson," she said quietly. "Grant is going to auction Taye's virginity here tonight and we have to rescue her."

"I know."

Cameron lifted her head to stare into his gray eyes that were unreadable at the moment. She lifted a brow, her ire rising. "You *know*?"

He gave her a boyish, crooked grin. "Well, why else would I be here?"

22

"You *know?*" Cameron leaped off the bed as if it were on fire. "You know, you no good son of a— You cad!" She yanked a lacy pink pillow out from under him and struck him as hard as she could with it.

Laughing, he threw up his arms to protect himself from her onslaught.

She hit him again and again with the pillow, growing more furious with each strike. "How could you let me go through all that downstairs? I could have been caught! That awful woman could have hurt me! How could you let me think I had to get you alone to tell you? How could you let me come up here and…and…" She stared at the rumpled bed and his glorious naked body stretched out in front of her. "Aren't you going to say anything?" she demanded.

"Well, I must admit, I did want to tell you that you make a most fetching whore. The best I've ever seen."

"Ohh!" she groaned in livid frustration. "You!" She threw the pillow at him. "You *truly* are no gentleman."

He laughed, tossed the pillow aside and climbed out of the bed. Cameron turned away from him and wrapped her arms around her waist, wanting to cry but too angry for tears. It seemed as if all she had done for the last two months was cry.

"Ah, Cam, come on." He walked behind her and put his arms around her waist, pressing his groin to her bare buttocks. She groaned at the heat that rose in her face in response.

"Leave me alone." She pushed him away with her elbows. "Help me get dressed." She began to scoop up discarded clothing and throw it onto the bed. "We have to get downstairs and figure out how we're going to get Taye out of this mess."

"Whatever you say." He stepped into his tan breeches and tucked himself neatly inside before working the buttons. "You're the master, Cam, and I am but your slave."

She narrowed her tawny cat eyes angrily. "You just wait until I have the time to give you a piece of my mind." She threw her slipper at him and then sat down on the bed to pull on her silk stockings.

Amazingly, the clock was just striking ten when Cameron and Jackson descended the stairs of the *Juchoir.* The parlor was filled now beyond capacity with men all smoking cigars and holding glasses of drink in their hands.

"Are these men all here to see Taye?" Cameron whispered.

Jackson tightened his grip on her hand. "It's going to be all right."

She lifted her lashes to meet his gaze. She was still angry with him for deceiving her the way he had, but she knew the only way to beat Grant was to join forces with Jackson. This had to be about Taye, not about her and Jackson. "You're sure this is going to work?"

"The best plans are the simplest," he assured her as they entered the room. "Believe me."

Cameron turned in the direction of a great commotion near the entry hall.

"Here she is at last!"

Cameron recognized Peppin Toussant's voice, though she couldn't see him.

"Step back, gentlemen, and give our guest of honor some room."

Cameron and Jackson remained in the rear of the parlor near the staircase, and as the men moved back, they pressed against the papered wall. She could see nothing but men's coats and their heads as they strained to see Taye, no doubt.

"Is she there?" Cameron whispered, holding tightly to Jackson's hand.

"She's there. Grant, too." His voice was now angry. Ominous.

"Does she look all right?"

"She looks scared, but she seems unharmed."

Cameron squeezed her eyes shut, praying this would be over quickly.

Taye was lifted onto a small stool so that the men who would bid on her could get a better look. Cameron tried to remain hidden by all of the bidders while trying to get a glance at Taye's face. When she finally caught a glimpse, she wished she had not. Taye's pale-blue eyes were glazed, her mouth rigid.

Everyone was talking at once so that the noise was nearly unbearable. Cameron tried not to listen to the lewd comments, but she knew her face reddened with embarrassment. She was ashamed, not for herself, not even for Taye, but for her father's memory, that he could have sired a son as despicable and depraved as Grant.

Jackson slipped his powerful arm around Cameron and lowered his mouth to her ear. She shivered and closed her eyes for a moment, comforted by his touch. "You need to slip out the back and through the kitchen the moment the bidding begins. The carriage I hired has two bays with those white feather things on their heads." He made an annoyed gesture. "Have the driver pull around to the kitchen and wait there."

"You're certain you can escape out the back without anyone seeing you?" she asked.

"I checked out the place yesterday as soon as Naomi told me what had happened."

Cameron's eyes widened. "Naomi found you?"

He gave a nod, looking out over the crowd as Toussant gave instructions on how the auction would be run. "How else could I have known?" He didn't meet her gaze as he studied the crowd carefully.

"You didn't tell me that Naomi found you," she whispered, exasperated.

He didn't look at her; his attention was focused on the noisy room. "You didn't ask. When I wasn't where you expected me to be, somehow she found her way to Baton Rouge." Jackson's arm tightened around her. "The bidding has started," he whispered. He gave her a pat on her bottom. "Go, bring the carriage around. We'll meet you and head for my ship. Naomi is already waiting there. I have a feeling we'll be pulling away from the dock rather quickly when your brother and Toussant realize they've been duped."

Jackson accepted a glass of watered brandy a chippy offered him. He listened as the bidding began. He wanted the others to get started, and then he would step in once he knew his competition. As he leaned against the wall and tried to appear casual, his thoughts kept slipping back to Cameron. He couldn't believe his good luck. He had been so certain he had lost her the day he left Elmwood when the senator was buried. And then, at the Hitches' party, she had annoyed him so greatly that he had almost been glad to let her go. Over the following days he had practically convinced himself he was better off without her. His new venture was dangerous; he had no right to drag Cameron into it. He didn't need to be saddled with a woman right now, a woman he had to worry about. He already had the weight of a nation on his shoulders. But then there she was in his arms, almost begging him to make love to her. Jackson was strong of constitution, but not that strong. Even his sense of honor had limits.

The bidding passed seventy-five dollars and the room began to grow lively. Jackson sipped his brandy and forced himself to think about what was happening here and not of Cameron. Not of Cameron naked in his arms, not of the sweet, honeyed taste of her, or the scent of her silken skin. He would have to take her on his ship with him. He couldn't leave her and Taye here. Perhaps they could sort things out then.

"I've a bid of eighty dollars," Peppin Toussant declared. "Going once…"

Jackson caught a glimpse of Taye's pale face. Christ, she was barely more than a child. How could that little sniveling bastard Grant do this to a girl he had grown up with? Hell, Taye was practically his sister. How could he do this to the good Campbell name? The senator would have horsewhipped the boy for suggesting such an evil.

Grant strutted back and forth in a suit of poor taste in front of the girl, puffing a thin French cigar as if he were some banty rooster. If Jackson could only get his hands around that pervert's scrawny neck, he would ring it as if the coward were a rooster destined for Sunday dinner.

"Going twice…"

"One hundred dollars," Jackson drawled lazily, remaining with his back against the wall.

The crowd of men and their fancy ladies turned to see who the new bidder was. Heads bowed as gossip was passed. He was notorious in these parts, which was a good thing. It would serve him well in the war. Men thought him more than a little dangerous, and that was just the way Jackson wanted it.

Toussant grinned, patting his massive stomach. "One hundred dollars to Capitaine Logan."

"Captain Logan?" Grant yanked his cigar from his lips, craning his neck. "Is that Captain Jackson Logan?"

"*Oui.*" Toussant belly-laughed. "Who else would have the balls, eh?"

The crowd laughed with him.

"No!" Grant hustled up to Toussant. "I won't sell her to him. Absolutely not." He squealed like a stuck pig.

Toussant turned to Grant, looming over him a full head. "She is not yours to say *oui* or *no*. You sold her, sir. The moment you stepped foot on my premises, she was mine. We had a deal." He spoke with a jovial smile on his face, but his tone was steely.

Grant took a step back.

"Anyone else for this fine piece of Mississippi fluff?" Toussant called, taking Taye's hand to kiss it gently.

Taye remained perfectly still, staring at the men who crowded around her, but not seeming to hear them or see them. She has the presence of a queen, Jackson thought, some dark Biblical queen with the face of an angel.

"Gentlemen, gentlemen, surely you won't lose such a prize without making a bid," Toussant urged. "Do I have a hundred and ten?"

"One hundred and five," called an aging Creole. "She will do nicely for my boy."

"Do I hear one-ten?" Toussant looked around the room. "Captain? Will you let her go for a mere five—"

Jackson nodded. "One twenty-five, gold, and that is my final bid."

A cheer rose up among the men. Several of the ladies oohed and aahed with delight.

"Going once, going twice, the virgin is sold for one night and one night only, sir."

"He must remain here," Grant babbled. He had some kind of festering sore on his face that was quite disgusting. "The agreement was that the winner would stay here under this roof!"

Toussant took Taye's hand and helped her off the stool. She moved mechanically like a sleepwalker who would not waken. "Meet in the back, sir, and we will make our exchange," Toussant instructed Jackson. "Cat for gold." He laughed and others laughed with him.

Jackson pushed his glass into the hand of a young woman passing by. "Thanks, sweet." He pulled his moneybag from inside his coat. He handed the money to Toussant without counting it and took Taye's hand. If she recognized him, she gave no indication. "Thank you so much, sir. It is a pleasure, as always, to do business. And now if you will excuse us, we have an evening of entertainment planned."

Toussant held the sack of gold in his hand, measuring its weight. "Enjoy, Capitaine."

Logan turned away from the proprietor, almost running into Grant.

"You had better not be up to anything," Grant sneered, looking more like a weasel than a man except that he had put on weight since Jackson last saw him. He looked like a stuffed weasel.

Jackson ignored him, headed for the staircase. Taye walked

beside him taking tiny, delicate steps. She was so thin, so pale, that her beauty almost seemed translucent. Thank God Naomi had reached him. A night in the hands of one of these men and Jackson feared she would not have survived.

"Do you hear me?" Grant whined, following as fast as he could, dragging his bad leg behind him. "She is this man's property now. He does not take lightly to—"

At the bottom of the elaborate carved staircase, Jackson turned sharply to face Grant. "You plan on coming with us upstairs, Grant?" He lifted his upper lip in derision. "No, you might just like that, you sick bastard. You look like one who's better at watching than doing. You'd better be gone when I come down. You understand me?" He presented his back to him. "Let's go, Taye," he urged gently. "That's right, just one step at a time. Good."

When Jackson turned at the corner of the upstairs landing he saw Grant still standing at the bottom staring after them. Jackson would have to be fast. He just hoped to hell that Cameron had found the carriage and had it waiting. Putting his arm around Taye to help her walk, he led her down the long hall, past the room he and Cameron had shared less than an hour ago and down the narrow back servant's staircase. He cut through the kitchen, ignoring the openmouthed stare of the big mammy standing over the stove, and walked out directly into the darkness of the alley.

Cameron stood near the carriage, silhouetted by a gas lamp out on the street.

She was his light shining in the darkness.

Cameron was thankful for the rocking motion of Jackson's ship, the *Inverness,* as she entered the tiny cabin with bread and cheese and some of Jackson's Scotch for Taye. The motion of the ship told her they were well underway and headed down the Mississippi.

On the carriage ride to the shipyards, Jackson had chatted as if they had been out for an evening of dining and a stage show and were returning home. He told Cameron that he had purchased this new ship built in Scotland. She was a fast, powerful iron steamer, 190 feet long and twenty-five feet wide. She drafted only nine feet, he told her proudly, with an incredible speed of thirteen and a half knots. He said there would be no blockader she wouldn't be able to outrun.

Right now, Cameron didn't care how long the boat was or if she had a crew of twenty or a 120, all she cared about was getting Taye out of Baton Rouge and away from Grant.

Cameron turned up the oil lamp that hung from a beam over the bunk bed that Taye rested in. "You awake?" she asked quietly, taking the Scotch bottle from under her arm to place on the floor.

"Yes." Taye's voice was barely recognizable. She sounded so lost, so utterly defeated.

Cameron sat on the edge of the bed, the bread and cheese on her lap. She poured some of the Scotch into the cup of water and pushed it at Taye. "Drink this."

Taye sat up and took the tin cup with two hands, as if she were a small child. At the first sip, she spit and sputtered. "I don't like it," she said softly.

"Drink it anyway."

Obediently, Taye took another sip and then handed the cup back to Cameron. Cameron hesitated for a moment and then took a big gulp. The whiskey was smooth and peaty, not bitter like so many liquors. It was no wonder her father had liked it.

Balancing the wooden trencher on her lap, she cut a piece of cheese off and put it on bread. "Eat."

Taye took the nourishment and lay back in the bunk again. "I didn't say thank you," she said nibbling on the corner of the bread like a mouse.

"You don't need to. You'd have done the same for me. You'd probably have not let it get this far."

Taye made a sound, as if that comment did not even warrant a response. "You risked your life, Cameron. Captain Logan risked his life. For me."

At the mention of Jackson's name, Cameron took another drink of the Scotch. Then another. Since they'd boarded the ship she hadn't seen Jackson. Once on board, he had emerged from the captain's cabin dressed in sailcloth breeches, a muslin shirt and boots, looking every bit the pirate Grant accused him of being. He ordered his first officer to get the ship out of its anchorage, and they had steamed south. Cameron and Taye had been escorted by one of Jackson's officers to this berth, and he had helped Cameron find food and water. He had promised he would locate Naomi on the ship and send her in.

"I can't tell you how ashamed I am of my brother," Cameron said, trying to find the right words. "I can't tell you how sorry I am. I don't know what's happened to him since Papa's death."

"It's not your fault. Something snapped inside him after the senator died, I think."

Cameron nodded thoughtfully as she took another sip from the cup. She was feeling better now, not so tense. Jackson had promised there would be no trouble getting out of the harbor. If Grant or Toussant led chase, it would most likely be on the open waters of the Gulf, he said.

There was a knock on the door.

"Come in," Cameron called.

Naomi ducked and entered the berth. Cameron jumped up, leaving the bread and cheese on the edge of the bed. She threw her arms around Naomi and hugged her. Whatever she had once thought of the girl who was said to be a voodoo priestess, Cameron couldn't help but love her for what she had done. After all, as a young slave woman who had traveled alone from Jackson, Mississippi, to Baton Rouge, Louisiana, her feat had been the most daring in all of this.

"Oh, thank you, Naomi. Thank you."

"Yer welcome, Miss Cameron," she answered shyly.

Cameron stepped back to get a look at the young woman in the lamplight. "When you didn't come back, I was afraid something had happened to you."

"Pshaw, tell the truth, Miss Cameron," Naomi teased in her liquidy voice. "Ya thought old Naomi and her man done run off with yer money." She reached into the waistband of her dirty skirt and pulled out something wrapped in a bit of cloth. "I had to spend some of it to get my way here, but here's what's left of what you give me."

Cameron pushed her hand away. "Keep it. If I had more, I'd give that to you." She glanced at Taye lying in the bed. "I'd have given anything to save her from what he was going to do to her."

Naomi shook her head. "Yer pardon for sayin' so, Missy, but I always thought Masta Grant, he not right in the head."

Cameron had to laugh. "You're not kidding." She went back to the edge of the bed and reached for the Scotch. She was beginning to really like the taste of it now. It was making her warm, offering a comfort she desperately needed after everything that had happened tonight.

"So is your man here? Wasn't Manu his name?" Cameron asked. "I'd like to thank him, too. Almost half the slaves got away because of that boat he left us."

She shook her head. "Manu stayed to make sure my mama got north to the first stop on that there Railroad. He gonna meet me soon as he can." She grinned. "We thinkin' 'bout travelin' west."

Cameron had to smile. "Well, I don't know what Taye and I are doing yet, but we'll talk later after I know Captain Logan's plans. Hopefully, I can help you and Manu get away safely."

"Well, good to see ya livin', Miss Cameron." Naomi nodded her dark head. "You too, Taye."

"Do you have a place to sleep tonight?"

Naomi nodded. "I met up with two other runaway colored girls in the woods. I couldn't jest leave 'em scared and alone so they come with me. Captain Logan, he's a fine man. He tole me they could stay in his ship with me long as we want. We got us a nice cozy place to sleep down below."

"Well, good night, Naomi. And thank you again."

Naomi slipped out and Cameron poured herself some more Scotch. She was really feeling quite well now. Everything that had happened tonight was beginning to seem like a bad dream.

She sipped the fiery liquid. "Have enough to eat?" she asked Taye.

Taye nodded and then lay back and stared at the ceiling. "Do you know where he's taking us? Captain Logan, I mean."

She shook her head. "We haven't had time to talk." Her lips felt numb and her fingertips and toes were tingling. "Away from here is all I know." So much had happened tonight that Taye could never know...would never understand. So much that she, Cameron, didn't comprehend. But she wasn't sorry, and given the chance, she'd do it again.

Taye turned her head. "You know, we were wrong. He is a good man. Captain Logan."

Cameron frowned, sipping from the tin cup. "He's a cad and a blackguard and...and a pirate, too!"

"If he was truly all those things, do you think he would have come here? Do you think he would have spent a hundred and twenty-five dollars in gold to rescue me? Who am I to him, Cam?"

"Hush, you're tired. You don't know what you're talking about." She blinked, realizing that everything looked a little fuzzier than it had a few moments before. It wasn't that her eyes were not focusing, only that all the edges seemed softer. Even her own voice had less of an edge. She patted Taye, her motion awkward. "Get some sleep. We'll talk tomorrow."

Taye nodded and rolled onto her side. Cameron was concerned that her friend was still acting so dispirited. After all, she was safe now. But Cameron knew she had been through a lot. Maybe it was just going to take a little while to recover.

Cameron finished the tin cup of Scotch and was just reaching for the bottle again when there was another tap on the door. "Y-yes?" Cameron stood up and swayed...but not with the boat.

The door opened and Jackson ducked and entered the small berth. "She asleep?"

Cameron glanced at Taye who lay on her side, curled up in a fetal position, her back to them. "I think so." She covered her mouth self-consciously, fearing she might belch.

"Good. Come on." He grabbed her wrist and dragged her behind him.

"Wait! What are you doing? Where are you taking me?"

He pulled her out of the room and closed the door behind them. "To my cabin," he said. "Where you belong." He leaned over to bring his face to hers, then frowned. "Have you been drinking, Cam, dear?"

She wiped her mouth with the back of her hand. "I thought Taye should have a drink."

He chuckled. "Looks to me as if Taye wasn't the only one who imbibed." He forged ahead and pulled her along the open deck. The ship was rocking gently and she could hear the hum of the steam engine. Silhouetted by a few hanging lamps, she caught glimpses of the crew, who seemed ghostly in the night.

"What if I don't want to come to your cabin?" she protested. What? Did he think he owned her? Just because once in the heat of passion, in fear, she reached out to him, did he think that left him with an open invitation to ravish her whenever he pleased? Well, she would certainly tell him!

He held tightly to her wrist, leading her through the darkness that he was obviously familiar with. "I don't care what you want. I care what I want and what I want tonight is to get a few hours of sleep with you in my arms." He glanced at her, a droll expression on his face. "That way I can keep an eye on you. Keep you from getting into any more trouble...at least for the night."

He opened a door that was similar to the one they had passed through, but upon entering the chamber, she found it much larger. There was a wide bed and desk built into the wall that was raised paneling in a dark oak. There was a large sea chest against a wall, a chair, and even a round window. The room was not nearly as large as Cameron's bedchamber at Elmwood had been, but it seemed quite efficient. Cozy.

She smiled, turning to get a better look at the room as he closed the door and lowered the latch to lock them in. "This is nice."

He sat on the chair and pulled off his boots. "Become the captain of your own smuggling ship, and you, too, can have such fine accommodations."

She covered her mouth and giggled. She really didn't know what was so funny. Just something about the way he said it.

He pulled off his white muslin shirt and hung it on the chair. She watched, hypnotized, as he slid off his breeches and walked naked to the bed. He had the most well-formed, muscular buttocks....

She moistened her lips remembering how they had felt beneath her hand.

"Come on," he said. "Dawn comes early, and I have the first morning watch." He sat on the edge of the bed and slid his hand under the thin mattress. She thought she saw the handle of a pistol before he slid the object back into hiding.

Cameron stood in the middle of the room looking at him, feeling a little dizzy. Dizzy and confused. Maybe she *had* had too much to drink. He lay back on the bed and tucked his hands behind his head. He laid there naked for her to see...to see all of him in his glorious...nakedness.

"Well, aren't you going to undress me?" she asked, puzzled.

"Nope."

Her brow creased. She was definitely confused. "You're not going to undress me?"

"You can't undress yourself?"

She kicked off one slipper and then the other, now looking forward to shedding the stolen clothing. "I... Of course I can."

"Then do it and get into bed."

She wandered toward him, stepping out of the dress. "You—you're not going to ravish me?"

He gave her that boyish grin that she so loved when she didn't despise it. "I think we've had enough ravishing for one night, don't you, Cam?"

Without answering him, she dropped into bed beside him in her undergarments. He raised his hand and turned down the oil lamp that swung on the rafter above, then lay beside her again.

Cameron fell asleep almost instantly, made content by Jackson's strong arm around her waist. It was the first time since her father's death that she truly felt safe and loved.

PART THREE

23

Cameron woke in the morning to bright sun pouring from the single window, and an empty cabin. Jackson was gone and she didn't know if she was disappointed or relieved.

She slid to the edge of the bed, throwing her bare feet over the side. She yawned lazily, stretching her arms over her head. She couldn't remember the last time she'd slept so well. In the night, she remembered rolling against Jackson, her buttocks pressed to his groin, his arm around her beneath her breasts. There was something about sleeping in bed with him that seemed so right.

And yet so wrong.

Cameron rose from the bed. She had a dull ache in her head and her mouth was dry. She walked to the desk and lifted a small pottery jug. Thankfully, it was full of cool, fresh water. Taking several gulps, she looked around the captain's cabin. She realized with agitation that the ugly lavender dress she had stolen off the clothesline was gone. It wasn't that she was fond of the dress, but it was the only thing she had to wear. She could hardly display herself by walking around the deck in front of Jackson's crew in her undergarments. No doubt, his men already believed that she was a scarlet woman, and seeing her even partially uncovered would confirm their worst suspicions.

Then she spotted the pair of dark breeches and the white shirt left folded neatly over the back of the chair. Tucked underneath the chair was a small pair of boots, too. She picked up the breeches and looked them over—too small for Jackson. He had obviously left them for her.

The pants were so slim cut, obviously a boy's, that there was only one way she could wear them. Cameron shimmied out of her pantalets and pulled the soft, worn breeches over her bare legs. Shedding her corset, she slipped the corset cover back on. She knew from experience how thin a man's shirt could be. She pulled the shirt over her head. As she had suspected, it was wispy thin and completely see-through. She sat on the chair and grabbed the boots. A pair of clean, short stockings had been stuffed inside. When she stood, completely dressed, she was surprised by how nicely everything fit.

Then she became annoyed at the thought that Jackson knew her body so well.

She turned in the room in search of a mirror. She knew her hair was a mess. She found no mirror, but in the sea chest she discovered a boar's bristle brush and a piece of leather she guessed Jackson used to tie his own hair back. She didn't even attempt the tangles of red hair, but smoothed it all as best she could into a tail at the back of her neck and tied it off. She wanted to get outside and breathe some fresh air, and she needed to check on Taye.

Cameron walked out of the captain's cabin into the brighter light of the day, and spotting the sun overhead, she realized she'd slept until almost noon. No wonder she was hungry. She would check on Taye and then find the galley to beg the cook for some more bread and cheese.

Cameron lifted her face to the warmth of the sun as she walked in the direction she recalled her and Taye's cabin was situated. It was already overly warm, and humid on the Mississippi River. She could smell the peat of the muddy banks. The thick, pungent smell reminded her of the Pearl River and home.

"Well, good morning, sleepyhead." Jackson appeared out of nowhere, looking tanned and entirely too handsome. He was smiling at her.

She shaded her eyes with her hand to look at him. "Good morning."

"Feeling all right?" There was a teasing tone to his voice, but it was not cruel.

"Just fine, thank you. Excellent." He didn't say anything more but just stood there looking down at her.

She could barely form words for his engrossed attention, hardly meet his eyes for what she knew she would see there. She should have been ashamed, ashamed of what they had done, of what she had permitted, but she wasn't, and it was all she could do to stammer, "L-listen, Jackson. We need to talk about our plans," she said. "Yours...mine and Taye's. I—"

"Miss Cameron!" Naomi came hustling across the deck, two thin slave girls of about sixteen years in her wake. They looked so alike, they had to be identical twins. "Thank the Great Mother's belly that I found ya. It jest won't do, us sleepin' below with them men." She shook her head. "Jest won't do. I had to stay awake all night with a timber in my hand to protect these pitiful gals."

Cameron frowned. "Protect them from what?"

Naomi eyed Jackson. "Men, what else?"

Jackson sighed and looked away. "I was afraid that would happen. I made it clear to my men how I feel about such shenanigans, but much of my crew is new and young." He ran a hand over his sleek hair that was pulled back in a queue like Cameron's. "I'll have my first officer speak to the entire crew concerning female guests again, but Naomi is right. She and the other ladies—" he indicated the young girls who stood with their gazes locked on their bare feet "—will have to have quarters above deck where I can keep an eye on them and my men."

Cameron smiled at the two thin, sloe-eyed girls. "I understand you'll be traveling with Naomi," she said. "It's nice to meet you."

Neither girl answered.

"They shy and a little scar't," Naomi explained. "This

one—'' she pointed to one girl ''—is Dorcas. This one is Efia. Ya can see they was born of the same belly. Hard to tell 'em apart 'til ya get to know 'em.''

''Well, I'm just glad Naomi could help you,'' Cameron said. She turned back to Jackson. ''I hate to cause more trouble than I already have.''

He grunted in response, but Cameron ignored him and went on. ''But do you have a place to put them?''

''In with Taye.''

Cameron thought the quarters would be terribly tight, but if there was no other choice, she would certainly not complain.

''Naomi can sleep with Taye, and the two girls can sleep on top,'' Jackson explained. ''The bunks are narrow, but these ladies are tiny wisps anyway.''

''Thank ya, Cap'n.'' Naomi bobbed her head, grinning. ''I tole Miss Cameron ya were a good soul.'' She shook her head. ''Tole her ya were.''

''Wait a minute,'' Cameron said. ''Where will I sleep? I'm not sure there's room on the floor for a—''

Jackson's expression hardened. ''You're sleeping with me, that's where.''

Cameron's eyes widened in shock that he would say such a thing right in front of Naomi and the other girls. ''I'll what?''

''You heard me.'' He turned to Naomi, ignoring Cameron. ''I'll get one of my officers to escort you below decks to get your belongings, and you can join Taye. You should be perfectly safe above decks. Feel free to walk around, stretch your legs and get some sun. Just stay out of my men's way.''

Naomi dipped a little curtsy. ''Thank ya, sir.''

The girls behind her dipped curtsies as well.

''Wait a minute, this is not settled,'' Cameron protested.

Jackson looked to Naomi. ''It's settled,'' he said. ''Go, Naomi.''

Cameron stood there in disbelief as he dismissed the girl who had been *her* servant until a week ago. She knew she had to get used to this new South, but it still galled her. "You can't tell me where I'm going to sleep," she huffed.

He walked away. "Sure I can. My ship."

Cameron followed him, her boots tapping on the sanded deck in unison with his as she hurried to keep up. "You might be in charge of this ship, but you're certainly not in charge of me," she shouted.

A sailor, swabbing the deck, glanced up with interest, grinning.

"You're causing a scene."

"I am not. You are."

The whole deck was alive with men working at various tasks, but at the moment they all seemed more interested in the conversation between their captain and the red-haired lady he had brought onboard.

"You can't make me sleep with you, Jackson Logan," she hissed, lowering her voice to a harsh whisper as she caught up to him. "What will your crew think?"

"What do you mean, what will they think?" He cast a glance over his shoulder as if she were senseless. "They saw me bring you onboard last night dressed in that purple dress. They'll think you're just one more of my lady friends."

"Lady friends? Is that all I am to you? Another one of your lady friends. One more woman to bed and toss aside?" She had to fight tears that scratched the backs of her eyeballs. "Damn you, Jackson Logan."

"It's time you grow up, Cameron. You're not Papa's little girl anymore, and I'm not your papa. It's time you decide whose opinions of you are important and whose aren't."

Cameron stood at the rail, fighting back the tears. What could she say? Why was she so hurt? She had no expectations last night when they had made love at the bordello. She had given herself freely, and she had enjoyed every moment she spent with Jackson in that bed. He had made no promises when he took her in his arms and she had demanded none. But it still stung.

"Listen to me, Cam." He reached out to touch her arm, but

she drew back. "I have a lot of work to do. In case you haven't heard, we're at war."

She shook her head. "I've been reading the papers all week in Baton Rouge. We're not at war." She spoke the words as if the sound of them would make it so. "President Lincoln says we are not at war."

"I don't care what you call it, Cam. It's war. Now, if you don't mind, I have kegs of turpentine in the hull that weren't loaded correctly and could easily become a danger if that's not rectified." His steely gray eyes bore into her. "As you will recall, we left Baton Rouge last night rather hastily."

Cameron lowered her gaze. It hadn't occurred to her that the *Inverness* might not have been ready to set steam. And she hadn't considered how many people had responded to her cry for help. Jackson's entire crew had worked together to get Taye out of Grant's hands and safely out of Baton Rouge.

"I asked my cook to make us a nice supper tonight. I have wine. We'll sit down and talk. We'll discuss a plan. Now go see how Taye is. She was asking for you earlier, but I thought you needed to sleep."

Cameron pressed her lips tighter. She wanted to argue with Jackson. She wanted to discuss now what his plans were for himself and for her. If he had turpentine onboard, he was headed somewhere to sell it illegally. The North had cut off all supplies in both directions. The Southern states that had seceded had not collected federal revenue as required and, therefore, had their ports closed by President Lincoln in mid-April. Northern states were not permitted to ship into Southern ports, or receive goods from those ports. Because officially the president would not recognize the South's attacks as acts of war, but rather as "rebellion," blockade-runners could not be charged legally with treason. But they would be imprisoned for the duration of the war. Cameron refused to be put in danger of arrest for Jackson's financial gain.

"I'd really rather discuss this now," she said looking up at him.

He turned on his boot heels. "Well, I'm not going to."

If she thought she could have gotten her boot off fast enough, she'd have thrown it at him.

In the end, Cameron capitulated. She attended to Taye, ate and then found a book in Jackson's cabin, *Moll Flanders,* which she spent the afternoon reading aloud to Taye. In the early evening, she convinced her friend to take a walk on the deck. It was the first time Taye had left the tiny cabin since they boarded the night before.

Linked arm in arm, they strolled along the ship's rail. The sun was beginning to set so it was cooler but the Mississippi still sparkled. The hum of the steam engine, though loud, was surprisingly calming.

"I'm having supper with Jackson tonight, Taye." Cameron had given up trying to refer to him in the more formal manner of Captain Logan. Who was she trying to fool? Taye knew where she had slept last night. Everyone on the ship knew. A part of Cameron was ashamed, but once again, in light of all that had happened in the last two months, her virtue really didn't seem that important.

"Good," Taye said patting Cameron's arm. "The two of you need to talk."

Cameron walked slowly. Taye seemed weak and fragile right now, and she didn't want to push her too hard. "What's that supposed to mean?"

Taye looked at Cameron, a hint of amusement gleaming in her blue eyes. "You truly want to know what I think?"

"Of course I do."

"Sometimes when you say you want to hear someone's opinion, Cam, you mean as long as it is the same as yours."

Cameron pressed her lips together, gazing out over the river. "I want to know, Taye. Truly I do."

"I think you need to seriously consider your feelings for Captain Logan."

"He's a despicable cad, and I hate him." She smiled at Taye. "That was easy."

"I'm serious, Cam. He's a good man."

"A good man? Taye, do you know what this boat is carrying? Turpentine. Turpentine that he removed from that port in Baton Rouge illegally and turpentine that he will sell illegally elsewhere. That's a good man?"

Taye shook her head. "You know I don't have a mind for politics like you do. I never did. I don't know what he's doing or why. I'm not even sure he's doing what you think he's doing. I'm just telling you, he's a good man."

Cameron's amber eyes flashed and she began to protest.

"Now you said you would listen to me."

Cameron nodded. "All right. I'm listening."

"If you'd just stop being so stubborn, you'd realize you still care for him. And, Cam, I think he cares deeply for you."

Cameron gazed out over the ship's rail. "We're in the middle of a war. We're on two obviously distinct sides."

"He is not pro-slavery."

"No," Cameron replied sharply. "He's pro Jackson Logan."

"Cameron, you need to explore your feelings for him. You need to make sure you don't make a terrible mistake you'll regret the rest of your life." Her voice caught in her throat. "A mistake like I made."

Cameron turned, grasping Taye by the shoulders. Jackson had dug up breeches and a shirt for her as well. Though Taye did not usually take to male clothing, she was so thankful to strip off the *virgin gown* Grant had made for her that she would have worn her underclothes on the deck before she would have put it on again. Efia had accepted the gown and been thrilled to have it.

"What are you talking about? What mistake did you make?"

Taye released Cameron's arm and walked to the ship's rail. "The night of the ball, the night the senator died, Thomas found me on the back staircase after I had heard about Fort Sumter. I was terribly upset and…and he tried to comfort me. We sat on the steps in the dark and we talked." Taye bit down on her lower lip, tears brimming in her blue eyes.

"He…asked me if after the war he could court me. He said he wanted to marry me."

"And you said no?"

"How could I say yes, Cameron? He's a white man. A lawyer. Me. I'm a mulatto, a slave's daughter."

"There will be no more slave's daughter because there will be no more slaves."

"You know what I mean," Taye whispered.

"You were afraid to dream," Cameron said, understanding perfectly. "To hope."

Taye nodded, gazing out at the riverbank on the far side, watching the tall grasses blow in the breeze. A line of brown pelicans flew overhead and for a moment the women watched their amazing grace in flight.

Cameron leaned on the rail, smiling at the sight of the birds. "So you sent Thomas away without telling him how you felt about him."

"And now I will never see him again."

"I don't know, Taye. We never did find out why he left so hastily, but I can't help thinking it had something to do with Grant. I have a feeling he'll find you."

"Don't say that." Taye's voice trembled. "Please don't say it."

Cameron slid her arm around Taye's waist and rested her head on her shoulder. "Don't cry, Taye. Everything is going to be all right. We've come this far. It's all going to work out, I swear it is. I'll make it work for both of us."

Taye nodded, sniffing back her tears. "Thank you," she whispered. She turned to her friend, her eyes still wet. "Now go to Jackson. Enjoy your dinner. Your evening. I'll see you in the morning." She squeezed Cameron's hand and released it.

"Why don't we both dare to dream, dear Taye?" Cameron smiled.

Taye nodded and Cameron gave a wave good-night and followed the ship's rail to the far side and the captain's cabin. She had barely had enough time to freshen up in the washbowl when Jackson entered barefoot, carrying his boots. His clothes were dry but his hair was wet as if he had just bathed.

"Fall in?" Cameron asked, going to sit on the edge of the bed because there weren't many places to sit.

"Only if you pushed me over." He gave her a lopsided grin as he dropped his boots on the floor near the door. "I have this bucket rigged up so I can clean up. I'm not a true sailor, you see. I can't go thirty days without bathing." He walked to the sea chest and pulled out the hairbrush she had used that morning. "You pull a string—" he demonstrated with one hand "—and fresh water pours over your head."

"The water lasts the whole trip?" She lifted her shoulder. "Wherever you're going?"

"I have some fresh water in barrels on the deck now, but I also use rainwater."

She swung her feet, beginning to relax a little. She had to admit that maybe Taye was just a little right. She did like Jackson and she liked being with him when he wasn't being such an opinionated, self-centered bore.

There was a knock and two cabin boys entered upon Jackson's command. One was carrying a small wooden table and an extra chair, the other a tray of food that smelled absolutely tantalizing.

She found it interesting that, though they were his servants, Jackson spoke kindly to them, teasing them as they worked.

Jackson closed the door behind them and slid the bolt home. Cameron licked her dry lips.

Still barefoot, but his hair now brushed in a dark, damp curtain around his face, he pulled out a chair for her. *"Mademoiselle."*

Cameron took the chair. *"Merci."*

He pulled his chair from across the table where the boys had set it and placed it beside hers. As he sat down he pulled off a large white linen napkin that covered the food.

"Oh," Cameron breathed. In the last few weeks, food had not been as plentiful at Elmwood as it had once been. And she had had no appetite for so long that she had forgotten how much she liked to eat. "Steamed prawns," she breathed.

"And clams, and fish, and you have to try some of this rice. I don't know what it is." He spooned rice with tomato and pepper bits onto her plate with his own fork. "It's spicy, but I think you'll love it. My cook's mother was some sort of Haitian princess, and his father is French Creole."

Cameron peeled a prawn and bit into it. "Oh, Jackson, this is so wonderful."

He opened the wine and poured them both a glass. "Sorry these aren't wine goblets," he apologized as he poured the dark wine into short leaded glasses, "but I don't usually do too much fine dining onboard ship."

"This is so good." She sipped some of the wine. "And the wine also."

"I'm glad you like to eat, because I do, too." He heaped prawns onto his plate. "Now let me tell you my plan, and you tell me what you think. The *Inverness* is headed for the Bahamas. I have cargo to unload there and more to pick up. I think you and Taye need to disembark there where you'll be safe. It's British held, so Taye will be in no danger." He poured them both more wine. "I've tried to convince Naomi that she should go, too, but she has her heart set on getting off in New Orleans. She says she has a man waiting for her near Elmwood."

Cameron smiled and sipped her wine. "I am not going with you to the Bahamas. I'll just get off your boat in New Orleans, too. I'm going home."

"Damn, I knew you were going to say that. Listen to me, Cam. We're not actually docking in New Orleans. That's the first place your brother will look for us. If he has any sense at all, he'll check with the harbormaster. I left half of my supplies back on the dock in Baton Rouge, so everyone knows I'll need to put in somewhere." He didn't let her get a word in edgewise. "Naomi will be passed to another ship and then rowed ashore. We have to put in somewhere, but we'll hold out until Biloxi. You have to be sensible about this. You know very well—"

"I will not be a part of your smuggling enterprises!" She pushed out of her chair, getting up and throwing down her napkin. "You know very well my father would not approve of your running blockades to assist the Southerners."

He laid down his napkin on his plate, obviously trying to stay calm, but she could tell he was angry. His face had turned red and he had set his jaw the way she knew he could. "Cameron, you stay out of this. There are things you do not know about my enterprises."

"My father would not want me onboard this ship," she fumed. She didn't know what had gotten into her. One minute she was so happy sitting beside Jackson, sharing in a meal with him. The next minute she was furious with him again. Maybe this wasn't about Jackson's disloyalty, but her own. How could she care so much for a man who would make his living assisting those who approved of slavery?

"So you finally admit you're shipping illegal goods?" She crossed her arms over her chest, her eyes flashing. "You're purposefully going against the president's declaration concerning closed ports. Grant is right. You're nothing but a pirate. Just a well-paid one in a fine coat."

"You want to talk about money?" He rose out of his chair and struck it with his hand, sending it sliding across the polished wood floor. "Let's talk about money. How do you intend to pay for your passage from Baton Rouge to Biloxi? What about Taye's passage? And Naomi's? And those other girls'?"

Cameron stared at him, shocked. "You're a friend of my father's...."

"And you know Taye's purchase didn't come cheap. I'm out a large sum of gold." He took a step toward her. "How are you going to pay me, Cam?"

She could not tear her gaze from his gray eyes that sparked with anger. "I don't have any money and you know it!

What I didn't give to the slaves when they ran, Grant took from me.''

His gaze narrowed, as if he were undressing her with his eyes right there in the middle of the cabin. He was like a wolf about to swallow its prey and she was that prey.

''Ah,'' he murmured, taking another step closer. ''But you have more to barter with than mere gold....''

24

Cameron lifted her chin in offended pride, refusing to break eye contact with Jackson. "Would you buy in exchange for my passage what I once gave freely to you?"

He took another threatening step toward her, but she held her ground. How far could she go? The cabin was small and it was *his* cabin. Even if she could escape out the door, it was *his* ship. None of his crewmen would dare come to her rescue.

Jackson's forehead creased in a frown. His dark hair was almost dry now and swung near to his shoulders as he spoke. His tone was angry, but there was some emotion that lay deeper, one she could not identify. "Is the thought of making love with me so repugnant to you?"

"Yes," she replied bitterly. "Repugnant, indeed."

Cameron saw him lunge toward her, but an instant too late. She gave a cry of fear and attempted to feign right, but he was too fast for her, too large and too strong. Jackson grabbed both her arms and she stumbled backward. When she backed into the door, she knew she could retreat no farther.

Jackson caught her wrists and pinned them above her head. He crushed his mouth to hers and her cry of protest was muffled as he forcibly parted her lips and thrust his tongue inside. It was a wicked, vindictive assault and yet there was desperation in it…a longing she had never sensed from him before. Even if he wouldn't admit it, Cameron realized he needed her. Even if he didn't want her, he needed her.

Cameron knew there was no need to fear Jackson, but she was still furious with him. She attempted to kick him, but he molded his body to hers so that she could not lift her knee. She fought him wildly as she tried to move her head, to pull away from his assaulting mouth.

She fought her own rising desire.

She hated him. She hated him for what he was. For what he would never be. And she hated herself because she loved him anyway.

"Let me make love to you, Cam," he whispered hoarsely in her ear. "Let me touch you the way you deserve to be touched."

"No. Help me!" she cried, but only halfheartedly. "Someone help me."

"You little ninny. No one will come to your rescue. They know better!"

Her arms and legs pinned, Cameron bit down in fury on what was nearest to her mouth. His ear.

"Ouch, bitch," he cried. "That hurt!"

"I'm glad it hurt," she ground out, panting and breathless.

His steely gray gaze met hers for an instant and then he swept her into his arms and turned for the bed.

"No, Jackson."

"Yes, Cameron. You can't have it both ways. You can't have me when you need me, and then play coy when you're angry."

"You don't understand," she panted. "Last night was a mistake."

"A mistake. Right. You want me. You just can't stand the thought that Miss Cameron Campbell has such base desires." He threw her down on the bed and yanked off his shirt. He reached for the top button of his breeches and Cameron scooted back on the bed as far from him as possible. She was desperate to escape, as enraged as a caged wildcat. It wasn't just his actions; it was his words she abhorred. But where could she go? How could she get away from him? Worse, how could she get away from herself?

Jackson slid off his breeches and then knelt, naked, on the bed and grabbed her.

"Please, Jackson," she begged him.

"Now that's what I like to hear."

"Can't we talk about this? Can't we—"

"I'm done talking." He pushed her onto her back and began to pull off her boots. One hit the chair, the other the wall. He reached for her shirt.

She kicked her legs wildly, but he had her pinned down at the waist so her frenzied movements were to no avail.

He yanked the man's muslin shirt over her head and threw it away. Next came the corset cover. Cameron called him every vile name she could think of, vacillating between indignation and anger.

He grabbed the waistband of her breeches and again their gazes met. With one hand he began to pull the garment off, and weaving his fingers through her long hair, guided her mouth to his.

Cameron choked back a sob that a moment before had been of rage and was now of desire. She opened her mouth to take his tongue, thrusting her own between his lips. He released the waistband of her breeches and pulled her roughly against him. Somehow he was now seated and she was cradled in his lap. With one hand he teased and caressed her breast while kissing her deeply.

Cameron's entire body trembled with desire. She suddenly wanted him more than she had ever wanted anything in her life. She kissed him until she was near fainting as the fury of their fight had given way to a frenzy of passion.

Cameron looped her arms around his neck as he lowered his head to take her aching rose-colored nipple in his mouth. She groaned loudly, making no attempt to restrain herself. She arched her back, guiding his mouth with her hand, lifting her peaked breast to his lips. Still holding her in his arms, Jackson slid one hand over her belly and into the waistband of her breeches. Cameron grabbed the fabric and shoved them down, aching to feel his hand in her most intimate place.

He discovered that she was already damp for him and she

moaned as he slid his fingers between the folds of her quivering flesh.

"Cameron, Cameron, why does everything have to be so difficult between us?" he groaned.

She caught his face between her hands and covered it with kisses. His face was rough with two days' growth of beard and she liked its coarseness against her skin. He smelled of soap and rainwater and the answer to a need deep inside her that only he could fulfill.

"I don't know, I don't know…" she whispered, breathless, on the verge of tears, in desperate need to feel him inside her. "I don't know, Jackson."

He took her mouth again with his and slid his fingers inside her. She arched her back, lifting her buttocks to meet his stroke. Cameron had not realized how desperately she wanted him until she rose again, and a heat she had come to recognize flowed through her. One more stroke and she nearly screamed with the pleasure of the climax that racked her body.

But still he did not stop. He began to stroke her again, more slowly at first, but then faster. He lowered her onto her back, and lay on his side, next to her, and smoothed her hair. Cameron rolled her head on the pillow, lost in the sweeping waves of her own desire and his willingness to fulfill her.

Again she was assaulted by a tidal wave of ecstasy, and again he halted his movement only long enough to let her catch her breath. When he began to stroke her again, she cried out, almost in pain from the pleasure. "No," she murmured. She was so filled with emotion that she did not know if she wanted to laugh or cry. She knew what she wanted, only she didn't know how to say it. "Please, Jackson, won't you come to me?"

Obediently, he slid on top of her, stretching his lean, muscular body over hers so that his hands were on each side of her head and his groin pressed into her aching one. She could feel the hot rigidity of his need for her, and she parted her thighs. Breathless, panting, fierce with a need that still had not been fulfilled, she reached down to boldly clasp him.

She hesitated for a moment, then began to stroke his swollen member as he groaned in response to her touch.

"Cam," Jackson whispered huskily. The anger was washed from his voice, and she heard only naked desire. "A man can only stand so much."

To the surprise of them both, she tipped back her head and laughed, and then, still guiding him with her own hand, she slid him inside her.

This was only the second time they had come together in this way, yet it seemed as if they had been joined for decades. Eons. All of eternity. There was a rhythm in Cameron's head that only Jackson seemed to know. They moved smoothly, as one, without any awkwardness.

Cameron closed her eyes and dragged her fingernails over Jackson's back. She heard his panting in her ear and she smiled at the thought that she was not only taking pleasure, but giving it.

Jackson moved faster. Cameron wanted to make this union last forever, yet she could not hold back. She moved with him, taking him deeply, lifting up to meet each stroke.

"Cameron," Jackson groaned.

She rose again adoring the sound of her name on his breath. "Jackson…"

Their bodies tensed in unison and they were swept up in the same moment by the same wave of ecstasy. Cameron felt as if she were falling, falling as Jackson tightened his arms around her. And then slowly she drifted back to earth and the world around them, still holding him inside her.

With a final groan, Jackson started to move off to relieve her of his weight.

"No," she whispered, her eyes still closed. "Just a moment longer."

He gently brushed the damp hair from her face. "Open your eyes," he murmured, his voice still husky.

She lifted her lashes to look into the pools of his eyes that were more black now than gray. "What are we going to do about this, Cam?" he whispered. "You are like an addiction for me. I don't know if I can live without you."

She pressed her lips together, knowing what he meant. Right now she wanted to be here with Jackson more than she wanted to be anywhere on heaven or earth. But she knew very well that they couldn't live in this world of just a bed, the two of them naked and entwined in each other's arms. At some point she would have to rise, and then all the world and its troubles would come tumbling back again. The moment she left Jackson's arms, she would be angry with him for a million reasons, and he would grow angry in return and walk out, slamming the door.

"Can we not think about it tonight?" she whispered, smoothing his cheek with her hand. "Just for tonight. For a little while."

"Ah, Cameron, you really are such an innocent, aren't you?" He kissed her forehead and then gently withdrew from her and rolled onto his side. He wrapped her in his arms and pulled her against him. "Sleep a little while," he murmured, kissing her bare shoulder, "and then let me wake you."

Cameron closed her eyes, reveling in the sound of his indecent suggestion. "Promise?" she whispered, afraid to raise her voice for fear it would all fade away.

"Promise."

"I am not certain you will catch Capitaine Logan," Peppin Toussant said, puffing on a thin French cigar. He sat in an overstuffed chair in a private parlor in the rear of the *Juchoir*. "He left two nights ago shortly after he vacated my premises, I am told, and his new ship is one of the fastest in the South's new fleet. The *Inverness* was built to outrun even the fastest blockaders, they say." He lifted a bandaged foot onto the hassock in front of him. "And if you do not catch up with him and return my property, you'll owe me what I paid you for her, Campbell."

"Don't be ridiculous." Grant paced in front of Toussant and scratched at the open sore on his cheek. The wound seemed far larger this morning and itched as if it were on fire. It was the damned Louisiana heat and humidity. Louisiana was a festering swamp. It never seemed this hot to Grant in Mississippi. "We'll catch him."

Toussant threw back his head and laughed, his hanging jowls shaking. "*We,* Monsieur Campbell. There is no *we.* Peppin Toussant knows who is better a friend than an enemy. Any man right in his head knows not to make Jackson Logan his enemy. He is a dangerous man."

"I'm not afraid of him," Grant grunted, scratching again. He could feel something trickling down his cheek, and when he glanced down at his white glove, it was soiled with streaks of blood and pus.

"Well, then you are a fool. You should be afraid of Capitaine Logan. A man like that—" Toussant shook his head. "I have heard tales of him that would chill your…" He let his odd voice trail off, then grimaced and swore softly in French. "What is that on your face, anyway? Have you the whore's pox?"

Self-consciously, Grant lowered his hand and continued to pace, dragging his damned bad leg behind him. He ran a hand through hair that was greasy and stiff. He'd not taken the time to bathe this morning, and now he wished he had. He could smell his own body odor, sour and putrid. Or was the smell coming from the wound? He moved to scratch his cheek again and resisted. "I've hired men. Men with bloodhounds that can track a negra to hell and back. If Captain Logan docked in New Orleans, they may already have her. He has to dock somewhere. He left without loading most of his supplies— flour, sugar, barrels of fresh water. They're still sitting on the dock here in Baton Rouge."

"I hope for your sake, Monsieur Campbell, that you are right." Toussant sipped a thick, rich coffee from a tiny demitasse cup, which looked like a plaything in his large, fat hands. "Because I will be paid or I will have the girl."

"You'll have the girl," Grant snapped. "By God, you'll have the girl." He lowered his voice, now speaking as much to himself as to the bordello owner. "She wouldn't have me. She thought me repulsive, I suppose. Not a whole man because of my leg. How repulsive does she think three or four men in the same night will be?'' He only wished he would be here to see her humiliation, to see shame stain her beautiful face.

''I'm giving you two weeks,'' Toussant said. ''If the yellow girl is not returned in two weeks, I will see my gold returned.''

That would be a problem; Grant didn't have the money in the bank he thought he had. He'd lost badly at the gambling tables every night this week. He had the cash from the sale of Elmwood's slaves coming, but that would take time. And of course he had his living expenses, and the price had been high to hire men and dogs to go after Taye and his damned interfering sister. Christ, she'd be lucky if he didn't sell her whoring ass as well. Grant knew she was the one who had gotten Logan involved in all this. She was playing the trollop with him, no doubt. She had him under some sort of spell and was leading him around by his stones.

No, it wouldn't be easy to come up with the coin Toussant wanted, especially since he insisted on gold. But Grant wasn't going to tell Toussant that. It wouldn't matter, because he was going to drag Taye's yellow ass across the Mississippi back here. Maybe after a year in a whorehouse she'd be ready to discuss his original offer. Perhaps she wouldn't find him so repulsive then.

''All right. Out,'' Toussant said motioning to the door.

Grant frowned, annoyed that Toussant spoke to him so rudely. ''I beg your pardon?''

''You heard me. Out. I can't have the likes of you in my place. I won't have you. Bad for business.''

''The likes of me?'' Grant grunted, stepping closer to Toussant. ''I'll have you know I am Grant Campbell, son of Senator David Campbell.''

Toussant threw back his head and laughed heartily. ''And everyone knows you are not fit to wipe the shit from your father's boots. Now get out before I have someone escort you out.''

Grant lowered his head and stalked out of the parlor, ashamed of the tears that filled his eyes. He would get even with Taye and that bitch sister of his for this embarrassment they had caused him. He'd get them if it was the last thing on this earth he did.

"You are awake early, Miss Cameron," Naomi said, waiting by the railing so she could transfer to the ship beside them by means of a rowboat.

The sun was just beginning to rise in the east, a brilliant ball of orange-and-yellow gasses. The Mississippi was calm here in the cove where they had set anchor sometime after midnight.

Jackson had tried not to wake Cameron but when he had slipped out of her arms, she had awakened, missing him instantly. "Go back to sleep," he had whispered. "It's not yet light out."

She recognized immediately that they were not moving, and she looked up at him questioningly. "Have we put into port?"

By a single lamp he dressed, pulling on his breeches first and then the shirt he had discarded on the floor earlier. "New Orleans lies nearby. I have agreed to let Naomi disembark, and I've a passenger to pick up."

Cameron had slid out of bed, naked but unembarrassed. "I'll go with you. I have no coin to give Naomi, but I can at least thank her and wish her farewell."

"Suit yourself."

Now, Cameron was glad she had climbed from the cozy bed to see Naomi off. Cameron reached out and hugged the slave girl. "Good luck to you," she murmured. "And thank you again."

"Ya jest keep yourself out of trouble, Miss Cameron," Naomi said, laughing. She seemed happy to be getting off the ship, happy to be heading to join her man. "And ya best keep that one out of trouble, too."

Cameron looked up to see Taye walking barefoot across the deck. Except for her long, dark hair she could have been a boy dressed in breeches and a shirt that covered her womanly shape.

"Taye." Cameron smiled. "You're up, too."

"I wanted to tell Naomi goodbye and thank her."

"Let's go, Missy," a man in a red bandanna said. "Capt'n wants to be steamin' within the hour. Don't want to be spotted if we can help it."

Taye hugged Naomi. "Thank you," she whispered fiercely. "Thank you so much."

"And you'll take care of my girls, won't ya? They wanted to come, Dorcas and Efia did, but Naomi gonna be movin' fast. See they get to their family in Delaware."

"I'll take care of them, I promise."

"Here comes the boat," the sailor beside them said. "Let the man climb up and then you'll get a leg down."

Taye rubbed her arms as if chilled by the early morning air. "Who's boarding?"

Cameron shrugged. "Jackson didn't say."

They heard the sound of a voice below and then a man's hands gripped the railing and he climbed up the Jacob's ladder the sailor had dropped down.

Cameron heard Taye gasp, and she looked up in the direction of the figure boarding.

"Thomas," Taye murmured in shock.

Thomas appeared over the rail. "Miss Taye?" The moment his feet hit the deck, he rushed forward and awkwardly took Taye into his gangly arms.

"Sweet God, Miss Taye," he declared, his face red, his eyes twinkling with moisture. "I feared I would never see you again."

"Oh, Thomas. I'm so sorry. I'm so sorry for what I said back at Elmwood." She buried her face in his coat. "I'm so sorry I—"

Cameron watched in awe as Thomas ushered her toward the stern of the boat where they could have more privacy. Naomi waved, winked. "I'll be seein' ya again some day, Missy. I can feel it in my bones." Then she disappeared over the rail.

"Time to pull anchor," Cameron heard Jackson say from behind her.

She turned to face him. "You knew Thomas was boarding in New Orleans?"

"I'm the captain of the ship," he said solemnly. "Of course I knew who was boarding."

Cameron's eyes widened. "Why didn't you tell me?"

He gave her that boyish grin as he walked by. "You didn't ask."

25

By mid-afternoon, the *Inverness* had steamed past New Orleans without incident and was working its way down toward the Mississippi Delta. Once they reached the mouth of the river, they would turn north across the Gulf of Mexico and head for Biloxi. Jackson had explained to Cameron that it would take three days' time to reach port because once they reached the Delta, they would have to anchor at night. The flats were not well charted because they were constantly moving, and would be too dangerous to attempt to navigate under the cover of darkness.

Three days, Cameron thought. She had three days to live here with Jackson in his cabin, in a world that really did not exist. She still had not come to terms with her feelings for him. She feared—no, knew she loved him and yet he made no such proclamation. Not that she was so foolish as to expect him to. As she saw it, Jackson's plan was for her to play his bed partner until they reached the Bahamas, and then he would leave her there in "safety." Abandon her again.

But this time Cameron was not seventeen and not nearly so naive. She would leave him before he had a chance to leave her. Cameron had decided she would get off in Biloxi and return to Elmwood. If Taye wanted to go to the Bahamas, she could, or if she wanted to return home one last time before heading north, that was all right with Cameron, too. They could go to Elmwood, bid a proper farewell and then travel to the Stuarts in New York.

A part of Cameron was tempted to remain on the boat with Jackson and prolong what she suspected would be the most bittersweet days of her life. But she was afraid it would be too hard to part when they reached the Bahamas. If Jackson didn't love her, she could not change that, but she could protect herself. Disembarking in Biloxi, going to Elmwood and then on to New York, was her best defense not only against Jackson, but herself as well.

Cameron heard the cabin door open and she looked up from where she lay stretched out on the bed. She had tried reading *Moll Flanders,* but had mostly just been daydreaming. She had come to look at this captain's bed as a haven from the world. The rumpled sheets, the scent of Jackson and of their lovemaking was a welcome escape from the trials and tribulations of the last two months.

"Jackson."

He smiled as he ducked into the cabin, but she could tell that he was distracted. Thomas followed behind him.

"Good afternoon, Miss Cameron," Thomas said awkwardly, his face coloring.

She had not gotten a chance to speak with him yet because she had wanted to give him and Taye some privacy.

"Thomas." She leaped from the bed and ran barefoot across the cabin to throw her arms around him. "Heavens, I can't tell you how happy I was to see your handsome face."

He blushed further at the compliment and stammered but said nothing.

"After you left so hastily the night Papa died—" she stepped back to look at him "—we didn't know what had happened to you. That was a terrible thing to do, Thomas. We were so worried."

He stared at the cabin floor, tucking his spindly arms behind him. "I—I'm sorry I didn't speak with you that night before I left. I told Taye how sorry I was but it was a matter of safety," he said cryptically. "Not...not mine, Miss Cameron, but...others'."

She thought of her initial suspicions that Grant had something to do with Thomas Burl's abrupt, unannounced departure. Now she was almost positive her qualms were right. But this wasn't the time to question Thomas. It was obvious he and Jackson had come here to speak privately.

"Well, I cannot tell you how happy I am to see that you're safe and well." She smiled mischievously. "And I know one young woman who is nearly ecstatic."

Cameron didn't know how it was physically possible, but Thomas blushed further. He had lost weight since she'd last seen him, and any pretense of good looks he might have had was gone. But his brown eyes were still dark and true, and Cameron could understand how Taye fell in love with this gentle man.

"Well, I think I will go see the other ladies." She glanced at Jackson. "And leave you gentlemen to talk."

Jackson said nothing, but the look on his face was one of thanks to her for being clever enough to realize they needed time to speak alone.

Cameron didn't know what was going on, why Thomas was here or how he was involved with Jackson, but she was beginning to suspect that there was something more here than met the eye. Thomas would never involve himself in any illegal activities, however. He was as devoted to the emancipation of slavery as her father had been. Did meek Thomas have some influence on Captain Logan? Cameron was afraid to hope.

"I'll see you this evening for supper?" she asked Jackson, studying his face in a new light.

He nodded. "I invited Thomas and Taye to join us, if that's all right."

She rested her hand on the cabin doorknob, unable to resist a smile. He was asking her as if her opinion mattered, as if they were partners or even—God forbid—husband and wife.

"That would be lovely."

That night they tied up in a cove at sunset in a flurry of activity. As Cameron, perched on a water barrel and hidden from view, watched Jackson work, she couldn't help but admire him. He had a way with his crew that was demanding but fair. The men, mostly little more than boys, seemed to look up to him and he served as an excellent example. Cameron had to laugh at the thought. Captain Jackson Logan, scoundrel extraordinaire, a role model?

Later that night, once the ship had settled for the evening, Taye and Thomas joined Jackson and Cameron for a late supper. This time, the cabin boys set up the small table from the captain's cabin on the stern of the *Inverness*. By the light of the moon and a single lamp, they were treated to another delightful dinner of shrimp and mussels and another concoction of spicy rice. Ignoring the war and what had brought them all together on this steamer, the four talked easily of mundane happenings. And for the first time in what seemed like months, Cameron saw Taye smile and heard her laugh. Taye and Thomas were painfully shy, painfully polite with each other, but Cameron sensed that matters had been smoothed between them, and she saw a sparkle in Taye's eyes that made Cameron hopeful for their relationship, even if she couldn't be for her own and Jackson's.

After the meal, the table was cleared and Thomas bashfully offered to escort Taye back to her cabin to join the other two women. Bidding them good-night, Cameron and Jackson remained on the stern, leaning against the rail to stare into the dark water.

"Hot night," Cameron said, running her hand across the back of her neck. "Doesn't seem like there's a bit of breeze."

"Want to go for a swim?" He offered her a sideways grin. "Might cool you off."

"A swim?" Just the thought of the cool water against her body made her almost shudder with pleasure. She gazed over the rail at the water that seemed far below. "But how—"

"A Jacob's ladder. I dropped it over earlier. I like to swim when I can." He leaned on the rail, already taking off his boots. "Besides, it's much nicer here on the river than it is in the ocean. No sharks."

She gave a laugh at the thought of him dodging sharks in

the Atlantic while swimming for pleasure. "I can't go for a swim. These are the only clothes I have."

Barefoot, he peeled off his shirt and dropped it to the deck. "So you'd better not get them wet."

She widened her eyes. "You're shameless."

"I could say the same thing for you, my sweet, considering what you did to me beneath my sheets in the middle of the night."

She blushed but was not embarrassed. Something told her that lovemaking would not be like this again for her. There would be no other man like Jackson, and she had decided she would enjoy every moment of pleasure they shared. Why not? She was probably already going to burn in hell for her shameful behavior.

He grinned as he reached down to unbutton his breeches. "Come on, Cameron. Where's that adventurous spirit I know? Where's the horsewoman who can take her mount over fences higher than she is tall?" He stepped out of his breeches to stand before her in all his naked male glory, and she couldn't help but admire his physique. "Afraid?" he taunted.

Cameron let out a snort. "Is that a dare, Captain Logan?"

"You bet it is." And then Jackson climbed onto the rail and dived into the water below without another word.

Cameron stood on the quiet deck for a moment in indecision. Senator David Campbell's daughter swimming nude in the river? Why, any crewmember could walk out to the stern and see her. If she wasn't spotted naked in the water, she still had to get out of the water and dress again. Of course, she couldn't swim naked in the Mississippi River with a man who was not even her husband.

Then she glanced over the rail. Jackson was stretched out on his back, floating in a circle. He waved up at her.

Cameron yanked off one boot and then the other. Next came the stockings. She arranged the boots neatly near the rail, folding the stockings as she tried to find her courage. She looked both ways to find that there was no one to be seen. She heard nothing but the sound of Jackson paddling in the water below and the soft whistling of the watchman on the bow. It had to be after midnight. Most of the crew was asleep in anticipation of another long day of steaming.

Taking a deep breath, Cameron slipped out of the breeches, letting the shirt cover her nakedness. Thank heavens the boy's shirt fell near to her knees.

Tentatively, she climbed up onto the rail. The water looked so much farther away from up here.

"Come on, Cam," Jackson called. "No one will see you. My boys know better than to interfere with the captain's bathing."

Cameron looked once more over her shoulder and then, balancing herself, pulled the shirt over her head and let it float to the deck behind her. She closed her eyes and dived in the way her papa had taught her what seemed like a hundred years ago.

Cameron glided smoothly into water that was cool and silky against her naked body. She came up for air smiling.

"Damnation, you're my kind of woman. It's twenty feet off that rail to the water. Some of my crew won't dive off the side."

She grinned, proud of herself, pleased he was pleased. She paddled up to him and slid her arms around his neck. He treaded water holding them both up.

"Good thing I'm a strong swimmer," he teased.

She pressed her wet lips to him. "Good thing."

He stopped kicking and both of them slipped under the surface. She slipped her tongue into his mouth and for an instant they sank in silky, cool darkness. Then she ran out of air and had to let go to paddle to the surface.

Jackson popped up beside her and gasped, taking in a great gulp of the fresh night air. "You'll be the death of me, woman."

She paddled around him and turned over to float on her back. "Can you tell me what Thomas had to say today in your cabin?"

"No."

She was silent.

He lay on his back and floated beside her. "Cam, it's a matter of national security."

She laughed.

"No, seriously."

She turned her head to look at him, wishing she could see his eyes in the darkness. There was something in his tone that made her almost believe him. "Is there something I don't know about you, Jackson?"

It was his turn to laugh. "Cam, I'm twelve years older than you are. There's a lifetime of me you don't know about."

"You know what I mean." She wanted to reach out to him, but she stayed on her back, floating. This was the most serious conversation she had ever had with him, and she didn't want to shatter the moment.

"Cam—" He started to say something, made a sound and halted. "I want to tell. *Have* wanted to tell you." He groaned.

"But you won't," she said quietly.

"Can't," he corrected. He turned upright, grasping her. They had been floating beside the ship and now he swam, pulling her along, toward the hanging Jacob's ladder. He grasped the thick rope with one hand so that he could steady himself and hold on to her with the other arm. "You have to believe me," he whispered. "I would tell you if I could."

She stared into his eyes. With nothing but the moonlight, she could not see into the gray pools but she heard a sincerity in his voice that she hadn't known he possessed.

Her heart swelled.

Could she possibly be wrong about Jackson? What if he was not the man he appeared to be? Her father had always liked him. Had the senator known something of this man that Cameron did not?

"I wish you could tell me," Cameron murmured.

He brushed his lips against hers. "I wish I could, too."

His kiss deepened and Cameron hung on to him, wrapping her arms around him. She thrust her tongue into his mouth, exploring the coolness inside. She wondered what he would say if she told him she loved him. Just blurted it out. But then she thought of all the times he had hurt her, and she just didn't have the courage.

Instead of speaking, she wrapped her arms around his shoulders and molded her body to his. She loved the way they fit so well together, his hardened, well-planed muscular body to her softer curves. She reached down to stroke his burgeoning manhood and he groaned, his breath warm in her ear.

"Unfair," he said. "I can't reciprocate or we'll both drown."

"You just hold us up," she teased, her voice husky with her own building desire. "I'll do the work."

He groaned, leaning back against the hanging ladder that swayed slightly with their movement. He wrapped his arm around the thick hemp and managed to tuck one foot into the rope that hung below the surface.

Cameron grew bolder in her sense of power over him. She had always thought of the sexual act as utterly controlled by the man. Even when she had learned that a woman could gain great pleasure, she still saw the man as the one in charge. But now she knew that she could direct his pleasure as well as her own.

"Cameron," he whispered in her ear. "Witch. You've enchanted me. Put me under your spell."

She laughed huskily and laved his nipple with her tongue, still stroking the source of his desire for her. And as she touched him, she was amazed to find that her own ardor grew. Just pressing against him, stroking his silky flesh, feeling his heart beat, made her pulse with desire for him.

"Cam, enough," he moaned. "Come here. Make love to me."

She threw back her head and laughed. "I don't know if I can do this," she said, trying to lift her body to meet his.

He held tightly to her. "Ah, I think you can, my love."

My love. He'd called her *my love.*

Grasping the rope ladder, Cameron lifted herself up and wrapped her legs around him, settling onto his rigid length, groaning with pleasure as he filled her. Balanced precariously, half in the water, half out, she began to ride up and down, allowing the natural rhythm of the water to aid her.

Together, they rose up and down, with him completely at her mercy, and Cameron moved to the cadence of the needs of her own body.

Cameron had never felt so alive in her life. She had never felt so powerful and yet so…loved.

She felt his muscles tense, and she moved faster, realizing he probably couldn't hang on to the ladder much longer. At the same moment, they both surrendered to the wave of ecstasy, and she felt herself falling. He released the ladder, and they both fell into the water with a great splash.

Cameron came up laughing and sputtering. He held on to the ladder and grabbed for her. "You're going to drown," he teased, laughing with her. "Come here."

She reached out to him and he pulled her into his arms. He pressed his lips to her temple in a tender kiss. "Let me think about this, Cam."

She knew what he meant. About their conversation. About his secrets. She nodded.

"Ready for bed?" he asked.

She kissed his cheek. "Bed, but perhaps not sleep."

His laughter rang out over the calm waters of the Mississippi, and for the very first time in a long time, Cameron felt an overwhelming sense of sanguinity.

Two days later Cameron and Taye sat side by side on the foredeck, shaded by water barrels, playing cards they had borrowed from Jackson's cabin. Nearby the twins Taye had befriended were talking quietly. Cameron liked the girl Dorcas, but there was something about Efia that she didn't quite trust. No matter what Taye or anyone else gave her, she always wanted more. More food, better clothing.

"So what do you think?" Cameron said, studying her cards. "Do you want to go to the Bahamas?"

"Thomas said it would be wise."

"I didn't ask you what Thomas said you should do. What do you want to do?"

Taye studied her closely with those pale-blue eyes, and Cameron wondered again if Taye was actually her sister. She still debated whether to speak of the matter to Taye, but remained unsure if it was a good idea. There would be no way for them to ever know the truth, and Cameron feared that the possibility that Taye was the senator's child might only confuse the young woman more. She already had a difficult time dealing with who she was as the daughter of a slave woman and a white man. To discover she was the senator's daughter and neither of her parents had ever told her the truth might only make matters worse.

"What are you going to do, Cam?" Taye asked.

Cameron sighed. "I don't know what I want to do. These last few days with Jackson have been— I don't know how to describe it."

Taye smiled and Cameron knew that she understood. Although she and Thomas did not have the physical relationship that Cameron and Jackson had, Cameron knew that Taye was in love with Thomas.

"Jackson says I should go on to the Bahamas with him," Cameron continued, lifting a shoulder in indecision. "In a way, I would like to be with him a little longer, but I don't know. Maybe that's only prolonging the inevitable."

She looked up to see Taye's face lined with concern. "What?"

Taye glanced down at her cards, looking guilty now. "He didn't tell you?"

"Who didn't tell me what?"

"Jackson."

Cameron tossed her cards on the deck. "Jackson didn't tell me *what?*"

Taye pursed her mouth in an obvious quandary.

Cameron grabbed her hand. "You have to tell me. We don't keep secrets, you and I."

Taye's face fell. "Jackson isn't going on to the Bahamas. He has to get off in Biloxi. The first officer and Thomas will be taking the boat on. But that doesn't mean he doesn't want to be with you, Cam," she added quickly.

"What do you mean Jackson is getting off?" Cameron had no idea how Thomas could be taking the boat on. He had no experience sailing, but that wasn't the issue right now. "He said nothing of the sort."

"He probably knew you'd be upset and didn't want to spoil—" Taye seemed to search for the right words. She knew very well what was going on between Cameron and Jackson, and surprisingly, she approved. Proper Taye told Cameron that she had the right to take joy when she found it, rules, even morals, be damned.

"He probably just didn't want to spoil what you have right now," Taye said.

"So now you're defending him?"

Taye got to her feet. "Cameron, I don't think we know exactly what is going on here."

"Perhaps not." Cameron strode away, her jaw set. "But I'll be damned if I'm not going to find out."

"You lied to me," Cameron accused.

Jackson picked up a wooden crate and carried it to the far side of the hold. It was stifling hot below deck; his hair was damp and sweat ran down from his temples. "I didn't lie to you."

"Semantics," she scoffed angrily. "You mislead me, then."

"Cameron, I fully intended to continue to the Bahamas, but Thomas came aboard with a message of vital import. This jeopardizes the entire trip, but I have to get off tomorrow and travel overland north."

She followed him as he returned for another crate. "You've known since Thomas came on the ship, damn you! Your talk in the water the other night was nonsense. You were just trying to placate me. And you won't tell me why."

"Nope."

"Damn you, again! I'm getting off, too."

He shook his head. "You can't go with me. I have to travel fast. It will be dangerous."

She dropped her hands to her hips. Had she been foolish to

think things could possibly change between them? He was up to his old tricks again already. "I'm not going with *you*. I'm going home to Elmwood."

He dropped a crate into place and spun around, grabbing her wrist. "Cam, you can't get off in Biloxi. You can't go back to Elmwood."

She jerked her arm from his grasp. "Don't tell me what I can and cannot do! I want to go home. I want to go home to my father's house, and no one is going to stop me."

"Stop being so selfish and listen to me. Taye cannot return to Elmwood. She can't get off in Biloxi. Thomas discovered by accident while in New Orleans that Grant, or Toussant, or both of them hired men to find Taye and take her back to Baton Rouge to the *Juchoir*. If we had docked in New Orleans, we would have been boarded by officials and she would have been dragged off as stolen property." He drew his face close to hers. "Is that what you want? To have Taye returned to those animals?"

Cameron whipped around so that Jackson could not see the tears of frustration welling in her eyes. She had known not to trust him. She had known something like this would happen. So why did it hurt so much?

"When are you getting off?" she asked, her back to him.

He just stood there behind her. "Tomorrow morning. Dawn, I suppose. The fewer who know I'm going until I'm gone, the better. I trust my men, but in times like these, it's better not to trust anyone."

He was talking cryptically again, but Cameron didn't care to question why. It didn't matter. All that mattered was that she and Jackson had gotten too close. She'd begun to trust him and now he was taking off again. The fact that she had the same intention didn't factor in.

"You should have told me," she said firmly, hoping he didn't hear the pain in her voice. "I was actually considering going on with you to the Bahamas."

"And you still should stay on the ship. The *Inverness* may not be headed for the Bahamas now, but it will most definitely be headed for safer waters. Baltimore even, perhaps."

Her lower lip trembled. She wanted to go home. "I'm getting off and you can't stop me."

"Fine. Then get off. Don't listen to me." She heard him pick up another crate, jerking it angrily off the floor. "Do whatever you damned well please, because you will anyway."

He almost shouted his last words, but Cameron was already out the door.

26

Cameron crouched at the stern of the boat among the stacked crates and barrels of supplies that had been loaded the moment they docked. It was her understanding that the ship would be underway again by midmorning, before too many people discovered the *Inverness* was in port in Biloxi. According to Thomas, if Grant had charged Jackson Logan with the theft of his slave, the authorities could be looking for him for questioning.

The ship had arrived in Biloxi just before sunset, but it was now after midnight. Jackson had come to the cabin to talk to Cameron before she went to sleep, but she refused to speak to him. He had walked out on her, throwing a knapsack over his shoulder saying he was going to catch some sleep elsewhere on the ship. He said they would talk later.

Cameron nearly laughed aloud. Right. Talk later. Not five minutes ago, Jackson had walked down the gangplank and off the ship carrying his knapsack. She didn't know where he was going, but she knew he wasn't coming back.

Of course, Cameron wasn't staying, either. She was going home to Elmwood. Home to collect a few belongings, home to say goodbye before she took Taye north to safety. She turned to Taye, who hid with her behind the barrels.

"Are you certain you want to do this, puss?" She studied her friend's blue eyes by the light of the bright white moon overhead. A full moon. "I think you and Thomas should stay together. I think the man has possibilities."

Taye smiled shyly, but then glanced up, her eyes filling with determination. "Thomas understands that I have to go home, but he's very upset that I'm leaving like this. He even wanted to send one of the men with us to protect us, but I told him we wouldn't have it. There's no need to put anyone else in danger." She smiled hopefully. "And it's not so far to Elmwood."

Cameron frowned—170 miles wasn't far by boat on the Mississippi. It wasn't far by covered carriage even, but it was a long walk. It was a longer walk if you were a white woman trying to hide three black women from the slavers.

"And you girls wouldn't rather go on with the ship?" Cameron asked the sisters who crouched on the deck behind Taye. Both shook their heads, their eyes wide and gleaming in the night.

"They want to go north with us. When Naomi found them, they were lost in the woods. They only went farther south with her because they didn't know the way home. They have family in Delaware, so that's where they want to go. I thought they should stay with us. It's got to be safer traveling together with you."

Cameron gazed out on the near empty dock, understanding her meaning. Cameron was an educated white woman. All of them would have a better chance if they stuck with her.

She sighed. She had no idea how they were going to make it home, but she was determined, and if these girls wanted to go with her, she wouldn't stop them. "You have your things?" she asked Dorcas and Efia. "Because we won't be able to go into any towns, except maybe me alone. We'll follow the road from here to Jackson, but we'll have to stick to the woods. Maybe even travel at night with the moonlight to guide us." She looked back to Taye. "And you said you have some money?"

"Thomas gave me what he had, but it isn't much. He says he has to go north to get any more."

"Well." Cameron gazed at the gangplank she had watched

Jackson leave by a few minutes ago. "Let's go. I think I know the fastest way to get out of here."

When Jackson disembarked, she had seen him halt at the end of the dock, at the street corner, to talk with a sailor in a striped red shirt. She had watched him as she spoke with the girls. He had only disappeared around the corner a minute ago. If he were going north as he said, he would lead them right out of Biloxi.

Single file, the four women moved noiselessly over the gangplank. As they hurried along the dock, Cameron whispered to Taye. "Thomas didn't come to say goodbye?"

"He said he couldn't actually know my plans, else he would be held responsible." She smiled. "He thinks we're leaving tomorrow morning when we were supposed to go into town for supplies before they set sail."

Cameron grinned. "Well, won't our gentlemen friends be surprised?"

Taye caught Cameron's hand and then hurried up the street, as if they were children again, running across a sunny meadow. They turned the corner where Cameron had seen Jackson disappear. Sure enough, he was only a little more than a block ahead of them. He kept to the narrower streets, cutting across alleyways. Cameron and the girls saw stray dogs and cats. They saw a drunken sailor sitting on a water barrel and several carriages careening down the street. As they crossed one alley, they heard the rich throb of native music and caught sight of a half-naked black woman dancing in the light of a small fire. They heard laughter and drunken revelry.

Cameron tried to hang back, but always kept the mysterious Captain Logan in her sight. Exactly where was he going? He seemed to be looking for something now, reading the posted street signs. When he turned onto a main street, Cameron waved for the girls to stay back. She peered around the corner of a butcher's shop and watched as he approached a doorway guarded by a soldier in a new gray army uniform. He spoke his name and was admitted.

Cameron ground her teeth. He was consorting with the enemy, making plans, no doubt, to increase his own profit by shipping Southern goods out, or Northern goods in. Watching the soldier, she wondered how she could ever have considered that she and Jackson could be together. She loved him, God help her, but she knew she couldn't live with a man—marry a man—who supported slavery. She just couldn't.

"What's he doing?" Taye asked. "Shouldn't we move on before someone sees us?"

"I don't know the way out of town," Cameron whispered. "And it's not as if we can ask. Look at me." She indicated the boots, breeches and boy's shirt. "I'd be detained for sure. I'm dressed like a sailor traveling with two slave girls."

"Three slaves," Taye said softly. "Without my emancipation papers, I have no proof of who I am."

Cameron squeezed Taye's hand reassuringly. "I'm going to get you out of this."

"I know you are."

After close to an hour, Cameron heard the sound of Jackson's voice. She peered around the corner again, motioning for the others to stay back and remain among the barrels lined up along the wall of the butcher shop. The alley stank of rotting meat and rodent droppings, but at least it was dark and shielded from the street.

"I thank you for coming, Captain Logan." A distinguished young man dressed in a gray uniform, this one with officer's insignia, spoke gruffly without removing the cigar from between his teeth. He was thin and blond and looked like so many of the young men raised on Mississippi cotton and the luxury of slavery. In a way, he reminded her of Grant.

"Now you understand, Captain," Jackson said apologetically, "I accept only gold for my shipments."

The officer chuckled. "They told me you were a shrewd son of a bitch."

Jackson shrugged, offering that smile that seemed to beguile not only women but men as well. There was something about his devil-may-care attitude that drew people to him, made them believe in him.

Cameron frowned. She was anxious to get on the road now. Anxious to get as far away from Jackson as possible.

A scream rented the air and Cameron spun around in horror to see Efia climbing onto one of the barrels.

"Rat! Rat!" she screeched. "Oh, gawd a Missy. Lord save my sorry soul. It's a big ole stinkin' rat!"

The slave girl had strung more words together than she had the entire time she was on the ship.

"Who's there?" the soldier on guard shouted.

"What the hell is going on here, boy?" Cameron heard the officer say as she reached up to yank Efia off the barrel. They would have to make a run for it down the alley.

"Let's go," she hissed, still trying to get Efia down, but the girl would have no part of it.

"No, no, Missy. I can't. It's a big ole rat."

"Heaven sakes, Efia," Cameron groaned. "That rat is halfway to Washington D.C. by now."

Footfalls pounded on the street as all three men tore into the alley.

"Run, Taye," Cameron shouted. "Take Dorcas and run!"

"Stop them," the officer ordered. Cameron heard more footsteps behind her. More soldiers. "They could be spies," the officer growled.

"Where do you think you're going?" a familiar voice demanded with great authority. It was Jackson. "Don't take another step, Taye, or I'll have you shot."

Taye halted midstride and turned around to look at Cameron, her eyes wide with fear. Cameron slowly turned to meet Jackson's gaze in the darkness, leaving the terrified Efia to stand on the barrel.

"Didn't I tell you to stay put here, Fanny?" he asked Cameron directly.

Fanny? Who was Fanny? What was Jackson talking about? But Cameron had enough sense to know she had to trust him. She had no other choice.

Jackson turned to the officer. "I can explain this, George."

"I hope the hell you can," he grunted.

Soldiers appeared at the far end of the alley, their shiny new army-issued pistols drawn. The women were trapped.

"It's really rather embarrassing."

The officer shoved his fat cigar into his mouth. "I'm listening, Captain Logan." As he spoke, smoke eased from his nostrils.

"A little side business, George." Jackson grimaced apologetically. "Doesn't affect our business transactions in the least."

"Selling *stolen* darkies? I don't need dealings with a man beyond the law."

"No, no, no. Not stolen. Runaways."

The officer narrowed his dark-eyed gaze, his bushy brows knitting until they met to form one eyebrow. "Not my business what you do on the side, Captain, though I have to say it disgusts me. Selling them like they're sides of pork." He removed his cigar from his mouth, pointing to Cameron. "But what about that one? She's no darky." He eyed her carefully. "Pretty thing."

"This one." Jackson reached out with his hand and grabbed her by the hair.

"Ouch!" Pain shot through her scalp as sharp as her surprise that he would be so violent with her. She tried to slap him, but he caught her around the waist and whipped her around, pulling her off her feet.

"Now, this soiled dove's a different story."

The officer laughed as Cameron struggled to escape Jackson's imprisonment. He held her at his side, waist high. She kicked furiously, but to no avail. He was so damned strong.

"I'm listening."

"Runaway from a whorehouse."

"You son of a bitch," Cameron ground out. "Put me down. I'll show you—"

George chuckled. "Lively piece of tit, isn't she?"

"I'm just sending her back to Baton Rouge. A nice finder's fee. You'd be amazed by the things you find under the docks if you look."

The officer knitted his big brow again. "Seems to me I heard some rumor about you being involved with some whorehouse. That wasn't the story I heard, though." He scratched his head. "I could have sworn there was something about stolen slave property. There's someone hanging around the docks looking for you to pull into port.''

''You know gossip, George. It's never accurate but always entertaining.'' He winked. ''Well, I'd best get on my way. I've got to meet a man to pawn off these darkies.'' He looked at Cameron. ''Now, Fanny, if you promise to be a nice girl, I'll put you down.''

''Christ, Logan. How do you think you're going to keep these women from running off down the street? Let me get you some rope. You, there.'' He called to one of the soldiers. ''Run and get the captain some nice strong rope.''

The boy, barely old enough to shave, returned a minute later with an armful of twisted hemp. Jackson held Cameron pinned against the wall.

The boy tossed the rope.

''Thanks.'' Jackson grinned as he caught the coil. ''Now, Fanny, we can do this easy or we can do this hard. Give me your wrists.''

Cameron stared at Jackson, wishing her eyes were daggers so that she could bore into his flesh.

''Come on,'' he grunted under his breath. ''Let's get the hell out of here.''

It was all Cameron could do to lift her arms to let him bind her wrists together.

''There we go.'' Jackson gave the knot he made a hard tug.

Cameron flinched, but she didn't say a word as the rough rope bit into her wrists. She'd have plenty to say when she got him alone.

''All right ladies, let's go.''

George puffed on his fat cigar. ''You don't want to tie the others?''

Jackson made a face. ''Nah, the rest are docile enough. It's this one I've got to keep an eye on.'' As Cameron turned to go the way they had come, he swatted her across the bottom.

She spun back and tried to kick him, but he dodged the blow and all the men laughed as they filed out of the alley.

''Good to do business with you,'' George said. ''Good luck, and I'll be seeing you in the future, eh, Logan?''

"Let's go," Jackson ordered and ushered the women down the alley.

"What do you think you're doing?" Cameron snapped the moment they were on the next street.

"Shut up and keep walking unless you want a Confederate bullet between your ears." He pressed his hand to the small of her back and directed them down another alley.

The moment they were out of the streetlight, Cameron halted and spun around. "Untie me," she ordered between gritted teeth. She was so angry with him she could have spit.

He leaned over her, nearly touching her nose with his. "Why should I?"

"Why—why should you?" she sputtered. "Because you have no right to tie me up like this."

"Cameron," Taye urged gently. "You have to keep your voice down."

Cameron stared hard at Jackson. "Untie me," she demanded.

"Tell me what you think you're doing following me. Dragging those women into this with you? Do you realize how dangerous those men are? Haven't you heard? There's been fighting in the new West Virginia."

"West Virginia? What do I care about West Virginia? That's a million miles away from here," she said.

"You won't think so when the fighting shifts south to Mississippi. They'll be fighting in Elmwood's backyard in a year's time." He reached down and none too gently began to work the knot at her wrists.

Cameron grunted in pain as the thick, rough rope cut into the soft flesh of her wrists. She didn't want to hear about the fighting. About the war. She just wanted to go home. "I wasn't following you. I was going to Elmwood."

"By way of regimental headquarters?" he snarled.

Taye drew close to them. "This isn't the place to talk about this, Cameron. We have to get these girls out of here if someone is looking for me. I wouldn't want them to be taken away as well."

"Damn it," Jackson cursed. "I'll have to take you back to

the ship, but then I've got to get going. I have an engagement north of Jackson that I cannot miss.''

"You're going to Jackson?" She felt a tug on her heart. She wanted to go home so desperately now that unwelcome tears sprung in her eyes.

To her surprise the tone of his voice changed. His face softened. "Cam, I can't take you home. I would if I could, but it's too dangerous.'' He reached out to push back a lock of tangled hair that fell over her face. "I wish you could trust me.''

Her lower lip trembled. "I wish I could, too.''

He slid the rope off her wrists and looked up at Taye and the two girls who were holding each other. "I'll take you back to the ship.'' He pointed to Cameron. "And I don't want to hear another word from you. Didn't you hear what he said? Someone is looking for Taye. Looking for me.''

Cameron felt beaten. "All right,'' she said softly. This wasn't the end of it. She was going home to Elmwood one way or another, but maybe Jackson was right. Maybe it was too dangerous, at least for Taye and the two girls. Cameron would have to set out alone after she got Taye back safely to Thomas Burl.

Without speaking, the four women and Jackson walked down the quiet, dark streets they had come. As they approached the docks, they began to hear what sounded like gunfire.

"What's that?'' Efia cried, immediately frightened again.

In the distance, they could hear men shouting and more gunfire exchange. Something on the dock was on fire.

Jackson swore. "Sounds like all hell is breaking loose.'' He turned to the women. "Taye, you stay here with the girls. I would say I'm going to go check out the situation alone, but I know Cameron will follow me anyway so I might as well keep her beside me where I can keep an eye on her.''

Taye smiled. "We won't move an inch, Captain.'' She herded the girls behind a pile of fresh cut lumber that smelled like raw pine. "We'll stay right here, quiet as mice.'' She looked to Efia. "Won't we?''

Both girls nodded rapidly.

Jackson glanced over his shoulder at Cameron. "You coming?"

She fell in behind him.

They took the alley down toward the waterfront, and as they came to the main street that ran along the docks, Jackson pulled a pistol out of the back waistband of his breeches. She hadn't even noticed it in the fabric of his linen shirt. "I tell you to run, no arguments. You run."

She nodded in affirmation.

The moment they came into view of the dock, Cameron gasped. There was a ship pulling out of its slip quickly while men from the dock fired on it. She could see the silhouettes of men on the ship running back and forth along the deck, firing back.

"The *Inverness,*" Cameron breathed in shock.

"Must have tried to board her. I told Thomas to be ready to get the hell out of here in a moment's notice."

Cameron crouched beside Jackson watching. The ship had begun to move forward, its steam engines groaning. "This is all because of me," she whispered.

"Thomas will get her out of here in one piece."

"I didn't know he knew anything about sailing."

"His father was a merchant like mine. Thomas grew up on the deck of a ship. His father sent him to law school and encouraged him to enter politics because he wanted him to have an easier life."

Cameron stared in amazement as men ran up and down the docks shouting. Someone jumped into a rowboat, but gunfire rained water around the little boat and the occupant leaped into the stale water and swam under the dock.

Then Cameron heard the sound of bloodhounds wailing. It was a sound a Mississippi girl could never erase from her mind. Slavers in search of runaways.

She laid her hand on Jackson's arm. "Guess we better go."

He looked to her, scowling, but he no longer seemed angry with her. "So you get your way."

She dared a smile. "How far you going, mister?"

He grabbed her arm and pulled her to her feet, hurrying her

back up the dark street. "Move along, Fanny. We've got to come up with a plan fast."

"Fanny? I was going to ask you about that. Just who do you think you are calling me *Fanny?*"

Half an hour later Cameron, Jackson and the three women stood on the edge of town contemplating where they would go from here and how.

"We can't walk all the way to Elmwood," Jackson said with annoyance. "Too slow. Too easy to get caught."

"Well, you said you were going north of Jackson. How did you think you were going to get there?"

"A horse, but that won't do. Even if I could beg, borrow or steal enough horses for all of us, people on the road would be suspicious of a white man and woman traveling on horseback with three women who appeared to be slaves all with their own horses," he said quietly, not wanting to offend Taye.

Cameron studied a darkened storefront that read James Bros. Mercantile. She glanced at Taye, Dorcas and Efia, all seated on the ground, hiding in the shadows of the store. All three were tired. Taye had not yet physically recovered from her ordeals and the sisters didn't seem used to any sort of physical labor. She didn't know what they did before Naomi found them in the woods, but she guessed it wasn't much walking.

Cameron gazed longingly down the road that Jackson told her led out of Biloxi, north to Elmwood. She would walk every step of the way with the women on her back if she thought she could get there safely.

But now she had Taye and the twins to think about as well.

"So the question is," Cameron said, thinking aloud, "how could we travel so that no one who came upon us would be suspicious?"

Jackson stroked his two-day-old beard. "Hmm. I have an idea, but it might take some ingenuity and some fine acting if we're questioned along the way."

She gazed into his eyes that she could not help but love. "Tell me. We'll do it. I'll do it."

"We're going to have to work together on this, Cameron. You've got to cooperate. We need to be gone before people start waking up. It's going to be all over town that the *Inverness* was in port."

"Just tell me what to do. I'm not afraid."

He brushed his fingertips beneath her chin. "You really aren't, are you?" He took a breath and then went on to the task at hand. "You'll have to find some clothes for yourself and for Taye. She needs to look more like the other two. She'll never pass for white."

Cameron nodded, appreciating his frankness for once.

"And you need a dress, a skirt, something simple. Plain. A bonnet to cover your face would be good. As we grow closer to Elmwood, I would hate to have anyone recognize you or Taye. Though I do like this on you—" he tugged on the thin white shirt "—it won't do for what I have in mind."

"I can find the clothes in half an hour's time," she said confidently.

He grinned. "That's right, you've experience snatching clothes off lines."

She made a face at him. "And what will you do while I find the clothes?"

They heard the sound of hoof beats on the street and both shrank into the shadows. Without thinking, Cameron pressed her hand to his broad chest. He covered her hand with his. "I'm going to find a wagon and a team of horses."

"Where are you going to buy horses at this time of day without drawing any suspicion?" It had to be almost four in the morning.

"Who said anything about *buying* horses and a wagon?"

Cameron looked up at him in shock. "You would steal a man's wagon?"

He lowered his face close to hers. "You're going to steal some woman's clothes."

"It's not the same thing." She bumped her nose to his. "Horses and wagons are expensive."

"Well, I have very little money, and what I do have we'll need to buy some food along the way."

"Why don't you have any money with you?" Cameron could hear Taye talking softly to the two frightened girls. She didn't know what they were saying, but it didn't matter. Once again, Jackson was becoming the center of her world. She brushed her hair off her forehead. It was hot and muggy in Biloxi and being so close to Jackson made her even warmer.

"If you must know, it's easier to travel inconspicuously like this. Like a working man." He indicated his simple dark breeches and inexpensive shirt and boots. "It's not safe for a man to carry too much money on these roads anyway."

"And you still won't tell me why you're doing this." She indicated his clothing. "Where you're going that it was important enough to get off your ship for."

He shook his head. "Can't." Then, to her surprise, he leaned over and brushed his lips to hers. He was obviously no longer angry with her. "Bet I can get back here with a horse and wagon faster than you can find two sets of ladies' clothes."

Cameron thrust her hand into his and pumped his arm. She liked it when he treated her this way—like an equal. She knew few men who were so confident of themselves that they could regard a woman this way. She grinned. "It's a deal, Captain."

He lifted her hand to his mouth and pressed his lips to it. "Be careful, Cam," he murmured, his kiss lingering.

She gave a nod and then slipped off into the darkness, not sure if she hurried now to get to Elmwood, or to be in Jackson's arms again.

27

It wasn't much after dawn that four hard-faced men in gray uniforms approached them on horseback on the road that led out of Biloxi.

Jackson slid his hand across the bench seat of the old wagon and rested it on Cameron's thigh. "Ready?" he whispered.

She tugged on the brim of her worn yellow bonnet to better hide her face. She had won the bet and beat Jackson back to the girls by five minutes with a calico skirt, a cambric bodice, two bonnets and a ragged servant's dress for Taye. She'd also found a bucket, some potatoes and onions and a pot with the handle broken off. They would all come in handy camping in the woods tonight.

Surprisingly, Jackson had seemed as pleased with her accomplishment as she had. He brought back two nags that looked to be on their last legs and a small wagon. In the back of the wagon was an assortment of blankets and other items that might be useful.

Cameron glanced over her shoulder and met Taye's gaze as the soldiers grew closer. "Ready?"

Taye gave a quick nod.

Cameron stared straight ahead again, her heart pounding in her throat. "We're as ready as we'll ever be," she whispered.

"Just let me talk," Jackson said. "And no matter what happens, stay calm. Play along."

"Good morning," one of the soldiers called, slowing his

horse to a walk as he approached the wagon, looking them over carefully.

Jackson pulled on the broad leather reins and nodded his head. "Mornin' to ya, sirs." He spoke as if he had a wad of chewing tobacco in his mouth the size of a wagon wheel.

Cameron had to keep her gaze focused on the ragged ears of one of the horses pulling the wagon to keep from sniggering.

"Where are you headed?" the soldier asked stiffly, his gaze shifting from the black women in the bed of the wagon back to Jackson.

Cameron noted the insignia on his uniform. An officer.

Jackson tipped the broad brim of a chewed leather hat he had found in the barn where he had stolen the horses. "North to Jackson. Overseer for Fell's Point just east of town." He halted the team and the wagon rolled to a stop. "Know it? Little tobacky, little cane, mostly cotton."

"I'm afraid I don't," the officer said haughtily. "I'm not from that part of the state."

Jackson looked as if he were moving the wad of tobacco around in his cheek. What was that in his mouth? Cameron glanced at the horses again.

The officer lifted his chin, indicating Taye, Dorcas and Efia all seated in the back of the wagon. "Those your darkies?"

Jackson gave a snort of laughter. "I look like a man who can afford slaves? The master's. Just bought 'em. Me and the missus, we come to fetch 'em." He slapped his shirt and then the wagon seat. "Want to see the papers? I got 'em here somewheres. Don't know what they say 'cause I never learned my letters. But Master Josh, he said I wasn't to bring any darkies home without proper papers." Jackson looked to Cameron. "Fanny, where the plum hell is them papers?"

Cameron pursed her lips. "Reckon they're somewhere," she grunted. "'Pends on where you put 'em, Amos."

"Well, Christ a God, woman. Can't ya do anythin' I ask? I tole you to make sure I put them papers in my pocket." Jackson continued to slap his clothes as if the fictitious ownership papers would miraculously appear.

The officer eyed the women again. "I see you have them properly secured. It's a good thing. The woods and swamps are full of runaways."

"Can't be trusted, their kind," Jackson said, finally giving up on the search. "And I lose one of them, the master will have my ass in a sling fer sure." He cackled.

The officer looked over his shoulder at the three men on horseback behind him. "Well, we'd best be on our way, gentlemen." He touched his pristine hat that had not yet seen battle. "Carry on."

Jackson lifted the reins as he tipped his brim. "Ha!" he cried and the horses bolted forward.

Cameron sat on the wagon seat beside Jackson, her back stiff until she knew they were well out of hearing range of the officers. Then she slumped over, pressing her face to his sleeve. He smelled so good. "Are you sure we can't travel at night? I don't know how many times I can take that."

Jackson glanced in the back of the wagon. "All clear, ladies. You can drop the ropes, just keep them nearby." He looked back to Cameron. "That was a stroke of genius, tying them up. Far more believable."

"What were you going to do if they asked to see those so-called ownership papers?" she asked incredulously.

"I don't know." He cocked his head, offering a boyish grin. "Shoot? Throw you out as an offering?"

She wanted to slap him. Instead, she looped her arm through his and pressed her cheek to his sleeve. "We're going to have to come up with a better name for me, Amos. I don't think I can live with Fanny for another 160 miles."

Jackson's laughter rang in the treetops.

Grant walked through the dark, empty house wondering morosely what he was going to do when the whiskey ran out. If only he'd brought more with him from Baton Rouge. His hand brushed the burning hole that covered most of his cheek and was now a crusty, oozing wound. Christ, what was it? No doctor in Baton Rouge could tell him, and it had finally gotten bad enough that he'd come home. He couldn't stand the way people stared at him. Even the negra whores wouldn't lay with him anymore for fear it was the French pox.

He pressed the cool glass to his face and groaned. It itched so badly that he couldn't sleep, couldn't eat. There was no relief until he passed out.

His boots echoed on the dusty, hardwood floor as he moved across the entrance hall and up the grand staircase. His slow, hollow footsteps echoed overhead. The house had been empty only a couple of weeks, but it seemed longer. It looked abandoned and uncared for. As he gazed over the railing he saw that most of the furniture was gone and what was left was draped with canvas dust covers. In the self-imposed darkness, they looked like veiled spirits. He shivered. Nothing looked right in this house any more. Nothing felt right. The place smelled funny, too. Not like home at all. Like—like a tomb.

Grant took the stairs slowly. He was in trouble, bad trouble. He owed a lot of money for things he'd bought in Baton Rouge—the new carriage, clothes, some gold rings for himself. And Toussant wanted his money back for Taye's sale. Only Grant didn't have the money, and he didn't have Taye, either. He'd gotten word yesterday that Logan's ship had pulled briefly into port in Biloxi, but supposedly the girl wasn't onboard. No one knew where she was, the little ungrateful whore.

The gold from the sale of his slaves had been spent, and he could not draw credit from his bank. There was some ridiculous dispute now as to whether or not he was the heir to Elmwood. Thomas Burl, the little sniveling weasel, had apparently just petitioned the state court to compare another copy of Senator David Cambell's will to the one that had been read and executed months ago. If Grant could get his hands on the turd's neck, he would squeeze the life right out of him. There was no other will. Grant knew it. Burl knew it. But his claim was enough to freeze Grant's bank accounts, accounts the senator had set up for him.

Grant slowly took the steps, one at a time, dragging his bad leg. It ached at night, almost as much as this damned crater on his face. Angrily, he dug his dirty nails into it. Pain seared across his cheek and pus oozed out of it that was sticky and foul-smelling, but somehow in the pain, there was a little relief.

He'd make Naomi rub his leg. Sometimes that helped.

It had been just plain good luck that the slavers had caught her so close to home, otherwise he might not have gotten her back. It would be hard to function with just one slave, but one was better than none. It was really too bad the slavers had had to kill the big buck with her. Grant could have found a use for him, too. If nothing else, he could have sold such a fine specimen.

At the top of the stairs, Grant entered the dark hallway. He didn't have much oil left for lamps so he didn't light the rooms anymore. Not that he needed to. He liked the darkness, except when he had the nightmares. He was always dreaming about spiders now for some reason. Big spiders, little spiders. Shiny black ones, hairy brown ones. He had never been afraid of spiders before, but he was terrified of them now, and he had no idea why.

Grant sipped his whiskey. He was growing light-headed and his lips were beginning to numb. Another glass or two and maybe he could get some sleep. He would have liked to eat something, but there really wasn't anything left. Apparently the men he had hired to close up the house had helped themselves to the larders. All Grant had been able to find was some food in the abandoned slave quarters. Maybe tomorrow if Naomi promised she would be good, he would let her go down to the cabins and see what she could find to eat in the little weedy gardens.

Grant pulled at his shirt as he approached the closed door to his bedchamber. He was hot and sticky and he smelled godawful, but he didn't have the energy to draw a bath. It was too much work to haul his own water.

He fished a key from his pocket and fumbled with it in the door. It was hard to find the lock in the dark, but after a moment, he slipped it in and the mechanism clicked. He pushed the door and watched it glide open.

''Naomi?'' he called in a voice that bordered on forlorn.

Then he heard the sounds of her chains clanking. As long as he kept Naomi chained to the bed, he wouldn't be all alone.

Cameron crouched beside the tiny fire Jackson had built and fed it twigs. The others were stretched out on blankets, already asleep. No one had gotten any sleep the night before so they were all beyond exhausted.

Jackson came back from checking on the horses. He had managed to find a good place off the main road to rest for the night. It was an old mill site, so there was fresh water. And since three walls still remained of the mill house, no one would be able to see their fire from the road.

Jackson carried a bucket with him. "I'm going down to get water. Want to come?"

She tossed the last stick into the flames and rose. She was stiff and tired, but amazingly content. Taye was safe and she was going to Elmwood. Was it the thought of Elmwood that was giving her strength, or was it Jackson?

He caught her hand and held it in his as they walked through the woods. She smiled at the thought of how safe Jackson made her feel. She had always thought of herself as an independent woman, a woman who could do anything she wanted to. And the last weeks had proved that. But there was something so good about knowing he was here. With Jackson at her side, she just knew she could get Taye safely to Elmwood. After that…well, she would worry about that later.

"I figure it will take us a good two days to reach Jackson," he told her. If the road gets too busy, we may have to hole up for a day and wait to travel at night. We can't risk running into one of the senator's neighbors."

"All right."

He glanced at her. Moonlight filtered through the treetops providing enough light to see their footing, but not much more. "You're quiet tonight."

"Tired," she said.

"Look, Cam, I want you to know that I left because I didn't want to argue with you anymore."

"You don't have to say this," she said. "You never made any promises. I have no right to expect anything from you."

He squeezed her hand tightly and groaned. "God, you make things so hard, Cam. I'm trying to say that I left because I was concerned for your safety. I would have come back. Met the ship elsewhere. I would have found you."

She wanted to believe him, but why should she? Hadn't he left her before? Fool me once, she mused, fool me twice— what was that old saying? It didn't matter. She wasn't a girl anymore. It was hard to believe that she'd ever been so trusting. But that was before, when the world made sense...before everything changed.

They made their way slowly down the bank, but instead of releasing her hand and walking to the rippling creek, he sat down, pulling her with him. There was velvet green moss on the bank to cushion their seats. Frogs croaked and crickets chirped. He slid his arm around her waist and she let him.

"Damn, Cameron, I don't know what to do with you."

She gave a little laugh. "You don't have to do anything with me. Just help me get to Elmwood. I can go on from there alone when I'm ready. I don't need your help," she said starting to feel defensive.

He turned his head to look into her eyes. "No, you don't need my help. You're as capable as any man I've ever known. The thing is though, I'm beginning to feel as if I have to help you."

"That's ridiculous. You've got your—" she made a fluttering motion with her hand "—whatever it is you have to do. And I have to do what I have to do. I can't leave the South without seeing my home again. I just can't."

"I hate to leave you there alone. What about slavers? What if that damned brother of yours turns up?" He shook his head, seeming to wrestle with some inner turmoil. "But I'm cutting it close as it is, and there's too much riding on this. I *can't* not go."

She didn't bother to ask him where he was headed or why because she knew it was pointless. It all seemed rather odd to her, but she couldn't put the pieces together. Why would a blockade-runner need to suddenly leave his ship and go else-where by land? What news had Thomas brought to him when he boarded in New Orleans? Just what were the men up to?

"Cam, what I really want to talk to you about is the future. About us."

She lifted her lashes and was suddenly afraid. Afraid of losing Jackson, afraid of gaining promises from him that he could never keep. "Shh," she murmured, brushing her lips against his. She flicked her tongue across his lower lip. "We've so little time left together, Jackson. Don't say any-thing. Just love me." She slid her arms around his neck and he drew her close. "Can you do that? Can you love me for just a little while?"

Jackson met her gaze and his gray eyes were filled with an emotion she dared not put a name to. Then he pushed her backward into the soft moss of the bank and she closed her eyes. She parted her lips, welcoming the thrust of his tongue, and for a little while she let herself forget who she was, how she had gotten here and how soon she would be alone again.

Two nights later, Cameron stood on the road beside the elm-lined drive that would lead her to Elmwood. Jackson had given the women the wagon, one of the horses and most of the supplies.

"Now, you understand that you cannot stay here long," he said tersely.

She stared up the long drive. The bare ruts had begun to sprout grass, and the drive looked abandoned like an old woods road. "A few days," she said, tired to the bone.

He held the horse's reins in his hand. At the barn in Biloxi he'd had the foresight to steal tack so he could ride on. "Damn, I hate to leave you here." He looked at her and then at the ground. He had several days' growth of beard now, and oddly enough, it seemed to make him even more handsome, more roguish in appearance.

"We'll stay a day or two and then we'll head for the Un-derground Railroad stop on the Mississippi border," Taye said. "I promise, Captain Logan. I'll make her go if I have to tie her up myself and drag her behind this mule.'' She smiled and Cameron knew she was hoping to make her smile as well.

"Go on with you,'' Cameron told Jackson. "Get to your business, whatever it might be, and then back to your ship safely. We'll be all right.''

He ran his hand over his head, still seeming to be fighting himself and his choice to go on without them. "I want you to take this, Cam.'' He pulled a pistol out from the back waistband of his breeches. "And don't hesitate to use it if you have to.''

Cameron looked doubtfully at the gun as he pushed it into her hand. It seemed rather heavy for its size and amazingly cool to the touch.

"Thank you, Captain Logan,'' Taye said and led the horse and wagon down the lane. The two girls in the back waved.

Cameron just stood there for a moment, not looking at Jackson, not looking at the departing wagon. "Go,'' she whispered, fearing her voice would crack. Fearing she would crack and begin to beg him to stay, to take her with him, anything but leave her like this. Instead, she bravely lifted on her toes and kissed his cheek.

Jackson let go of the horse's reins and grabbed both her arms. He covered her mouth roughly with his, taking possession of her in a way no one else ever could.

When neither of them could breathe, he pulled away, meeting her gaze with fierce gray eyes. "I'll find you, Cam. When this is all over, I swear on your father's good name that I'll find you.''

She nodded, afraid to trust her own voice and then she turned away. Ignoring the sound of the hoofbeats retreating behind her, refusing to look back, Cameron hurried to catch up with Taye, the heavy pistol still in her hand.

"You all right?'' Taye asked, leading the horse and wagon into the dusky evening.

Cameron nodded. She reached for Taye's knapsack and dropped the pistol into it. "Here. You take this. I don't want it. I don't want to have to use it.''

Taye slipped her small, warm hand into Cameron's and gazed at her sideways with a sweet smile. "Come on. Let's go home....''

28

Cameron approached the three-story whitewashed house slowly, staring at the lower windows that had been shuttered. In the fading light they looked like eyes, and the house almost appeared asleep. The yard was overgrown with weeds and it looked as if a vandal had taken an axe to the front door to gain entry. He had either given up, or someone had chased him off. It was odd, but even with the air of sorrow that seemed to hang from the rafters, there was a bloom of happiness in Cameron's heart. She was home at last, home if only for a few hours.

"I'm hungry," Dorcas said from the back of the wagon. "I hate to ask, afta all ya done for me, but ya think ya got anythin' to eat here, Miss Cameron?"

Cameron continued to stare up at the house that loomed before them. It was almost dark so it was difficult to see, but she could have sworn she caught a glimpse of a shadow pass before one of the upstairs windows.

Grant's room.

Cameron's heart gave a trip. Grant was supposed to be in Baton Rouge living it up, gambling and running whores. It had never occurred to her that he would come back *here*. Why would he? He hated Elmwood. There was nothing left here for him. No reason for him to return to this lonely, empty house...unless he lay in wait for them.

She glanced at Taye and spoke, hoping her voice did not

tremble. "Take the horse and the wagon to the stable. Get the girls to climb up into the loft and throw down hay. The old mare needs water, too."

"I hope there's hay left," Taye said. "You heard those boys we met on the road yesterday. They said vandals had been through stealing anything that wasn't nailed down."

"Or defended," Cameron mused softly, returning her gaze to the upstairs window.

"Where are you going?" Taye asked. If she knew that Cameron was suddenly apprehensive, she gave no indication.

"Just inside." Cameron tried to keep her tone even, though her heart was pounding. Taye was nearly back to her old self again and Cameron would not jeopardize that, not for anything. "Maybe I can get in through the back."

"You got a key?" Efia offered. "If ya had a key, Miss Cameron, you could get in."

Cameron studied the house more carefully now, looking for signs that perhaps it was not as empty as it had first appeared. "I seem to have forgotten my key," she said lightly. "Silly me."

Cameron parted from Taye in front of the house. The wagon rolled on toward the stable and Cameron cut across the overgrown lawn. The tall grass was beginning to turn dry and brown in the heat and it cracked beneath the boots Jackson had given her.

Eyeing the house, she walked around toward the back. The house that had once bustled with activity was utterly silent on the hot, breezeless evening. In her mother's garden she smelled the faint scent of roses, but as she passed her mother's favorite pink rosebush she saw that the flowers were small and dry and shriveled. Was this what had become of the Campbell family? Had they shriveled and would they now die out?

Cameron's gaze shifted upward to the second story. In the twilight, she could see her father's upstairs veranda. Studying it, she could almost picture him seated in his chair, a cigar in his mouth, gesturing as he offered argument on one political notion or another. She couldn't resist a sad smile, but then it fell away.

So where was he? *Grant.* She knew he was waiting for her. She could feel his presence as dark and festering as that wound on the side of his face.

"Where are you, Grant?" she whispered as she watched and waited.

Cameron heard Grant's sad voice before she saw him. "You did come back," he groaned, sounding near to tears, full of misery and pain she had never realized he felt.

She watched warily as he stepped out of the shadows of the door that led to their father's bedchamber, onto the veranda. "I had to," she whispered.

"No, you didn't have to. You could have run. You could have let me chase you down." His tone was strange now, dreamy. "I would have, you know. Chased you down. Made you pay." He lifted one thin shoulder. His clothing was dirty and stained, which was so unlike him. "But now you have come to me."

"I had to come back because this is my home, Grant. You are still my brother."

He shook his head. "No. No, I have no sister. Never wanted a sister."

She frowned. "You should not say such things. You and I, we're all that is left of the Campbell name."

"Left of the Campbell name?" Grant growled. "What do I give a shit about the Campbell name?"

Cameron could feel her anger rising. She glanced up at her brother who was still partially obscured by the shadows of the roofline. "I will not have you dishonor our father that way," she ground out.

"Our father! Our father!" He came across the veranda toward her and it was then that she saw their father's pistol in his hand, gleaming in the last light of the day. "Your father, you mean! He was never mine. I was never his son."

"That's not true, Grant. Papa loved you."

He tipped back his head and laughed, a tragic, frightening laugh. "Loved me? He never loved me. How could he?"

She could see the infection on his face now and it sickened her. It was a great deal worse now than when she had last seen it. The wound had spread across his entire cheek, turning it an ugly shade of red and black and the center glistened with discharge. It looked painful.

She shook her head. "You're not making any sense. Put away the gun. I'll come up and we can talk."

"No! No, you stay there." He held the gun at arm's length, his hands trembling. His red face bloomed brighter. "You know what I'm saying is true. He always loved you. He loved you so much there was no room in his heart for me."

Cameron didn't know what to say. It made no sense to argue with Grant when he was in this state. He had to have a fever. The infection on his face was preventing him from thinking clearly. Rationally. "Grant. Papa loved you. It…it was only that you made it so hard for us to love you sometimes. You always seemed so discontented with us. I know I felt it was that way with me." She shook her head, watching him and the gun closely. "But we never meant to make you think we didn't love you."

"How could he?" he said, seeming to speak as much to himself as to her. His voice was eerie. Haunting. "How could he love me? He thought me a coward."

"Grant." Cameron tried to keep her voice steady. She reached out to him. "You know that's not true. Papa—"

"Shut up!" He shook the gun and she froze. "Shut up before I shut you up! I'm talking." He stomped his foot. "For once I am talking and everyone else is listening. You will listen to me!"

Cameron slowly lowered her hand to her side. "I'm listening," she said softly.

He still held the pistol out, but it was getting heavy. His hand drifted downward. "I don't understand why it had to be this way."

"What way?" Cameron despised her brother, yet there was a part of her that pitied him. How could she not pity such a shell of a man? "What do you mean? I don't understand what you're talking about. Why did what have to be this way?"

"Life." He glanced down, his eyes suddenly filled with a hatred that shocked her. "You know he always loved her."

"Who?" Cameron watched him carefully, trying to figure out what he was talking about while still watching the direction of the gun barrel. He wouldn't really shoot her, though. He just wanted a captive audience; he had always been a bully.

"Sukey." He spoke with such detest. "Papa married our mother, but that black bitch was already here in the house when our mother arrived. Did you know that?"

Cameron glanced down at the grass at her feet. She wished she had had an opportunity to talk to Papa about Sukey. She wished she had known more. She wished she could have better understood. "I think Papa loved Sukey very much."

"He loved her more than he loved *our mother!*" His voice cracked. "More than he loved me. He loved you all more than he loved me. Even Taye." Grant wiped his runny nose with his sleeve. As he did so, his finger tightened around the trigger of the pistol.

The hair rose on the back of Cameron's neck as she realized how close to madness her brother really was. It had been dangerous for her to approach him this way. Foolish. She slowly slid one foot back, hoping he could not detect her slight movement in the twilight.

"You know," he called down, his voice a little steadier. "I understand. I loved Taye, too."

"We both love her," she offered, hoping she could redirect the conversation.

"No." Spittle flew from his mouth. "I mean I *loved* her. I would have given her anything. *Done* anything for her. But she rewarded my love with nothing but—but scorn."

It occurred to Cameron that her brother had a rather odd way of showing his love, but she didn't dare voice her opinion. Not when he had the weapon and she had nothing.

"But she thought I was a coward, too."

Cameron had no real desire to injure her brother, but she wished she had Jackson's pistol now. "No one ever said—"

"Didn't I tell you to shut up once before, bitch?" He waved the pistol violently at her, and Cameron froze as he drew closer to the edge of the veranda. She pressed her lips together, trying to guess how far she would have to run to get under cover should he fire at her.

"*She* thought I was a coward just like *he* did," he screamed shrilly. Then his voice grew frighteningly calm again. "But I wasn't a coward, was I? Hmm? I did what no one thought I could. I've accomplished what no one thought I would." He held the pistol steady on her, beading her through the eye site. "You know, *I* did it."

Cameron got a strange feeling, one Sukey would have described as "a ghost walking over her grave." The hair rose on her forearms and shivers shook her body. Cameron was almost afraid to speak this time. She didn't want to hear anything else Grant had to say. She just wanted to run. But she couldn't help herself; she *had* to ask. "You did what, Grant?"

Still holding on to the pistol with one hand, he ran his other hand fondly over the lighter colored wood on the veranda rail. The wood that had been replaced after their father's death.

Cameron took half a step back, any glimmer of calm left, shattered in a blink of the eye. "No, Grant…"

He glanced downward at his sister, a treacherous smile on his face. "You think he fell?" he snorted. "No. I sent the senator on his way." Grant stepped closer to the rail, raising the pistol again. "To hell, I hope!"

Cameron covered her face with her hands, tears streaming down her face. She felt as if she were falling, tumbling in a darkness so deep, so black, that she would never see light again. Never in her greatest nightmare had she felt such utter betrayal. "No," she cried. "Grant, please, no."

"So now, Papa is dead. Sukey is dead." His voice grew stronger, as if he drew strength from their lifeless bodies. "Taye has been made to stand before all those men and be degraded. And you, little sister, dear. You know the shameful truth of the Campbell family. Patricide." He grinned. "The greatest sin of them all, don't you think, sister dearest?"

To her shock, he threw back his head and laughed wickedly.

Cameron lowered her hands, not bothering to wipe away her tears. Determinedly, she pulled herself from the emotional darkness that threatened to leave her incapacitated. Her brother was a madman and she had to get away from him. If he would kill their father, he would have no qualms about killing her.

By her calculations, the smartest thing to do was seek the shelter of the lower veranda rather than run farther out into the open. If she could make it there, he wouldn't be able to shoot her from above.

"So now, everyone who ever hurt me is dead, gone. Ruined. Everyone but you, that is, sister."

"Grant, listen to me." She spoke evenly despite her heart racing in her chest. "If we could just sit down and talk about this. Let me look at that nasty…welt on your face. We could talk. We could—"

Without warning, Grant fired the pistol directly at her. Cameron screamed as the gun exploded. Dark soil burst in front of her hitting her arms and legs and the bullet plowed into the grass at her feet. "No, Grant!" Cameron tried to scramble backward as he leaned over the rail to get a better shot and took aim at her again.

Time seemed to stand still. Cameron saw the evil hatred in her brother's eyes. She saw his finger flex to fire on her again, from closer range this time. She screamed.

Gunfire exploded in her ear. She heard the whistle of the bullet and waited for the blossom of pain. But to her shock, Grant pitched forward, crashed through the railing and tumbled to the ground. Cameron spun around smelling the black powder in the air, tasting its bitterness on her tongue. Her gaze met with Taye's pale-blue eyes.

"I'm sorry," Taye said softly with an utter calmness that was as shocking as the fact that she had pulled the trigger. "He killed the senator and he would have killed you."

The girls threw their arms around each other, but said nothing. The pain was too raw. Tears ran down Cameron's cheeks, but Taye remained dry eyed as they walked to the place where Grant had fallen.

Cameron knew her brother was dead even before she squatted and rolled him gently onto his back.

"Dead?" Taye asked, holding the pistol at her side. Still,

she did not weep. The girl was stronger than Cameron realized.

Cameron nodded. Taye had saved her life.

"Miss Cameron? Taye?"

Hearing a familiar voice, Cameron looked up to see Naomi running toward them across the lower veranda, a lamp swinging in her hand. As she ran, something clinked like a chain. When Naomi drew near, Cameron saw that the girl's face was a mottled blue and green. Her eye was nearly swollen shut and she had a nasty cut in the corner of her mouth. She looked as if she had been badly beaten and Cameron didn't have to wonder by whom.

"Naomi," Cameron breathed.

The young black woman's gaze fell to the body lying in the grass and she walked over to stare into his lifeless eyes, lifting the lantern to get a better look. "Knew it would come to this," she murmured. "Seen it in the bones."

In the lamplight, the wound on Grant's face was horrifying. This close, Cameron could smell the putrefying flesh. "God in heaven, what is it?" she breathed, reaching out to close her brother's sightless hazel eyes. "I've never seen such a lesion. What could have caused it?"

Naomi drew back her lips, lifting a haughty dark brow. "Some would say it was a spider bite, Missy," she drawled matter-of-factly. Then her dark eyes narrowed and her voice floated on the heavy, hot night air. Cameron could have sworn she heard the echo of slave drums that had been silent for weeks.

"Old folks claims they got them little gray ghosty spiders back in old Africa, little teeny gray spiders what creep around at night and hunts for jest the right place to lay they eggs. Someplace warm and safe fer the little'ns to grow and hatch, someplace wheres theys blood to drink. And the old folks, they say them little'ns suck and bite and dig an' scratch and claw 'til they free. I hear'd that story lots of times." She nodded and a half smile tugged at her bruised lips. "Some would say ole gray spider bite Master Grant...but some would say it was somethin' else."

Cameron looked up at Naomi. She didn't believe in curses or any of the voodoo magic Naomi believed in but there was something about the woman's face...

Cameron stood up and pressed her hand to her lower back. Suddenly she was so tired, she could barely hold her eyes open. "I'll drag him inside tonight so the animals don't get to him," she said, amazed by her own lack of emotion. "We'll have to bury him tomorrow and then we'll move on."

"Ya got that right, Missy Cameron. We shouldn't tarry here too long. 'Federate troops movin' through. They say they burnin' what ain't occupied. Yankees pushin' south fast. They don't want to leave nothin' the Yankees can use."

Cameron studied Naomi's battered face in the lamplight. She didn't want to ask what had happened to her, how Grant had gotten her under his thumb. She'd obviously been chained up and gotten free. Cameron would give the girl time to tell her later. "Your man, Naomi. Did you find him?"

Naomi's eyes turned bright with tears. "Dumb fool. He didn't go on the way he was s'posed to. Waited for me at our special place." She rubbed at her eyes with the heels of her hands. "He's dead, Miss Cameron. Slavers got 'im."

To Cameron's surprise, her own eyes filled with tears and a lump rose in her throat. She could not cry for the loss of her brother, but she could cry for the loss of a slave man she had never met. She sniffed and rubbed at her nose with the back of her hand. "I'm sorry," she whispered.

Naomi nodded and set down the lamp. "What's done is done. 'Least I had him for a time." She took a breath and looked up again. "Me and Taye will see what we can scare up to eat. I got another lamp inside. You want help haulin' him in?"

Cameron shook her head. She knew her brother's body would be heavy for her to move alone, but it didn't seem right that Taye or Naomi should help her, not after what Grant had done to them. Besides, she needed a little time alone. "Find Dorcas and Efia, too. They're probably scared out of their wits with this gunfire."

"You brought them girls?" Cameron heard Naomi say softly as the two women went into the dark house.

Without thinking about what she was doing, Cameron retrieved her father's pistol and tucked it into the back of her breeches the way Jackson did. Then she grabbed Grant by the armpits and slowly dragged him across the lower veranda, ignoring the bloody trail she left behind. She had to stop several times because he was so heavy, but she eventually reached the door that led to her father's study. She could leave his body there for the night.

Finding it locked, she went into the house through the main rear door Naomi had used and came back out onto the veranda through the small side door that led from her father's study. Without thinking about the gruesome task she performed, she dragged Grant inside and then fetched the lamp.

She closed herself up alone with her brother in their father's beloved study. There was no brandy left and the big leather chair was gone, but Cameron sat on the edge of her father's elmwood desk and closed her eyes. When she did, she could almost feel his presence. As she sat there in the darkness, she thought of Grant and how sad it was that he had brought this upon himself. That his sick hatred could have been so great that he would have killed their father.

She thought of her beloved Papa and Sukey buried and gone. In the last months, it seemed as if she had lost everything. Nothing was as she had once thought it would be, all of her bright hopes were tarnished, broken, abandoned.

She opened her eyes and stared into the darkness, wiping at her tears that seemed so useless now. Taye was right. There was nothing left in this house for her any more. There was nothing left of Elmwood for her. All that was here now was tangled weeds, barren fields and empty stables.

She felt so alone.

A sob rose in her throat as she remembered Jackson's arms around her only a short time ago. Had she been wrong to insist on coming home to Elmwood? Could she have gone with him, wherever he was going? Would he have taken her if she had asked?

Cameron felt so lost. So forlorn.

She stared at her brother's still body by the door and then her gaze shifted. She studied the walls, the bookshelves now empty. So many good memories. Then her attention fell to the small writing desk that had once been her Grandmother Campbell's. It hadn't even been covered with a drape. Probably because it was old and didn't appear to be worth much.

Indifferently, she walked over and opened it, pulling down the front panel. She smoothed the worn writing surface with her palm thoughtfully, feeling the grain of the wood beneath her fingertips. Her gaze drifted to the drawer meant to store an inkwell. Grant had cleared the desk of their father's papers and the little odds and ends that had collected there over the years. She wondered, however, if he had remembered the secret compartment. Curious, she pulled the drawer out and set it aside, then reached up inside the desk and slid the panel that could be felt but not seen. As she turned her body to better access the secret compartment, her gaze fell once again on her brother. She pressed her lips together, overwhelmed by the emotions of the day.

Her fingertips touched a piece of paper and a small cloth sack with something hard inside it that felt like pebbles. She had no idea what the sack was, but as she removed the items, she wondered if she could hope this was Taye's emancipation paper. It was silly, she knew, for Grant had surely burned it. But what *was* hidden in the desk?

There was a light tap on the door and Cameron's head snapped up.

"Cam, can I come in?"

It was Taye.

"I brought him in here," she called, not wanting to speak his name before Taye. "But you can come in, puss, if you don't mind."

"I'm not afraid of dead men, only those living." Taye slipped inside the study and closed the door behind her. "What are you doing in here, alone? You should join us in the kitchen. We found potatoes and onions and some turnip greens that Naomi said would make a delicious meal." She glanced at Cameron's hand. "What's that?"

Cameron looked at the paper folded neatly in quarters and a tiny velvet sack. "I don't know. I found them in the desk's secret compartment." She drew them closer to the lamp. "But look, your name is on the letter. In Papa's handwriting." She turned to Taye and offered the paper as if it were a treasure. "Here."

Taye stared at the folded sheet of paper in Cameron's hand. "Why would the senator leave me a letter?"

Cameron felt her heart pitter-pat in her chest. Dare she hope she knew what the letter contained? "I don't know," she breathed, offering it again. "You'll have to read it and see."

Taye shook her head, clasping her hands behind her back. It was hard to believe this slight, beautiful woman had killed a man she had known her entire life just an hour before. "I couldn't. You read it to me."

Cameron drew closer to the lamplight on the desk again and slowly unfolded the letter. "Dear Taye," it said in her father's dark, thick scroll. Cameron read aloud slowly.

"'I apologize for not having the courage to say this to you in person, dear daughter.'"

Taye gasped.

Cameron broke into a wide grin and went on. "'But I want you to know how proud I am of you. I want you to know how proud your mother and I are of you. Enclosed in the bag you will find my gift to you, dear Taye. Please take the jewels and use them as you see fit. Perhaps with this small fortune, you will be able to live in a place where you can be appreciated for who you are and not prejudiced against for the color of your skin.'" It was signed, "Your loving father, David Campbell."

Cameron looked up at Taye who seemed stunned.

"My…my father?" Her blue-eyed gaze met Cameron's.

Cameron gave a squeal and threw her arms around Taye's slight shoulders. "That means we really are sisters!"

Taye hugged her tightly and then pushed away. "Wait a minute. Do you mean you knew about this?"

Cameron shook her head. "I only suspected, and that wasn't until the night your mother died. But there was no proof. Papa and your mother were both dead."

"So you didn't want me to get my hopes up," Taye finished for her.

Still grinning, Cameron took Taye's hand, opened it and pressed the velvet bag into her palm. "Something tells me you have just become a wealthy lady."

"*We* have become wealthy," she corrected, still in shock. As she eased the drawstring on the bag she kept shaking her head slowly. "I can't believe this. It's like a dream come true. When I was little, I used to pretend I was your sister. I used to practice calling the senator *Papa.*" She tipped the bag, and to their amazement, glittering green jewels rolled into her palm.

"Emeralds," Cameron breathed. "They're so beautiful."

"So many," Taye whispered. "They must be worth a large fortune." Her hand shaking, she poured them back into the bag and tied it shut again. She looked much like a little lost girl. "I don't know what to say."

Cameron laughed and was surprised by how good it felt. "I do. Welcome to the family, Taye Campbell!"

29

Taye, Naomi, Dorcas and Efia all slept the night upstairs in the big, empty house that had once been so alive with the sounds of life. Cameron, however, could not sleep. Instead, she spent the night in the study with Grant's body and her father's memory.

Cameron found that she could not summon much regret for her brother's death. Not now, knowing that he had killed their father. It wasn't that she was glad he was dead; she wasn't. Even though he had done all these terrible things, Grant had still been her brother. Even the senator would not have wanted her to be glad of his son's death. But so much had happened, and she was utterly overwhelmed. And though she was thrilled that Taye was her half sister, she wasn't even sure what that would mean to them. Somehow, knowing they were sisters and the last of the Campbell line, made the task of getting Taye north to safety weigh more heavily upon her shoulders.

On the trip north from Biloxi to Elmwood, they had talked to many people on the road and it was quite evident that Mississippi was trying desperately to prevent her slaves from escaping north to freedom. There were hired bands of slavers everywhere, and even soldiers were called on occasion to round up darkies for service in the army. Cameron had to get these women north of the Mason-Dixon line and she had to do it quickly; it would only get more difficult to travel with the black women as the war escalated.

Cameron spent the entire night thinking, praying, drifting in and out of sleep, dreaming of days long past. She thought of iced lemonade on the veranda, shared with her father's laughter and lectures. She recalled the feeling of light-headedness as she flew over a fence on her beloved Roxy's back. She remembered the sound of Sukey's lovely voice as she sang softly to herself while at work. There were so many good memories that it was hard for Cameron to be sad. She thought of all the goodness that had come from Elmwood, and knew she would hold those memories dear for the rest of her days. But as dawn came, her thoughts drifted naturally toward the future.

All night, interspersed with memories of parties, rowing on the river and picnics on the lawn, images of Jackson Logan had flitted through her head. And now, as dawn rose pink in the horizon, she wondered if Jackson would play some part in her future. She was at such unrest with her feelings for him. And what of his feelings for her? There had been moments in the days since the *Juchoir* that he had been tender. Did he love her? Did she have the courage to find out?

In the end, Cameron decided that she must tackle one thing at a time. She couldn't continue to dwell over Jackson and their relationship. She needed to put all of her energy into getting the women who depended on her to safety. Perhaps then she could decide what to do about Jackson. After all, how hard would he be to find if she truly wanted to locate him?

As dawn's light brightened the study, Cameron left the house. She needed to find a shovel and begin digging in the family graveyard. Even taking turns with the other girls, it would be hours before she could bury Grant. Then they needed to make plans, pack whatever they could find and map out their path north. Cameron had kept no information on the Underground Railroad except what was in her head, but she thought she knew where to make her first contact on the border between Mississippi and Tennessee. There, she prayed she could find help, maybe even gain information about what happened to some of Elmwood's slaves.

Cameron walked out onto the lower veranda from the study

and through her mother's dying garden. The relentless Mississippi sun beat down harshly upon her head and she wondered if there was a trunk somewhere in the house with servants' bonnets. She had dozens of stylish hats, beribboned and lovely, but wearing one would cause observers to remember her. No, the fancy bonnets would have to gather dust here at Elmwood. They would all need practical bonnets to walk in this heat, or even to rest in the daytime if they had to travel by night.

Cameron walked around the side of the house, wiping her sweaty brow. She was hungry; she'd not been able to stomach Naomi's meal last night. And what she wouldn't give for a cool bath right now. As she wandered toward the front of the house she contemplated a quick swim in the river. She could go for a swim and then wake the girls.

She waded through the brittle weeds still damp with morning dew, oblivious to the caw of a flock of crows overhead. As she walked, she tried not to look up at the shuttered house standing so forlorn and ghostly in the light of the early morning. As she crossed the lawn near the front porch, her gaze strayed to the elm-lined drive, and an image of carriages rolling up flashed through her head. She remembered the music of her father's last ball and the—

Cameron stopped short and shaded her eyes with her hand, wondering if her head and her empty stomach were playing tricks on her. Was there someone coming up the lane? The image shimmered like a mirage in the July heat. There was most definitely a man approaching. A stranger, and strangers were bad news these days. Her next thought was of the safety of the other girls. She had left the pistol in the study. Did she make a run for it?

Then Cameron recognized the gait of the man walking toward her as nonchalantly as if he were out on a Sunday stroll. Could it possibly be?

Cameron wanted to run down the driveway. Instead, she forced herself to walk. Step by step she neared him until she could see the silly grin on his face. She ran the last few steps, and he swept her into his arms.

"Jackson," she groaned, hating herself for needing him so badly. "You came back."

He covered her face with kisses. "I came back. No idea why. Walked half the night, telling myself I was a fool." He grasped her face between his hands and stared into her eyes. "But I just couldn't leave you, Cam." He sounded disgusted with himself. "Couldn't do it."

She smiled, her heart filled with a happiness she was not sure she had ever experienced. Jackson had come back for her. No matter what he said, how he behaved sometimes, the fact remained that he had come back for her.

"I have so much to tell you." Suddenly she frowned. "Heavens! What happened to you?" She brushed her fingertips over a nasty gash above his eyebrow. He had a bruised cheek and his lower lip was swollen. He'd been in a fight for certain.

He lifted one shoulder in a devil-may-care shrug. "Got in a little tussle. Not to worry. Business taken care of and a little extra on the side."

She laughed, afraid she might cry. She lifted on her tiptoes and kissed his swollen lip. Then his cheek. "I'm so glad you came back," she confessed, knowing she laid open her feelings by saying so.

"Me, too, but we can't stay." He slid his arm around her waist, and arm in arm they headed up the overgrown way toward the house. "You need to pack whatever you can carry. The girls, too." He glanced at her with those gray eyes that haunted her dreams. "If they're going."

"They're going."

"And we have to head north. I need to get to Washington D.C. as quickly as possible."

She lifted a brow, but didn't ask why. There would be time for that later. "I can get the girls to pack, but I need your help. There's something I have to do before I go."

"Cam, I'm serious. It's too dangerous for us to stay here with those girls, and I have to get to D.C. with or without you. Now if you think I'm going to get involved in another one of your—"

"I need help burying my brother." She suddenly felt weak in her knees.

Jackson halted, grabbing both her arms to steady her. "Grant's dead?"

She wiped at her scratchy eyes. "He tried to kill me. It was Taye." She pressed her lips together. "Taye shot him." She lifted her head, tears brimming in her eyes. "He told me he killed Papa."

Jackson pulled her against his hard, lean body and she breathed deeply, letting the scent of his dusty skin and overwhelming maleness soothe her.

"I'm sorry, Cam." He hugged her tightly. "So sorry."

"Sorry Grant's dead?" she asked, feeling a little forlorn.

"Nah. Just sorry it had to end this way." Jackson leaned back and brushed her hair from her eyes. "And I'm sorry you had to find out that he killed your father. But you mustn't blame yourself."

She shook her head. "I don't."

"Good. We can talk about this later. Now, is Taye all right?"

She was unable to resist a sad smile as she shook her head in amazement. "She's tougher than I knew. We found Naomi, too. Grant had her chained to his bed."

"The bastard," he spat. "Taye just shot him? He didn't deserve that good. He's just lucky I didn't get my hands on him first." He slipped his hand into hers. "Come on. Let's see what we can find in the way of a shovel. I can do the digging for you if you want while you get the girls organized."

"No," she said. "I have to help...to at least be there." She walked beside him, matching his stride with determination. There it was, that flicker of hope in her heart again. "It's one last thing I can do for Papa."

The heat had become unbearable by the time Jackson and Cameron put Grant to rest in the family graveyard. There was no marker and no time to make even a rough cross, but once Taye was safe, Cameron would return to Elmwood and see that stones were placed on her brother's grave, as well as Sukey's. She would do it for Papa...for the memory of a brother she'd once loved.

While Jackson and Cameron dug the grave, Taye and Naomi set the other two girls to making preparations for the long and perilous journey north. The plan was to take the horse and the wagon into town so Jackson could sell them for money for food. The emeralds remained Taye and Cameron's secret for the time. Besides, they couldn't be sold here in the South. They were worthless stones in a place that needed food and ammunition.

The women had found bags and sewn straps to them so that they could be worn on their backs. They had packed blanket rolls to sleep on and all the food they could find. When sunset came, the plan was to head north for the Tennessee line. Cameron and Jackson had discussed it while they set to the terrible task of burying Grant. The decision had been made that they would all travel the Underground Railroad. It would be the safest way to get the four black women north, and perhaps Jackson and Cameron could be of some aid to other runaway slaves.

Cameron and Jackson joined the women for a small meal of bread Naomi had baked in the Elmwood kitchen ovens with the little cornmeal and flour she could find. It wasn't much of a meal, but because Cameron shared it with those she loved, it seemed like a feast.

"So you're going north, too," Taye asked Jackson. "Not back to your ship?"

Jackson lay back against a tree trunk, his battered hat tipped to shade his face from the sun. "I'm needed in Washington as soon as I can get there. Thomas will finish our business in the Gulf and then come to Baltimore. If all goes well, I think there's a distinct possibility that we may see Mr. Burl there, if that's what you're asking." He winked at Taye.

Taye blushed profusely and threw what little water was left in the ladle at him. The water hit him in the face, and Efia and Dorcas grew round-eyed with shock.

Naomi laughed and slapped her skinny knee.

Cameron grinned.

"Ah, could you throw a little more of that cold water my way, Taye? I was thinking—"

"Shh," Cameron interrupted. She rose from where she sat beside Jackson in the grass, gazing beyond the house to the drive. "Do you hear something?"

Jackson was up beside her in an instant, adjusting his hat so that he could see better. "Get the packs, now, Naomi," he ordered under his breath. He glanced at the twins. "And not a word out of either of you or I'll gag you both, you understand me? We'll not have a repeat of what happened in Biloxi."

Cameron stared at the elm trees that stretched in two parallel rows toward the main road. "What is it?"

"I don't know. My guess is soldiers."

Naomi and Taye ran back across the lawn, carrying the bags they had left on the front porch.

"The horse and wagon," Cameron said, turning for the barn. "I'll get it hitched up."

Jackson grabbed her arm. "Ah, hell, I hear horses. Riders on horseback. There's no time to hitch the wagon. I don't know who's coming, but we're getting out of here."

There were six bags with the supplies evenly distributed. Taye pushed the pistol she had shot Grant with into Cameron's hand. "Take this," she whispered. "I can't." Her blue-eyed gaze met Cameron's tawny eyes. "I just can't."

Cameron nodded. "And you have the *other?*"

Taye brushed her lips against Cameron's cheek. "Sewn into the hem of my dress for safekeeping." They had agreed last night that no one should know about the emeralds. It wasn't that they didn't trust the other women, but that they did not want to offer any temptation. Cameron had not even told Jackson.

Naomi pushed packs in Dorcas's and Efia's hands and grabbed one for herself. Taye picked up another bag and heaved it onto her shoulders. Jackson grabbed the last two.

"I can carry my own," Cameron said, taking one from his hand.

He lifted his palms in surrender. "Yes, ma'am. I don't care who hauls what, as long as we haul ourselves out of here before those men arrive."

All of them took off at a run, through the cornfield, away from the house and the drive, toward the river. They could hear the hoofbeats pounding now. They could hear male voices. Shouting.

"You ladies know this river better than I do. How are we going to cross?" Jackson asked as they cut through the woods near the slave quarters.

Cameron refused to look toward the slaves' graveyard, and she noticed that Taye avoided the site as well. "I don't know," Cameron said. "It took boats to get the slaves across."

"Old Pearl, she's drier now this time a year. Not much rain," Naomi offered. "I know a place where's we can cross and barely get our feet wet."

Jackson stepped back to let Naomi take the lead. "You show us the way to go. I'll pull up the rear. Keep an eye on our backs."

Sweat trickled down between Cameron's shoulder blades as she ran through the woods. Dry leaves crackled beneath her feet, and it sounded to her as if they were a herd of horses plowing through. They could hear the men, whoever they were, nearer now. They must have reached the house by now. It was just as Cameron spotted the shimmering water through the twisted vines that ran up the pin oak and hickory trees that she thought she smelled smoke.

At the river's edge, they headed south along the bank, leaping over fallen limbs, ducking branches. Here by the river, the smell of the mud was thick and the scent of the rotting vegetation pungent. But the scent of smoke was growing stronger.

"What are they burning?" Cameron asked, glancing over her shoulder as she ran behind the other women.

Jackson grabbed her arm, hurrying her along. "Keep going, Cam. Don't think about it now. We have to get these girls out of here. If we get caught, they'll all be carried off." He lowered his voice so that only she could hear. "You know they'll take Taye as well. No one will believe she's a free woman."

"And then they'll be asking questions about Grant," Cameron thought aloud. It wasn't until this morning that she realized the full impact of what Taye had done last night. She knew Taye had saved her life, but some might not see it that way. Some might say Taye had murdered Grant.

Jackson slowly released her arm and loped beside her. "I'm telling you, don't think about it. Just keep going."

They followed a turn in the river where Cameron remembered playing on fallen logs with Taye and Grant as children. They had caught tadpoles with their bare hands and set them free in the muddy water.

"Right here," Naomi called. "See. Ol' Pearl, she get right narrow. Shalla' too." Without hesitating, she lifted her pack up and stepped into the water.

Naomi's calculation that they would barely get their feet wet was not entirely accurate. In the middle of the river, Dorcas and Efia had to swim. Taye lost her footing, but Jackson grabbed her by the arm and lifted her up, preventing her from going under and getting her bundle wet. Although she protested greatly, it was obvious she was still weak from her time spent locked up in Baton Rouge when she had refused to eat.

Cameron reached chest-deep water and wondered if she too would have to swim, but then it began to grow shallow again.

"You all right?" Jackson called from just ahead of her, still holding on to Taye.

Cameron nodded as the others ahead of her splashed her in the face. The water would actually have felt good had their bath been under different circumstances.

On the far side of the river, they climbed one by one onto the bank. Birds twittered in the trees and the leaves swayed slightly in the hot afternoon breeze. In this heat, it wouldn't take long for their clothes to dry.

"Lord a mighty, I got to rest," Efia moaned, falling onto the grass.

Jackson walked past her. "Rest all you want, sweetheart, but we're pressing on."

Cameron was the last to drag out of the water, and as she did so, she turned around. She heard a sound escape her lips as she caught sight of the billows of black smoke rising over the treetops where she knew her home was. Her lower lip trembled. "They're burning Elmwood," she murmured. "They're burning my home."

Jackson took her hand. "I told you not to look back." His expression softened. "I'll build you a new one when this is all over, Cam." His tone was cool, but not unfeeling. "Now, come on, we have to keep moving."

Cameron forced herself to turn away from the sight of the billowing clouds of smoke, from the acrid scent of burning timber. They were headed upriver again, back toward Elmwood.

"You're sure this is safe?" Cameron asked Jackson.

He grabbed her arm to steady her as they ran along the bank behind the other girls. "Hell, no. I'm not sure it's safe. All I know is that we have to go north toward Memphis. That's what Naomi said this morning."

The wet, bedraggled group ran along the riverbank with Naomi in the lead. Efia was crying softly and Dorcas was pushing her along. They passed the place where Cameron had sent the slaves across the river, and she could not help but gaze at the spot where Sukey had fallen.

Cameron saw Taye staring too, and she looped her arm through her best friend's…her sister's. "Don't think about it now," she whispered. "Just run, Taye."

Taye turned to look at Cameron, her eyes filled with tears. They ran side by side. "She's in a good place now," she panted. "With Papa. That's what I keep telling myself."

Cameron suddenly heard dogs. She heard the baying of hounds on the trail of human flesh, and she turned to look over her shoulder at Jackson. Oh, sweet heaven, what else could go wrong?

Efia broke into little gasping wails of terror.

"There. I see one of 'em," someone shouted as men burst through the trees on the far side of the river. "Cripes. A whole passel of darkies."

"Stop or we shoot," another one shouted. Warning shots rang out in the trees and Cameron heard the whistle of bullets as they went by.

Jackson pushed past Cameron and gave Efia a shove. "Run," he cried. "Run!"

30

Cameron dropped back to run beside Jackson. "If they get across the river, we haven't a chance," she panted, her sides aching from running so far.

"So hope they don't find the low spot, and we don't get caught."

Cameron threw a quick look over her shoulder. She heard splashing and men cursing. One of the slavers tried to wade across, then realized how deep the river was in the middle and turned back.

"We've got to find a place to hide," Jackson murmured. "These girls can't run much farther. I don't know this area the way you do. You have to think of a place where we can get under cover."

Cameron shook her head, frantic. "I can't. There's nothing really here but fields and swamp and the river."

"Think, Cam," Jackson murmured. "There's got to be some place to get out of the open. An old cabin in the woods, a barn—"

"The mill!" she burst out. "It's a little farther up on a branch of the river." Cameron gulped great mouthfuls of air. The women in front of her were beginning to slow. "It's right on the main road so it's risky, but it's been abandoned for years. Some of the walls crumbled in a storm."

"But there's a place to hide?"

Cameron nodded, almost too out of breath to talk. "A cellar,

I think. You can't reach it...from the mill house any more...but we can...get to it by way of the riverbank," she panted.

"Excellent. Perfect." He grinned, rubbing her shoulder with his arm. "Near the water is perfect. The dogs won't easily pick up our scent."

Cameron forced herself to take an extra couple of steps, still running so she could catch up to Taye. "The mill," she told the women. "Take the fork in the river and head for the old mill house on the road to town."

Taye looked to Cameron with concern.

"Jackson says it will work."

"You trust him?" Taye whispered.

Cameron offered a grim smile. "With our lives."

She led the wet, weary group toward the branch of the river where the old mill house lay. At Jackson's suggestion, they crossed back and forth over the waterway to confuse the bloodhounds, should they track them this far.

Cameron led the group across the main road and over the bridge, recalling that this was where Taye had fallen into the millpond as a child. Back then, the water had been dammed and was much deeper, though.

Halfway across the bridge, they heard the sounds of hoofbeats again.

"Guess their dirty work is done," Taye muttered looking down the road to where Elmwood lay.

"I hate to say it, but burning is normal procedure for an army," Jackson said grimly. "It makes sense strategically not to leave anything that would aid the enemies' hand."

"This way," Cameron whispered, refusing to think about her beloved home burning to the ground. She loved Elmwood, the home her grandfather had built, but she loved her sister more. Cameron dropped onto her bottom in exhaustion, and slid down the steep bank on the slippery hill.

From above, the stone mill house looked almost entirely demolished. First there had been a fire when Cameron was twelve or so. After that, Elmwood had bought its flour and cornmeal elsewhere. A few years later, a storm of hurricane-force winds had collapsed the already weakened walls.

But the cellar was still intact as she remembered it from the year before when she had lured Taye on one of her adventures and the women had explored the ruins. If she recalled correctly, there was a room below ground whose walls were still sturdy.

"Let's go, let's go," Jackson ushered, running down the steep bank to the water. "The soldiers are coming."

The women splashed through the shallow stream behind Cameron and she ducked into the cellar. She stepped aside to let one woman after another pass. Jackson brought up the rear, his pistol drawn. A moment later they heard the thunder of horses' hoofs on the wooden bridge, which sounded as if it were directly overhead. The pounding echoed off the stone walls, and Efia uttered a little yelp of fear.

Jackson spun around, his gray-eyed gaze icy with warning. Efia paled and clamped her hand over her mouth.

Cameron motioned for everyone to get down, and the women collapsed on the damp dirt floor.

Jackson stood near the doorway he nearly had to crawl through. Cameron set down her pack, her heart still pounding, her breath still coming in short gasps. "You think…the slavers…were with the soldiers?"

He shook his head. They must have run more than two miles, yet he was barely out of breath. "Nah, coincidence most likely. I doubt those were professional slavers. Probably just a couple of Mississippi boys looking to make some extra money. I imagine they prowl the river regularly since slaves trying to escape use the waterways as guides north."

"Rivers and the stars," Taye said.

Naomi nodded. "Most follows the drinkin' gourd." She pointed up. "They say that the stars in the pitcher points the way t' freedom."

The twins murmured agreement. "Da drinkin' gourd," one said. "Ole Dan, that's what he tell us."

Cameron stood near Jackson and gazed out at the bank. She couldn't see the men riding over the bridge, but she could still hear the hoofbeats and the occasional male voice. Even here, below ground, she could smell smoke.

Jackson slipped his arm around her as the sounds of the soldiers began to die away. "You all right?" he whispered.

She turned to look into his gray eyes and nodded.

He offered a crooked grin. "Good, because I would have hated to come all this way back to get you just to lose you to a couple of bloodhounds."

She wanted to punch him. Instead she lowered her lashes and tipped her chin up to let him brush his lips to hers.

When she opened her eyes he was still gazing into them.

"We need to talk," he said quietly. "I don't know what the hell I'm doing here. I should be on horseback headed for Washington."

At that moment Cameron's heart swelled with hope. Jackson hadn't come right out and said it, but she knew he had come back for her and that had to be a sign that he loved her.

"Well, I'm glad you came back, and I'm glad you'll be with us. I don't know if I can do this alone."

"Sure you can." He licked his thumb and rubbed at something on her face. "Dirt," he said.

She smiled, knowing somewhere deep inside that he did care for her. Maybe even loved her. But this wasn't the time or the place to talk about their relationship. Cameron wasn't any more ready to talk about it than he was. Right now, she was just glad to have him with her. Perversely enough, he made her feel safe…protected. "So how long should we stay here?" she asked.

"Dusk. Then we need to get moving. We'll travel all night, see where we are in the morning."

"How far do you think it is to Memphis? That's the first stop I know of on the Railroad. Naomi might be able to get some word of her mother there."

"It's a little over two hundred miles." He still held her in his arms, his wet body warm against hers.

"On foot," she breathed, knowing how difficult the journey would be.

He nodded. "Be safer that way."

She frowned. "Hey, you left with a fine horse. What happened to her?"

He laughed, knowing full well the horse had been thirty years old if it had been a day and probably on its last legs when he stole her in Biloxi. "Oh, I traded that fine piece of horseflesh."

Her brow furrowed. It was cool and dark in the cellar, and even though the others were with them, she felt quite alone with Jackson right now.

"For another horse," he explained.

"And what happened to *that* horse?"

"Long story, but she's being delivered later. Now, don't you worry your pretty little head, sweetness."

He kissed her forehead as if she were a child or a spoiled daughter, and this time she did punch him.

It took them more than a week to reach the Tennessee-Mississippi border. They walked at night with Jackson pushing them to a grueling pace. In the daytime they slept, eating what food Jackson brought to them from the woods, usually squirrel or rabbit. While they slept or rested during the daylight hours, Cameron knew he went into nearby towns, perhaps to buy ammunition or hear the latest gossip of the war, but he didn't offer information on those trips and she didn't ask. She was trying to give him some time to think through his feelings for her and trust her with his secret.

On the morning of the ninth day, Cameron and Jackson left the others in the woods and approached a small clearing on the outskirts of southern Memphis. Nestled in the clearing was a small white clapboard church.

"Now what?" Jackson asked, surveying the picturesque church with its new white paint and stained-glass windows.

"I don't know," Cameron murmured. She brushed what dust she could from her soiled breeches and made an attempt to smooth back her hair. "I look a mess, don't I?" she said. He flashed her a boyish grin, and she smiled back at him and shrugged. "Here goes. All I know is I'm supposed to tell someone here that James in Jackson sent me." She took the sturdy steps to the door and opened it with more composure than she felt.

Together, they walked into the church that was cool and shadowed and smelled of newly lemon-polished wood. A creaking sound startled Cameron, and she and Jackson both reached for their pistols at the same time.

An elderly negro woman appeared from between two pews she had apparently been dusting. "Can I he'p ya?" she asked, rag poised in her hand.

Cameron slid the pistol back into the waistband of her breeches. "Yes. I hope so. James sent me, James from Jackson, Mississippi."

The woman stepped into the aisle and approached them, eyeing them carefully. She was a small but sturdy woman dressed in a flowered green dress with what looked to be red silk mules on her feet. Cameron couldn't resist a smile. She had never seen a black woman in silk bed slippers before.

She broke into a wide grin. "Ya be liken Elsie's shoes, eh?" She held a finger. "But they not fer ya, Missy. Ya gonna have to get yer own."

Cameron laughed at ease with the woman though she'd known her less than a minute.

The woman eyed Jackson and then Cameron critically. "So, 'zackly what you white folk want out of Elsie?"

Cameron glanced uneasily at Jackson, then back at the negro woman. "Safe passage. James said you could help if we made it to Memphis."

She slapped her thigh, laughing aloud. "Ya mighty confused, Missy. Far as I know, ain't no need for no whities to have use of *my* transportation."

Cameron stepped closer. "It's not for me," she whispered. "It's for my friends."

The woman's eyes grew wide with understanding. "Where are they?" she whispered, her liquid voice suddenly hushed.

"In the woods."

"In the bright of day? God a mighty, Lord Divine, get them folk 'round the back and in the door afore half of Memphis is come to Sunday meetin'."

Cameron and Jackson did exactly as they were told, gathering the women and ushering them in through the back of the church. There, Elsie and another older woman waited in a small room off the sacristy.

"Good morning," the snow-haired woman said, offering her hand. "I am Mrs. Matthews."

Cameron hated to accept it, since she was filthy dirty and knew she probably didn't smell very good, but the woman's greeting was warm and friendly. "My name is Cameron," she introduced. "And this is Jackson. And this is my sister Taye." She thrust out her hand to grab Taye's.

Mrs. Matthews's brows arched, but she said nothing.

"And this is Naomi, Dorcas and Efia."

Each girl bobbed a hasty curtsy.

"And I understand all of you will be needing our services?" Mrs. Matthews asked.

"I promised the girls we would stay together," Cameron said. "Taye and I will be going to New York eventually, and Dorcas and Efia have family in Delaware." She glanced at Naomi. "Naomi's mother passed through here a few weeks ago, and we're hoping you can help us find her."

Mrs. Matthews nodded. "I keep excellent records. If she's passed through the doors of Faith Baptist church, I'll be able to tell you." She smiled, clasping her hands. "As long as you understand the danger, I am willing to carry you to the next stop." She glanced at Jackson. "All of you but him."

Jackson took a step toward Mrs. Matthews. "I go, or they don't."

She lifted an eyebrow, looking back to Cameron.

"Please," Cameron said. "We've traveled all the way from Biloxi. We want to see this through together."

Mrs. Matthews raised her hand. "The less I know of you, the better." She glanced at the other girls. "This will make matters more difficult, but I have an idea." She looked to Elsie who had conjured up bread and cheese and water and was passing it to each of them. "Are we singing Saturday night, Elsie, dear?"

"Ya'll sing most every Saturday night, Miz Matthews,"

Elsie said proudly. "Got the purtiest voices in all Tennessee, some say."

Mrs. Matthews looked back at Cameron. "If you and the gentleman are willing to do what is asked of you—*whatever* is asked—you'll be transported as well."

Jackson touched the corner of his hat brim. "Whatever it takes, ma'am, to see that these ladies are safely on their way."

"I'm not doing this."

Cameron giggled, pulling the gown she had been given over her head to cover her clean breeches and shirt. She discovered that Elsie not only polished pews and conjured up meals, but also did laundry for those who passed through Faith Baptist church.

Cameron smoothed the lily-white satin choir gown over her hips. They were standing in the church with a dozen other men and women who apparently attended the church and really were the Faith Baptist choir. Everyone else was donning their gowns over their Sunday best clothes. "You have to wear it, Jackson. It's our cover."

"I can't sing," he growled, holding the gown at arm's length.

She covered her mouth to stifle another giggle. "You don't have to sing, only pretend you're singing."

"This isn't funny. I haven't been trained to—" He stared down at her, his gray eyes hard and penetrating. "I am not putting this damned choir robe on. I'll lay in the false bottom of the wagon with the girls."

"There's no room for you there. Mrs. Matthews already told you that," she whispered. Then she snatched the robe from his hand. "Now don't be such a baby."

He groaned and shook his head as he allowed her to pull the satin fabric over his head. "Christ," he grunted. "What a man doesn't do for love."

She snatched the gown down so that she could look at his face. "What did you say?" Suddenly her heart was in her throat. He *had* said love, hadn't he?

"Nothing. Let's just get this over with." He jerked the robe over his clothes.

With amusement, she watched him stomp off, his shiny white gown fluttering behind him.

"Cameron?"

Someone tapped her on her shoulder and she spun around to meet Mrs. Matthews's gentle brown eyes.

"Cameron, I must make certain you understand your instructions. There can be no errors, my dear. None at all."

Cameron pressed her lips together, nodding. "I understand. We ride with the choir in the back of the wagon to this church in Memphis. After the performance, Jackson and I will get into a wagon that looks exactly like the one we came in."

"There will be others dressed in robes just like these," Mrs. Matthews explained.

"And the driver will take us safely to the next stop. Taye, Naomi, Efia and Dorcas will be safe in the false bottom until we reach our destination."

"It's not a comfortable ride," Mrs. Matthews confessed. "But it has worked well for us. We've only lost one family in the last two months and that was only because they refused to follow instructions."

Mrs. Matthews's words brought home to Cameron just how dangerous traveling on the Underground Railroad was, and the risk those who helped took upon themselves. She threw her arms around the older woman, surprised by the tears that shone in her eyes. "My sister and I have nothing to give you now, but we'll send some money later. I can't thank you enough for helping us, and for finding the information on Naomi's mother."

"With any luck at all, she's already in Philadelphia, waiting for her daughter." Mrs. Matthews kissed her cheek. "Now go safely, and go with God. I think our choir is almost ready to load into the wagon. Are you ready, my dear?" She clasped Cameron's hands in hers.

Cameron cleared her throat and sang one long sweet note. And then with a smile, she headed out the door to look for Jackson.

* * *

Late that night Cameron and Jackson lay side by side on the floor of a hayloft somewhere northeast of Memphis, Tennessee. The loft smelled of clover hay, drying tobacco and bird droppings, but they were all safe and well hidden.

The transfer in the Faith Baptist church choir wagon had gone off without a hitch. Jackson stood among the men in his choir robe and pretended to sing. Cameron knew many of the songs and sang with the choir. After a reception where refreshment was served by the hosting church, Cameron and Jackson had exited the rear door, joined a group of robed men and women and rode off down the streets of Memphis. Well after dark, and safely north of the city, they were brought here. They would remain here until the following night and then be on their way again—how, Cameron didn't know.

"Still awake?" Jackson whispered.

"Can't sleep."

He rolled onto his side and propped himself up on one elbow to gaze down at her. "So did anyone say where we were headed tomorrow?"

"Toward Knoxville, I think."

He fingered her hair. "Listen, I came this far to be sure you would make it to the Underground Railroad. But...I need to move on. Go north ahead of you."

She didn't respond. She couldn't because a lump was rising in her throat.

"I could meet up with you," he said quietly. "After my business is done."

Cameron felt as if she were falling. He was going to do it again. He had come back for her, but now he was leaving. She struggled to find her voice. She wouldn't cry. She would not beg him to stay with her. "We're moving too slowly?" she said.

He leaned closer, sliding his hand over her stomach. They lay on the end of a line of sleeping men, women and children. There were more than a dozen runaway slaves in all hidden here in the barn loft tonight.

"Moving too slowly and— Hell, Cam." He ran his hand

over his forehead, brushing back his hair. "There are others with you now. Others whose lives could be at risk by association with me." He exhaled. "I don't want to do this, but there are people who need to know where I am. I have to make contact and I can do that here in Memphis."

"But not with us tagging along," she whispered. "And you can't tell me why."

He smiled. "I think you're getting the hang of this."

She fought her tears. She wanted to ask him if it really was business that was pulling him away or if it was her. Had his remarks back at the church, about what a man did for love, upset him so greatly that he had to leave her again? Was he so afraid of loving her that he couldn't stay?

Cameron reached up to stroke his cheek. It was smooth-shaven. They had all had baths tonight, and someone had been kind enough to lend him a razor blade. It was the first time his cheeks had been clean-shaven in weeks.

"I need to go," he said softly. "But I could meet you, in say...Baltimore?" He brushed his lips against hers.

The ache in her throat, in her belly, was easing. A strange sense of warmth, fatalism maybe, was beginning to replace it. She had never told Jackson she loved him. Those words had never passed between them. There had been no promises. "You don't have to say you'll meet me," she murmured, surprising herself.

"I wouldn't say it if I didn't mean it," he said firmly.

She slipped her hand around his neck and drew his mouth down to hers. "No more talk," she whispered as she rolled to face him, all too aware of those who slept so near to them. "Just love me, Jackson. Love me one more time."

With a groan of surrender, he took her mouth with his. He threaded his fingers through her clean, thick mane of hair and held her head so that he could kiss her more deeply. His hands skimmed her shoulders and then brushed her peaked breasts.

Cameron closed her eyes, pressing her lips together to remain silent as the first waves of pleasure washed over her. Heavens, he knew her body better than she did.

He pushed up the thin fabric of her man's shirt and grazed

a large warm hand over her breast. He rolled the bud of her nipple between his thumb and forefinger, and she lifted her head to bury her face in his shoulder to keep from crying out.

He rolled the fabric of the shirt up and leaned over to catch the deep-rose tip of her breast with his mouth. Cameron sank her short fingernails into his back, hoping she didn't scratch him too badly. As his tongue circled her nipple, she rolled onto her back, trying desperately to be silent. All she could hear was the coo of doves, the snores of an elderly woman and her own pounding heart in her head.

Jackson rolled on top of her, stretching his long, lean muscular body over hers. She instinctively lifted her hips, bunching his linen shirt in her fists. She could already feel him through the fabric of their breeches, hot and rigid for her.

As Jackson kissed the curve of her neck, she released him long enough to slide down her breeches. She moved as slowly, as quietly as she could. She knew she shouldn't be doing this. Anyone could wake up at any moment. And yet her desire for Jackson was so desperate at this moment, so overwhelming, that it wouldn't have mattered who was asleep near her.

"I'll find you, Cam," he murmured. "You have to believe me. If we're to make this work between us, you have to learn to trust me."

Trust him? How could she trust him? With resignation, she blocked out his words and all the perplexing feelings that went with those words. She didn't want to think right now. She only wanted to feel. To feel him deep inside her, possessing her one last time.

Jackson silently slipped off his breeches and Cameron parted her thighs. His fingertips brushed the tight web of red curls between her thighs and she had to shove her hand into her mouth to keep from crying aloud.

Jackson slipped into her with one long, powerful thrust, and she lifted her hips to accept him. He covered her mouth with his and began to move rhythmically. Their joining was quick and fraught with the tumultuous emotions of the last days. He took her hard and she welcomed his power, pushing her hips to meet his thrusts. Her muscles tightened suddenly, and she felt that familiar indescribable warmth that exploded into a thousand shards of bright light. A beat later, Jackson groaned into her tangled hair, his body stiffened and then relaxed in release.

Panting, Cameron looped her arms over his shoulders holding him as tightly as she could, taking her own breath away. She didn't know if Jackson would really meet her in Baltimore, but she knew she would have to let him go in order to find out.

31

"Where's Captain Logan?" Taye rested a hand on Cameron's shoulder.

Cameron turned from the open barn door that was used to hoist hay up into the loft. Their kindly host or hostess, a nameless face, must have opened it last night so that their "guests" would catch some of the nighttime breeze. Once it was fully daybreak, Cameron knew the door would have to be closed so she wanted to take advantage of the light and warm fresh air while she could.

Cameron did not look at Taye, but folded her arms over her chest. "Gone."

"Gone." Taye didn't sound surprised. "I knew he was afraid we were moving too slowly, that he wouldn't get to Washington in time."

Cameron glanced at her, trying not to be irritated. "In time? What is that supposed to mean? In time for what? I suppose you know what Jackson's big secret is."

She shook her head. "Thomas said that the less we knew, the better."

"But they are *not* the scoundrel blockade-runners they appear to be?"

"I think not." Taye sounded amused. "I think if Captain Logan had been what you thought he was, he would never have been welcomed into our father's home so warmly."

Looking back now, it occurred to Cameron that Taye was

probably right. She should have guessed from the beginning that perhaps Captain Logan was not all he appeared to be. Oh, he was certainly a scoundrel, but beneath that blackguard heart there was goodness. She knew it now. She had just been too blinded by what he had done to her all those years ago, that she had not seen the truth right before her. And now was it too late?

Cameron looked at Taye again. "He left me. Don't you see? He left me again. He doesn't love me. He will never love me."

Taye tenderly pushed a lock of Cameron's tumbled hair off her face. "Did he say that?"

"No," she scoffed. "But how foolish could I be to think—"

"What *did* he say when he told you he had to go ahead without us?"

Cameron lifted her lashes, surprised by how pushy her sweet Taye had suddenly become. "Well, he said he had to go because he had to get to Washington…and that he would find me. He told me this morning before he went that I should find him on the docks in Baltimore." She gave a laugh that was near to tears. "That's ridiculous. Find him where on the docks? When? We have no idea how long it will take us to get to Baltimore."

"I think you just have to trust him," Taye said softly.

Cameron gazed out into the thick green canopy of the Tennessee forest. It had rained during the night and the leaves shimmered with dewdrops that were already beginning to evaporate. Somewhere a rooster crowed. "That's what he said."

"And I think you have to trust yourself and your own instincts." Taye paused. "Do you think he loves you?"

Cameron exhaled. It was going to be another stifling hot day. Perspiration already trickled down the center of her back. "I don't know what to think. He risked his life to save you because he knew I love you. He saved all of us."

"And put his own self at risk to do it," Taye pointed out. "As well as this mission of his, whatever it might be."

"I know, I know." Cameron rubbed her forehead. She

couldn't think clearly. She had been so happy when Jackson had come back to Elmwood for her. It had never occurred to her that he would leave her like this yet again.

"I think he loves me," Cameron said slowly. "But what if I'm wrong? If I'm wrong, I'm right back on Papa's veranda again, left with a broken heart."

Taye rubbed Cameron's shoulder. "But what if he does love you? What if it's just taking him a little time to come around to it?" She whispered conspiratorially, "Wouldn't it be worth it?"

Cameron turned to meet Taye's blue-eyed gaze. "How'd you get to be so smart?"

Taye lifted her arms to hug Cameron. "I suppose I had a big sister to teach me."

Weeks later, Cameron trudged wearily through a field of chest-high weeds and briars somewhere in the Maryland countryside. The trip had been a long one, made even longer by rainy weather and a coughing illness that had passed through the ragged group and forced them to hole up in an old burned house for close to a week.

The group was relieved to be so near safety, but they were all still on the alert, knowing that they weren't safe yet. Although Maryland hadn't joined the Confederacy, it was still a slave state, and Taye and the others would just as likely find enemies as friends. They couldn't take the chance that they'd come all this way to be captured before reaching freedom.

It was pitch-black out, a moonless night. The stars were just beginning to twinkle in the sky and give a little light. Mist hung low over the field and turned lone trees into ghostly apparitions looming out of the gloom.

They had been walking since dawn and it had to be close to midnight. They'd had no food all day and just a little water, and Cameron was deathly tired. Two days ago her boots had rubbed blisters on her heels, and now they burned with every step she took. It was all she could do to put one foot in front of the other.

There had been talk more than an hour ago of stopping for

the night. Everyone was exhausted, and Efia had been complaining for hours. But their guide, a small black woman who looked to Cameron to be about forty years of age, insisted they had to keep moving. "We're getting close," she had said in a soft, gentle voice. It was the only time Cameron had heard their guardian speak since she had met the group of runaway slaves near a cow pasture at dusk.

Cameron glanced wearily at Taye, who walked with her head down, and wondered how she was holding up. Taye looked over, and even in the darkness Cameron saw her smile. It was then that Cameron realized she shouldn't be bemoaning her growling stomach or the blisters on her heels. They were approaching the territory where Taye and Naomi and all of the others in the group would be free.

They approached a woods line of old oaks and newer pines, and the guide halted. "We're here."

Cameron looked up, not realizing until this moment how sleepy she had become. She ran her hand over her face that felt grimy. At least it was cooler here farther north. "We're where?"

The woman folded her hands neatly over her pressed apron and lifted her bonneted head. "Freedom." She dragged the heel of her sturdy boot in the soft humus at the woods line. "You're safe from here on in."

Naomi gave a hoot of joy and raced across the line the guide had drawn in the soil. She backed up and passed over it again, flapping her dress and spinning in a circle.

There were hoots and hollers of pleasure as one by one the slaves stepped over the line in the dirt and into the dark forest. One of the women who had been with them all the way from Tennessee, a woman who had lost a child to the Mississippi River, began to cry softly.

Taye and Cameron were the last to cross the line.

"This is where we split up, friends," the guide said softly. "Those who are going across the bay to Delaware can go with the man with the black hat." She pointed at a figure who appeared through the trees. "You others keep walking for about a quarter of a mile. You'll reach a road, and you can follow that right into Baltimore.'' She turned away, headed back the way she had come, alone in the darkness. ''Go with God.''

The twins stared after her.

''Go with the man like she said,'' Taye urged. ''Hurry.''

The comrades parted with hugs and kisses and more than a few tears. Cameron was amazed by her feelings for these dark-skinned men, women and children who had been strangers to her only weeks ago. Even the twins, who had been trying at times in the last few weeks.

''Quick, now,'' their leader in the hat warned. ''We need to cross open water before daylight.''

Everyone called a final farewell and waved.

Cameron turned away and watched for a moment as their guardian disappeared into the shadows of the fields, and she was overwhelmed by a sense of relief, and oddly, accomplishment.

''Oh, no,'' Cameron said when she realized the soft-spoken woman was gone. ''She never even told us her name. How will we send her money?''

Taye looped her arm through Cameron's and led her into the woods. ''Didn't you know who she was?'' she whispered as if they were girls again, sharing secrets.

Cameron shook her head. ''How would I?''

''I suppose that's true. Being a white woman in a Southern white world, you wouldn't. That, my dear, was a very famous runaway slave who has ushered hundreds of slaves to freedom.'' She smiled, seeming pleased that she knew something Cameron didn't. ''That was Harriet Tubman.''

Cameron looked over her shoulder one more time but the guide was gone. She turned back, brushing her cheek against Taye's shoulder as they picked their way through the woods. ''Once we get to Baltimore, I want a hot bath, a big meal, a real bed to sleep in, and then I want you to tell me how you knew who she was. And I want you to tell me all about her.''

''You've got yourself a deal,'' Taye said. ''Now come on. That bath and a bed sound like something out of a fairy tale.''

*   *   *

Cameron, Taye and Naomi were fortunate to catch a ride in a wagon with a Quaker man headed for the docks of Baltimore. By early morning they found themselves dirty and bedraggled but smiling as they were left on the street at the harbor. Cameron and Taye climbed down and Naomi moved from the bed of the wagon onto the buckboard seat.

"Guess this is goodbye, least for now," Naomi said. "Mr. Jasper here, he says he can get me a ride on to Philadelphia so I'm goin' while the goin's good." She shook her head. "My mama won't doubt my magic no more when she sees I made it."

A lump rose in Cameron's throat as she reached up to hug Naomi. "Good luck, Naomi. And thank you for everything." She stepped back to let Taye hug her.

Naomi wiped at her damp eyes with the back of her arm. "Now you two take care of yourselves. Ya being sisters and all. Sisters is bound to look after one t'other."

"We will," Taye assured her.

Taye and Cameron held hands and waved as the Quaker's wagon rolled off. Then they were alone on the street where the sounds of gulls and the scents of fish, salt water and damp wood were strong on the late afternoon air.

"So," Taye said, swinging Cameron's hand. "Shall we find Jackson?"

Cameron pulled her hand from Taye's and folded her arms over her chest. "This is silly. How am I supposed to find him? The *Inverness* is obviously not docked here."

"We'll ask."

Cameron shook her head. She was tired and she wanted to figure out what they were going to do for sleeping arrangements come nightfall. They had Taye's emeralds, but they would have to find someone in Baltimore willing to buy one of the emeralds just so they could have a place to sleep tonight and a decent meal to eat. They didn't have time to look for Captain Logan who was probably long gone.

Cameron sat down on a small barrel at the end of one of the docks. "This is silly."

"It is not. But if you're tired, I'll ask around." With a smile on her face, Taye sashayed off in a clean but worn dress she had traded her boys' clothes for from a woman in West Virginia. While Cameron didn't mind the men's clothing, Taye couldn't wait to get rid of her breeches and shirt.

Taye was gone a long time. Cameron watched boats pull in and out. She watched sailors unloading crates from the deck of one of the ships. A carriage rolled by and she gazed longingly at a woman in a pretty green dress holding a parasol over her head. Cameron's gowns were all gone, and she realized how much she missed her pretty things. She missed all those silly lace petticoats and straw bonnets she had once owned.

Just when Cameron was beginning to worry about Taye, she spotted her coming up the street. "He's here," she called excitedly.

Cameron had to suppress the impulse to look around. She knew what they had discussed about taking chances. She was taking a chance with her heart just coming here, but she was so afraid of being disappointed again. And how could Jackson possibly know she was here? He would have arrived days ago, and he was supposed to be in Washington, wasn't he?

"Did you hear me?" Taye ran up, her cheeks rosy. "I talked to a nice man. The captain of a ship. He said that Captain Logan is here in Baltimore."

Cameron felt her heart give a little.

"And guess what else he said."

Cameron shook her head, numb.

Taye grabbed Cameron's hand. "The *Inverness*! It's expected into port within the next day or two!"

"How is that possible? She was headed for the Bahamas."

"I don't know. I don't understand, but that was what the man said."

"Oh, Taye," Cameron smiled, happy for her. "Thomas will be aboard, won't he?"

Taye's cheeks colored. "I hope so." She hung her head. "There's other news, too. About the war. Congress has authorized a call for another five hundred thousand men." She bit down on her lower lip. "There's been fighting. Mostly in

Virginia and West Virginia, some in Missouri. There was a big battle some place in Virginia called Bull Run only two days ago.'' Taye's blue eyes sparkled with unshed tears. ''Cam, the Union lost the battle. The man I spoke to said everyone is pointing fingers. They say that the commander, a General McDowell, attacked too soon, before his troops were trained. We lost.''

''There, there. It will be all right. You'll see.'' As Cameron rose from the barrel she was perched on to hug Taye, she spotted a man riding down the street toward the dock, leading a horse behind him. It was an Arabian mare. Cameron would have recognized the warmblood's physique and carriage anywhere. And this Arabian seemed even more familiar than just any mare.

It wasn't until after Cameron recognized the horse that she looked at the man again. Her lower lip trembled and a lump rose in her throat. She was so shocked that she couldn't move for a moment.

The rider approached, dressed in a dark-blue coat, breeches and a pristine white shirt. He tipped his hat. '''Morning, ladies.''

Taye gave a squeal of delight.

Cameron was still frozen, unable to move a muscle as she watched Jackson dismount and pass the reins to Taye. His gaze was locked with Cameron's and she couldn't look away.

Taye walked the horses back onto the street to give them a little privacy.

''I knew you would make it safely, but I was afraid you wouldn't come,'' he said softly. For the first time in his life, he sounded anxious.

''I was afraid you wouldn't be here,'' she managed to reply, her voice quivering. Her throat was dry and she didn't feel as if she could catch her breath.

''I've had a boy sitting here watching for you for days,'' he explained.

Then Jackson swept her into his arms and spun her around, lifting her off her feet. ''God, you feel good in my arms,'' he muttered thickly.

Cameron wrapped her arms around his neck and would not let go, burying her face in his white cravat.

"You even brought my horse. How did you find my horse?"

"Remember that scuffle I had in Jackson just before I came back to Elmwood to get you?"

She nodded.

"Well, that fellow and I were just coming to a price on her. The good man even shipped her for me."

Cameron didn't know what to say. All she could do was bury her face in his coat and try to hold back her tears.

Jackson smoothed her hair, dragging his mouth across her cheek. "Oh, Cam, I'm so sorry I had to leave you, but I had something to take care of. I'd made a promise to see it through." He tilted back her head, brushing her hair off her forehead. "And now I want to make a promise to you, Cam."

She shook her head, overwhelmed and suddenly feeling weak-kneed. "Not now," she whispered. "Just help me onto Roxy, and take me somewhere where I can get a bath."

"Excellent idea, because you, Taye and I have a date tonight. I already bought gowns and all the frills for both of you—hoping you'd be here in time." He slipped his arm around her waist and ushered her toward the waiting horses. "I was afraid you weren't going to make it in time and that I would have had to go alone."

The man wasn't making any sense. "A date? Where?" Cameron asked as they walked over to where Taye stood with the horses, her blue eyes shining with delight.

He grasped her waist and lifted her easily into the saddle. "Where?" he said as if she had asked the silliest question on earth. He reached for Taye to put her up behind her sister. "Well, the White House, of course."

32

∽⌒⌒⌒⌒∽

Cameron would have thought she was too tired to bathe, dress and make the journey from Baltimore to Washington by train. She was sure that, once she ate, she would want nothing more than to curl into bed with Jackson and sleep for at least two days.

But Jackson's enthusiasm was contagious. He took her and Taye home to the great Georgian brick house he had grown up in on the outskirts of Baltimore. He had servants fill copper tubs with scented water, and the two women bathed side by side, dining and drinking wine while they soaked in tubs in the bedchamber Taye would occupy while a guest in Jackson's home. After their baths, two shy maids delivered boxes to the two women. Together, donned in new filmy dressing gowns, Cameron and Taye pulled through the boxes, squealing with delight at the sight of lacy pantalets, silk stockings and gorgeous billowing petticoats. They opened the two largest boxes last, and both collapsed on the bed in awe of Captain Logan's taste in fashion.

For Taye, there was a pale-blue broche balzerine gown trimmed in white. With a rounded neckline and short puffy sleeves, it was daring, but modest. When the maids pulled it over Taye's head and fluffed the six white petticoats beneath, she declared she felt like a fairy princess.

"Now your turn," Taye said, moving slowly as if she feared she would rumple her gown merely walking in it. Cameron was already dressed in a crinoline, honey-colored petti-coats and new-heeled slippers. She lifted her hands carefully so as not to muss her hair. Taye had worked so hard to brush it out until it was glossy and then piled it on her head in ringlets of red curls. The maid pulled the green moiré gown with its gold satin underskirt over her head and began to adjust the *en demi-coeur* bodice that was edged with ribbon ruching.

Taye exhaled in amazement as she offered the golden elbow-length satin gloves that matched the trim of the gown. "Cameron, I believe that is the most beautiful gown I have ever seen."

There was a tap on the door that had been left ajar, and Jackson walked in dressed elegantly in black tails and black breeches with a top hat tucked under his arm. "And I must admit she is probably the most beautiful woman I have ever seen." Jackson took Cameron's hand and spun her around so that he could get a better look at her. "I was told in the dress-maker's shop that this new color is all the rage—Azoff green." He lifted her hand to his lips. "It is lovely, but I must confess I like you in the breeches and muslin shirt as well."

Cameron and Taye met each other's eyes and burst into laughter. Jackson only shook his head and offered his other arm to Taye. "Shall we go, ladies?"

The trip from Baltimore to Washington by train was entirely too quick, too magical. Before Cameron knew it, she and Taye were alighting from a carriage and walking up the steps of the White House. There were others, too, handsome men and ladies in beautiful gowns, all guests of President Lincoln and the first lady, Mary Todd Lincoln. Among these people, Cam-eron didn't feel quite grown-up, but instead like a little girl drifting in a dream.

"I expect the *Inverness* to dock tomorrow," Jackson told Taye as they mounted the steps. "And onboard I believe there is a young man very anxious to see you."

Taye fluttered her pale-blue fan that had been painted with dragonflies. "Captain Logan, please. You will make me cry."

Cameron glanced sideways at Jackson as they ascended the

long flight of marble steps. ''I thought the ship was going to the Bahamas with that turpentine you were going to sell illegally.''

Taye's eyes widened as she glanced around them, obviously fearful someone would hear them.

Jackson chuckled, appearing not in the least bit concerned how loudly she spoke or what she accused him of. ''If you must know, my ship had a bit of bad luck in the Gulf of Mexico. The crew was fortunate enough to get away with its life, but much of the turpentine was confiscated.''

Once inside the White House, they were escorted down a long carpeted passageway toward the Red Room, where they would be received.

Cameron narrowed her tawny eyes suspiciously. ''And now your ship returns to Baltimore where you happen to be? How convenient.''

''Convenient, indeed.'' He grinned and then lifted his head to nod to the first gentleman in the receiving line. ''Good evening, sir,'' he said with almost a princely manner.

''Jackson, good to see you in one piece.'' The man with the handlebar mustache pumped his arm enthusiastically. ''I hear we nearly lost you to a gaggle in Tennessee.''

Cameron eyed Jackson, wondering just what this man was talking about, but Jackson ignored her.

''Ah, the tales are always more exhilarating than the truth. Senator, I would like you to meet a good friend of mine. This is Miss Cameron Campbell, daughter of the late Senator David Campbell.''

''Miss Campbell.'' The senator took her hand between both of his, his green eyes shining. ''It is indeed an honor to meet you, my dear. I knew your father well....''

For the next hour the sights and sounds of the White House reception overwhelmed Cameron. She had only been to the great house once before when her father had sneaked her in when she was just a girl. Now she was grown-up, and a guest, no less. Everyone seemed to have known her father and scores of both men and women wanted to express their condolences and tell her what a good man the senator had been.

Not only was the conversation stimulating, but the food was exquisite. The French champagne was better than she had ever tasted in Mississippi, and then there was the music and dancing. She had not realized how much she missed dancing until the first sweet notes of a waltz were played. Both Taye and Cameron waltzed with Jackson, and Cameron wasn't certain who enjoyed the dances more, him or them.

It was well after midnight when Cameron finally realized that if she didn't sit down soon, she was going to drop. Jackson had been amazingly attentive all evening and he seemed to immediately recognize when she was too tired to go on.

"Ready to leave?" he asked, brushing his lips against her cheek.

"I hate to go. This has been the most wonderful night, but I think we're both tired, Captain. It was a long walk from Mississippi," Taye teased.

"Well, we shall go then. But there's one more person who has asked to meet you before you go," Jackson said mysteriously. "This way, ladies."

Jackson directed them into a small reception room. "Here he comes now."

Cameron turned to see an unusually tall, thin, dark-haired man who reminded her so much of her father that a lump rose in her throat. "The president," she murmured under her breath in disbelief. "The president wants to meet me?"

"Mr. President," Jackson said as the tall man walked over to them.

"Captain Logan." President Lincoln offered his hand. "I was hoping I would see you tonight. I've been speaking with Mr. Seward." He lowered the timbre of his voice so that their conversation became private. "The information you brought us will be indispensable. I cannot tell you how many Union lives you have undoubtedly saved." He was not a handsome man, but when he smiled, there was a warmth in his dark eyes that Cameron found mesmerizing. "And don't tell me, this must be Miss Cameron Jackson, the senator's daughter."

Cameron stood frozen for a moment, utterly confused by what the president had just said. What was he talking about,

Jackson saving Union lives? Did he have him confused with another man? Suddenly coming to her senses, realizing she'd just been introduced to the president of the United States, she curtsied deeply, lowering her head in complete awe. "It's a pleasure to meet you, Mr. President."

"And a pleasure to meet Senator Campbell's lovely daughter."

"And this," Jackson introduced, "is Taye Campbell, the senator's youngest daughter."

Taye curtsied. "Mr. President."

"It's good to meet you, too." The president nodded, studying her face. "Yes, I do believe I see the family resemblance."

Taye's cheeks pinkened and she waved her fan frantically.

"Mr. President," a man called from behind them. "Sir. We must speak of General McDowell."

President Lincoln sighed. "If you will excuse me. I would much prefer to stand here and speak with you lovely ladies, but I hear an old goat bleating. Thank you so much for coming." He looked to Jackson. "I understand we will be speaking soon. Thank you again, Jackson."

Jackson bowed formally and both of the women curtsied as the president took his leave. Cameron just stood there in the empty room for a moment. "I've met the president," she said softly.

"I believe I've had enough entertainment for the evening." Jackson glanced at Cameron. "And I believe Cameron and I need to have a talk that has been long in coming."

She lifted a feather brow. "I believe you're right, Captain. Because I think you and I have something to talk about."

He grinned innocently and offered both arms. "Shall we go, ladies?"

Jackson had reserved two rooms in the most elegant hotel Cameron had ever seen. It had great crystal chandeliers in the lobby, rooms that were heavily paneled in oak and beds larger than she had ever seen.

Cameron said good-night to Taye at her door. One of the

maids from Jackson's home was already waiting in Taye's room when they arrived.

"Should I come over and he'p Miss Campbell wi' her dress when I'm done, Capt'n?" the young black woman in a bright-pink dress asked.

"That won't be necessary, Liza. Good night." He nodded.

"Good night," Taye called. "And thank you, Captain."

Jackson groaned. "I think it's time you start calling me Jackson, don't you, Taye? After all, we're going to be related."

Taye's eyes grew round and she stared at Cameron.

Cameron looked at Jackson as if he'd lost his mind. "Let's go," she said. "I'm tired of these games. It's time we had that *little talk.*"

Jackson escorted her into a room that was the size of two of Cameron's bedchambers at home. Several ornate chairs and a love seat were grouped near a marble fireplace. The six tall windows that ran the length of the room were draped in rose velvet, and two huge floral arrangements of roses in the exact color dominated an antique walnut table. Priceless Persian rugs covered the gleaming hardwood floors, and dozens of candles flickered from two magnificent crystal chandeliers. Cameron's breath caught in her throat. It wasn't until this moment that she realized just how wealthy Jackson was. More wealthy than her father had ever been, for certain.

She tossed her gloves on the massive poster-bed that was covered with an elegant green silk counterpane and heaped high with matching pillows. "All right. Time is up," she said firmly. "Start talking. What was that man insinuating when he said he thought 'we' had nearly lost you? What was the president talking about—you saving lives?"

Jackson locked the door behind him and tossed his black top hat to the bed. It landed upside down on her gloves. He slipped out of his coat, threw it over a chair and moved languidly to a table where several glasses and bottles of liquor had been set out. "A little champagne?" he asked as he poured himself some brandy.

"Brandy. And my explanation, if you please."

"Brandy. Excellent choice." He poured an equally healthy portion. "So, my dear, where to begin?" His tone was annoyingly nonchalant.

She folded her arms over her chest, thrusting out one foot. "Let's start with who you *really* are and what the president was talking about."

"That." He waved a hand. "Nothing. It was nothing, nothing at all."

Cameron walked toward him. *"Jackson."*

He shook his head. "All right. I knew the ruse would be up sooner or later." He pushed her glass into her hand. "But let me first say that I never wanted to lie to you. I only wanted to protect you. It had to be this way from the beginning. Very few people know, and it's imperative that it remain that way."

"But Papa knew," she said softly, looking over the rim of her glass at him. "That was why you were so welcome in our house, despite your claims of being uninterested in politics."

He nodded solemnly.

Cameron sipped the dark amber liquid, and it burned a delicious path down her throat. "What is it Papa knew, Jackson?" Her voice was husky from the potent drink.

"That…while I do ship—"

"I believe it's called blockade-running."

He tapped her glass with his. "While I do appear to be *blockade-running,* I am actually an operative for our war department. I would have eventually been working for your father, had he not passed."

As Cameron listened, Jackson's voice seemed to reverberate in her head. Her emotions were spinning. She was immediately afraid for him and the danger she knew he must face, but part of her was thrilled. Captain Jackson Logan might be a scoundrel, but he was also an honorable man.

"Being in the shipping business, and being the man I am known to be, it was, shall we say, a natural succession?"

"But what is it you *do?*"

"I make friends with those I ship for in the South, men I have done business with for years, and they tell me things they should not tell me. I pass the information off in Washington, and they do with it what they can.''

"You're a *spy?*" she breathed.

"I think that's too dramatic a term."

She closed her eyes, trying to think, trying to absorb everything he was telling her. "But how will you ever keep up such a ruse and not have anyone figure out what you're doing? You said your turpentine was confiscated. I assume you mean by our own government so the Southerners will not prosper. But you cannot have everything you ship confiscated." She gave a little laugh. "Else you wouldn't be a terribly successful blockade-runner."

He laughed with her and grabbed her arm, leading her to the bed. He sat on the edge and pulled her down beside him. "That is going to be a little tricky, but it can be done. Right now I have a shipment of bandages, medicines and chamber pots that the *Inverness* will successfully carry through the blockades off the Carolinas and make safely to port in Charleston."

"Chamber pots?" She laughed and took another drink.

"They are quite fine, really. Hand painted with gold leaf." He finished his brandy and set his glass on the polished marble floor. "English made and not at all harmful to our troops. The ladies will love me for bringing the necessities of life."

Cameron shook her head, studying his gray eyes. "You did not come up with this since April."

He shook his head. "It has been in the making a long time." He glanced at his boots. "We had hoped we would not have to go to war but—"

"But if we did, your persona would already be in place." She laid her hand on his hand that rested on his knee. "I don't know what to say, Jackson."

He shrugged. "Nothing to say. I am still at heart the man I am." He looked into her eyes. "Just the good with the bad."

"So we really aren't on opposite sides of the war?"

He took her glass and set it on the floor beside his. "No, we are not." He paused and then went on. His face was so serious. "I'm sorry I couldn't tell you before, even when I was ready to back on the boat. But the information they sent me to Mississippi to gain had to reach the war department. If something had happened to me and you had known any-thing—*anything,* Cam, you'd have been killed. Taye would have been killed.''

Cameron's head was spinning. She didn't know if it was the brandy, or because she was tired, or because she just couldn't absorb the enormity of what Jackson was saying and what it all meant. She knew she loved him. She had known for some time, but she had allowed the war and what she thought to be his beliefs stand between them. Protect her from him, really. And now that barrier had fallen away.

''Listen, Cam.'' He took her hand in his. ''Now that I've safely reached Washington and had time to think, I'm ready.''

She couldn't tear her gaze from his. ''Ready for what?''

He slid to the floor on his knees, still holding her hand in his. ''Cameron, I've thought long and hard on this. I've thought of nothing else. You make me crazy, woman, but I don't think I can live without you.''

She just stared at him. ''Was that a proposal?''

He looked sheepish for a moment. ''I think it was.'' He pressed his sensual lips together, lowered his gaze and then looked at her with those penetrating gray eyes again. ''Cam-eron Elise Campbell, will you be the wife of a blockade-running scoundrel who hopes he can do a little something for his country on the side?''

For a moment, Cameron couldn't move. His words barely registered. ''You left me in some barn in Tennessee, and now, now you want to marry me?''

''I left you because I had to.''

''But you can't tell me why.''

''Well, I could,'' he said quite seriously, ''but then I would be forced to kill you.''

Against her will, she cracked a smile.

''But this offer is good for tonight and tonight only,'' he told her, growing serious again. ''And I can make very few promises. I will continue to serve my country. I will continue to captain my ship. I won't stay anywhere long, and I cannot promise what the future will hold. You'll have to be a very independent woman to be my wife. You'll have to have your own interests, your own life beyond me."

"Like my horses," she managed to say, her voice filled with emotion.

He nodded and then went on. "I can't make many promises, but what I can promise is my fidelity, my protection and my love. Forever my love."

"Your love?" she whispered. "You love me?"

He continued to look into her eyes. "Of course." He seemed surprised she had to ask.

"Say it," she whispered.

"I love you, Cameron."

She stood up and he caught her in his arms as she swayed. "And I can only hope that you love me, as well," he murmured in her ear.

"Oh," she breathed, afraid the dream would end before she could tell him yes. "I do love you, Jackson, and I will be your wife. I've loved you since that first day we met when I was seventeen."

"I think I've loved you since the day I was born." He offered a roguish grin. "It just took me a little longer to realize it."

"Oh, Jackson," she whispered.

He leaned over her, pulling her close and covered her mouth with his. He threaded his fingers through her copper hair, and kissed her until she was breathless and the room spun.

And then he kissed her again.

New York Times Bestselling Author

JOAN
JOHNSTON

CHARITY

Nothing could have prepared beautiful, bold Charity for meeting
identical twin sisters Hope and Faith Butler at Hawk's Pride—
and seeing a mirror image of herself.

HOPE

The stunning discovery that she is a triplet cannot distract
Hope Butler from her heartbreak—the man she has loved all her life
is about to marry someone else.

FAITH

Guilt stricken by her sister's abandonment, Faith Butler vows to see
her sisters happy, no matter what it takes. Even if she has to
break up one wedding, arrange a couple more...and seize her
own chance for happiness.

Three sisters. Three lives. Three hearts.
Reunited in a brand-new story of passion and secrets.

SISTERS FOUND

Available the first week of December 2002 wherever paperbacks are sold!

ROSEMARY ROGERS

66927 WICKED LOVING LIES	___ $6.99 U.S.	___ $8.50 CAN.
66852 A RECKLESS ENCOUNTER	___ $7.50 U.S.	___ $8.99 CAN.
66831 SWEET SAVAGE LOVE	___ $6.99 U.S.	___ $8.50 CAN.
66621 SAVAGE DESIRE	___ $7.50 U.S.	___ $8.99 CAN.

(limited quantities available)

TOTAL AMOUNT	$_____
POSTAGE & HANDLING	$_____
($1.00 for 1 book, 50¢ for each additional)	
APPLICABLE TAXES*	$_____
TOTAL PAYABLE	$_____

(check or money order—please do not send cash)

To order, complete this form and send it, along with a check or money order for the total above, payable to MIRA Books®, to: **In the U.S.:** 3010 Walden Avenue, P.O. Box 9077, Buffalo, NY 14269-9077; **In Canada:** P.O. Box 636, Fort Erie, Ontario, L2A 5X3.

Name:_____

Address:_____ City:_____

State/Prov.:_____ Zip/Postal Code:_____

Account Number (if applicable):_____

075 CSAS

*New York residents remit applicable sales taxes.
Canadian residents remit applicable GST
and provincial taxes.

MIRA®